Crossing the Distance

Crossing the Distance

EVAN SOLOMON

Canadian Cataloguing in Publication Data

Solomon, Evan
Crossing the distance

ISBN 0-7710-8151-0

I. Title.

PS8587.O4196C76 1999 C813'.54 C98-932970-4
PR9199.3.S64C76 1999

We acknowledge the financial support of the Government of Canada through the Book Publishing Industry Development Program for our publishing activities. We further acknowledge the support of the Canada Council for the Arts and the Ontario Arts Council for our publishing program.

Text design by Ingrid Paulson
Typeset in Bembo by M&S, Toronto
Printed and bound in Canada

McClelland & Stewart Inc.
The Canadian Publishers
481 University Avenue
Toronto, Ontario
M5G 2E9

1 2 3 4 5 03 02 01 00 99

To my parents, Carl and Virginia.
And to Jordan, Diana, Muriel and Tammy.
All love.

Once the realization is accepted that even between the closest human beings infinite distances continue to exist, a wonderful living side by side can grow up, if they succeed in loving the distance between them which makes it possible for each to see the other whole against the sky. . . .

– Rainer Maria Rilke

August 1, 1999

Betrayal isn't something you choose, it's something that chooses you. I know that more than ever now, especially when I think about the events that came together to destroy the people I love. Of course, my memory of things is different from that of the police or the newspaper reporters or the producers making a movie of the week; that's no surprise. We're all spinning out versions of the truth until the facts disappear and everything becomes a matter of belief. Which is how it has to be.

It's so cramped up here in the cabin, but I don't go out much to exercise my leg. Hard to believe that only five months have passed. Now the days are sweltering, stretched out by yellow summer light, and the heat wrenches and bends my thoughts as it used to do to the air above the highway when my brother and I would drive up north to go camping. That was when we were young, and trust was still something solid and obvious, a smooth stone that you could pick up with your bare hand and skip across the water. It used to feel like that on our trips, canoeing for days on a vast lake that was always blue with the certainty of a promising future. That's how I want to remember it, anyway.

And I want to remember everything, justify everything, comprehend everything so it will all make the kind of sense everyone needs it to make. But I can't seem to do that. Maybe the details of the story are forever out of reach. Maybe too heavy to carry, or too light to grasp. At best they flicker in the distance with incandescent answers, fireflies in the dark bush, then they disappear when I have to rely on them – which is mostly in the long loneliness of night.

I spend most of my time flipping through this journal, reading myself back to myself, searching for some code I can break that might reveal the precise moment when all the unconditional things in my life became conditional. But there is no moment like that, is there? At least, I haven't found one yet. There's only the memory of this story and, somewhere in it, the memory of a person I recognize as myself.

This is what happens:

SLOW MOTION

It begins terrifically with a mid-winter murder; at least, that's how the media wished it would begin. Blood and bodies for startling pictures, innocence and guilt for dinner-time viewers. But this isn't about a murder, although there is one of those. And this isn't about catching a criminal, although there is that, too. This is about the territory in between those stories, and that's not so simple to map. Still, beginnings are comforting, and that's what's needed right now, so it might as well begin here, on that Sunday night when Rachel Anne Poiselle was shot in the side of the head while she was catching up on some work at her university office. Terrific enough.

Just for the record, because records are also comforting, the bullet grazed her just above the left ear where her short, dirty blond hair was pressed back by a swipe of gel. When the ambulance finally arrived, the attendants found her willowy body balled up tightly, the knees of her black pants pressed against her smashed head. She had punctuated a fifty-foot trail of blood on the marble floor of the hallway like a gruesome exclamation mark. They expected her to die.

By morning the media turned her name into a headline. A few people actually remembered that two years earlier she'd published a controversial book proposing that children spend as much time playing video games as they do reading. Citing results from a four-year study she'd conducted, Rachel argued in her scholarly but still engaging prose that video games were not evil, brain-squishing mechanisms devised by corporate profit-mongers, but rather valuable tools of learning. "Video games teach children how to manage chaos," she wrote, a pithy phrase that her publisher printed boldface in all the publicity kits. "Pattern recognition will be the essential skill of the future," she concluded, "and electronic gaming is the best classroom." To Rachel's surprise, even to her embarrassment, as she later told Jake, her analytic book caught the wave of information-age hysteria and became *the* trendy new theory, transcending the ivory walls of academia. Eruptions of praise from critics and technology gurus sent the media into hyperbolic overdrive, everyone eager to ally themselves with the latest buzz: *She's done to education what Super Mario did to checkers*, gushed one reviewer, whose bio, like that of several other reviewers that same week, proclaimed him to be the true heir to Marshall McLuhan. *Such an original, delightful read that it should immediately be turned into a video game of its own*, a tabloid suggested inventively, placing the review neatly beside a half-page ad for the Sony PlayStation. One overzealous reviewer on a peppy computer TV show even urged people to *Buy this book, again and again. It's a two-thumbs-up read, way up!*

Rachel's publisher, Gwendolyn Lyman, imbibed the praise like expensive cocktails at an open bar and insisted, against

Rachel's better judgement, on putting Rachel's picture on the cover of the second edition. Technology needs a pretty face, Gwendolyn said. More women read books, Gwendolyn said. It will stand out on the racks, Gwendolyn said. You'll get on TV.

Her persistence won Rachel over.

Rachel went on talk shows, newscasts, radio programs; she did print interviews, Internet chat forums, her quick wit and deft turn of phrase charming even the hosts and callers who accused her of destroying the education system. And she tried to smile all the time, as Gwendolyn begged her to do. Smiling, smiling, even as she despised the phoniness of it all. And Jake could tell, even then, that she did. Still, Gwendolyn was right about her face. It turned out that her features were aligned in a mysterious way that producers call "camera friendly." "You simply eat the lens," a photographer whispered to her cryptically, all the while explaining how easily he could airbrush five pounds from her waist and digitally paint out the slight space between her front teeth and the lines around her eyes. "Just keep smiling."

Uneasy as it made her feel, the campy publicity was nonetheless a pleasant distraction from the encrusted world of academia, where Rachel's colleagues now glared at her from their office doors. They avoided her as if she were infectious, a huckster pandering to pop culture and betraying the subverbal contract of all academics: always remain irrelevant to the general population.

But that was two years ago, and the media had long since moved on to other stories. Rachel slipped back into a comfortable obscurity, teaching her classes, researching her next book, and collecting small royalty cheques. Until the shooting, that is. Because when the ambulance attendants found her covered in blood and rushed her to the hospital, Rachel became a media darling again – no longer as hip academic, but in the more glamorous career of a famous corpse.

□ □ □

Things fall apart. That's what Jake is thinking, sitting in his private hospital room as the news of the shooting dances through the airwaves into homes across the country. A doctor listens to his heart, measures his blood pressure, and finally tells him he's in shock. Jake believes the doctor's diagnosis is wrong. He orders him to leave. Shock is something real, a treatable condition, and Jake believes he's beyond treatment. He feels absolutely nothing.

A few hours later a nurse arrives and gives Jake a blanket and three small pills for his nerves, which he mistakenly chews. Choking violently, the nurse quickly hands him a glass of warm water and rubs his back. Her hand feels like a cold kitchen spatula. It's six in the morning and Jake is shaking from a chill he doesn't feel. The nurse whispers hospital things like, "It's okay, you just had a bad fall. You should be proud of yourself, you brought that woman to the hospital, and we're doing everything we can. The pills will help you sleep, Mr. Jacobson." But he can't sleep. Jake has seen Rachel Poiselle, has seen her crawl along the hallway, has heard her cry for help, has looked into her blazing green eyes. Has slipped on her blood and blacked out. He vaguely remembers the ambulance driver putting him on the stretcher and wheeling him towards the white-and-orange van. His last thought as they slammed the hinged doors and flicked on the siren: *Theo would not have blacked out.*

Jake examines the private room where the nurse took him

earlier that night. There are no pictures on the beige walls and only one bed, solitude being an ultimate modern luxury for the terribly ill. The hospital staff have put him here because they don't want the swarming media bothering him, asking him uncomfortable questions about the shooting. Being famous is like being sick, Jake realizes, strangers have the urge to help you. A television set bolted to a shelf near the top corner of the room plays without volume. Seinfeld waves his arms at his stupid friend George, but the show looks lifeless without the laugh track. Jake watches for a minute, then grabs the remote and surfs the channels: sees Kathie Lee Gifford grinning while a chimpanzee holds her wallet above its head; extreme-sports boy with a Mohawk haircut flipping on a skateboard tunnel; slow-motion aquatic sequence of a beautiful woman rescuing a man on *Baywatch*; black-and-white footage of the battle of Stalingrad; infomercials for super memory enhancement, for the Fruit-Juicer, for spray-on hair, for the Abdomenizer (*Just 7 minutes a day!*); a herd of buffalo thundering across a plain somewhere. . . . It all blends into a bizarre film montage of everything Jake has ever seen or imagined seeing until, unsurprised, he eventually comes upon his own face. The Network call-in show he hosts, *The Jake Connections*, seems to replay at the oddest hours. In front of his panel of guests, Jake looks fatuous but fit, as all people under thirty-five do on television with the proper amount of make-up. A line of text crawls slowly across the bottom of the screen: "This program is a repeat, please do not call in." Jake pauses and looks at himself in reruns.

Two of his guests are skinheads, the other two are black men, and even though the screen is silent, Jake can see that they're screaming at each other. He can't remember the show and watches himself moderate the dizzying debate, watches as it gets out of control, the camera jumping back and forth between the shouting skinheads and the furious black men, watches his TV self gesticulate with his long hands and his hazel eyes roll back in mock TV condescension as he segues into a new topic, and suddenly Jake's stomach muscles seize up. He drops the remote to the floor and doubles over, nauseous. Finally he gets up and moves towards the window overlooking the city, trying to breathe regularly as his other self moves fluidly back and forth on the screen. There's a loud crack as he bangs his head hard against the frosted dark glass.

Things fall apart.

Jake waits for the pills to do something, anything, but he feels no different than usual. The nurse reappears to see if he's fallen asleep, and when she sees that he hasn't she haltingly asks him to autograph her clipboard. "Make it out to Helen," she whispers excitedly. "I'm a . . . I mean, *she's* a really big fan of your show." As he automatically scribbles something down, Jake recalls an interview he once conducted with Richard Alpert, the Harvard professor who went traipsing around India feeding huge quantities of acid to wandering gurus. Amazingly, nothing seemed to affect them, and this chemical immunity convinced Alpert that there might be something more powerful than LSD. He promptly discarded his Jewish upbringing, changed his name to Ram Das, quit Harvard, and hit the talk-show circuit to pursue higher consciousness. Jake sees stranger things than that every day on his own program – murderers and mystics, cross-dressers and con men – but he wonders if he's now experiencing the transcendent state of the Indian gurus, and hopes, if he is, that it will somehow help.

An hour later, Helen pokes her head in again. She's carrying another clipboard which she uses to balance a muffin, but Jake, impatient for the promised artificial sleep, gives her the big blank stare Jack Nicholson used in *One Flew Over the Cuckoo's Nest*. Eyebrows arched up his forehead until they almost touch his mussed brown hair. Varnished eyes. Wide, sinister smile, making his long nose point downwards over his full, but pallid, lips. Helen quickly puts the muffin on the table beside him and bolts from the room. Three years ago Jake had been a patient at the hospital for an emergency hernia operation and the nurses then had been as aggressive as this one was kind. He'd thrown up for hours after the anaesthetic wore off, and a bitter nurse named Fritz kept ignoring his desperate requests for a glass of water. He was actually Filipino, or Chinese: muscular and mean, and walking around with an unsuitable name like Fritz. Jake can't remember the man's appearance, can only visualize a smudge of colour where Fritz's face should be. Suddenly names don't match faces, bodies don't match voices, places don't match locations. Everything an effect designed to simulate something else more meaningful, but Jake can't figure out what that might be. His arms tingle and lose their feeling and he can't focus his eyes. The pills finally start to take effect and his thoughts drift to faraway places . . .

There's his mother walking across the ice at the cottage, almost a mile away now, her blue snowsuit blending into the sky. She enters the horizon and disappears. The sun blazes silver, but gives no heat to the barren Georgian Bay landscape. Soon it sinks over the evergreen trees like a coin falling through water and the air almost freezes. Hours later, Theo runs to get her. "It's okay, Momma, come back now, it's getting late and you've been out too long, your lips are blue. Jake, build a fire, Momma's in trouble."

Momma misses the husband she never loved and she's become difficult – she cries sometimes and wanders off drunk across the ice until Theo or Jake must retrieve her. Mostly Theo, because he loves emergencies. Mostly Theo, because he's an outdoorsman, because he can stay out in the cold the longest, because if Momma fell through the ice it would be Theo who would dive in, Theo who would have the strength to pull her out, Theo who would give her A.R. until the ambulance arrived.

The sound of a real ambulance echoes through Jake's head, then fades away. A door slams. The P.A. calls for a doctor and Jake sees two people dash by. Nothing seems real: it's just another hospital drama he's seen thousands of times before. Every doorway another screen, every room another set piece, every noise another cue. Switch channels before the story lines are resolved. An old man in brown pyjamas rolls by in a wheelchair yelling, "I need to pee, I need to pee!" Jake's fingers fiddle with the bloodstained buttons on his jacket and a thickness envelopes his head like a hot July smog. Unseasonal.

His memory drifts.

"Pipe down, Jacobson, or I'll pipe you!" says the eleven-year-old Jake at the family dinner table, imitating his French teacher, Mr. Yvettes. Jake runs his hand down Theo's back and gooses him. His brother is laughing uncontrollably, and so is Pop. Jake smiles, smiles widely, and wants to tell that same classroom story again and again because for once it makes everyone happy. But Momma orders him to sit down at the table and eat his dinner, stop being a clown. Momma is drinking herself into a foul mood. Pop laughs and then coughs into a napkin, folds it, but the red spit seeps out and Theo looks away. Theo is already plotting his escape from their home. In the summer he'll join a group in Wyoming and work on a reservation where some Native Indian boys have killed themselves by drinking liquid paper. No one knows. No one knows that behind the laughter Theo is dreaming of a freedom he's never experienced at the dinner table; that Jake's father is worrying about his debts and the spot on his lung; that his mother is trying to forget the quotidian details of her failed marriage. All of them – except Jake – living lives other than those unfolding within the blue walls of their kitchen. The other lives within a life. But back then, Jake doesn't want to understand these things. He wants everyone to keep laughing. He's just a charmed boy who has no secrets yet, his young voice floating above the catacomb of his family's mysteries.

Theo never tolerated mysteries. He's always been certain and committed, as he is now out in Fenwick Park. Theo's strong, six feet tall with a rectangle-shaped, hairless face marked by two embossed cheekbones, unironic as oak tree bark in winter. A stark face concerned with ultimate things, that's how the rabbi described it to Momma when Theo refused to be bar mitzvahed. "I have my own faith," the thirteen-year-old Theo announced simply, and he never attended a religious service again.

When they were very young Theo used to punch Jake on the shoulder and he'd tell Jake to stop following him around. But once he made a mistake and hit Jake in the face. Little Jake cried; a streak of blood ran down his lip and dripped onto the blue carpet in the front hall of the house, making a stain. Momma took Jake into her arms and kissed him. *Jakey, Jakey*, she cooed. Her breath smelled of gin and lemons. Sweet. Theo cried too: he was sorry, he went too far. They all hugged and then Theo looked Jake in the eyes and tearfully promised never to hurt him. "I swear on my life," he said again and again, wiping his nose with the back of his sleeve. Momma forgot to clean up the blood on the carpet and carried them into the den where they curled up in front of the TV with a plate of Ritz crackers and jam, drifting off to sleep to the sound of Johnny Carson's show.

Theo travels and letters from him are rambling and frequent, often just cryptic updates on his latest unlikely adventure. Jake loves how familiar the words are, how Theo's bad punctuation and sloppy writing locate an intimacy in distance, an ease that belies his long periods of absence and their different lives. Jake keeps all the letters in a drawer at his desk at the Network so he can read them while he waits for his producer Kelly Gordon to give him notes on the day's topic. He keeps everything Theo gives him.

Dear J, heat in Calcutta could burn your asbestos underwear off and turns out the new medicine group I'm working with think Mother Theresa is the Pro-life Wicked Witch sticking bible propaganda down starving people's throats and they want to drive her out of business. They invited a crew here from the BBC to do a M. Theresa exposé and tell the world what a sick bitch she is, supporting pro-life nutters and stuff. In my humble opinion they're typical leeches looking for a sexy story (no offence, sort of) and it's all sort of pissing me off so it'll be too bad when the tight British asses from the Beeb find their cameras missing tomorrow and then I'll have to pack up and get out of here quickly. . . . J, hey, no news from you? Too busy at the Network to write me? Well, you're the rising star, or that's what people tell me, and Pop is probably glad that one of his sons isn't a screw-up, that is, if he gives a shit. I wired him a thousand bucks and haven't heard a word from him since, can you believe it, so I guess he probably just blew it. And no, I'm not going to get a computer, so forget about it. Letters are a lost art, you should remember that, because people like you are killing it. Not that I'm any writer, as you can see, but I trust the simplicity of pen to paper, it has its own kind of loyalty to something, but I don't know what the fuck I'm talking about do I? I guess I like its permanence. Anyway, wish you were in Calcutta so I could show you what's going on, no neon lights or all that bullshit and everyone sleeps at night in the street as if drugged by something in the air and it gets so quiet. I just wander about till dawn, walking over hundreds of sleeping bodies, feeling like I'm a ghost in everyone else's dream. I'm drinking too much, can you tell? And people think I'm too intense. . . . J, returning home from China soon, getting kicked out actually by the Red Chinese, as usual my pro-democracy friends aren't the most popular crowd, what with the rally and all, but I did manage to stick it to the government man Chulong who's followed me half around the country making sure I don't start another Tiananmen – slipped some very interesting mushrooms in his wonton and got on the first train to Shanghai. Chu found me (of course) and wasn't happy and neither were the higher-ups so no more Chinese food for this cowboy. . . . J, sorry for not writing, but you must understand that there are not even mailboxes here in Rwanda and I have to wait for a fucking chopper to come and grab the mail. How's Pop feeling? Guess I won't be there for the surgery, but take care of him and make sure his goddamn creditors don't visit him in the hospital – oh, and tell Momma I say hi and blah blah. . . . Feeling depressed, touch of malaria perhaps, that woman I told you about had to get back to Paris so your big brother's all alone again – she told me I was going to kill myself if I didn't sleep more and then we got in a fight about how to run this whole fucking relief project. She actually called me a relief-worker fascist – I woke up the next morning and she was gone. I think she just got homesick, but then again, work makes us free, right? ha ha. . . . Let's go to the Bay as soon as I get back if Momma is feeling okay, that is, and take a nice long paddle, I really miss you. . . . J, so, you got your own show on the Network! Jesus Christ, you're famous, hooray for you. But don't forget about your big bro out here in the *real* world doing some *real* work . . . J, *hi* back, thanks for the advice, but I'm staying out here in B.C. – you probably don't know how much old growth they're cutting down every day (sorry, don't mean to get granola, but you should stop watching your own show and get the true news). . . . J, six months in and things are finally getting hairy – as you know, because I saw the fucking coverage your holy Network gave to what's happening here. You call that shit news? I think the logging companies are sucking your Network reporter's dick every morning. Could you check that out please? If that's what it takes, well, damn, I'll blow the guy all night to get our side on the air! Jesus, Jake, if you want to know what's happening, just ask, don't buy all that crap the loggers are feeding you. By the way, you still with that prof Rachel? Sounds serious. She going to steal you away? I picked up her book at a store out here. Can you spell b-o-r-i-n-g? But I'm the stupid brother, right? Over my head. Love to meet her though, maybe when I get home. . . . J, what the hell is up with you? I saw that episode you did on logging rights, it was like watching Jerry Springer. Where do you get off putting a bunch of loggers on the air with a green loser like that? Who was he anyway, not one of us. Very amusing, and I'm sure you got great ratings when the guy took a swing at the logging exec, but it really pissed me off. I don't even want to tell anyone that you're my brother, 'cause you're practically a wanted man out here. Smarten them up, Jake. At least I can count on you to help us out. By the way, it's freezing out here suddenly. Send me some long underwear. Please. . . . J, Hey, hi and all that, those bloody loggers almost drove over me yesterday, did you catch the clip? I know you did, Mr. Saturday goddamn night. Don't worry, it was just a P.R. stunt, you understand that, just did it for your cameras. But I've got an interesting idea that could turn this whole thing around, so stay tuned. . . . Okay, listen to me carefully, Jake, 'cause I hate to have to write this. I heard you covered the crisis on your so-called news show again and showed a clip of a couple of protesters smoking dope and partying. Thanks for the press. Hey, whose side are you on? I'm out here risking my ass for something and my own brother is smiling pretty trying to nail it to the wall. You got some 'splainin' to do Lucy! Or should I say Geraldo? Stick to your bisexual-overweight-midget-nazi-tell-all shows and leave my stuff the fuck off the air. I hope that doesn't happen again. By the way, you never sent me that underwear, you prick. Gotta go. . . . J, sorry, no time to write any more, but you seem to think you know what's going on anyway, at least from their side of the equation. I bet

> your fucking pay cheque has the pulp and paper industry name on it. Anyway, we'll get to that later when we go away together. The rain here never stops, beating on and on until even your goddamn soul shivers. . . . Miss you J, really need to see you when this is over. . . . Love, Theo . . . love, Theo . . . love, Theo.

Theo is invincible. Pretty much. Pretty much because now he's in serious trouble: a logger is dead, and the police are in a fury. Where is he, why hasn't he written? Theo is angry at him, that's strange. "Don't tell anyone I called you," Theo says, leaving a breathless message on Jake's answering machine, "Everything's fine, that logger deserved what he got. I'll be in touch. . . ." He's running, running.

Jake doesn't run. He's back at the faculty where Rachel teaches, but he doesn't run when he sees her crawling along the bloody hall. It's Sunday night and Rachel's working late to finish marking some papers for her Monday class. She's expecting Jake to come and pick her up, take her to dinner and, if they aren't too late, a movie. But that's not what happens. This is how it looks:

Rachel Anne Poiselle is crawling along the bloody hallway of the English department, crying out for help. Blood pours from her head onto the floor, over her hand, which tries to stem the flow. Her voice rises and falls in the keening rhythm of terror. She claws forward with excruciating effort, like an animal with a broken hip. Finally she manages to raise her head and sees Jake standing at the end of the hall. Relief washes over her, but it instantly transforms into exhaustion. She collapses into her pain to wait for rescue. It doesn't come.

Jake pauses, pauses for too long. Swaying back and forth

on the heels of his shoes, he looks at her blankly, coolly examining the blood on the hallway floor, the blood discharging from her head. Jake knows he should help her, should try to sooth her pain, but he feels completely disengaged, like a film strip imprinting light images. He has this thought: Rachel looks beautiful covered in blood. Exotic, almost like a photo. Her hair is matted and shines, like when she sweats or comes out of the hot shower. Only this time it's black blood. Frame forward: her hands still seem strong and alive, clawing the floor. Beautiful hands he knows so well, hands that cover his body when they're in bed. Zoom in on the face: her teeth are white, so white and complete next to the horrible damage on her head. Next frame: her voice is strong, almost sensually engulfed by terror. And finally this: Jake has the powerful urge to make love to her.

Then, for a moment, everything goes black. He vaguely recalls a shadow down the hall flitting across his line of vision, the faint glimpse of a small red light, but he can't make it out. He must have moved toward it, though, because the next thing he remembers he's in Rachel's office, examining the tipped-over chair, the blood on the floor, the smashed computer screen. He moves slowly, taking more pictures in his head. An open window. A gun lying on the floor. He reaches for the phone and dials 911. The dispatcher is precise, forces Jake to be specific in a way he can't quite follow, to locate the urgent details of the situation. Jake hangs up the phone and sits down on Rachel's desk, not understanding why he's there. He feels blind, groping sloppily for meaning. Minutes pass. And finally it comes, a rising sensation telling him what he ought to do. Something tightens in his chest, a feeling of vertigo accelerating towards the edge of his shrouded mind like rain across the surface of a lake, tearing the precise line between water and air into an ambiguous mist of uncontrolled weather. He stands up and understands: Rachel is hurt. He has watched her, delayed. He's seen something important, the small red light, but now there's no time for reflection. Lost time to recover. He runs back to Rachel, hears her voice calling for him from down the hall. Even through her pain she's ordering him to save her life, instructing him to get an ambulance, to move more quickly. Closer now, Jake runs frantically down the slick red hallway towards her, and then, suddenly, he loses his balance. His shoes slip on the blood and he's down, head explodes against the floor, foot stops against something soft. Rescue bungled. His last thoughts are of something opaque, a blurred picture of someone familiar and then the sound of hail lashing an unbreakable window. Rachel fades to black.

The hospital P.A. system erupts, calling somebody to surgery, and it jolts Jake out of his reverie. Now he's annoyed at Helen because she hasn't given him enough pills to put him to sleep. *Where is she*, he whines to himself, *why hasn't she checked up on me? Maybe I need some help? Maybe I'm in shock?* He thinks about the nurse again, her square body, her efficient fingers more used to hospital tools than humans, her whispered words of comfort. Even the nurse seems to know what happened last night, but Jake can't remember the exact details. With dry lips he silently mouths: *Rachel is dead, Rachel is dead.*

They've been together for eight months, that's all. Two years earlier they met on the set of his show, when Rachel was promoting her book, *Pattern Recognition.* It was a good interview: she answered his questions deftly, had a quick sense of humour, and the callers enjoyed talking to her. They bantered during the commercial breaks, laughing at each other's remarks, but as soon as the show finished she quickly headed for the exit, mumbling something about a dinner she had to attend. Frantically, Jake cornered his producer, Kelly Gordon, in the hallway.

"So, what's the deal?" he said, pushing Kelly against the wall to let one of the set hands walk by.

"Great show all around."

"Not the show. Her."

"What about her?"

"Status?"

"Taken."

"Don't joke."

"Three years. Same guy. Live-in."

"Shit."

"Truth. A well-known writer. I forget his name. All this important data was in your research pack, as usual. You might read it occasionally. We do go to a lot of trouble."

"The way she talked, the way she touched my arm at the break, I thought she was, I don't know–"

"Flirting?"

"Yes."

"That was *you*. She was busy talking about her book."

"Oh, for Christ's sake." Jake moves away, wiping the make-up off his cheek with the sleeve of his suit.

"Don't do that," Kelly cautions, pulling his arm away and thinking about spiralling wardrobe costs. She yells down the hall: "Get Make-up out here with some cream! Now!"

"I'm such an idiot," Jake mutters.

"Don't say that, honey. I really thought you two were lovely together," Kelly consoles, a grin slipping across her wide, overworked face. "And if you want, I can tell you the exact same thing about tomorrow night's guest. Because I live to serve, sahib." She raises her hands and takes a mock bow.

"Fuck off," Jake laughs.

"Gladly."

Kelly heads down the hall as the make-up lady dashes up and slaps a massive dollop of white cream on Jake's face.

A few months later Jake sees Rachel and the "well-known writer" at a party. They stand in the corner of a small room, letting people come to them, as if the party was actually being held in their honour. He watches them closely, trying to hide behind a group of prematurely balding men swapping first-mortgage stories. Jake notices that, unlike most beautiful women, Rachel doesn't look bored, as if dragged out of the glamorous world of the beautiful people in order to fulfil some quotidian obligation she has to the more plain-looking folk. Nothing about her communicates obligation – not the way she holds her lover's hand, not the attentive way she listens to someone talk. She generates ease with an almost political instinct, frequently touching people, squeezing an arm or brushing a shoulder as if to neutralize any power imbalance her presence may cause – just like she did to Jake when she was on his show. Her dark, almost over-ripe green eyes move slowly, soaking in details, but when something intrigues her they flash wildly, as if some stored-up information has just split through the glassy surface and begun to pour outward. Jake sees how people are drawn to her, wanting to hold the attention of her eyes. And when they can't do it for long, they go to a different corner of the party to talk about her.

She's almost six feet tall, thin as a wood shaving, with small breasts pressing under her tight black sweater. Her lips make a pouty red circle on her face as if someone has crushed a raspberry against her white skin. When she laughs, which is frequently, her lips open to reveal a perfect set of white teeth, save for a small gap in the front two where he can almost see her tongue. She leans against the wall with her head bent forward to listen, her blond hair pressed carelessly over her ears, some strands spilling over her forehead, almost bordering her eyes. She smokes steadily and politely exhales to the ceiling, where the smoke catches the light and glows. From across the room, Jake listens to her husky voice, listens to the way she twirls dull words around to make them humorous, prowling subtly for ideas and brushing people with her hands, as if her fingers might alchemically set the people around her at ease. All vanity and selflessness, Jake thinks, and more compelling for the contradiction.

Out of pride, perhaps envy, he refuses to join the parade lining up to talk to her. He decides she's a phony – at least, he decides that after she doesn't rush over and thank him for the interview. It's as if she doesn't remember him at all. He feels his ego bruise in bitterness, and turns to easier prey: her boyfriend. A diminutive, pompous academic whose non-fiction books were often quoted, but rarely purchased. *Asshole*, Jake mumbles. He leaves early without speaking to her. He stays up all night, restless and alone.

Six months later, at one of Dylan O'Sullivan's soirées, Jake spots her again.

"Do you see that woman?" whispers Dylan, as he steers Jake around the bar towards Rachel. She's surrounded by four men. "That's Rachel Poiselle, the author. Very, very hot. I'd hawk my fucking Rolodex to do her. She's single, you know."

"Really?" replies Jake quickly, not sure whether he ought to trust Dylan's information at this point in the night. After all, he's already seen Dylan imbibe tequila, vodka, scotch and some Moroccan hash – the consummate, albeit indiscriminate, host. "I had her on the show once," Jake says, trying to feign uninterest and manoeuvre the gapingly bombed Dylan away from her before he sabotages Jake's chances.

"Yeah, I saw that episode," Dylan says. "You practically drooled on your mike." He laughs stupidly.

Jake stiffens but can't help probing for more information. "Isn't she always with that schmuck . . . what's his name? The writer."

"That's all over," Dylan says, his voice rising dangerously. "The dope cheated on her, can you believe it? With one of her own students! He should unzip his fly and air out his fucking brain, losing her. Look at the dials on her screen."

"Well, Dylan, why don't you take your tongue off the floor and go give it a shot," Jake says, adding quickly, "You've tried everyone else."

"Funny boy," Dylan replies, downing another drink that has somehow appeared in his hand. "Don't think I haven't tried, but she won't give me the time of day. Told me television arts producers were shallow. I'm quoting. So I dredged up some shit about James Joyce to impress her and she called me out on a scene from *Ulysses*. Naturally, I blew it. I never bothered to read the fucking book in school, but who did? Her, of course. I haven't even skimmed as much as she's read. You ought to take her down a peg, superstar. Let's go."

Dylan drags Jake over to Rachel, who's too engrossed in a discussion with a few earnest academic types to notice their arrival.

"Excuse me, Rachel," Dylan interrupts, swinging his hand sloppily over her shoulder. "I want you to meet my very good friend, Jacob Jacobson. He's the star of the whole goddamn Network, as I'm sure you already know."

"We met once on my show, I think," Jake says, giving her an unsubtle reminder.

Rachel's eyes cloud in a confused look and she slips out

from under Dylan's arm. "Sorry," she says, "but I did a lot interviews for the book. What show was that?"

Dylan explodes in disbelief, spraying the men in front of Rachel with his saliva. "You don't watch *The Jake Connections*? Oh shit. And I thought it was only us producers who weren't worthy."

"I guess we're all a little unworthy, Dylan," Jake says, forcing a smile. He finds himself wishing that Dylan's liver would immediately pickle and send him crashing to the ground. Turning back to Rachel, he grimaces. "Why would you know it? It's just a daily game show. But we give away huge prizes."

"You do look like a game show host, now that I think of it," she replies, catching the vitriol in Jake's voice and throwing it back at him.

"Hey, fun, fun, people, this is a party," Dylan mutters, suddenly wondering if he's somehow offended Jake and will therefore suffer a mysterious career setback at the Network. As the paranoia grips him he slurs into ass-kissing mode. "Rachel, *The Jake Connections* is the most popular show on the Network. Right, Jake? Maybe on TV in general. Or in the world. Am I right or am I right?" Dylan staggers, as if his efforts at flattery have somehow unsettled the roiling stew of booze in his stomach.

"Right, Dylan," Jake continues, biting down on his words. "It's kind of like *The Price Is Right*, only we play with politicians. They bid on Third World countries and we award the winner one at the end of the show."

"Oh, I remember you now," Rachel says, pulling on a cigarette. "But you're much wittier on TV than you are in person." She grins playfully and Jake grins back, moving closer to her and squeezing Dylan between them.

"TV changes people so much," he says. "I'm taller on screen too. And black, of course. I also have an English accent."

"Bully for you." She lifts her glass in a mock toast.

"Excuse me, I have to freshen up," Dylan mumbles, bolting towards a group of five lawyers he's spotted passing around a joint.

"I hear your book ended up selling well," Jake says to Rachel, continuing the banter. "I hope my unmemorable show helped. Our viewership includes most of my immediate family."

"I'm sure I owe most of my success to you."

"I take VISA."

"I've heard you're show has changed since I went on. It's more . . ."

"Trashy?" Jake offers happily.

"That's the word."

"We prefer to say popular."

"Pick your euphemism."

"You know, they've developed a cure for cultural snobbery."

"You're getting defensive."

"That's because I have something to defend. You?"

Taken aback by his quickness, she appraises him more thoroughly. "A talk show host. A professional talker. Now, how does one go about becoming one of those?"

"It's a Wiccan ritual. Very bloody."

"Was this some childhood dream of yours, to talk on TV? I'm always curious. How do people like you happen?"

"We pupate. In pods, actually."

"Not a fireman? A doctor? No. You always wanted to be a talk-show host?"

"Twelve years old watching Johnny Carson with my father and during the opening monologue I turned to him and said:

'Pop, when I grow up I want to be a talk-show host.' And he replied, 'Son, you can't do both.' "

She grins. "Astute man."

The group of men around Rachel shuffle their feet uncomfortably, instantly aware that they have become redundant.

"Am I interrupting something?" asks Jake disingenuously.

"As a matter of fact, you are," Rachel says, immediately touching the fellow beside her on the shoulder to bring him back into the conversation. Jake notices how he brightens instantly. "Ned was telling me about a book he's writing on the nature of genius. He argues that it's not necessarily a genetic trait, but something that can be acquired through study."

"Well, there's still hope for me then!" retorts Jake, hoping Ned will have enough intelligence to decipher the "fuck off" vibes he's sending his way. Ned doesn't budge. "I guess I can safely assume that Ned is a genius. Is the book a bestseller?"

"Actually, it's not quite finished yet, it's a project that I'm still trying to sell and–" Ned stutters uncomfortably.

"Ned's just finishing his doctorate," Rachel cuts in, rising to his defence. "A brilliant thinker." She exhales some smoke, not bothering to point it to the ceiling. It wafts in front of Jake's face.

"Not as brilliant as you, Rachel," Ned says smugly, reaching up to pat her hand. Jake notices Ned's smarmy manoeuvre and he suddenly feels nasty and reckless. He hopes Rachel will somehow find this erotic.

"Why don't we have the whole class on then?" Jake announces, putting his arm around Ned's shoulder and forcing him to disengage from Rachel. "What about it, Ned? Show and tell a couple of good Ph.D. theories? Viewers really go for an action-packed hour of post-structural neo-deconstructive psychoanalytical mumbo-jumbo."

"As opposed to what?" Rachel snaps, pulling Ned away before Jake takes him apart. "The incest-victim, crippled-transvestite-exposé you usually go with?"

"It's an idea."

"A bad one."

The verbal gymnastics grow sour and Jake picks up on Rachel's boredom. The crowd around them drifts off uncertainly, Ned heading quickly for the door.

"Well, you do quite a job of making people feel miserable," Rachel says finally, making motions towards the exit herself. "Aren't TV personalities supposed to make people feel the opposite?"

"How do you feel?" Jake counters, trying to keep her interest by changing the subject back to her.

"Embarrassed, but more for your sake than mine."

"They didn't look like the most fascinating bunch."

"Unlike you?"

"Try me."

"I guess I can safely assume that you're just a tad arrogant."

"As opposed to what, your humbility?"

He's running dangerously low on verbal ammunition and she decides not to let it go unnoticed. Smiling sadly at him, she parts her lips to reveal the tips of her teeth. "My humbility?"

"Humbleness, humblenicity, whatever." Jake throws up his arms in confusion, his aggressive tone collapsing. "Oh, hell, I give up. I'm sorry. I'm just so tired of Dylan's cocktail parties, you know? All these culturally competitive bottom feeders schmoozing someone else higher up on the social ladder, trying to be so goddamn fabulous and witty, but no one ever talks honestly – at least not to me."

"Maybe you just have that effect on people."

"Thank you."

They pause for a moment and lock eyes, hers widening as if to ask him to stop the relentless chatter, but Jake breaks her gaze immediately. He can't stop talking. He's too nervous, too exhilarated by her attention, and fears that if he loses momentum she'll simply find someone more interesting and forget about him. Stupidly, painfully, he bullies onward.

"So what happened to your lover, the little author guy?"

"The 'little author guy' slept with one of my students and left me," she says without flinching. "It devastated me, if you really want to know. Couldn't leave my apartment for months."

"Did it make you a better writer?"

Her eyes quickly flash greens and blues. "Do you ever get tired of being such a prick?"

"I'm serious. I want to know if the pain helped your writing."

"I don't know," she says, shaking her head in confusion. She shifts her weight from one foot to another and fidgets clumsily with her plastic lighter. "Maybe. Yes. I don't think about it like that."

Interpreting Rachel's momentary lapse as a suitable opening, Jake instinctively resorts to a more brazen strategy. "I think you should ask me out for a drink," he blurts out, tapping her lightly on the shoulder.

"Ask *you* for a drink?"

"That's right. Pick a date."

Her tongue flickers over the space between her two front teeth. "Is there oxygen in your world?"

She swivels on her heel and heads for the door, and Jake, seeing his plan backfire, decides his only hope is to push things so far that her distaste might transform into attraction – or, at the very least, interest.

"Call me at the Network on Monday," he snaps, grabbing her arm and pulling her around. "You can dial me up from the main line. We'll have lunch."

Before she can pull away, he strides quickly out the exit, leaving her standing alone, stunned, in the middle of Dylan's disintegrating party.

Throughout the next week Jake waits for her call, but it doesn't come. Finally, losing his patience, he phones the University of Toronto and books an appointment with her faculty secretary under the name of Bob Barker.

"Well, well. The TV wonder boy comes crawling," she says from behind her cluttered desk when he shuffles into her office. Her computer makes a blip as if it's just saved some data.

"You never called me."

"I'll bet that hasn't happened before."

He walks over to the shelf and picks up a copy of her book, bouncing it in his hand as if to weigh it. "Sorry about the other night."

"You ought to be."

"I'm suing myself for verbal assault, on your behalf."

She punches a key absently on her computer, as if tired.

"So what about dinner?" he asks.

"Is that a metaphysical question?"

"You're being difficult."

"And you're being slick."

"Truce?" He extends his hand, but she ignores it.

Jake says, "I want to have dinner with you. Will you come?"

"I don't think so," she says, turning her attention back to her computer. For a moment he pauses, listening to a pattering sound, and then he notices her foot tapping nervously on the marble floor beneath her desk.

"I'll pick you up at six-thirty," he says.

"I finish at seven."

At dinner they continue their banter, but the aggression soon turns to curiosity, and by dessert, to whispers. She invites him back to her apartment and pulls him into the bedroom almost immediately. Jake is taken aback by her easy abandon, the way her hands press against the small scars that cover his skin without concern or question, the way she bites his shoulder to hold back noises of pleasure, the way she instructs him on how to touch her. They stay awake until five in the morning, letting dawn cool them into sleep. After that they're together every night, discovering new borders and shapes of emotion. Where they first spoke cleverly, now they hardly speak at all, lying in silence for hours, letting their bodies settle into a new vocabulary of intimacy. Within two weeks he wants to tell her he loves her and tries to keep it inside. But his mouth opens to the words anyway and she replies in kind. It's too early for either of them to believe what they say, but they say it anyway because it's an idea they want to admit to knowing nothing about. Their promise is to learn about it later, through hands and eyes, through the text of sleep.

□ □ □

When Jake wakes up an hour later in his hospital room, he walks to the window and stares at a crowd of reporters who have gathered ten stories below. Vendors selling hot dogs and roasted chestnuts hover on the perimeter of the gathering quietly waving their steaming paper bags. Cameramen with high tripods record the scant beginnings of what looks to be a growing protest. The news has already spread, Jake thinks. The semi-famous Rachel Anne Poiselle has been shot. The very famous Jacob Jacobson is somehow involved. All the ingredients of a good news story. Jake squints to read the badly painted letters on a banner carried by three people: STOP THE MASSACRE OF WOMEN! How did they get here so early? Jake wonders, but then he realizes how the accidents of famous people have a way of rerouting schedules and creating their own time cycles.

A woman wearing a black checkered keffiyeh holds a megaphone and leads a ragged group of six or seven people in a chant, her arms rising and falling as if she's pumping water from a well. The small crowd moves their lips in unison and sway slowly, little puffs of hot breath blurring their mouths into angry expressions. Star bursts from the camera lights glisten in the grey dawn as reporters do live updates for their morning shows. Jake hears nothing. He stares over the crowd, down University Avenue, past the tall downtown buildings where early-morning traffic snarls, and out towards the shore of Lake Ontario. Tilting his head, his eyes catch the black skyline and move upwards until he stares directly into the freezing sun of a white sky. *Rachel is dead, Rachel is dead.* He repeats this line like a mantra and moves back to the bed, closing his eyes to another kind of blackness.

□ □ □

"Hey, Jacobson, you up? I got some questions I'd like you to answer."

Jarred awake to a loud voice. Jake rubs his eyes and looks up to see that the nurse with cold hands has been replaced by a large, yellow-haired man who has set upon his stale muffin with the kind of desperation reserved for the starving. The man lifts his head for a moment, his mouth cemented with bran, and stares intently at Jake through big rimless glasses. He smiles warmly, crinkling the skin beside his eyes, but it's quite obvious to Jake that the man is trying to communicate something approximating the exact opposite of warmth.

"Got to ask you about last night," the man says, his words muffled by the food.

Jake examines him, shaking his head, as if the image he's seeing is distorted. Something's wrong with the man. He looks normal . . . pressed beige pants and suit jacket that might have come from a Bay Days sale set off by a slash of blue Bic pens in the breast pocket. Maybe it's the sideburns – old mutton chops, too long and out of fashion, even for the chic retro look. No, it's the left ear; more precisely, the fact that the man doesn't have a left ear. Pink scar tissue covers a very small stump that moves hypnotically as the man chews on the muffin. It's gruesome really, especially when contrasted with his well-kept air. For a moment the fog in Jake's mind lifts.

"You lookin' at my ear, aren't you," the man says as he sees Jake's eyes focus. "It's okay, everyone takes a secret peek."

"Sorry," Jake whispers.

"Forget it." The man flashes the I'm-not-really-smiling smile again. "Even my wife says it makes me look like a goddamn alien. So take your guess. Go ahead."

Jake sits silently, squinting his eyes in confusion.

"Don't be shy," the man says, bending over to give Jake a closer look at the mottled skin where his ear used to be. Patches of hair grow randomly beside the small, dark hole. "I know what you're thinkin'."

"You do?"

"Yeah, yeah. How'd I lose the ear, right? You wanna know, but you're afraid to ask 'cause you think I'll be offended or something, and I'm just sayin', take a shot. I don't mind at all."

"It's okay," Jake mumbles, averting his eyes.

"No, go for it. You wanna ask, so ask. Was it a birth defect? Was it a car accident? Whatever you think, bring it on."

The man lifts his hands and waves them at his chest, urging Jake to say something.

"I don't know," says Jake finally, shrugging his shoulders.

"One guess. Just one."

"Alright, okay. I'll go with fire."

"Very close." The man grins delightedly. "Actually, it was a blow torch. Mind if I eat this?" The man holds up the half-devoured muffin. "Someone must have left it for you."

"Blow torch?" Jake repeats, overcome by a wave of nausea.

"Mohawks, my friend," the man explains. He pronounces it *Mo-hacks*. "Just before the Oka stand-off in Quebec." He stuffs the last of the muffin in his mouth. "Nearly scalped me, if you'll pardon the slur, although I don't think that's a slur, just history. Whatever. Got to be careful with Indians though, even talkin' about them."

"What happened?" Jake sounds like a child at show-and-tell.

"Long story, but since you almost guessed. . . . They got hold of me one night when they were on some sort of recon mission, the Mo-hacks that is. I was out patrolling the stand-off area alone, makin' sure they weren't leaving the reserve to smuggle in guns. Stupid to be alone, I know, but hell, we were at those barricades for days, and I was just trying to cool off. They were throwing rocks earlier, threatening to shoot us cops, all for your camera people, mind, but fuckin' scary all the same. Anyways, I'm just walkin' and suddenly I'm grabbed from behind by four, maybe six guys, dragged into a car, beaten up pretty good, and then knocked out. Drugged too, I think. Woke up the next day missing my goddamn ear. Massive burns to the tenth degree. Doctor almost barfed when they brought me in. Cops kept it quiet, didn't want to upset the media, elevate the crisis and all. Worst goddamn thing that's ever happened to me, but people go on. Got a promotion and a citation because of it. That's just what you do, brother, you endure. Get scalped by a gang of Mo-hacks and then you just move the fuck along. Good muffin." He scans the room for another.

Jake has difficulty processing the man's story. He covered the Oka crisis when he was a reporter for the Network and he'd never even heard a rumour about a cop getting assaulted like that.

"Nobody got *scalped* in Oka. I was there."

"Huh? Well, like I says, we never told anyone. But you can't trust you media types to get the whole story," the man adds quickly and winks at Jake.

"Who are you?"

"Quite a crowd out there," the man says, ignoring Jake's question and pointing out the window. "None too happy with things."

The watery feeling suddenly returns as Jake tries to remember the details of the Oka crisis. His thoughts slosh uselessly around for facts, and then, like a car blowing a tire on the highway, swerve off into other memories. The man in front of him starts to resemble his brother Theo. *Theo's coming home and wants to go camping–*

"By the way, I'm detective Ian O'Malley. Irish descent, in case you're wondering," the man says, switching topics again and flashing a badge. "Big cliché, I know, an Irish cop, but hell, it's a cliché 'cause it's true, right?"

But Jake's mind is drifting and he can barely hear the man. Theo wants to travel somewhere together as soon as he returns from the logging protests at Fenwick Park.

"Not too many of us in Quebec," O'Malley continues, in the same methodical rhythm he used to devour the muffin. "That's where I'm from before I moved here. Frenchies gettin' to me with all that separation bullshit. Know what I mean?"

"Maybe we'll go to Algonquin Park," Theo says, "where we used to go to get away from Momma and Pop, get away from the fighting. It'll be great in the winter . . ."

"Jewish?" O'Malley mumbles as he begins to gnaw on the soggy paper of the muffin holder.

For a moment Jake jumps back into the conversation.

"Sorry?" he says, shaking his head.

"I'm saying, you're a Jew. You know, with a double name like that: Jacob Jacobson. I always try to know the ethnic origin of the people I'm dealing with. Helps the communication if you just get it right out in the open. I have this theory: If everyone knows everyone else's story then we'll all just get along fine, if you know what I'm sayin'. Grew up with some Jews down near my house in NDG. Nice people, no trouble. Never had any with a double name though. Jacob Jacobson. Strange." O'Malley rubs the stump of his ear with thick fingers as he ponders the ethnic mysteries of Jake's name.

But Jake can't understand the man. He's canoeing somewhere up north with his brother, bending his neck back to feel a warm rain cover his forehead and lifting his arm up to wipe his brow. The gesture makes it seem as if he's sweating, but he isn't. O'Malley makes a note in his book and smiles again.

"Like to ask you a couple of questions about last night, Mr. Jacobson. If that's okay?"

"You're too busy with that fucking show now," Theo says, angrily complaining that they can't make time to go away together. "When I

get home I'm selling Pop's old canoe," Theo threatens, *"we never use it now anyway."*

"I should tell you, Mr. Jacobson, that you have the right to an attorney, but I don't think . . ."

Two weeks ago Theo sent a short and cryptic postcard from Fenwick Park. *"Don't be afraid to be afraid, Jake. Love, Theo."* What does he mean? What kind of letter is that? He's angry about the coverage the logging protest is getting. *Angry at me.* Now Theo's disappeared, no letters, no calls. And one of the loggers at the protest is dead.

"Mr. Jacobson, hey!" O'Malley snaps his fingers three times. Snap. Snap. Snap. "You okay, bud?"

The strange man with the torched ear is talking.

"Mr. Jacobson, why don't we just talk straight? Shit, we're men of the world; you're a famous guy, and so am I, sort of." O'Malley leans in towards Jake's face. "You ever see my *Crime Re-Play* segments? On at 6:22 p.m. every Tuesday night on Channel 9, local news. I host the report – you know, car thieves, hold-ups, B and E's. We do re-enactments of crimes with scratch amateur actors and I come in at the end and ask the audience for any tips. Write 'em all myself too, it's just this talent I got. I try to keep it very gritty, very *real*, like on *NYPD Blue*, right? I'm no Jacob Jacobson, mind – hey, I'm missing a goddamn ear – but I understand the medium. Talk to the camera like it's your bloody wife or best friend. And don't let anyone see the bad ear! I know what I'm talkin' about. You know, we're kin, both of us public people. I'm even toyin' with the idea of writing a book about life on the streets. Everyone thinks they're an artist, right? So let's be up front and everything will be fine. Last night there was a gun involved in this Professor, uh, Poiselle incident, see, and it seems that you told the dispatcher that you saw it or somethin'. Can you tell me what happened?"

Jake tries to focus on the question but keeps getting distracted by the man's ear. If the man's on air, he wonders, why doesn't he get some plastic surgery or a prosthetic ear? Are there prosthetic ears? Jake imagines a box full of them at the dollar store. Artificial body parts for sale, cut rate. Everything disassembled. He notices the arm of the man's glasses resting precariously on the deformed stump, bobbing up and down as he talks, and Jake waits for it to slip off and send the thick rimless glasses crashing to the floor.

"Hey, uh, Mr. Jacobson, I know this is hard and all, but just tell me what you told the dispatcher."

Jake feels his mind tugging itself away from the conversation, like a boat revving to leave a dock it's still moored to. He hopes his mental ropes will hold, he knows this is an important conversation, he watches the man's lips move. But something in Jake's head is not connecting.

"Mr. Jacobson, please, you told 911 that you saw a gun, didn't you? That you know where the weapon is, isn't that right? Thing is, we don't have the gun in our possession. What exactly did you see?"

Jake cocks his head to the side, unable to answer.

"Oh, for fuck's sake, snap the hell out of it!" O'Malley suddenly yells, whipping off his glasses.

"I'm sorry," Jake says, gritting his teeth as the boat breaks its moorings and leaves the dock. "I just don't think I can help you."

Through his pleasant memory of canoeing with Theo in Algonquin Park, Jake vaguely hears Detective Ian O'Malley's voice say, "Mr. Jacobson, I think you should start looking for a lawyer."

July 17, 1996

Jessica Aikey. Matthew Alexander. Charles Beatty. David Hogan. Kyle Miller. Carol Fry. Jean Zara. Marcel Dadi . . .

I decide to write down some of the names of the dead passengers aboard the TWA flight that crashed off of Long Island. I'm not sure why. I guess I'll try to get to know them over the next few months as the mysterious "they" sort out the details of the disaster. The media gives it a long, one-word title, which I like better: "the-worst-airline-disaster-in-American-aviation-history." It sounds like the title of an e.e. cummings poem.

Here are the words that I hear most often tonight: terrorists, bomb, mechanical failure, black boxes, rescue effort, survivors, France, Long Island, baggage, passenger list, no survivors, and we'll-be-back-with-more-on-the-worst-airline-disaster-in-American-aviation-history.

I take down all the names the news people mention because the names will be the most important and least memorable part of the mystery. So, instead of watching TV and listening to FDA excuses and TWA apologies, instead of going on-line and checking the conspiracy pundits who blame the CIA or the local Arab terrorist squad, I stick to the passenger list. Lists of all kinds help in a disaster. I'm just doing my bit.

After a couple of hours I reread the names I've jotted down. I've only got a partial list of the victims. "There were no survivors in the-worst-airline-disaster-in-American-aviation-history," says Dan Rather, says Peter Jennings, says William Stonebane. The mantra of the day. It's become a pretty empty phrase by now, but it's still used a lot, I think because telling people there are no survivors signals to us, the vigilant viewers, that we can finally stop thinking about the people on board and get on to the real question: What the heck happened to that big old plane? No survivors is a nice segue line into more compelling discussions of engine failure, plastic explosives, and security lapses. Hardware. Engineering. Stuff that needs no funeral. Leave the messy details to the priests, TV likes mysteries.

Rereading my unfinished passenger list out loud, I try to compete with the volume of the TV and imagine who they were. Some of the people on the plane were students. Some were husbands, some wives, some friends, and some long-time colleagues. There might also have been child abusers, petty thieves, drug addicts. Maybe there was a man on board taking a secret trip with the woman he's having an affair with and now his poor wife is home grieving for him, forever ignorant of his terrible infidelity. It doesn't matter. None of them deserved to die like that, invisibly, aware at the last second that their most hackneyed fears of an airline disaster have actually come true. The black humour of a death that's statistically improbable. What would I have thought, strapped into a seat, as the fireball approached? Maybe: an airline disaster? Of all the ways to go, can't I get a better ending than that? Who's the author of this story, anyway?

But I'm bullshitting myself. Accident survivors often confess that during the final moments before impact they had no thought at all. No fear, no prayer, no memory. Just a blankness, a nullity, a feeling of being disengaged from their body and watching the accident happen from above. Somehow I'm comforted by this information.

I get up and go retrieve a phone book and start randomly adding names to the list. After awhile I can't discern which names came from the TV and which came from the phone book. It's all pretty random unless you read the names carefully, which most of us don't. Did Beth Trudell die in the crash, or is she living happily in upstate New York? Check the list. Maybe Beth was not on the plane, but since her appearance in the phone book, it's possible that she too has died in an improbable accident. Struck by lightning? Hit in the crossfire of a gang shoot out? I don't know. I wonder if I read the new list on TV, would anyone know the difference? Who listens to the actual names, except the families? Why make it public? Would anyone in the audience know who Beth Trudell is, what phone book she appears in? Maybe she's just a made-up name.

All night I watch TWA disaster footage and I realize that it doesn't matter who's on the victim list. Each life is a fiction, a set of events that someone decides to remember, an imagined constellation in someone's blurred night sky. And we remember so few people, we pay so little attention to the people on the lists because there's no difference between death and life if nobody knows your story. That's the only real law of media.

I make the list longer and longer and promise myself to fax it to TWA with a note asking them to "Please locate the following people who have gone missing." I add my own name to the middle of the list, head to the kitchen and minutes later I'm enjoying a Lean Cuisine. Chicken Parmesan, piping hot, straight out of the microwave.

REVERSE ANGLE

This is how the librarian gets involved:

The anticipation of his smoke break so occupies Tasso Darjun's mind that he fails to notice both the two police officers standing in front of the revolving doors of the Network building and the Channel 7 Street-Beat news van parked across the street. Why do the callous reporters insist on having their covert, late-night cigarettes in *his* library, he wonders, stepping over a puddle of slush and pulling his grey cap over his ears, when they could just as easily slip into Studio 50, like he does, and smoke in the little storage space behind the flats of the set? Uncomfortable and cramped as it is back there, at least the studio has a powerful air filter that efficiently sucks up the offending – and recently outlawed – stench. And as an added bonus, he thinks, the security guard never checks there to disturb him.

Tasso jumps up onto the curb and a blast of wind hits him on the chest so that his black woollen coat billows like a cape, almost knocking him into a snowbank. Was it arrogance on their part, lack of respect for the sanctity of books, or simply a matter of convenience? he ponders. Indeed, the library houses one of the few windows in the Network that the renovators didn't seal shut so, to a certain extent, Tasso understands why the staff covet it in winter. Cowering outside the front doors in the bracing cold, as the anti-smoking rule has forced so many people to do, was no way to enjoy a fix of nicotine. The library provided a warm and convenient place to have an indoor puff – a veritable Tropic of Cancer, as the library was often called by the addicts. Still, he'd asked them many times to stop, even told them about his hideaway in Studio 50, but nonetheless they persisted. And so every morning the stale smell of tobacco assaulted his nose, mingling unpleasantly with the pure, woody smell of his well-organized research books and stacks of magazines. "Damned reporters and their smoking," he mutters, picking up his pace.

He's getting irritated and knows it's useless. The scent will stay but his morning will evaporate. And Tasso adores his mornings, adores the 6 a.m. brisk walk up Spadina Avenue, adores being the only person at the library, *his* library, where for one long hour before the hysterical news day begins he can sit in silence among the clippings and books and tapes he has cherished and ordered for so many years. Bliss.

He keeps his head down to shield his face from the biting wind, nimbly negotiating his way across the ice, deriving secret pride from the fact that he never compromises his stride. Twenty-five years without slipping or falling on the treacherous ice of his adopted country, an accomplishment few natives could brag about: two kilometres to the building in the morning, two back to his flat in the evening, summer through winter, one thousand kilometres a year, body moving like a metronome.

Tasso is a man of order, and his disapproval of the reporters' sloppy habits comes more from that than from any reactionary policy against smoking. Tasso himself enjoys exactly two cigarettes a day, but makes sure that they offend no one. The first is at 12:45 p.m., immediately after lunch, when he slips into the cavernous studio, where such illustrious shows as *The Jake Connections* are recorded, and crouches in the storage area near the ventilator to light up a single Benson and Hedges Gold. Charcoal filtered. His second cigarette is lit at exactly 6:05 p.m., when he leaves the Network building to begin his walk home. His custom is to pause outside the revolving door on Spadina Avenue, turn eastward to face the defaced 1959 bronze plaque – "Network-TV: Truth in Journalism?" (the question mark etched deeply a few years earlier by a downsized reporter) – open his Benson and Hedges King Size and take out another long, thin stick. Indeed, the Network reporters make jokes about it on occasion, about his "little turn towards Mecca." "How's the mother of all cigarettes, Tasso?" they say, or, "Lighting the evening incense for Allah?"

Tasso ignores both the distasteful remarks and the inaccurate observation. He's not Muslim, but Hindu, a distinction often lost on the heavy-handed TV reporters for whom the building had once been an exclusive domain. But under the new president, Greta Watt, so much has changed. The Network is now dedicated not only to greater ethnic diversity, but also to more financially diverse activities – films, databases, administration, and the more sinister-sounding "on-line services," whatever that is – and established reporters like William Stonebane tend toward bouts of snobbishness. They let elevator doors close as Tasso scurries towards them, calling out, "Hold it, please!"

They demand their research from the library with rude (and poorly written) e-mails – "National news need ALL New York Times files on Monica Lewinsky's high school record, by 3pm, urgent!!! Hi-lite any stuff on sex!!!" And worse, they stay late working on their stories, smoking illegally in the library near the open window, sometimes leaving their cigarette butts crushed disgracefully in the floor where Tasso smells them in the morning.

There is also, Tasso theorizes, something more personal to all this muted hostility than just the modern frustrations of news people. It has to do with Tasso's relationship, albeit tenuous, to the controversial young star, Jacob Jacobson. Last year Jacobson did Tasso a special favour and hired Tasso's daughter, Raitna, to work on his show as a summer intern. Stonebane and the old guard immediately interpreted this as an alliance against their version of the Network, and Tasso's own sense of neutrality, cultivated so carefully over the years, was suddenly compromised. He was politicized now simply by showing up for work. It's all so complicated and sad, Tasso thinks, recalling his old life during the war in Goa, so long ago it barely has shape as memory. He shivers in the cold and unconsciously quickens his pace as his mind stretches back to another life.

The beautiful old city of Goa instantly splinters. It's the Goan war of 1961, when the Indian government invaded the Portuguese colony, wanting to take everything back for their new country. Neighbours stop talking to each other as political alliances become public; his family supports the Portuguese, most others do not. Soon they are at war with each other, and a young, outspoken Tasso is elected to lead a small band of soldiers. He remembers the thrill of sabotaging Indian trains, of setting land mines on supply roads, remembers the lust of a rebel woman brimming with the passions of fear, remembers sleeping at a different hide-out every night, the frisson of rebellion, of sex and war. But the thrill doesn't last. Suddenly there are torn bodies in the street, old homes burnt to black rubble, and then his mother and father are splayed out dead in the living room, bullet holes in their chest and in the white plaster walls above them. And days later his beloved is dead, too. Everything accelerates into chaos and failure, jail sentences loom for the rebels and the war is over, everything old changed forever. The defeated subversive Tasso Darjun and his baby daughter have to escape to a new land, riding on an old cargo vessel that takes them to the back room of some distant relative in Canada.

Canada. Tasso lets the syllables dance on the tip of his tongue as if he's trying to summon some taste from a bland piece of food. Ca-na-da. He looks down at the slush puddles that might well be the national symbol of his adopted country and darts around them. It could be worse, he thinks wistfully. He could be rotting in an Indian jail or stuck serving drinks to stoned American hippies, like some of his friends on the beaches of Goa. But he has his library and his daughter and his morning walk. A new and quiet life he's worked hard to build and protect. If the old staff treat him rudely, at least they can't take away his security.

So he doesn't look up when the Channel 7 camera crew scrambles from the van and begin to film him. He doesn't notice the two detectives nod at each other and put their hands on the butts of their revolvers. As he approaches the building, Tasso automatically reaches to his side, unclips the key chain hanging from his belt loop, and uses his thumb to single out the magnetic pass card to the front door of the Network building. It's gauche to hang keys from his belt, he knows it. It's custodial, boorish. Back in Goa he would never have done that. As a Brahmin, wearing tools of labour was strictly out of the question, even in the Portuguese colony. It wasn't the Brahmin way. And, more importantly, it wasn't the Western way. He remembers how hard he studied English and Portuguese with the private tutors his parents hired, how thrilled he was as an eight-year-old throughout the family trip to Europe, his mother constantly telling him stories about the wonders of Oxford University, where his father had always wanted to attend, and where young men went to study philosophy and science so they might land a good job and be able to buy a big flat and shop on Saville Row. The colonial dream of assimilation sent him off to sleep almost every night. But the war came and destroyed that potential life, forced him to contrive something smaller, this one, here in Canada. And if it's custodial to clip the keys to his new life on his pants, then so be it. This is who he has become. *Never again*, he inwardly vows as he deftly steps over a patch of ice, *never again will my life be stolen from me*. It's the same promise he has made over and over again since he was a young man on the cargo boat, clutching his baby daughter in the steerage section, floating blindly towards a new future.

A bright light blasts into Tasso's face, breaking his thoughts.

"Hey! You work at the Network, don't you? That's a Network passcard in your hand. Do you know Jacob Jacobson? What do you think about Jacobson's involvement in last night's shooting?"

The person barking the questions grabs Tasso's arm and shoves a microphone in front of his face. Instinctively Tasso lurches to the left, wrenching himself free.

Then more voices.

"Slow down, buddy, she's Channel 7 news, the Beat on the Street!"

"Just keep the fucking camera rolling, Herb."

"Hurry up, the cops are coming."

"What are you doing here so early in the morning, sir? Why are you running away?"

"Ask him if he knows Jacobson!"

"For Christ's sake, let me do my job. Sir, sir, wait a second please. Do you know Jacob Jacobson?"

The wind howls, snapping at Tasso's coat. The woman with the microphone keeps screaming strange questions into his face. Gripping his key chain tighter, Tasso tells himself, *Keep walking, keep walking.* He bumps into someone, slips for a moment on sheet of ice, and only recovers by stepping into a deep slush puddle. He feels the cold water climb over his galoshes and soak his ankle. *Keep walking.*

Suddenly another man appears in front of him and sticks a small black tape recorder in his face.

"Gerald Dennis-Stanton, *Gazette.* What's your relationship to Jacob Jacobson?"

Tasso thrusts him violently aside. *Walk. Walk.*

"He pushed me!" yells Stanton indignantly. "Did you see that, Charlene? Did your cameraman get that? Where are you going, buddy, we're not gonna bite." Stanton starts back after Tasso.

"The little man's not talking, Stanton," says Charlene Rosemount from Channel 7 Street-Beat news as she strides ahead of the *Gazette* reporter. "I think he knows something."

Tasso rapidly increases his pace until he's almost running for the entrance to the building, but the news people follow tenaciously. An old colonial fear creeps into his belly, a fear he thought had long subsided when he left Goa. He gives into it, puts his head down and goes hard towards the Network staircase. He wants to get inside and lock the doors of his library, but when he glances up he sees two large men racing towards him, blocking his way into the building. *What's happening?* For a second he has the urge to dash across the road – to escape – but after all the years of walking up the same street he continues on. He can no more change his route for the two men bearing down on him than he can for a puddle of slush. Anyway, it's too late. Now they're upon him.

A huge yellow-haired man stands over Tasso's head breathing stale cigarette and coffee into his eyes, his hands coiling like vines around Tasso's arms. Blurred, but still recognizable, another man stands behind the first, holding a gun pointed at Tasso's head. Police? Tasso goes limp with fear. The news people catch up and a bright camera light glares into Tasso's eyes again, glazing them into black discs.

"Now why the fuck are you running from us?" demands Ian O'Malley as he pulls Tasso close. "Going inside the Network? I don't think so. No, no, no. I wanna ask you some questions." O'Malley's big rimless glasses begin to fog up with body heat.

"Is this the guy, O'Malley?" pants Stanton, winded from the short run. "Does he have something to do with the shooting?"

"Get this, Herb, make sure you get this on tape or I'll have your balls for breakfast," Charlene says, her voice slick with urgency.

"Would my balls be part of your low-fat diet?" Herb says, smiling wickedly from behind the bulky Betacam.

"Just get it." She plunges her microphone in front of Tasso's mouth, accidentally clipping his nose with the cold metal bulb.

Stanton tries to butt in. "Give us a statement, O'Malley." He thrusts his little black tape machine into the fray. "Why are you arresting this guy?"

Without hesitation Charlene elbows Stanton sharply in the ribs.

"Stanton, if you're in my picture, so help me I'll fuck you to death," she hisses. "This is my story, paper boy. Watch and learn."

"Prozac anyone?" mutters Herb under his breath.

"I heard that!"

All Tasso can discern from the bizarre choreography around him is the steam coming out of the strangers' mouths, the black gun staring at his face, and microphone bobbing dangerously close to his teeth. But more than the fear, Tasso's mind focuses on the wetness creeping up his leg, leaving a salt stain on his newly pressed pants. For the first time in twenty-five years, he's slipped on the ice.

"Shut that fuckin' light off," orders O'Malley, holding Tasso with one hand while using the other to take a swipe at Herb's camera. "Roger, move these scavengers outta here. This guy's not going nowhere."

Roger puts his gun back in its holster and quickly moves on the press pack.

"Easy, partner! I'm Gerald Dennis-Stanton, chief crime reporter with the *Gazette*. Just tell us what's the deal." Stanton lowers his tape recorder but remains still.

"You heard the man," Roger grunts. "Back off."

Grabbing Dennis-Stanton by his camel hair coat, Roger heaves him into a snowbank and then turns menacingly towards the woman from Channel 7.

"You touch me with those filthy paws and I'll slap a lawsuit on your pig ass so fast you're head'll spin," snaps Charlene without moving. "Keep that tape rolling, Herb. O'Malley, cut the macho bullshit and tell me who you have here?"

"Well, Miss TV," answers O'Malley, his glasses almost totally fogged, "that's just what we're gonna find out."

He kicks Tasso's legs apart and frisks him quickly, taking out

Tasso's wallet and the key chain with the magnetic pass card. The cold wind cuts through Tasso's exposed clothes and the stench of old cigarettes on the cop's breath makes him nauseous.

"Ian O'Malley, Metro Police detective." O'Malley flashes his badge at Tasso. "Why're you runnin' from us at this time of day? You got somethin' to hide?"

Tasso stares at him and says nothing.

"Am I speaking too fast? All right, let's try a little basic communication lesson. I'm Irish; you're what, Muslim? I grew up next to some Muslims, very nice people. Never any trouble. So why can't we talk like two civilized people? I have a simple question. What are you doing at the Network so early, running from these good people? What do you know about Jacob Jacobson's involvement in last night's shooting?"

"Maybe the guy doesn't speak English," Stanton mumbles, getting up from the snowbank and brushing off his coat.

"Shut the fuck up, will you?"

Silence. Very slowly, Tasso's mind peels back the thin layer of fear and replaces it with practised calm. Canada. Ca-na-da. There's nothing to fear.

O'Malley keeps talking. "Okay, my friend. Maybe you want to talk some more down at the station? Rog, let's take him in for questioning."

Tasso looks directly into the policeman's eyes and says quietly, "I'm the Network librarian."

There's a long pause as O'Malley checks Tasso's wallet. He sees the security card and looks up at Roger in embarrassment, taking off his glasses and rubbing the stump on the left side of his head. The hum of the video camera is barely audible in the wind.

"Oh, shit," spits Charlene Rosemount, the disappointment in her voice almost crystallizing in the cold air. "Stop the tape,

Herb. O'Malley, would you mind telling me why the hell you people are shaking down the librarian?"

"Us?" O'Malley yells at Charlene. "You went for him like you knew something."

"I only went for him because I saw *you* were going for him first. Is he involved in the shooting, or what?"

"If you would shut your maw for a second maybe I can find out." O'Malley nods to his partner. "Rog, ask him what he's doin' here."

"Sir, do you know anything about last night's incident?"

Tasso shakes his head. "I'm just the librarian."

Roger looks helplessly towards O'Malley, who shrugs.

"I'm very sorry about this, sir," Roger says, fumbling for an explanation. "It's early in the morning and we saw you running away from us and thought that, you know, what with the shooting and all . . . well, we got orders to check out, uh, suspicious-looking people, and with Jacob Jacobson working here, uh, we didn't want evidence tampered with. You know what I mean? No harm, no foul, right? Everyone's pretty jumpy, just doin' our jobs."

Jacobson? Shooting? Tasso searches his mind to try to find a reference to this news story, but comes up empty. He just wants to get inside. Now, more than ever, he needs to be alone in his library, back to his peaceful routine. Straightening his coat, he takes his wallet and key chain back from O'Malley and says quietly, "If you're quite finished with your investigation, I think I should be getting to my post."

PLAY

Seven a.m. In shock but on the move.

Over his jacket Jake wears a white doctor's coat that he's stolen from the hospital laundry hamper. It's splattered with blood and smells of some emergency-room worker's rancid sweat. Morbid thoughts come momentarily to his mind as he makes his way into the freight elevator. Perhaps the coat came from the very doctor who operated on Rachel, Jake imagines. The elevator door opens and Jake bows his head and scurries past the check-in desk, through the admitting room, and towards the automatic sliding doors. Two nurses pass him without so much as a second look. Perhaps, he thinks, it's *her* blood on the coat, smeared there when a doctor leaned over to massage her heart as she died. Jake can't shake these dark ironies as he follows the blue line on the linoleum floor past the empty stretchers lining the hall and out through the doors.

The white hospital coat camouflages him as he makes his way through the exit. In his arms he clutches a small bag containing an assortment of pill bottles. He's stolen them from a medicine cabinet he broke into while he was roaming the hospital floor in the middle of the night, too restless and frightened to sleep. As the faceless people in hospital attire flow by him, he remembers the long night, remembers the moment he noticed the on-duty nurse leave her station to make her rounds. Then quickly, like a thief, he stole into her room and pulled hard on a locked door, tearing the hinges off so he could get some *real* drugs, the kind the nurse obviously failed to provide. On the shelf were pills, dozens of bottles lined up carefully, and he remembers grabbing a handful and stuffing them into his pockets, not even checking the labels, then walking quickly back to his room, chest heaving, hoping the nurse would not turn the corner and ask why he was up. Around his neck a stethoscope, also stolen, completes the disguise. He thinks briefly about Helen, the nurse who gave him food throughout the night – about the trouble he's about to cause her when she discovers that the drugs from the cabinet are missing. About the trouble that will ensue when the detective discovers that he's no longer in his room. But he can't worry about anyone else. He needs to get away from the hospital, to try to forget Rachel's desperate face, forget about how he stood there blankly as she lay dying. The pills buzz and hum through his mind like ambient noise.

Tucking his chin into his shoulder, Jake blends in with the people rushing in and out of the hospital and manages to avoid the attention of the encamped media. Half-running towards the street, he discovers that his feet are now as numb as the rest of him. His body moves unchaperoned by his mind. It darts quickly away from the crowd and hails a cab. Opens the door, slides onto the seat, and disappears from the hospital, where helpless voices push alert nurses up and down corridors and police detectives come looking for him.

In the front of the cab, the driver smiles broadly, displaying a sparkling gold tooth.

"Where to, doc?"

"Just go anywhere. North," Jake says frantically.

"North where?"

"Go, just go."

"You pay me enough, mon, I take you to da north fuckin' pole!"

The driver hits the accelerator, flips on the meter, and the taxi screeches out into traffic. Jake watches as the man furiously slides in and out of cars, hitting the brake every few seconds with a jolt. It's almost the morning rush hour and everyone drives as if they're being followed by something dangerous. Forward, stop, forward again. He's in a car. He's moving. He has an ally.

The driver's skin is so black that his shaved head glistens as it moves, confidently checking mirrors, scanning the road, and bending forward in an apparent effort to move the car more quickly. The radio plays a slow reggae song out of time with the frenetic pace. Jake examines the picture on the cab licence pinned to the roof. The name Leon Pastiche is typed neatly under the photograph. It must have been taken a number of years ago, Jake imagines, because in it Leon has a full head of hair and wears what looks to be a newly pressed white shirt and a tie under a baby blue suit jacket, all of which fit him awkwardly. He smiles broadly at the camera, eyes alight with pride, and it reminds Jake of the awkward innocence of a high school graduation picture.

Jake notices a miniature red, green, and gold Jamaican flag on the dashboard, and it lifts slightly in the blowing air of the car heater. A jolt of familiarity arrests his gaze and he recalls that a similar flag used to be pinned up next to his bed when he was a child. It was a gift from the Jamaican nanny who took care of him for years, and she gave one to Theo as well to teach them about her home country. They were spoiled like that, when their father had money and vague plans to make a family work. Pop once said that Jake loved that nanny more than he loved his own mother. One day Pop said that when Jake was crying hysterically the nanny let him breast feed on her nipple – even though she wasn't pregnant. He had calmed right down after that. Latisha, that was her name. A tall, big-boned woman with a sweet voice, made sweetest for her baby Jake. Momma might have fired her if she had found out about that breast-feeding session, but Pop never told her. It was Jake's first secret. Momma was rarely home anyway, mostly out at social events and charity balls, flirting with men and being beautiful, still young in such a way that too much alcohol made her elegant instead of sloppy. Latisha would stay home with Jake, repeating his full, ancient name over and over: Jacob, Jacob. She regaled the uncomprehending baby with details of the Bible story of Jacob and Esau, reciting, almost verbatim, long passages describing how Jacob stole his elder brother's birthright and how he wrestled all night with an angel at the spot named Peniel. She told him how blessed Jacob was to be able to see a divine being of God and escape with his life, which is why, she said, he was allowed to reconcile with his brother twenty years later. Sometimes, Pop told Jake, sometimes Latisha would just continue right on with the story, long after Jake had fallen asleep, whispering the details of the biblical Jacob's bitter exile as an old man, and then Latisha would bless baby Jake herself, again and again, holding him up high near the ceiling in her hands, her voice a thick vibrato, like an organ playing in an abandoned church. And this is where Jake first imagined all life began: floating above the world on a sonorous voice that lifted children with good stories and promises of infinite kindness. And finally Momma would come home and say, "Put the boy down, Latisha, you're going to drop him one day." She never did.

In fact, it was Latisha who got dropped. Deported back to Jamaica when Pop ran out of money and had to let her go. Years later Latisha wrote to the family asking for a loan to help her family get by. Of course, Pop still had no cash, none of his own anyway, and Jake remembers Theo knocking on doors all around the neighbourhood, trying to raise a few dollars to send over to her. He managed to rustle up eighteen bucks and asked Jake to contribute his allowance to the cause. But Jake didn't want to. He wanted to buy a new skateboard, and lending money to an adult seemed somehow wrong. So Theo simply broke into Jake's piggy bank, stole his money, and mailed it off to Latisha first class. He included a forged note from Jake saying, "Hope this helps a bit, thinking of you, Best, Baby Jacob." Later that year, while Jake was watching his mother get ready to go out one night, he heard her telling Pop that Latisha had been killed.

"Apparently she was gunned down in Kingston during a robbery or something," Momma explained as she carefully put on lipstick, red like fresh fruit. "Poor woman. Her daughter wants to come over now, but God knows what she'll do here. It's just tragic. Are you ready? We're already late."

Listening to his mother's hurried summary of Latisha's life, Jake realized for the first time that perhaps everything could not be lifted up by sweet voices and acts of love. Accidents had their own gravity. And riding in the back of the cab, Jake wonders whose voice he's now depending on to keep him up.

"Hey, mon, the meter's runnin'. I can drive all day if dat's what you want." Leon Pastiche glances back at his passenger, curious but impatient.

Jake is catapulted back to the present.

"Sorry?"

"You got an address yet, mon?"

"Just keep driving."

"Is your dime, mon. You wanna go north, I can take da Don Valley Parkway. Fast at dis time of de day."

"Don Valley? No," Jake says dreamily. "Keep going."

But he repeats the phrase "Don Valley" in his mind, visualizing the brown, sludgy tangle of water that is the Don River as it cajoles its way through the urban ravine, how it spans the length of the city, eventually moving past Hogg's Hollow, the neighbourhood where Jake grew up. So he knows the Don River from his childhood, knows it from hours spent wading along its reedy shores, from splashing his friends on hot summer days and sometimes even trying to catch fish in its polluted waters. But mostly he knows it from one particular night when he was eleven, and whenever he drives on the Parkway he always looks across the great steel viaduct bridges, down to the shrivelled river below, and he remembers what the water felt like the night Theo almost drowned him in it.

The cab slices smoothly in and out of traffic and Jake rocks back into the clear memory of the night he followed his brother and Theckla Garrow down to the Don so he could listen to them talk. Something happened to Theo and him that night, a border of some kind fell between them, one they refused to formally recognize but could never erase, not then, not ever. Jake realizes that he's never even spoken about it with Theo, and he wonders if perhaps Theo has forgotten about it altogether. But no, he thinks, Theo would remember this. It was a long time ago and they were just two unformed boys growing up in the Hollow, but these are things you can't forget. This is how it used to be:

At night Theo lies awake and waits. He wants to sneak out of the house to meet his next-door neighbour, Theckla Garrow, to smoke cigarettes and drink beer and listen to Theckla's exotic ideas about the world. He listens carefully to the night sounds. Outside his window the occasional car passes along the street and Theo watches the willow tree catch the sound and hold it, changing its rhythm so it hangs listlessly in the night sky like a kite. Down the hall he hears his father sleep, the liquid in his lungs hissing with laboured suction. It's a sound his mother never gets used to. She paces, walking downstairs to smoke cigarettes and drink gin and tonics, waiting out the night until solitude turns to oblivion. She usually passes out with her head on the kitchen table, her long black hair strewn over it like knitting material. Sensing her sedation, Theo will put on his North Star running shoes and a hooded Adidas sweat shirt and slip out the side door.

He never hears a sound from Jake's room. Jake sleeps in complete silence, as if he's disappeared into dream. But he hasn't. Unlike his brother, Jake doesn't count the night sounds. He listens only for Theo, listens for his brother's nightly escape, the sigh of the screen door gently opening, and he lies fully clothed under his blankets, waiting to follow. Even back then, Jake knows that Theo will lead him towards a life he can't find on his own.

Theckla waits at the fence to the Rosedale golf course, which lies at the end of a cul-de-sac near the Jacobsons' house. Theo is late and she's already smoking. As he runs along the gravel road where the fence blocks out the course's third hole, he begins to picture the details of Theckla's frame. Long before she's in sight, he visualizes her breasts pushing out the white cotton of her tight New York Dolls T-shirt into her long auburn hair, which bends compliantly. Her lips will be curled and wet around her cigarette, covered in dark brown lipstick – a piece of birch stranded between the sandy banks of the Don River. And her body will be in the classic *contra posta* position: one hand resting on her jutting hip, the other working the intricate motions of smoking and ashing, shining like alabaster next to the cigarette's orange glow. She'll look both perfectly relaxed and perfectly impatient, her opaque blue eyes committing alternately to each mood. This, in Theo's mind, being the very definition of cool.

Jake stays fifty yards behind Theo, running across the front lawns of the neighbours' houses so his footsteps don't make any noise. He knows where Theo's going anyway and doesn't need follow too closely.

Theckla is fifteen, three years older than Theo, and old enough to be angry at the world. Theo's quite sure that he's in love with her even if he doesn't know how to explain this to himself. He wants to grab her white hand and bring her body near, wants to kiss her, wants to marry her and listen to tales of her father's travels and his love affairs with other men and her memories of a mother she has never seen.

As he arrives, she says, "I've been here for twenty minutes. Let's go."

"Sorry. I had to wait till everyone was asleep."

"Did anyone hear you go out?"

"No, no one heard. I swear."

"What about your stupid little brother?"

"I told you, he's asleep."

"Let's go."

She throws her cigarette down on the asphalt and scrambles up the fence, throwing her leg over the top of the sharp wire ridges and jumping six feet to the ground. Theo follows slowly. He can't climb as fast as Theckla and suspects no one can. His pant leg gets caught at the top and he hears it rip as he jumps down. Concern for his new corduroys takes his mind away from the sharp pain that shoots up his ankle as he lands on the dewy grass.

"You ripped your pants, you piss punk."

"Yeah, so what?" Theo hates it when she calls him "piss punk," but that's how she is. Abrasive. Rough. Her smile always suspicious and condescending, as if she has an inside joke with an invisible co-conspirator that Theo would dearly like to meet. He tries to play it cool, and copies her languid pose. "Got a smoke?"

"You're too young to smoke. Come on." And she's off down the centre of the green fairway where somehow the moonlight is brighter. He has to follow.

Jake lets them go ahead before he wriggles under the fence, still small enough to get through a depression used by dogs and too afraid to climb. Swinging wide to the right of them, Jake keeps to the cover in the bush along the river, picking his way through the vegetation and trying to listen to what Theckla tells his brother.

The Rosedale golf course is the oldest and most expensive in the city, and it connects to Hogg's Hollow, where the Jacobsons live, at the third hole. At the turn of the century the whole place used to be a swamp surrounding the Don River, with thick oil-coloured greenery choking out the daylight, bulrushes and poison ivy snarling indecently on the banks. Hogg's Hollow itself, with its "no sidewalk" policy and roundabouts of middle-class brick houses and large front lawns, sits at the bottom of a steep hill of trees – birch, oak, maple, and evergreen. Occasionally an old tree crashes down during a storm, smashing onto one of the roofs below, and Jake and Theo come out and watch the fire trucks come to make sure everyone is okay. They always are. Hogg's Hollow is not a place where accidents happen in the open. Dogs are run over by station wagons and kids fall off bikes, but tragedies occur silently, inside houses, as if the long-drained swamp remains only in spirit, settled somewhere inside the Hollow's families' shiny hearts.

Every spring Jake and Theo wait for the floods, which no one can stop. Basements are ruined, mildew festers, floor tiles bubble as the water table rises and falls to the call of a natural master that none of the architects or engineers have ever tamed. In fact, there's an informal competition among the men of the neighbourhood to solve the flood problem. Some have their weeping tiles dug up, some raise their floors, some put in sump pumps. Nothing works. The silt clogs the tiles and the pumps, the mildew rots the raised floors, and the only people who benefit from the competition are the contractors. At summer barbecues, neighbours joke that the contractors perform a secret rain dance in March and spend their winters in rich Florida condos.

The two young brothers, however, don't remember their father taking part in the flood-control game. He never bonds with the other fathers around dams and levees, engineering and plumbing, and the boys believe this is why their father is regarded with a certain degree of suspicion. He has no interest in stopping the spring flood. He simply abandons the basement to natural cycles, as he eventually abandons everything else to them. Only once does he have a carpenter in the house, and that's to board up the entrance to the basement altogether. "Floods are just a goddamn part of life here, okay." That's what he says to Jake and Theo's mom when she complains about the smell. "No matter what you do, something always seeps through."

Off in the distance Jake can hear Theckla's voice hang in the humid night air, and he moves a little closer so he can discern the words.

"You know what, Theo?" Theckla says, which means that she is about to start one of her meandering talks, which is what Theo has snuck out to hear. "I love this place, I love the fact that it's so kept-up, so clean and, like, proper." She talks quickly, as if to pace her stride, and Theo has to scramble to keep up. "Imagine taking this much care of something just to, like, whack around a filthy little ball. I mean, Jesus, they even rake the sand for God's sake. I just don't get it. Fucking rich people have the craziest ideas. And you know what? I heard most of them don't even walk. They, like, drive little white carts from hole to hole, following the ball around all day sitting on their fat asses, you know, counting each whack of the ball like it's the fucking most important thing in the world." She takes a long drag of her cigarette and pauses to wait for Theo. "Hurry up, will ya? And you know what else?" She doesn't wait for Theo to answer. Her questions are rhetorical and only make her talk more quickly. "My father and his boy toy would, like, suck every dick in the club just to ride around in one of those carts and count balls and strokes, if you'll pardon the pun. Do you ever think of how stupid that is, Theo, devising something so useless just to feel like what you're doing is important – you know, like, when there's so much else to do in the world that's important? Keeping score of a ball, now that's some lonely goddamn idea! Fuck, I just *love* this place. It's a monumental piece of arrogant waste, and the more monumental it gets, the more I love it, you know, like, the more peaceful it becomes. It just screams out to the whole world, 'Hey, it's okay to fuck with everything; everyone's doing it!' Know what I mean?"

Theo actually has no clue what she means, but he's used to that. Theckla is rambling and Theo's job is mostly just to nod and listen. She might love the golf course or hate it, or love hating it. It doesn't matter, because he's mesmerized by the passionate way she responds to it. He wishes he were thinking thoughts like hers, he wishes he would stop obsessing over her breasts, stop worrying about acting cool, about the rip in his corduroy pants. . . . But in the growing silence that's all he *can* think about. Now, however, it's his turn to say something, and that's always the worst part of the night. He would rather just do things, not talk about them. He can smoke, walk, swim in the river, rip up the sand traps and dig holes in the greens if that's what Theckla wants. But talking. No. That's what she does. That's what Jake does, too. Jake talks all through dinner, telling stories, entertaining the family. Theo's fascinated by the skill but can't do it himself. If he talks, she'll think he's stupid, and he doesn't want to appear stupid to her. Theckla despises stupidity and announces her intolerance of his with loud hissing exhales of cigarette smoke and wicked verbal jabs about his underdeveloped mind. But there's little he can do about that because, as far as he's concerned, nothing sufficiently interesting has ever happened to him.

"Yeah, golf's pretty stupid. Gimme a smoke, would ya?" His attempt is instantly greeted by a loud hiss.

"Oh, Christ, Theo, I'm not talking about golf. I'm talking about people wasting their fucking lives. You're worse than my bloody therapist. Here, take it." She flips a cigarette onto the wet grass.

From the bushes Jake watches his brother bend to pick up a smoke. Theo has never smoked in front of him and Jake makes a mental note to himself to steal some cigarettes from his mother and try it out for himself.

"How's your mother?" Theckla is always interested in Theo's mom, party because she doesn't have one of her own and partly because she knows Theo's mom drinks too much, and a disease like that is interesting to her.

"Fine, I guess. She took us to a play the other day. A magic show. Very boring."

"I bet she's screwing someone, getting it regular on the side," Theckla speculates matter-of-factly, walking away from Theo.

Jake stiffens at the casual cruelty of the statement and silently moves closer to listen. He went to the show with Theo and had enjoyed it thoroughly.

"That's what I think, anyway," Theckla continues. "I saw her all dolled up one afternoon when I skipped school, you know, when your old man was at work or whatever the fuck he does. I saw her walk out your door in a fancy dress. She checked herself in the car rear-view mirror, then roared off down the street. Man, if I was you I'd tell your dad to straighten her out. Belt her or something, I don't know, whatever it takes. You're gonna lose your mom, Theo, that's what's gonna happen, trust me. That's what moms do, they take off."

"Yeah, well, not my mom. She just likes to go out a lot." Theo doesn't need Theckla to fabricate a life for his mother. He's already seen his father try to do this and fail, has seen how his parents never managed to work the trick of a happy home life. So he decided long ago, for his own comfort, to let his parents have whatever private life they could get somewhere else.

"Okay, if that's what you want to believe, fine," she snaps, dissatisfied by Theo's denial. "You know, I used to think my dad just liked to go out a lot with his good friend Sebastian, you know, like, take his little student out for coffee, have him over for lessons. And then one day little fucking student boy toy moves in and, like, Dad says to me, 'Theckla, Sebastian's going to be staying with us now, is that okay?' As if I had a choice! So I'm like, 'Sure Daddy-o, perfect, I really like Sebastian, and I'm really happy that my new mother has a beard!' Wake up, Theo. If you don't want to know things, one day someone is going to force you to find out about them. That's the way life is. Trust me. At least, that's what I think. Let's go over to the river."

They turn directly towards Jake, and he panics. If he tries to run they'll catch him spying and Theo will be furious, won't let them hang out together any more. Frantically Jake searches for an escape route and realizes that the only thing to do is to slip into the river. Scurrying down the bank, he wades into the cold, muddy water of the Don, which never makes a sound, as if its current is embarrassed by its pitiful strength. Jake's feet sink into the silty bottom, and he slowly lowers his body down until only the top half of his head remains above the surface. He prays he'll disappear into the shadows, invisible.

The night is cool, even though it's early June, and Theo can see Theckla's white skin begin to tighten into little bumps. Near the bank of the river, just above Jake, Theckla leans against a big willow tree and lights another cigarette.

"You gonna smoke that thing or just suck on it?"

Theo shrugs and moves towards her hand where she holds

the flame of the lighter. Bending down to light his cigarette, Theo can smell her, recognizes the sharp odour of her hair gel mingling with the clean night air and cigarettes. He lingers close to her. She clicks her lighter closed.

"You know what?" Theckla says, introducing another "talk." "This river's dead. It's been so polluted that even the river rats have died. Now it's only good as a little ornament in the golf course, makes it look all natural and pretty, you know what I mean, but it's just useless. And if there was no golf course here, well, then what good would it be at all? There's nothing you can do with a dead river, that's for sure, it just stinks. I told my father that I swim in it in the summer, that I drink the water, and you know what he said? He said, 'That's great, honey. I'm really glad that you're getting some exercise.' I could fucking jump into that river and float right through the golf course and right out to wherever it goes and my dear daddy-o wouldn't give two shits. Although it might make the fucker pay some attention. I'm telling you, the only way people notice anything is if you *make* them pay attention, know what I mean? Love by force, it's the only way. Remember that. Look at this river; like, how's it going to make us pay attention?"

"I don't know," Theo mumbles.

She picks up a stone from the bank and throws it into the water, missing Jake's half-submerged head by less than a foot. Jake holds his breath.

"It can't call attention to itself, so no one cares," she continues. "It just stinks a bit, and you know what? Even that's not enough. I bet half the people here think all rivers stink. I bet they can't even imagine a river that doesn't stink. Jesus, I hate this place."

"My brother says he's seen ducks in here," Theo ventures and immediately wishes that he'd kept his mouth shut.

"Jake? He's full of shit, there's no ducks in here. I've been coming here for ten years and I've never ever seen a duck or a fish or anything."

"You're probably right, Theckla," says Theo, backing off. "There's nothing here."

She exhales loudly and stares at him. They try to listen for the current and can't hear it. Theckla picks up another rock and throws it at the water. "See? It's dead, dead."

She keeps bending down and picking up rocks and sticks, throwing them into the river, and Theo quickly copies her. Soon they're raining debris down onto the water, finding bigger stones on the river bank and tossing them in, making spectacular splashes. Excited by Theckla's enthusiasm for something other than talk, Theo works furiously along the shore, lifting impressive boulders and ripping branches off trees, while Theckla whoops and hollers in delight as the debris crashes down on the black surface of the water.

"Let's dam this fucking river, let's flood the golf course so no one can come here any more," Theckla cries out, hurling a piece of driftwood into the river.

"Dam the river! Flood the course!" Theo cries out, jettisoning rock after rock into the water.

"Flood the whole fucking neighbourhood!"

Hiding beneath the surface, Jake holds his breath, the rocks falling on his back, hitting his head, his shoulders. He doesn't want to leave, he wants to stay and listen, but he's been hit too many times, and as the pain increases he starts to cry, his tears mingling with the muddy water, his lungs burning. Finally he has to come up for air, and when he does Theo unknowingly throws a stone that clips him in the face, almost knocking him out. Jake dives frantically back beneath the surface of the river, letting out a muffled noise and taking water into his chest. He swims away as far as he can, while the distorted noise from Theckla and Theo drums around him. He emerges twenty feet away, blood trickling down his forehead. Gasping for breath, he crawls towards the cover of some bulrushes on the shore, choking and crying into the dirty grass.

"What's that noise?" Theckla says, abruptly stopping.

Theo doesn't respond. He tears a limb from a fallen tree and tosses it gleefully on the water.

"Stop it, Theo," Theckla orders, heaving from the exertion, her cheeks flushed and her hair frayed. "I think I heard something in the water."

"I'll check it out," says Theo, immediately scrambling down the bank.

Pressed against the shore, Jake tries to hold back sobs as he hears his brother pick his way through the brush, moving directly towards him. Too scared to move, Jake prays that the night will somehow envelope him, make him disappear.

Moonlight reflected in the water glances off Theo's eyes, brightening them in flashes, as if turning them off and on. He moves through the dark brambles with sure feet, swatting the brush in front of him with a long tree limb, trying to flush out the source of the sound Theckla heard. When he's less than six feet from Jake he stops and peers deeply into the night. He shuffles forward cautiously, probing the undergrowth with his branch. And suddenly, as if he's seen something, he raises the limb above his head and brings it crashing down.

Now Jake knows he's been discovered. Terrified that Theo will punish him in front of Theckla, but somehow, too, exhilarated by the possibility of exposure, he watches Theo move closer, each swing snapping branches and crushing the bush around him. In seconds Theo stands directly over him, holding the weapon high in the air. Jake's whole body trembles as he waits for the tree limb to come smashing down upon him. The moonlight flickers onto Theo's face and for a moment their eyes lock. Jake swallows and, unable to hold his brother's gaze, he blinks. Tears roll down his face, as if to communicate some kind of apology Theo will understand. His body shifts involuntarily beneath the water, splashing waves against the bank. And then, ever so slightly, Theo cocks his head to the side and smiles. He lowers the branch carefully, barely letting it touch the top of Jake's drenched head. And then, so quickly that Jake has no time to react, Theo turns away.

"There's nothing in here, Theckla," Theo calls out, throwing the stick into the river a few feet away from Jake. He makes his way back to Theckla. The water ripples as the wood concusses the surface and Jake, mystified, watches it float lazily downstream.

"Must have been a raccoon, or something," Theo says when he reaches Theckla's side. He kicks some mud off his shoe. "I guess I scared it off."

"Come here," Theckla whispers fiercely.

Theo doesn't move. He's already next to her and he doesn't know what she means.

"Closer. Come closer."

Still not moving, he wipes his dirty hands on his pants, and mutters, "You got a smoke?"

"You have no clue what's happening here, do you?" she hisses. "No bloody clue."

"What do ya mean?"

"Why I bring you here. Don't you get it?"

And then Theo feels useless and so stupid, as if all he can do is tear up the land like an animal and listen to Theckla speak and hope she doesn't call him *piss punk* for ripping his pants. She leans against a willow and it creaks slowly in the night breeze, the budding tendrils swaying around them. Theo moves up beside her and a slight breeze carries the sharp odour of cut grass from the fairways, which, for Theckla's father, is the smell of civilization. But cut grass reminds Theo of his ignorance, making him feel naked in front of the wild eyes of Theckla Garrow.

"We're not finished the dam," Theo says, nodding towards the water where he left Jake.

"Forget the dam. We'll never flood this place. It's too big. Put your hands on my arms, I'm cold."

And so he touches her arms, gently at first, and then he slowly squeezes his hands around them and looks down shyly at the thick roots of the willow tree that snake in and out of the ground.

"Put your head on my neck."

He hesitates. She twists her left arm out of his hand, grabs his hair and presses his face hard into her neck. He lets go of her other arm and feels her lift the front of his sweatshirt. He tries to move, but she holds his hair firmly. And then, without warning, her hand is down his pants. She squeezes his thin penis. He freezes, not knowing what to do, thinks that she'll notice he doesn't have very much pubic hair, then curses himself for being so shallow and stupid and scared.

"Listen to me, Theo," Theckla whispers harshly. "Your brother's right. There are ducks here, and birds and fish and who knows what else? But so what? For me the water's still dead. Just because you see signs of life, that doesn't mean anything is alive. It just means that people are afraid to see what's really happening. It's blind inertia, that's all it is, it's things going on because no one's noticed that they're dead yet. We're the only ones with open eyes, Theo, the only ones. Oh, Christ, you don't even know how to kiss a girl yet."

She pauses and holds him, whispering, "Piss punk, piss punk."

And this is what Jake remembers as he rides in the back of the cab, fleeing the hospital where the police want to question him about Rachel. His young self, half-drowned and shivering, huddling bloody against the bank of the Don River so he can watch his older brother discover love. And high above the moon shines midnight and the twelve-year-old Theo buries his head in Theckla Garrow's taut neck, his hair pulled hard as if stuck with clothespins, his penis locked in her cold white hand while the soundless current of the dead river moves past them all on into the night.

The car lurches forward, startling Jake out of his reverie. From the corner of his eye he notices that Leon Pastiche has a pink-brown scar that meanders up his neck and wraps itself over his right ear like the dirty brown water of the Don snaking through the golf course. Where it disappears from view, Jake imagines the scar bisecting Leon's cheek, persuading itself through the flesh of his jowls and perhaps ending very thinly at the nose, as if it had hit a dam. He doesn't notice it in the picture, largely because the plastic covering is smeared with taxi cab grime and also because when the photo was taken Leon had a thicket of black hair covering his majestic scalp. Jake bends forward to look closer at the driver's head. He thinks of his own body, of the curling red lines on his chest, the quick slashes on his arms, the cigarette burns on his shoulder that Rachel used to touch so gently. Running his hand up his shirt, he feels the thin scabs he's made there, and then slowly he digs his nails into one of them until it peels away. Then he feels it sting and warm with blood, tingling on his numb body. His own scars are a secret, a secret from himself.

"What happened there," Jake asks absently.

"Dis?" replies Leon, clucking his tongue again and pointing to his scalp. "Oh, sheeit, my mon. Dat come from an operation you doctors do to me to sew up my head."

But Jake isn't really listening to Leon. Now he's thinking about Rachel before she was shot. He's blocking the bloody picture of her out of his mind and remembering what it used to be like when she would ask him about his body, ask why he cuts his skin. He usually evaded her questions, but she knew how he did it anyway, had once caught him standing in front of the washroom mirror late at night running a nail file over his bare chest. She'd seen him stare at himself in that detached way as the bloody red lines became embossed on his skin, and then she'd pulled his hand gently away, taking him back to bed. She also knew how he would inconspicuously butt a cigarette out on his arm at parties as he listened to someone bore him with their comments about his show. She knew that he did it; she just wanted to know why. But Jake had no answers for her, or none that he could properly explain. Somehow the stinging calms him, lets him keep working, or listening, or fall into sleep when she's not beside him. But Rachel always wanted to know the stories beneath the skin. This is how she wanted to love him.

Reflecting on this, Jake has a strong urge to feel his body the way Rachel might have. Feel the deepness in himself where the effect of the pills can't reach, a place in his blood, where he knows he's located. He runs his fingers back across his chest, following the wet scab line from his heart to his nipple, digging his nails in again. It burns solid and absolute, releases something real from his dead body, as if he's just paid off a debt to Rachel she didn't know he owed. He pulls his hand out of his shirt and feels his chest heat to its own blood.

"Sorry, I didn't hear you," Jake says through gritted teeth. "What happened to your head?"

"Had a tumour da size of a soccer ball, mon, damn near killed me." Leon laughs and switches lanes without signalling. "Grew up next to power lines so I guess I grew a battery. Now I'm da fuckin' Energizer bunny."

Leon glances back at Jake in the rear-view mirror to get a reaction to his joke and suddenly his face hardens. He examines Jake's green eyes, his unshaven face, the dark hair in its blunt Roman cut.

"You know somet'in'?" says Leon quizzically. "You look damn familiar to me, you know dat, I t'ink I seen you before."

"Maybe," Jake replies noncommittally.

"Yeah, you look like dat guy on de television, dat Jacobson guy. Anyone ever tell you dat?"

Jake shrugs. So he's recognized. What does it matter? His chest burns deeply and he savours it. "Oh, right. Yeah, that's my show."

"No shit? You? I knew it!" Leon exclaims delightedly. "Last night I seen you on da television. Damn it, mon, why you dressed up like a doctor?"

"Oh, I'm, uh, doing some research."

"Well, well, Meesta Jacobson in my cab. I'm honoured. Who knew TV people even drove? I t'ought you jes' beamed your ass everywhere. Now, why don' you do some research on your destination, Meesta TV, 'cause I still don' know where da fuck I'm takin' you."

Jake pauses and wonders where he ought to go. He doesn't want to be alone, so he can't return to his apartment, and his mother would certainly not be awake yet. He vaguely remembers that there's a staff meeting scheduled at the Network.

Good. If he goes to work, everything will settle into a safer routine. He'll record his show tonight. The feeling of disconnection will pass. He'll take calls and rile up his guests, smile for the camera, let millions of people just like his cab driver take his face into their homes and make use of it. Perform for them. That's what Theo would do. He would keep working, not let anything stop his purpose. And Jake knows his purpose is to be on TV, to take a half hour of the country's time and use it to tell other people's stories.

"The Network building on Spadina. Could you take me there please," he asks hoarsely.

"Sheeit mon, why you no tell me before? Dat's de other way."

Leon glances over his shoulder and spins the car in a U-turn, throwing Jake against the door.

Now Jake's whole body trembles with a sharp pain and somehow he feels better for it, more located. The pills he's ingested smudge his thoughts. He's floating out of control, caught in the traffic of his memory, reckless but out of danger. He gazes dumbly out the window as the washed-out colours of city life accelerate and blend. Construction causes cars in Chinatown to move in spastic rhythms like a scratched record, and Jake watches how the road workers ignore the stress they cause with the practised regal detachment labourers acquire after long, monotonous hours. Even on this frigid day, sidewalks brim with food stalls of salted fish, dried mushrooms, and hot peppers. Radios hum with the Canto-pop beat of Chinese disco stars, mingling through the glass with Leon's reggae. Above the stores Jake sees how the faded signs of Jewish tailors and shoemakers, who settled a generation ago in this neighbourhood, are now peeling away into the history of the city. The street transforms without the ceremony of violence, swirling cultures into a great morass of electronic connections and real estate deals. Leon cuts in and out of small openings with his horn blazing, his middle finger now almost constantly erect, muttering "fuckin' Chinks" at the pedestrians who dart in and out of the frustrated cars. And then they are past it, shooting down below King Street towards the great old Network building.

Leon pulls the car over next to the front door and Jake pauses to look at the place that might save him. He never fails to admire the way the crumbling stone walls of the Network abut the new glass-and-steel additions. It reminds him of some Depression-era photograph Theo once showed him of a poor farm family who have been visited permanently by once-rich relatives from the city. Jake remembers the faces of the two families looking out at the camera: stunned and ashamed by their unlikely union, but at the same time surrendering to that deeper, uncoded inevitability they all understood to be the future.

"T'irteen dollars, my mon. I give you a receipt for fifteen dollars, all right?"

Jake pauses before he gets out of the car, realizing that he doesn't want this man to leave him. He wants some continuity, wants to be in someone's care, however tenuous.

"Listen," Jake says quickly. "If I give you fifty bucks, would you wait for me for an hour? I may need you later."

Leon looks at him, puzzled by the request, but Jake hands over three twenties.

"You wan' change?" Leon asks, counting the money.

But before Leon gets an answer, Jake jumps out of the cab – blood-stained coat flying, skin burning – and bolts into the Network building. As the door behind him swings shut, Jake glances back and notices Detective Ian O'Malley and his partner with Charlene Rosemount and Gerald Dennis-Stanton huddled across the street in front of the Channel 7 news van, so busy arguing about their bungled attempt to arrest Tasso earlier that day that they fail to see him duck inside.

Leon Pastiche opens his mouth into a gold-toothed grin and recounts his money. Then he turns up the heater in his idling car and settles in to wait for his generous passenger, the cold wind howling like feedback in a giant speaker, looping endlessly between the helpless forces of the city and the sky.

THEO

This is what happens to Theo three days before Rachel is shot:

It's early morning in the old-growth forest of Fenwick Park, and the sound of chainsaws and trucks echoes through the slash piles and fallen trees. The sun complies with the noise and backs away deep into the grey sky. Vickers-Langston has won a contract to take down four hundred square acres, so Fenwick Forest is being clear-cut. This isn't a big job, but it's an important one, and the company wants to finish it quickly before the band of protesters manages to create a media sensation about spotted owls and fragile ecosystems.

Ranklin Demoins is focused as he works his chainsaw, making the first deep cut into a tree. His bearded face seems to flicker under the shower of wood chips, and from Theo's hidden position behind a clump of aspen trees, it's like watching a man illuminated by a strobe light. The tan sawdust catches in Ranklin's facial hair, temporarily aging him well beyond his twenty-eight years. Theo can hear the sound the saw makes, a high-pitched tremolo, as it bites into the hundred-year-old wood. He watches closely and waits.

All at once Demoins's saw hits something metallic, kicks wildly and recoils. The saw makes a screaming sound, as if over-revving its engine. Then the whirring teeth of the chain tear off the blade and lash backwards, catching him on the shoulder blade and, like a bull whip, snapping viciously upwards into the soft part of his neck. Demoins is thrown to the ground as if kicked by a mule. Involuntarily, his fingers squeeze the trigger of the machine and the high-pitched sound whinnies as the chain slashes across his neck again before finally jamming. The engine cuts out.

Ranklin has hit the steel rod Theo pounded into the tree earlier that day, anticipating this very moment. It comes just as planned. Even before Ranklin goes down, Theo has reached into his bag and taken out a video camera. He points it at Ranklin and records. Records Ranklin Demoins cutting the tree, records as Ranklin recoils, drops the saw, and grabs for his neck. The picture's too dark, so Theo flicks a button to turn on the flash. The bright light knifes through the thick bush. Theo zooms in. Blood spurts into the air from Ranklin's neck, maybe a foot high, before breaking into drops and falling back to the ground like cherry pits. Then a thick stream ascends again, and then again to the rhythm of a desperate heart. Demoins's body is coursing with adrenaline and he expends huge amounts of energy simply trying to bring blood from his heart to his brain. But the route has been severed. The heart – stupid, senseless – continues its relentless pounding. Theo has never seen a death like this, but even as he begins to break cover and run towards Ranklin Demoins, he suspects that the jugular has been severed and there's nothing he can do – even if he wanted to. As he moves, the video blurs out of focus until it's no longer a picture, and Theo thinks how everything passes beyond itself at least once.

Ranklin Demoins is still conscious, lying with his gloved hands pressed to his throat. He's bleeding into a bed of pine needles and wood chips. He can't scream because he's choking on his own blood, and his chest rises and falls rapidly, red and frantic. The copper smell of blood mingles with the scent of fresh-cut fir.

As Theo sprints out from his camouflage towards Demoins, he screams into the remote grey British Columbia sky: "*Help! Man down! Man down!*" He calls out because it's the right thing to do in an emergency, but he knows no one in the empty bush will hear him. The wind blows his words up into the careless cirrus clouds overhead.

Theo kneels down beside Demoins and trains the video camera on the man's face, watching the autofocus sharpen the image. Then he leans in and whispers urgently into Ranklin's ear.

"I'm sorry, I'm so sorry. Don't be afraid. This wasn't meant to happen to you. You're part of something bigger . . . I'm sorry you have to suffer like this."

Demoins opens his eyes, disbelief overpowering pain, and he summons his last energy to spit black blood into Theo's face. Some of it splatters on the camera lens, but the tape patiently records Ranklin pass into convulsions. Theo doesn't wipe off the blood. He lets it drip down his cheek like sap, leaving a dark, viscous track. He moves his head closer to Demoins and says clearly, "You're dying for a purpose. I'm sorry. Be angry, then you'll understand."

A thin, grey rain begins to fall and the leaves around Ranklin Demoins and Theo bend down and spring up in response. The forest feels smaller because of it. Theo quickly kisses Demoins on the forehead and tastes the dying man's sweat and blood on his lips. Then he turns the video camera towards his own face and lets it run for five or six seconds while he stares into the glassy black lens with no expression in his eyes. He wonders if the tape will find something in him he doesn't already know. He doubts it. He already knows everything he needs to about himself. He shuts the camera off and gets up, retreating into the bush, away from the sound of saws and trucks and the choking noises of a dying Ranklin Demoins. But even as he runs, Theo knows few people will understand what has happened. He knows they'll fear it because they refuse to admit the truth, that an ordinary life is imbued with meaning only when it becomes symbolic of something greater than itself. And sometimes that requires blood and misunderstanding. This is what Theo thinks he has captured on tape. This is his process of rationalization. It allows him to believe that what he's done will be forgiven by the very forest that now swallows him up and erases his escape.

□ □ □

Later that day at the tiny office of the Fenwick Old Growth Mission, Theo stands in the middle of a group of seven people who look agitated and uncomfortable. The walls are covered with posters of lush forest, and printed stickers that read "Clear-cutting is Murder" are scattered on some beat-up office desks. Like everyone else in the room, Theo's been in the bush for months and looks it. He wears dirty blue jeans and battered hiking boots. A plaid logger's jacket with the sleeves unbuttoned hangs from his broad shoulders as if it were a cape. His face is tanned beneath the stubble of his beard, and on his wrists dozens of cheap silver bracelets with Native designs carved on them jangle as he paces.

"You're being unreasonable, Nigel," Theo says, aiming his comments at the leader of the group. "*You* invited me here and now you're turning on me."

"Well, I didn't, didn't expect this, did I?" Nigel mutters. "You've got to go . . . got to get the hell out of here."

Nigel Fornhaven is irate and his thin cheekbones glow red above his wispy beard. When he talks, Nigel uses half-sentences, then repeats them and moves on, as if he's walking on a road he suspects is full of land mines. He waves his arms around frantically, even though he'd prefer to remain calm and hold his arms to his side. But they keep flailing out below the elbow like penguin wings, and it would destroy him if he saw how painfully silly he looks. Nigel is a skittish man, and his face has a perpetual look of hunger honed after years of noble, albeit unsuccessful, protesting. It's very much the look of an animal searching for food after a long winter. And at this very moment his dream would be to wave his penguin arms so fast that Theo Jacobson would blow away and leave his organization alone.

"Relax, Nigel," says Theo in a condescending tone. "No one suspects *you* did it."

"Me! You tell me, tell me to relax? Oh, that's just . . . just . . . we'll be relaxing in the goddamn slammer. The police have already called a dozen times. Now, I said go, I said that, and you . . ." Nigel's sentence trails off into a fit of sputtering.

Theo, sensing Nigel's weakness, turns aggressive. "Listen to me, chickenshit. You wanted attention, so I got you attention. More in a single day then you and your rent-a-day bullhorn have done in months." Theo moves his arms up and down ever so subtly, effectively imitating Nigel's penguin problem. "The world's been ignoring us, Nigel, and we're losing this thing. But not any more. A little blood catches people's attention. Ranklin Demoins is our weapon. He makes the story personal. Half the news agencies in the country are already here."

Theo performs for the crowd, not so much for the pleasure of performing as for the necessity of it. It works him up, releases the adrenaline rush of righteousness as he remembers the terrifying moment in the bush when Ranklin Demoins went down. It allows him to transform his fear into inspiration, his best trick, and he loves to turn it. He gazes around the room and everything appears exaggerated with multi-perspectives and composite details, as if he were looking through the eye of an insect. He sees the people around the room wavering, unsure of whom to support. He sees their doubt rising like tear gas, choking off their ideals. He sees the hours of planning, the precious fund-raising dollars, the carefully penned signs. He sees the media cameras watching them. In his mind these disparate images coalesce into a single, magnified picture, a picture that holds the whole DNA of the conflict: the face of Ranklin Demoins. Undeniable and now dangerous, this final image shimmers so realistically in front of Theo's eyes that he almost reaches out and runs his finger along it, as he might do to the edge of a blade.

"We're not, not in the business of murder," Nigel replies nervously.

"I'm here to save the forest," Theo says simply. "What are you here to do?"

There's a pause as Nigel tries to keep his composure. He suspects that Theo will win a war of rhetoric and he'll lose control over the very protest he's spent years organizing. But he also knows that Theo has a weak spot.

"How do expect me to support you, Theo," Nigel says, sucking in air so he won't stutter, "when your own brother is on national TV making a mockery of us? Tell me that."

Theo lunges at Nigel and grabs him by the shirt collar. "Leave my brother out of this."

But years of protesting have made Nigel stubborn, and he refuses to back down. "We all saw his show, Theo. Saw what he said about the protest. He made us look like crazies. Turned the public against us. He knows you're here, doesn't he? Everyone does. Even he thinks you've lost it. You're out of control."

Theo brings his face close to Nigel's, their chins almost touching. He knows Nigel has scored a point, but it doesn't matter. He's already done something concrete, and he knows action will defeat rhetoric. Events have already been set in motion and he feels the future inside him already playing itself out. "I don't talk to my brother any more," he lies. "Haven't in years. But the point is simple: Whose rules are you going to play by, Nigel? Your own, or some TV-friendly version? I know where I stand."

"People like your brother make the rules, Theo, not me."

Theo lets go of Nigel's collar and moves towards a table. He picks up a video camera, turns it on, and points it at Nigel.

"All right, pretty boy, then play by his rules," Theo taunts, walking around Nigel with the camera. "Here's a camera. Make nice for all the people and tell them that they should put down their potato chips, quit their jobs, and come out here to peacefully save a bunch of fucking trees. Tell them what big bad Theo did to that nice logger? I'm sure that'll work. I'm sure if you do it right, Nigel, the public is just going to leap up and throw their doughy bodies in front of those logging trucks. Go on, start saving the world. I'll send this tape right over to my brother and then we'll all be able to go home happily. You don't need me. Get a few cameras around here and everything will work out dandy."

Nigel puts his hand up to block the lens of the camera. "Don't, don't embarrass yourself."

For a moment Theo holds the camera on Nigel's face and zooms in so closely he can see the sweat beading on Nigel's brow. Then he drops it to his side and shakes his head sadly. "I'll give my brother your regards," he mutters as he walks out of the room.

□ □ □

On the road two days later, heading for Toronto, Theo hunches forward in his car, which is moving well over the speed limit. The highway bisects the tawny Prairie horizon with a confident monotony that suggests endless harvests and granaries of survival. He ignores it, chain-smoking cigarettes and drinking black coffee to stay awake. Sometimes, while he drives, he points the video camera out the window, recording the whiteness of the journey towards Jake. He wants to record everything now.

Taking a swig of cold coffee, he occupies himself by replaying in his mind what happened in his motel room as he was packing to leave Fenwick Park. Jake was on TV, was talking about the crisis in the park.

The room is ugly on its own – a bric-a-brac collection of defeated furniture (two polyester-covered chairs, a sagging single bed), the kind Theo has often seen at roadside "yard" sales where the unsold goods quickly find their way to a town dump – but it's uglier now since he's lived in it. The green army sheet on his bed needs washing and the fast food debris that litters the floor is weeks old. Above the empty corn chip bags, beer bottles, and pizza boxes, he's tacked a map of Fenwick Park, the red circles highlighting the areas marked for cutting. There's a stack of protest signs in the corner, along with a hammer and four dirty T-shirts piled on top of the dresser. On the night table beside the bed there's a green, fake wood lamp, and the white frayed fringes of its shade hang listlessly near the clattering radiator. Under the light lies the video camera. It's plugged into the wall, batteries recharging.

Theo sits on the end of the bed in front of the television, as unwashed and unkempt as the rest of the room, his steel-toed boots needing new laces, logger jacket still on. He's watching his brother's show, *The Jake Connections*, with intense interest. The picture cuts between shots of Jake in his studio and pictures of Fenwick Forest. Jake is talking about the possible murder of an unidentified logger, found dead that day, the suspected victim of a "radical environmental group headed by Nigel Fornhaven." The video footage of the protest, taken from a news helicopter, reveals a sprawling scene of logging trucks and media vehicles jammed beside a string of Volkswagen vans. The crowd of people – loggers, policemen, reporters, and protesters – moves about in four distinct groups, like water droplets spilled out upon a table, each held together by an invisible surface tension. This is what Theo hears:

Jake: Today, terror among trees. In the ongoing war at Fenwick Park, tensions escalate with what looks like the murder of a logger. No one has claimed responsibility for spiking the tree, but police suspect the killer was a member of the radical environmental group camped out in Fenwick. Our question: How far would you go to protect something you believe in? Today we meet Jessy Hickenson, whose son was killed two years ago in another part of B.C. when he was hit by a car driven by some Tree First protesters. Thanks for being here, Mrs. Hickenson. And joining us via phone from his prison cell, the head of Trees First, Campbell Boyd – the very man who was driving the truck that killed Mrs. Hickenson's son. All right, Mr. Boyd, is there anything you want to say to Mrs. Hickenson right off the top? Would you like to apologize to her?

Campbell: No way, man. I'd just like to say that your son shouldn't have been a capitalist pig logger. He got exactly what he gave.

Hickenson: [standing up and screaming] You're a goddamn murderer, that's what you are! A cold-hearted murderer!

Jake: Calm down, Mrs. Hickenson, please.

Hickenson: After what he's put my family through, he should be put down like a dog.

Jake: Well, that's a healthy attitude. But we'll discuss capital punishment another time. Now Mr. Boyd, do you have any comments about what's going on out in Fenwick?

Campbell: I sure do, if that woman would be quiet. I would say, this is one small victory for Mother Nature, dude! If I was there, I'd have done worse.

Hickenson: Murderer, killer!

Jake: Well, it's good to see that our penal rehabilitation system is working so well. All right, the switchboard is lighting up, so let's take some calls. Hi, you're on *The Jake Connections*, and our question today is, How far would you go to protect something you believe in? Do you think the wackos out in Fenwick Park have a point when they say that this is a war?

Caller: Yeah, hi. Love the show, Jake, you rock!

Jake: Why thank you. You rock too. Do you have a question?

Caller: Yeah. I don't see the big deal here. Those protestors are trying to save Mother Nature. Like, duh! I'd say that's a good cause, given the state of the planet. What's the deal with these whining loggers?

Jake: Good point, but this is a bit different. It's not just protecting Mother Nature, it's killing for Mother Nature. If that's okay, then what's next: mass murder to save the panda? Nuke the Brazilians to save the rainforest? This is the same idiotic logic we used to hear from the military: "We had to destroy the village to save the village." Righteousness gone mad. No, as far as I'm concerned, nothing is worth killing for. Let's take another call. Hello, you're on the air. What cocks your gun?

Caller: Hi, Jake. I'll tell you what cocks my gun. Psychos like that greenie guy in prison. I'd put one in him no problem and sleep like a baby the same night.

Jake: Thoughtful comment. Thank you. I'm sure the logger's family feel the same way about the guy who just killed their son. Let's go to another call.

Watching his brother's face fill the screen, Theo flushes with anger. He remembers how it used to be, remembers the incandescent clarity of paddling on a lake, when they were young and still recognizable to each other. Before Jake went on TV. Reaching over to the night table, he picks up the green lamp and hurls it at the TV. Glass explodes as the light smashes through the screen. A haze of frazzled electrical parts drifts over the room. He grabs his video camera from the night table and records the debris. Five minutes later, his bags are packed and he's back in his car, driving feverishly east, heading home towards Jake, before the police in B.C. can find him.

NETWORK NEWS

At the Network, the day after the shooting begins like this:

"Well, Greta, I'm sure you've devised a suitable spin strategy for today's lead story," intones news anchor William Stonebane. As if folding an expensive cravat, he carefully lowers his long body into the velvet-covered chair across from the Network president's mahogany desk.

The morning light glows dully on the bay windows and warms the already well-heated room, but Stonebane refuses to loosen his tie. He's not here to relax, and the beads of perspiration on his neck soak into his white collar, staining it the same dull grey as the day itself – as if the tortured mood of the weather is beginning to physically inhabit his whole body. His eyes move from Greta Watt's dyed-brown hair, down past her flat nose to her double – no, he thought he could discern a third emerging – her triple chin, then slowly back again, a carnivore scanning his meat before selecting an area to begin his meal. He blows some air quickly through his nose.

"I imagine you must have had something akin to an electrical shock when you read the papers," he says, pitching his famously deep voice – "the Voice," as he is known by everyone in the newsroom – even deeper to emphasize the word *shock*.

"I've been too busy preparing for the staff meeting to read anything, William. At least, I was before you barged in," Greta replies, shuffling some loose papers that don't appear to need shuffling.

"Haven't you looked at the wire service yet?"

"Not yet."

"Listened to the radio?"

"No."

"Been on the Net"

"Again, no."

"And the morning papers?"

She sighs impatiently and doesn't respond.

"Right. Well then."

Stonebane throws a copy of the *Gazette* onto Greta's desk, but she doesn't reach for it. They stare at each other for a few seconds as if the silence might communicate more helpfully than words, and finally both purse their lips into a diplomatic half-smile that conveys mutual dislike.

"Please, Greta," Stonebane says unctuously. "Do me the honour and read the front page story. After all, your star Jacob Jacobson is mentioned quite prominently."

Reluctantly she picks up the paper, never unlocking her eyes from his, and then cautiously bends her head down to begin reading.

William Stonebane has been imagining this delicious encounter since he first arrived at his office forty minutes earlier and read the news about Rachel Anne Poiselle. More precisely, he's been imagining this encounter, or one just like it, for two years, since the day Greta Watt gave Jacob Jacobson his own nightly talk show. As far as Stonebane was concerned, the new show set a new low for Network standards. Designed specifically to slake the apparently unquenchable thirst audiences have for the outrageous and tawdry ("Only our show does it with an intelligent and genuinely witty host," Greta was quoted in the press release), *The Jake Connections* caught fire as soon as it was launched. Letters and e-mails poured in about the racy, confessional style of reporting, newspaper editorials ranted against guests attacking each other on the set, and magazine profiles waxed dreamily about the handsome young host with the silver tongue. This mysterious combination of both praise and distaste took the show from controversy to mass popularity in a matter of months – and suddenly Jacobson, not Stonebane, was the major star of the Network.

As he waits for Greta to finish the article, Stonebane thinks how strange it is that such an auspicious day should begin so routinely – as all his days do. He arrives at his office eight-fifteen in morning, pours himself a stiff cup of Viennese black coffee, and checks his leather-bound date book to see if his assistant Thatchly has scheduled in anything important. "Monthly Staff Meeting: 9 a.m. Sharp" he sees circled neatly in big red ink. He sighs at the thought of having to suffer through another dreadful speech from President Watt about budgets and firings and other administrative minutiae that rarely affect him, and he walks over to window to meditate on various ways to avoid it altogether. The leafless maple tree outside his office sways in the wind, the branches hitting the window with a clatter. Winter in Toronto is Stonebane's favourite season, black-and-white city shadows evoking memories, the cold stinging his exposed hands like Mr. Bladeshire's schoolhouse strap would do when he acted up at his boyhood boarding school in England. As he gazes out onto the street below, he notices a Channel 7 Street-Beat van parked against the sidewalk, its metallic roof glistening in the brilliant cold like a piece of broken glass. He makes a mental note to ask Thatchly to check up on what story the local reporters are staking out so close to the Network, and then he moves back to his desk chair.

Greta turns the page to follow the story about the shooting, and the rustling of the paper startles Stonebane from his thoughts.

"Done yet?" he asks.

"I'll let you know," she snaps.

As he watches her pore over the newspaper, he quickly slips back into the recollection of his strange morning . . .

Thirty-nine minutes before the staff meeting (he regularly checks his gold Rolex as time is crucial to a good newsman) he decides to catch up on the news events of the night. Adjusting the lumbar support in his chair to work out a small kink in his lower back, he takes the paper from his valise, unfolds it on the surface of his desk, and reads the headline: MURDER 101: PROF SLAIN AT UNIVERSITY. His left hand gently rubs his shimmering scalp as he reads, a behavioural tic Thatchly has commented on more than once. There's no secret to it, really, he always insists. He simply likes the feel of his famous head, likes the contours, the two distinguished bumps at the top, the neatly cropped white band of hair that rings his high dome, radiating thoughtfulness and sobriety. In fact, he likes his whole body and takes pains to keep it up the way others keep up their gardens or their golf averages. Even at his age, his muscles and lymph nodes have yet to betray him with the sickness to which so many of his friends have succumbed. Just last week he tested negative for prostate cancer, and his urine, if increasingly weak in stream, is still remarkably strong in health. His doctor is always pleased to know that Stonebane works out every day at the gym for thirty minutes, keeping his body as firm as it can be for a man in his mid-sixties. His sagging skin still delineates lithe, hardened muscles. After years of experience, Stonebane believes quite strenuously that viewers don't trust fat people – a salient insight his ghost writer insisted he leave out of his autobiography, *Written in Stone: How One Man Reshaped the Craft of Journalism* (ninth on the bestseller list for a full week, thank you very much).

His meditations stop instantly when he sees Jacob Jacobson's name mentioned in print. *"According to Detective Ian O'Malley,"* the *Gazette* story by Gerald Dennis Stanton runs, *"Mr. Jacobson refused to answer questions about the shooting. Early this morning, Jacobson disappeared from the hospital. Police have not formally named him a suspect, but do admit that they are trying to locate him for further questioning. Just what he was doing at the university on a Sunday night has yet to be explained. Meanwhile, several dozen people stood outside the hospital throughout the night to hold a vigil for the slain professor. A larger protest is planned for the morning to mark the tragic death of a heroic woman."* A surge of adrenaline rushes through his body as Stonebane devours the article, peaking into near dizziness when he reads the phrase "named him as a suspect."

At that very moment, his assistant Thatchly bursts through the door.

"Did you hear about it yet?" Thatchly asks, his lanky body quivering with such excitement that his voice, high-pitched at the best of times, threatens to shift into soprano.

"Hours ago," Stonebane lies, quickly folding the paper on his desk and tucking it into his valise. "Incredible, isn't it?"

"I was going to call you last night, but I didn't want to disturb you at home, Sunday night and all. I know how you need your sleep."

"You should have come right over. This is a major story."

"God, it really is. It's Lewinsky major, it's Lady Di major, it's just, just . . . well, it's just perfect, William, perfect!"

"Was he really there, is it true?" Stonebane asks solemnly, trying to calm Thatchly down with the thick modulations of the Voice.

"Look at the paper!" Thatchly yelps, throwing up his hands giddily. "Yes, yes, he was there, he was found with blood all over his clothes."

"How do you know that? Have you confirmed it with the police?"

"Confirmed it with the police? William, I was there, for God's sake!"

"What are you talking about?" Stonebane leans forward in his chair and furrows his brow, as if to psychically drag the information from Thatchly's mind.

"Last night. I came into the office to get some things ready for the staff meeting. You know, I heard a rumour that Watt is thinking of closing the library and shuffling around some of our reporters, so I wanted to write you up a little memo."

"The point, Thatchly, get to the point," Stonebane growls.

"Anyway, I was just finishing up when I heard on the newsroom police scanner that there'd been a shooting down at the university. It's right on my way home, so I thought, what the hoo, I'll just pop by and take a look, maybe phone in to the night staff if anything interesting came up. And, wouldn't you know, as soon as I arrived, I saw Jacobson. I mean, they were putting him in an ambulance and the police were cordoning off the area. I'm crazy at this point, just dizzy with questions."

"An ambulance?"

"He was covered in blood. Who knows what horrible things really happened in there? There's a rumour – I have yet to check up on it, mind – that the woman was Jacobson's lover. Celebrity domestic violence! That's just too sensational for words. In any case, I tried to get something from that detective, O'Reilly or O'Hara or something Irish-sounding. You know, he's that stupid brute who does those crime-re-enactment spots. They're not so bad actually. We should consider that format for our show."

"Did he tell you anything?" Stonebane ignores the uncalled-for programming advice.

"You know how the cops are. Not a word. But this is the thing, William. I didn't need *his* details. I've got my own. In all the confusion, I slipped under the police tape and snuck up to the office where she was shot to look around. And the blood! You've been to war zones, God knows I haven't, so you probably know that there are more than four pints of blood in the human body, and I think every drop of hers was on the floor."

"So what happened? She died right in her office and was dragged down the hall?"

"There's confusion on that point. The hospital hasn't even formally confirmed that she's dead yet, but apparently some doctor tipped off the *Gazette* reporter, Stanton, and that's why he decided to run with it. She's a goner as far as I'm concerned. All that blood! I even got some on my silk shirt when I went into her office."

"Soak it. Cold water takes the stain out," Stonebane says, always an authority on appearance.

"Even a day later?"

"It's dicey."

"I've probably ruined it then," Thatchly mutters bitterly.

Stonebane switches the discussion back to the main issue. "What else do you know?"

"Not much. I overheard that cop O'Leary say to his partner that Jacobson is the prime suspect. I actually heard that and wrote it down in my notebook. My guess is that they'll prepare a warrant for his arrest sometime in the next day or two."

"Mother of God," Stonebane whistles, finally leaning back in his chair. He rubs his bald dome vigorously. Outside, a leafless tree clatters against the glass, as if trying to break in.

"The local stations are already parked down below," Stonebane says, thinking of the Channel 7 van he noticed when he first arrived at his office. "Those snapping little hacks are going to try to get some mileage out this, embarrass the whole Network. Somehow we've got to take charge of this story. Be first on all breaking reports."

"Oh, I can almost guarantee you that we will," Thatchly whispers, moving around the desk and bending his lips into a smirk.

"Explain."

"Let's just say that I've got something no one else does."

"You know how I hate surprises, Thatchly."

"Not this one you won't."

"Well?"

"I really shouldn't tell you yet," Thatchly says, clearly enjoying his role as the tease.

"Don't make me punish you, young man."

Thatchly lifts his eyebrows, but sees Stonebane scowl. "It's better that you don't know yet, William," he says firmly.

"There are still a few sticky things I have to clear up, so I won't be able to make the meeting this morning. Apologies. But trust me, please, this will be worth it. Be patient."

Thatchly puts his hand gently on Stonebane's shoulder and gives it a little squeeze.

"All right then," Stonebane demurs as he feels the heat of Thatchly's hand pass through his pressed white shirt. "I trust you, of course. Now, we've got twenty minutes until this staff meeting. I must get over to see Greta."

□ □ □

Greta Watt finishes reading the *Gazette* article – twice, just to make sure she's got all the details – and turns her head to the side to avoid Stonebane's intense stare. Four round spheres of sweat form on her upper lip, bobbing on top of the layer of facial powder like plump spiders on their webs. If Jacob is somehow implicated in this shooting she knows her plans to redesign the arid schedule of Network programming will suffer a serious, possibly a fatal, setback. After all, Jacob is, as she's announced so often to the press, the cornerstone of her strategy, his free-for-all hosting style moving the Network closer to the successful formula that pioneers like Oprah and Springer capitalize on every day to grab audience share. It's the very kind of TV she was appointed president to create and the very type of programming old codgers like Stonebane despise, but if Jacob's reputation is destroyed, so too will her plans for the Network. On the other hand, if she tries to protect Jake and doesn't run with the story about his involvement in the shooting, a competing station surely will. The Network will get killed in the ratings war, and that too would be devastating. Programming, ratings, her protégé Jake: the conflicting loyalties of leadership stab sharply in her stomach. She looks back down at the paper and tries to stall for time, but Stonebane catches her eye.

"Quite a story, don't you think?" he says, his voice low and thick, as if he's just finished a delicious meal and is settling in to enjoy a stiff cognac. "That Stanton fellow is an excellent reporter. We might consider recruiting him for our staff."

"Interesting stuff," Greta replies tersely, hoping to avoid a confrontation for which she's not prepared. "But I have to get back to my work. Thanks for the heads up."

"It's more than just interesting, Greta" Stonebane purrs, not moving from his seat. "Let's not be blasé. I'd venture to say it's a veritable windfall for the station. Of all people, surely you must see the volcanic ratings potential in this interesting little turn of events."

"I'm very busy, William."

"But surely not too busy for news like this. After all, the biggest news story of the year has just dropped in our laps and we're obliged to exploit it, as you might say, 'to the max.' This kind of glamorous crisis is your forte, isn't it? So let's not waste any time here. Let's cobble together an hour-long special for tonight's broadcast documenting the rise and fall of our young newsman Jacobson. Maybe grab an exclusive interview with him. Up close and personal with the suspect, something like that. Live, of course. Let him give his side of the story to our audience. A blockbuster special for which I am happy to offer my services as host."

"He hasn't even been named a suspect," Greta says warily, even as she mentally calculates how lucrative a special on the killing might prove to be.

"My sources say he will be by the end of the day," Stonebane replies smoothly.

"How do you know that?"

"I can't reveal my informant, Greta, but let's just say it's someone high up in the police force." Stonebane's face doesn't show even a hint of anxiety as he stretches the truth into a lie. "The point is, we must capitalize on this golden, albeit tragic, moment. To put it crudely, Jacob's loss, no matter how damaging it is to his career, is our gain."

"We haven't even heard from Jacob yet," she says, still weighing her options. "I want to get his side of things before I make up my mind."

"He's disappeared, for God's sake! Read the paper. For all we know, he's being be picked up by the police right now and some other station is going to scoop us. This is not the time to be sentimental, Greta. It's ratings week, and you know as well as I what this will do for the Network."

She stares intently down at the paper as if some advice might be encoded in the story. "I'll think about it," she says finally.

"Think?" he repeats incredulously.

"Consider, cogitate. To exercise the process of reason. Look it up."

"There's no time to think in the news business, Greta. You know that. It's all instinct."

"Don't tell me how to do my job."

"Obviously someone has to."

Before their discussion escalates into a full-blown argument, Greta gets up from her chair and quickly turns her back towards Stonebane. The light from the window beats down on her face and she closes her eyes to let it wash over her, as if it might enter her and diffuse in her bloodstream like a pill, dulling her irritation. This is not her first run-in with Stonebane; far from it. She recalls the difficulty they had two years ago, when she left her job as head of the wildly successful cable channel RealLife TV to become president of the illustrious Network. She was so nervous arriving that first day, hired in a surprise move by the reclusive billionaire owner of the Network, Mr. Kingston Marble, in order to revamp the venerable station and bring it back to profitability. After years of pioneering work in cable, suddenly her talents were publicly (and profitably) recognized. She was anointed one of the most powerful people in broadcasting. When she actually met William Stonebane for the first time, in this very office, she remembers, she was genuinely thrilled to shake his strong hand. After all, he was a legend, the most famous newsman in the business. His mellifluous voice signified six o'clock to millions of viewers; it *was* six o'clock. And now he was working for her.

But that first meeting didn't go well at all. Stonebane, insulted that he had not been consulted during the hiring process, immediately adopted a confrontational attitude. He lorded around her new office as if it actually belonged to him, rudely grilling her about her track record.

"I guess I should say congratulations," he had opened, the Voice conveying both caution and disdain.

"Pleasure to finally meet you," she smiled. She decided to be as diplomatic as possible on her first day. "I've enjoyed your work for many years."

"Yes, well, I'm afraid I'm not as familiar with yours." He stroked the top of his head gently, as if stirring some thought. "But I see here that you developed some rather novel programming over on that cable channel." His long finger tapped on a piece of paper he held delicately in his hand, which, she realized to her horror, was actually a résumé of her work. "Of course, I don't watch cable, too confusing, what with so many little niche channels way up there on the dial these days. So enlighten me, if you would, as to the mandate of your station, this RealLife TV. I'm so keen to find out."

"It's really self-explanatory," she answered, awareness dawning on her that, in the flesh, this man was actually quite unpleasant. Still, she gamely maintained her friendly demeanour. "Our programs had to be created from actual footage taken from the, quote, 'real life' experiences of the average person. Reveal people as they really are, in the raw, no filters."

"Scintillating." He gazed up at her with those stormy blue eyes. "And explain to me, if you don't mind, what this show called *AfterLifeTV* was all about. Odd name – but, of course, very catchy, as they say."

"My own creation," Greta said, forcing herself to laugh pleasantly. "A controversial program at first, but it's now syndicated in ninety-six countries. We managed to turn death into a real cash cow."

"Meaning . . .?"

"Meaning crews went out and filmed funerals and I'd stick them on air. No whiz-bang, no effects, nothing. From body to burial, we'd shoot the whole process."

"Forgive me. I don't follow."

"A basic concept if you think about it laterally. Dying is the most dramatic event in anyone's life, right? And since I didn't have much of a budget, nothing like what I have here, I figured I could experiment with death's television potential. Air some *real* funerals, not just the Lady Di's of the world, but also the funerals of the average Joes. Show the tragedy of the working man, show how his sorrow is as majestic as anyone else's, blah, blah, blah. My reporters scanned the obits for various contestants – that's what we called our main characters – and then they'd go off and interview the bereaved for a few days. Before and after the funeral, you know, to give the story an arc."

"I see. And your, um, 'contestants,' is that it? They didn't find this intrusive?"

"Of course not," she chuckled. "They were dead! I think they appreciated the attention – but then, I'm no theologian."

"I mean the families," he said icily. "They willingly complied to this, this idea of yours?"

"Like ants to a picnic. Always gave us full access. Amazing, isn't it? We filmed sons as they struggled to write eulogies for their dead parents or widows as they sorrowfully cooked food to get their minds off their deceased husbands. Sometimes we'd even show how the morticians prepared the bodies, get right in there on the table for the washing and dressing. Tastefully, mind you, and very *real*. Even something as trivial as coffin selection could be a most dramatic thing. Cedar or mahogany, two doors on the lid or one, the Cadillac model or the K-car. It was fascinating really, the stuff we'd get. Tears and confessions, revenge and bitterness, the whole emotional gamut. Death is not a single event as so many people imagine. It's really an intricate, elaborate process. Full of life, in its own way, and very powerful on screen."

"I can only imagine."

"That was the whole point. With my show, you didn't have to imagine any more. All the mysteries of death were right there in living colour."

Stonebane shook his head, mystified. "And this thing you called a program actually found viewers? Cable truly is another universe."

"Truth is, we struggled for a while, fiddling with format and so on, until we aired the infamous 'Pulling the Plug on Your Loved Ones' episode. That changed everything."

"Illuminate me."

Greta winced at Stonebane's prickly manner, but bullied onwards nonetheless, keyed up by the memory of her past success and determined to give her new employee a grace period to adjust to the new regime. "Got a call one day from a young woman – big fan of the show – and she asked if I could come down and film the moment when her family stopped the life-support system of their grandfather. Caused a big debate at the station, but in the end I told the producers, if it's real, we ought to show it. And we did. I think he was in Toledo, or Baltimore, and he'd been in a coma for something like ten years. I sent three cameras down, a real budget breaker. One for a close-up of the contestant's face as he expired, one to shoot that little green heart monitor as it went flat, and the other to shoot the family, all holding his hand, gathered together like the *Pietà*. We publicized that show to the max! There was an avalanche of audience response, we were swamped. After that people were literally dying to get on our show, if you'll forgive the pun. We went to hospital rooms and homes all over the world and filmed people as they expired – the Alzheimer's victims, the cancer patients, and especially the AIDS victims, who got to be quite popular in the late eighties. Very Kevorkian stuff, mind you, but we never did anything illegal. Press dubbed it "DeathTV," of course. Yap, yap, yap went the nattering nabobs of negativity who didn't understand what a revolutionary thing we were doing, how we were humanizing the most inhumane of all events. But the ratings? Unbelievable. Made *AfterLifeTV* a franchise. You must have read something about that?"

"No, no, I really don't think I did," Stonebane whispered, rolling his tongue on the roof of his mouth as if he'd just tasted something sour. "And this show here," Stonebane said, pointing to another name on the list. "This *BirthTV*? Let me guess. You televised the inner workings of a maternity ward."

"Such a quick study," Greta said, letting a bit of impatience slip through her veneer of camaraderie.

"You're serious, aren't you. Televising births?" He shook his head in amazement.

"Right in there with real-life mothers and fathers," Greta continued, seeing his discomfort and now finding herself wanting to exacerbate it. "It was another simple but brilliant idea. The only thing more dramatic than death is birth. I'm telling you, filming a young baby enter the world after all that screaming and pushing and blood is a finale that nothing on TV can match. Not *ER*, not *NYPD Blue*, nothing. Of course, birth is an advertising gold mine as well. Maternity is a business worth four billion dollars a year, all those anxious moms out there ready to spare no expense on their precious puppies. We were charging rates that would rival what we're charging right here on the Network."

"Is that so?"

"Birth is a licence to print money, William. There were waiting lists of over a year of parents wanting to be on air. We shot home births, hospital births, Leboyer-style births – you know, when the mom gives birth right in a bathtub. That's something I never got used to, what with the baby swimming around like a tadpole in bloody water. Eerie, but still, makes for a helluva show. When a mother had complications on air, the letters of support would pour in. It was so intense that we finally hooked up to the Internet and broadcast the show as a simulcast so viewers could write to each other in real time. It was extraordinary, truly interactive TV."

"How progressive," Stonebane muttered.

"And I'll tell you something else."

"Please."

"That story in the *Gazette*? You remember a year ago they published a story alleging that we overcharged families for video copies of the show about their birth?"

"Again, the vicissitudes of the cable world remain a mystery to me."

"Ignorance isn't something a newsman ought to brag about," Greta quipped, her diplomatic manner stalling before she could recover. "Anyway, the story was slander. The kind of lowbrow journalism that I cannot condone. Some hot-shot reporter named Stanton went out looking for dirt and contacted a family who were angry that we wouldn't put their birth on air. They fed him that crap out of bitterness and he printed it. But he was wrong, we never charged anyone a dime. We took him to court. Still bogged down there, mind you. And the thing is, we could have charged them. They're suckers, these people, they'll pay anything to see little Junior pop out and scream himself purple. I know, I'm a mom. But we had a deal to make five free official copies for any family we put on air, and we always stuck to it. We developed a real relationship with the people on our show."

"Clearly."

"First-time parents always got the best ratings, because there's simply nothing as nakedly fearful as the face of a rookie dad as he watches his young wife give birth. We'd call those guys spermies. They're so desperate and vulnerable looking, completely compelling. Once – oh, you won't believe our luck – once this poor, young woman, couldn't have been out of her twenties, lost her first child right on air. The umbilical got caught around the kid's neck or something. Awful. Doctors tried an emergency Caesarian, everything, but the baby just expired. The father, a real spermy, he literally collapsed on the floor in a dead faint. And you know what we did? We took the footage of that show, cut it in with footage we took later that week at the baby's funeral, and ran it all on a special episode of *AfterLifeTV*. The whole pitiful cycle of life in one hour, from birth to death, and we captured it! That's synergy. It was simply the best TV I have ever produced. Period. Must have won a dozen prizes. I can get you the tapes if you want to see some of them."

"Spare yourself the effort," Stonebane demurred. "My imagination should more than suffice."

"You have kids?" she asked, making one final, desperate attempt to warm to the man.

"I'm a happy bachelor, married to my work."

"I know the feeling. I have two boys from a first marriage, but he got custody of them in the divorce battle. Very messy. It's a heart-mulching process, divorce. Judge actually called me an absent mother."

"I'm sure I don't need to know that."

Greta stiffened and decided, finally, to dislike Stonebane as much as he evidently disliked her. "In any case, that's all in the past. I've got a lot of plans for the Network and, well, I look forward to hearing your feedback in the near future."

"Why not start with some feedback right now?" Stonebane said, glaring at her with simmering anger.

"Be my guest."

"Very well." He folded her résumé neatly in half, then into quarters. "I just want you to know – and I say this with the utmost respect – that if you try to put any of that ghoulish tripe on air while you're working in this office, it will be over *my* dead body. And I don't think that's the kind of funeral millions of Network viewers really want to see, is it?"

She gasped. "Are you threatening me?"

"Merely clarifying a few things, Greta. Remember, you may be president in name, but this is *my* network. It survives on my reputation, and the reputation of hundreds of people just like me. Is that *real* enough for you? We practise the Craft of journalism here. Good, solid, objective news. And I tell the stories at my discretion. There are no interactive funerals, screaming mothers, or whatever else pops into your head. Got it? You're not in cable any more, Dorothy."

His voice, dredging the very bottom of its mysteriously dark tonal range, trailed off like the aft a great ship sinking into the black waters of an uncharted ocean. And with that, William Stonebane strode out of her office and ended their first meeting.

Now, two years later, they're back in the same office, having their usual confrontation over her vision of the station. But this time, she realizes, Stonebane's position is significantly weaker. His dead body, which he once offered so boldly, is now a realistic option. In the last quarter, the ratings on his show were so precarious that the major sponsor, a company that manufactured a popular remedy for piles, threatened to drop out. When the top anchor can't even hold his hemorrhoids client, everyone in management knew it was a mandate for change. Stonebane's core audience, Greta read in the most recent viewership survey, is dying off. To prop up the show, the marketing department has desperately hit upon every possible demographically related advertiser: the diarrhea people, the bran people, the denture people, the prostate people, the hair-dye people. But to no avail. Every company that makes products for those aging Stonebane faithful who practically lie laminated to their couches while their bodies corrode has refused to come on board the teetering *World Report*. The ratings are too low, the programming out of date.

Greta realizes that this is the perfect time to hit Stonebane with more bad news about his show. Put him on the defensive and avoid the subject of Jacob until she gets some real data and can devise a proper strategy.

"Given the circumstances, your offer to host a special is really most generous, William," she says, slowly turning back to him. "After all, ratings are so crucial."

"I knew you'd see it that way."

"Oh, I still haven't made up my mind about Jacob. But on the subject of ratings, you and I do have a few things to sort out."

Stonebane squints his eyes to two fiery slits.

"Such as?"

"Such as the sagging ratings on your show," Greta says calmly. "You do know that Preparation H is thinking of cancelling their spots."

"Impossible. They've signed on for the year," Stonebane says, shifting uncomfortably in his chair.

"Save me the embarrassment of showing you their letter, William." Over the years she's lost the capacity to be intimidated by him. "You know as well I do that your numbers are low. I'm going to be making some changes to your show, effective immediately."

"I really don't see how any of this has anything to do with the Jacobson affair," Stonebane blusters.

"It has to do with ratings, William. You're the one who brought the subject up. And I'm glad you did. Meagre ratings mean meagre budgets, and meagre budgets mean cuts. So, as of this morning, you'll have one less producer on your show. Not only that, your people will have to start doing their own research."

"I'm afraid I don't follow," Stonebane says, feigning ignorance.

"Let me spell it out, then. I'm cutting a producer from your unit and I'm letting the librarian go. We have a good computer data base available and it's just too expensive to keep him any longer. He'll be gone at the end of the month."

"You're firing Tasso?"

"No, I'm letting him go. He'll get a decent package."

"But he's been here for years. He's indispensable to my staff. This is outrageous!"

"No, it's progress," she corrects him. "Everything in the library, in the whole world for that matter, is going digital, William. It's not 1955 any more, in case you haven't noticed. You'd better find someone immediately to train you on how to use the new system."

"We can't make real news without a librarian at our disposal!" Stonebane bellows. "Who'll gather our background material? Who'll dig for stock footage? You're hacking away at the very heart of the craft. That's just not the way we work around here."

She rolls her eyes. "It is now. And if your show doesn't improve during ratings week, we'll have to take more radical measures."

Stonebane bristles. "Are you threatening me?" he asks, undoing the collar button to his now sweat-soaked shirt.

"Threat is such a strong word," she says, pausing to let the implication dangle in front of him awhile. "But I look forward to your feedback, as always. And if I do decide to do something about Jacobson, you'll be the first to know." She glances down at her watch. "Now, we're almost late for the staff meeting, so I suggest we both get moving. I hope I've made myself clear."

Gathering the notes from her desk, Greta flings open her door and strides purposefully out into the newsroom, leaving the great William Stonebane sitting dumbly in the velvet-covered chair, his shoulders collapsed under the dull ache of morning light.

october 24, 1997

It's raining when I get here, which is good for everyone because it brings an element of cliché to the night. It's supposed to rain when you find bodies, and I can almost hear everyone secretly thanking the weather gods for helping out the drama. At least something feels familiar. Heard they'd found the victims while I was lying awake in bed, bored as usual, listening to the night action on the police scanner I bought years ago.

Can't sleep these days anyway, just lie here under the covers and watch my restless self stalk the apartment like a thief. Once tried telling Pop about this empty feeling when he was lying alone in the hospital, but he thought I was patronizing him, called me a cold bastard and told me to smarten up. Asked me to buy him some magazines to read, and I brought back a *Hustler*. Read it for the articles, I said, but he didn't find that amusing. Still, he's wrong about me. It's not a coldness though, maybe a loss of connection, an inability to be fully present at any moment. It's as if my body is always walking somewhere ahead of me, waiting in the shadows for me to catch up. I never do.

When the news breaks on the scanner I get up and dress quickly, hoping to get there before the media ghouls, but that's wishful thinking. Everyone waits for the murder calls, they're the feature presentations of news. I'm chewing peppermint gum to get rid of sleep breath and leave the door unlocked behind me.

They were all shot in the back of the head with the same weapon – an old Saturday night special or something. That's what the cop on the scene tells me. Gives me a wink and grin as he stares at the bodies, as if to say, Nice ass on one them. Being blasé is *de rigueur* on these occasions, and we all walk around slowly talking about other things – cars, movies, mortgages, as if there are no bodies in front of us. Never talk about the bodies as people, that's rude. They are just the "vics." The etiquette of mutual distraction is enforced with a certain degree of vigour.

Serial killer: that's what the headlines will say in the morning. This is the all-time favourite pair of words to the press. Papers will sell on these words. I try to avoid the arcane cop vocabulary of "vics" and "perps." It's their refuge and I don't really want to join their invisible fraternity of cynicism, not yet anyway. But then again, I'm here, aren't I? I left my bed to drive over for no reason, I lay awake listening to my private police scanner, so it's too late for defence mechanisms. My strategies tend to fail at the best of times, so here in the middle of the wet night I don't expect much of myself. I blend in and blow small, snapping bubbles with my gum.

The bodies were dumped in the alleys where I imagine the women went to have sex with a john. I'm probably wrong, but I can't think of a better reason. I walk around the yellow police tape with a hood over my head, listening to the rain spit and the voices around me spill onto the wet street. Three bodies. "A bunch of whores, I think," someone says casually. "Got an extra umbrella?" As usual, the only witnesses are dumpsters and fire escapes, and I imagine the cops trying to question them: "All right, dumpster, what did you see? Come on, you and the fire escape, up against the wall, we know you saw something." I must be really bored.

Turns out they really were street hookers, and – surprise! – the one with the nice ass was a transvestite. He's splayed out on his stomach, blood mingling with garbage on the asphalt, his wig thrown off and lying in a puddle like a dead squirrel. The chalk marks blur in the rain, making everything appear exhausted and ill defined.

I close my eyes and try to imagine the life of a prostitute. I remember playing a similar game as a kid when I rode the subway to school, looking at the other passengers. The Mating Game. It was simple really. I'd simply imagine the sex lives of the other people on the train and what it would be like to screw them. I was a frustrated high school virgin at the time and believed that adulthood meant you got to have a lot of regular sex, so this game provided a compelling form of entertainment.

Was the man in the suit reading the paper a real estate salesman? And, more important, did he get laid last night? Or did he get a blow job? The lucky bastard. What kind of lover was he? A biter, a slapper, or just an ordinary joe who settles happily for the missionary position? Hard to tell, he looks so calm and asexual. You can never tell what anyone is really like once they're dressed for work.

If I had had sex back then – an unlikely but elaborately imagined situation – I probably would have strutted around the subway car, chest puffed out, gleefully describing the details to any passenger who would listen. "Excuse me, sir, forget the paper, I just have to tell you that last night I balled my brains out. I know, you wouldn't think it to look at me, but it's true: all night like a crazed animal, doggy style, standing up, on our side, sex oils, handcuffs, silk scarves, the works." And then I might have asked others about their nights and we'd all swap stories like real adults and go off to work feeling satisfied.

Of course, the game also entailed my imagining what

people on the subway looked like naked. The size of men's penises, the shape of women's nipples, the colour of their pubic hair. Great stuff. On particularly long rides the Mating Game became more complicated. I'd wonder what would happen if there were some freak accident and all the passengers somehow got stranded and had to choose mates for survival. Who would I get? Would the twentysomething woman in the blue pants pick me because I was young and showed potential, or would she go for the poker-faced real estate guy? Would I end up with that old woman in the corner, and if I did, would I learn to like it? In this bizarre scenario I was forever being chosen by someone I didn't want, stuck for eternity in a union of someone else's making.

Now I'm all grown up and playing the same game with dead prostitutes. *Plus ça change* . . . I try to imagine them before they were killed, hustling passing cars and surviving on barren street corners by relying on some secret resistance mechanism you might find in a cactus. They endure everything – the heat, the cold, the usual hassles, their ears trained to smudge the sound of shouts and abuses into white noise. They must discern no difference between an insult, the screech of brakes, and the sound of a man having an orgasm. A functional deafness might be their primary weapon of survival. They just watch and categorize: the businessmen who need a quick blow job before going home to their wives, the loners who substitute a fuck for affection, the perverts who like to be pissed on, tied up, or spanked (they pay the most). And they desperately try to judge which men are the violent kind. These men mean bruises and broken bones, bloody lips and no money. But they all look the same. Violence is always hidden so deeply inside.

I open my eyes and wonder how misguided I am. I expect I'm pretty much beside the point in general, dreaming of lives I've never known, but I'm getting used to that. I reconstruct most things from what I've seen on TV or read in books. *Shhp, shhp, shhp* go the flashes of the police camera, as if telling a short secret. The cops make muffled noises to each other like applause. Three bodies, two hookers, and a transvestite. No suspects.

Walk around for another hour wondering why everyone is more edgy than usual. Cops snap at the crowd and no one talks to each other. Bad night for eavesdropping. I guess dead prostitutes are something different from the usual murder, not so much victims as talismans. Prostitutes are the canaries in the mine of the city. Their twisted limbs don't evoke pity; they send out a chilling signal that even the fearless have become afraid. Even the criminals have a more criminal enemy. The city grows older with fear. *Shhp, shhp, shhp* go the whispering cameras. What secrets are the flashbulbs telling, everyone wants to know. The bodies looked washed out, the colour of water left for too many weeks in a vase. My feet are wet, I should have worn boots. Puddles everywhere.

The police photographer kneels down and focuses on details. Bent arms, clenched hands, open mouths. Shhp, shhp, shhp. He shoots the legs and hair and eyes and tongues and shoulder blades; he documents it all in ugly still life, all for closed files, never to be published. I wonder if he thinks of his job as an art form, if he has an aesthetic theory about his work. Maybe he's a closet artist, and like Michelangelo he needs to study corpses to refine his work. It certainly is hard to tell. He works so quickly.

The police check for identification, and soon the body parts have names and residences. Then, to everyone's surprise, a family appears for one of the "vics" and a mother and son collapse on one of the bodies and start to wail. Suddenly everything seems too familiar. The sound of grieving loved ones doesn't belong in this scene, seems out of place. The crowd dissipates quickly, avoiding an unasked-for bond with the bereaved. Even the reporters look uncomfortable. No one likes the emotional confusion of a dead prostitute's family. Turn the page. Change the channel. Look away.

I try to forget what I've seen and ride the subway home, examine the sleepy passengers and imagine what they all look like stripped of their clothing, shivering and naked to the world.

DEAD AIR

The staff meeting begins in twenty minutes and Jake is unwell. His body resembles a coil of wire as he curls it stiffly on the carpet beneath the huge boardroom table. It's been almost an hour since the cab driver first dropped him off and he has slipped unnoticed into the nearly empty early-morning Network building. The security guard at the desk didn't even bother to look up from his paper when Jake let himself through the door. Vaguely Jake remembers taking the elevator to the seventh floor and creeping into the boardroom where he knows the staff will gather. His body passed through a panoply of side effects from the pills he ingested earlier. First dizziness, then vision spots, then a crescendo of exhilarated panic, the surface of his skin tearing and buzzing until it threatened to disintegrate. Almost upon arrival he collapsed under the long table, taking the self-protective position of an embryo. *Rachel is dead*, he thinks. *Rachel is dead.*

Now the cocktail of pharmaceuticals settles upon a deep,

thumping deadness that seeps into his head, a pall of chemicals smothering his opaque thoughts the way smoke creeps under a locked door to fill a room. He wants to reconstruct what happened to Rachel in that hallway. To see clearly. But the pills – or possibly something different, he's still not sure; a gap of some kind in his memory – make it impossible. All he sees is the flash of disjointed pictures: her broken face, the bloody corridor, the small red light flickering in the distance. And something else too, something dense and indeterminate near her office. A shape of some sort, darting across his vision. It's all blurred, frightening image fragments. The hand on the marble floor. The mouth opening and closing. Focus on the green eyes shining. The blood soaking into the blue dress. Close-ups of the fingernails and feet. Panoramas of the body in the long hall.

He hears her voice scream out his name, a hectoring sound that cuts the anaesthetized feeling. He presses his knees hard against his chest as thoughts swirl and twist; again he finds himself swimming through the liquid of memory, that other place he takes refuge in, beyond the gravity of touch, beyond the decisions of skin and hands and fingers and lips. Beyond body into a place without pain or feeling or responsibility. Like a hit of adrenaline, the intelligence of numbness releases into him and he floats on image streams: Theo raising a large stick above his head, his mother wandering alone on the ice, Rachel's voice screaming and screaming until it moves so close to him that it becomes something else, the sound of his own breathing, rapidly in and out, a tight, choking sound as if he can barely move the air into his lungs. And from this sound another image emerges, his father, lying under a thin blue sheet, eyes closed, all his features collapsed into stillness. Jake submerges himself into the clarity of his last memory of his father.

Sitting on the edge of the hospital bed, Jake had held his father's hand for hours. The flesh was supposed to get cold but it didn't because Jake kept rubbing it, the grey skin sliding smoothly over the bones. *Please Pop, please Pop, stay for a little.* But his father was gone. Theo told him on the phone, said simply, "You'd better get down here, it's all over. I'm with Momma now." Theo was there because Theo was always available to handle an emergency. Jake arrived as soon as he could, after his show went off the air, but it was too late. Pop was dead. The room smelled of piss and hospital food and somehow of wet leaves in fall when Jake and Theo would rake the backyard to prepare it for winter.

When he saw his father's body he expected a bolt of shock, a terrible pain, but there was nothing like that. He simply felt as if his insides had been erased, quick as the crash of a computer, from the full memory banks of sorrow to nothingness with a simple click. So he walked over to the body on the bed and picked up his father's hand and stroked it, remaining silent for hours. The skin, that's what he still remembers most; the skin seemed so separate from the skeleton, his father's exterior just a rubber costume thrown on top of a wooden bench. The eyes began to bag around washed-out pupils, the jawline disappeared, a slackness that made it seem as if the peculiarities of his father's appearance Jake had so loved – the deep furrow in his forehead that once came from laughter and then later from worry, the hooked nose squashed forty years earlier in a street fight, the cleft chin that would quiver in frustration when word of a bad business deal came in – it was as if all this had been meaningless, a disguise. The truth about Pop lay somewhere deeper, in some inaccessible place, and Jake had missed it. Had only touched the skin. This was all he had left, the features of a life, the whole vocabulary of emotion washed out of the body. It was the grammar of pure surrender.

A nurse stood at the door and with a small shrug of resignation seemed to tell Jake that he should go home. It was 4 a.m., the nurse was tired, and Jake watched her shoulders sink sadly. Two weeks earlier someone down the hall died and Jake had watched the same nurse's back as she stood in that doorway and used an identical shrug to communicate loss to that family. But the gesture looked different from the front, more intentional, as if an ambiguous shrug was the best advice you could give to someone trying to understand loss. He did nothing all night but watch his father become accustomed to death because that was all he could do.

Pop wasn't supposed to die that night. He had been so stable earlier when Jake left to record his show that even the doctors were surprised by the sudden turn of events. They had no explanations for Jake and quickly left the room after a few sorry words, as if the embarrassment of death offended them. Theo and Momma left Jake alone too and went home to write the obit and make funeral arrangements. That's what Theo told Jake they were going to do. So Jake sat on the bed, staring stupidly at his dead father, wishing words would come to him, but they didn't. Just this emptiness generated by the friction of touch.

□ □ □

Now Jake's skin vibrates as he crouches under the long boardroom table, and he doesn't want to think of his father's death or of Rachel's death. He wants to stop thinking altogether and just go blank. He's frightened and his life seems out of control, like a still photograph he once saw of a car as it careered off a suspension bridge, poised in mid-air, in the breach between land and water, neither flying nor falling, pinned forever to the blue sky. Not yet even an accident, but dead before death. Reaching into the medicine bag he stole from the hospital, he takes two more pills and puts them in his mouth. They stick in his throat and he gags, spitting one white and one brown tablet into his hand. *Prozac? Lithium? Do these have such an immediate effect?* Momma would know the answer. He remembers how she took so many pills after Pop died: sleepers, relaxants, anti-depressants, anxiety relievers, mood controls, anything to help her survive the long, dangerous distances between the days. This is how it was:

After Pop dies Momma battles depression, tells Jake she too wants to die. He doesn't know what to do for her, tries to comfort her with more regular visits, explains that she's just mourning the loss of Pop – which neither of them really believes. He writes Theo about it and Theo immediately flies home from China and rushes her to a psychiatrist to get help. Momma's alone now, Theo explains to the man. Crippled by the debt my father left behind, crippled by her bad habits. She lets her once lithe body get fat and slatternly with depression, cries in front of the TV, drinks gin and lemons all day, phones Jake at work and hangs up when he answers. Failures and accidents everywhere. She needs something powerful to support her and the doctor prescribes Prozac, the miracle drug. Before he leaves again for China, Theo makes sure the drug works for Momma. Takes her to the cottage on Georgian Bay for a retreat, bathes her, brings her juice, and cooks pastas and her favourite mushroom soup. During the day Momma wanders across the ice into the blazing sun, comes home almost frozen, her fingers blue where they used to be yellow with tobacco. Theo stays to protect her and she let's herself slide into his care. Momma turning colours as she mourns, remembering and forgetting as fall does during its turning. Finally Momma recovers, releases everything from her past and says she's born anew . . .

Thinking about this, Jake realizes how badly he wants his own pleasant little chemical dinghy to buoy him through the roiling water around him. Throwing back his head, he tries again to swallow the pills, but the effort proves useless. His throat is bone dry and he feels the pills lodge themselves halfway down. Coughs again. Head lists and memories slosh. Rachel crawling down the long hall ebbs back, replaces his mother.

A voice intrudes on the silence. "Is anyone in here?"

It barely registers in Jake's mind and he gags painfully on the pills.

"Hello? Who's that?" the voice queries. For a split second the haze in Jake's mind lifts and he recognizes the voice as Tasso's. Then he manages to swallow the pills and drifts back into his memories.

Always first to arrive at the staff meeting, Tasso moves nervously across the room towards the source of the noise. He bends down to peer under the table.

"Mr. Jacobson!" he gasps, taking a step back. "What are you doing there? We have a meeting here in ten minutes."

Jake doesn't answer him, tries to hold onto the slippery walls of his solitude.

"You're in some kind of trouble, you know that, Mr. Jacobson?" Tasso says anxiously, not quite sure what to do. "The police are looking for you."

The voice presses against Jake's brain, like a finger touching a water droplet, and his thoughts spill out into Tasso's reality. After a few seconds, he crawls slowly out from under the table.

"Tasso?" Jake whispers. His skin is clammy and glistens.

"Yes. Of course. Tasso Darjun. The librarian."

"Oh. Right. You, um . . . a glass of water, could you get me . . .?"

"Mr. Jacobson, listen to me, the staff will be here any minute and the police–"

"Is Theo here?" Jake interrupts. "Have you seen him?"

Tasso's mind races, thinking about his encounter with the police earlier that morning, how they were searching for Jacob. "Mr. Jacobson, please."

"I'm so goddamn thirsty," Jake mumbles.

"I think you'd better get out from there," Tasso says, wondering how Jacob made it inside in the first place. Wouldn't the police have stopped him? "People are going to arrive very soon."

"It's my turn to watch Pop and I'm late." Jake ignores Tasso. In his mind he's touching his father's hand, back and forth along the loose covering of skin.

"I don't understand," Tasso says, puzzled by Jake's non sequitur. "Have you talked to the police, Mr. Jacobson?"

Jake coughs again, feeling the pills slowly make their way down his throat.

"They want to know about the shooting," Tasso presses on. "Are you all right, Mr. Jacobson? You look ill."

Jake raises his body slightly and crawls along the floor towards Tasso. His head spins. "My show goes to air tonight and I should get ready," says Jake, taking off the bloody hospital coat and the stethoscope and handing them absently to Tasso.

Tasso holds the items uncomfortably in his hands, unsure if Jake has heard a word he has said.

"I think those are bloodstains, Tasso," Jake whispers, his

voice draping over the words like a drunk passed out on a couch. "I couldn't save her."

Tasso can barely hear Jake and has to lean in to understand.

"Take this too," continues Jake, holding up the black satchel he stole from the hospital. His mind dances crazily with strands of thought: Rachel, Momma, Pop lying on the bed. "I don't need them any more. Took some pills, but I'm fine now. Tired. Don't want to see anyone. Not yet. Can you help me? Please. I have to pee. Can you take me to the washroom? Then I'll call Theo and he'll take care of everything. Goddamn pills. I'm so tired."

Jake's eyes suddenly glaze over and his head lolls to the side. Now his skin feels heavy, it's as if he's wearing one of those lead aprons the dentist lays on him when he gets his teeth X-rayed. He can barely hold himself up. With one last effort, he straightens his neck, looks up helplessly at Tasso, and promptly blacks out.

Tasso moves tentatively to examine the prone body of the famous talk-show host, nonplussed by what he's just seen. The whole day has been seriously out of order, and, as if to conform to its randomness, Tasso craves his lunchtime cigarette. A nice long haul on his Benson and Hedges Gold to calm his nerves and help him put everything into perspective. He gazes at the bag full of pills that sits beside Jake's body and then down at the bloodstained doctor's coat and the stethoscope he holds in his hands. Odd artifacts in a newsroom. Nowhere to file these, he reflects, nowhere to file anything that happened today, for that matter.

He thinks back to earlier in the morning, after the inquisition by the police, when he rushed to his desk to read the story about Jacob. It startled him to be sure, but upon reflection he decided not to believe a word of it. After all, he reasoned, Jacob had helped his daughter in the summers, gave her a job when no one else would. Paid her a decent wage. Jacob could simply not be a murderer. It wasn't possible for such a good-hearted man to go bad, he decided.

With Jacob's wasted body now in front of him, Tasso confirms his earlier analysis. Obviously, Jacob hadn't run from the hospital as the paper so sensationally claimed. He'd simply come to work, just as he did every day, only so early in the morning that no one had seen him yet – and here he is, plain as day, to prove it. He's probably hurt and in shock, Tasso thinks as he bends to examine him more closely. A famous man hounded by the paparazzi, but not a killer on the run. The news story is just tabloid junk, Tasso concludes, still tempted to take a cigarette from his pocket and light it.

He touches the tip of his nose where the microphone clipped him and remembers the violent tone of the policemen, the foul smell of coffee-tainted breath and cigarettes mixing with the cold air. The gun pointed to his head, the hands frisking his body: "We're looking for *suspicious* people." He observes his pant leg, the salt stain clouding his pressed trousers. No, he wouldn't help *those* people. In any case, Jacob isn't asking for much. Just wants some assistance going to the bathroom, right? Tasso decides that it's his duty to help.

Grasping Jake under his arms, Tasso drags him into the washroom at the end of the boardroom. It takes him a few minutes, and when he finally gets Jake inside, he shuts the door behind him, panting as much from the exhilaration of his decision as from the strain of his task. With a bit more effort, he manages to sit Jake awkwardly against the toilet. He holds him up with one arm to make sure Jake doesn't choke.

"Mr. Jacobson, wake up, please," Tasso says, talking closely to Jake's face, but too shy to slap his cheeks.

Jake doesn't respond and Tasso goes to the sink, folds a stack of paper towel, and holds it under cold water to use as a compress for Jake's head. "Open your eyes, Mr. Jacobson. You're at the Network now, it'll all be okay." He dabs the wet cloth on Jake's forehead until it looks as if Jake's face is covered in tears.

Outside the washroom door Tasso hears the voices of the producers and journalists as they come into the room for the meeting. Instinctively he glances at the damning evidence around him, the bloody hospital coat and medicine case, and he wonders if he ought to just open the door, wash his hands of this whole mess, and turn everything over to the police. But at the thought of the police, anger from the morning's events reddens his skin. He hasn't tasted anger in a long time, and he's tempted to savour it. In any case, he realizes as the noises outside the door increase, his decision's made. It's too late to leave the washroom now. If the staff find him with Jacob they'll ask all sorts of difficult, intrusive questions and he'll get dragged into the very kind of complicated situation he's tried for so long to avoid. Might even jeopardize his coveted job. And Jacob, he notes, is clearly in no condition to answer questions. *Stay put,* he tells himself, *wait the meeting out.* He quietly locks the washroom door.

Built during the great renovation of the Network, the boardroom was once a series of monotonous cubicles used by the white Network mandarins, all lined up in regimented patterns that communicated both power and imprisonment. During the time when executives still got perks, the place where Tasso perched Jake on the toilet seat was the top executive's private washroom. For some reason the renovators decided to keep it attached to the end of the new boardroom and somehow it lends the room a touch of the old grandeur, a reminder of a time when space was happily given over to the vanities of employees who expected lifelong tenure at the immutable Network. It's the architectural equivalent of a hope bracelet.

Having attended so many similar staff meetings during his tenure, Tasso can imagine with a choreographer's precision how it will proceed. The staff will come in quickly like ticket holders to a general admission concert and race for a coveted chair, but they'll leave five seats empty. The first is for Greta Watt, who takes her rightful position at the head of the table. To her right sits the executive producer of the *World Report*, Ludwig Zeemanvitz, leaning back and compulsively smoothing his hair across his bald spot. William Stonebane sits beside Zeemanvitz, and his sycophantic assistant Thatchly usually parks himself one seat over, from where he slips notes to Stonebane throughout the meeting, thereby creating a low level of paranoia throughout the room.

The last reserved seat, Tasso knows, belongs to no one. Located at the foot of the long table, right in front of the door he's just locked, it's reserved by default. This is the chair no one wants, but during the monthly meeting when the room is always filled to capacity, someone must take it. It's to this chair that Greta usually directs her whole speech, and the unlucky person sitting in it functions as the de facto representative of the whole staff, the newsroom personified. If the meeting turns nasty, as it most often does, there's a good chance everything will be subconsciously blamed on whoever is sitting in what is unaffectionately known as "the Chair." Tasso recalls that last month the lippy arts reporter Dylan O'Sullivan got the Chair. This went a long way in explaining why Ludwig Zeemanvitz abandoned Dylan as his unofficial protégé in favour of the financial wiz reporter, Tobias Kantor, or T-Bill as he's known on Bay Street.

As the room quietens down, Tasso pictures the person in the Chair, how they'll roll it around to the corner of the table, bending their head forward in a contrite posture as if awaiting a death verdict. He knows that seeing one of their comrades in a state of misfortune will relieve the rest of the staff, and they'll proceed to set cellular phones and note pads on the table like cutlery, blowing on and slurping their hot coffee to distract themselves from the oily air of general discomfort. Every face will communicate the same thing, intense interest and fear, as they all hope to leave the room as quickly as possible and get back to their jobs where they'll begin to complain – because complaining is the best way to reassure themselves that they have a job at all.

□ □ □

"I'd like to get going," Greta Watt calls out from the head of the table. Her voice is too loud, the volume burning off some of her pent-up anxiety about the current status of Jacob Jacobson. "Please fill up the seats. There's still one there at the end."

Sudra Buchdeera, the politics producer, and the sports reporter, Martin Gimper, a.k.a. the Gimp, end up near the Chair, and naturally neither one wants it. Sudra, however, is not in the mood to be coy. She's angry at Dylan O'Sullivan because he e-mailed her a description of an elaborate sex fantasy entitled "The Anchor Position" which involved screwing her late at night on the glass top of William Stonebane's famous news desk. Ever since a rumour circulated about a secret club of producers and reporters whose membership required doing this very deed, it's been *the* topic of conversation in the newsroom. Apparently T-Bill did it with his producer Fiona Dartmouth last week, helping him cultivate a roguish aura that belied his pressed-suit, plastic-hair image. Dylan obviously reckoned it would do equally beneficial things for him, but Sudra sent him back a terse reply (elegantly entitled "Fuck off") explaining that she was not the type of reporter who screwed co-workers, and certainly not at work, to which Dylan quickly responded that if fucking off involved fucking of any kind, he was up for it. The whole episode made Sudra suspect that O'Sullivan's self-proclaimed interest in women's issues was of a somewhat different nature than her own. And with the breaking news about Jacob being implicated in the shooting of a woman, Dylan's request was more than a little offensive. Mulling over the shameless venality of men, Sudra smoulders.

"Ladies first, Sudra," Martin Gimper says to her softly, gesturing lamely to the Chair.

"Ladies first, my ass," she snaps back. "It's all yours." She has to physically restrain herself from lashing out and kicking the Gimp in the crotch for his mildly sexist tone.

Neither of them moves.

"No really, Sudra, I'm fine standing. Go ahead, I insist."

"Plant it, sports boy, just fucking plant it," Sudra hisses, and the Gimp knows he's lost. He slips dejectedly into the Chair, and immediately rolls it to the left, flashing a defeated look at his producer, Janice Dawson.

"Very good, let's begin," Greta says as she stares straight down the long table at the Gimp. Years ago she'd taken a public speaking course to help overcome her one weakness as a leader, and despite the inane nature of most of the self-confidence exercises they taught – she really didn't feel it was necessary to look in the mirror before each speech and repeat, "You don't have to be Martin Luther King, you just have to be you!" as Tongue Tip #4 suggested – the course did give her one valuable tool: the SOS. It was one of those cosy, self-help anagrams, this one standing for Stare Out Straight. "If you feel at all nervous in front of a large crowd," the instructor told the class, "send yourself an SOS. Pick a central point in the room and direct all your comments to that special safety spot you've zeroed in on. Remember people: SOS if in trouble." She's almost embarrassed to think of how often she's used the advice.

"There are a few very important announcements to make and I'm sorry to say that they're not very pleasant," she says. "Our audience numbers on certain shows dropped again this month by almost a full share and the advertisers are nervous." She breaks her SOS code for a second and steals a glance at Stonebane, but he's studiously picking a piece of lint off of his shirt and doesn't notice. "True," she continues, "our documentary on the secret prison sonnets of Jeffrey Dahmer did well, but we simply haven't had a lot of winners like that since. On the whole, it's been a rather sluggish month."

As if on cue, everyone in the room puts their heads down to their coffee mugs and mutters in perfect harmony with Greta: "I'm going to have to impose Draconian measures in order to get this place back to profitability." This is her standard verbal foreplay before announcing a financial execution of some sort, and she's used it so often recently that it's become part of the monthly orgy of pain.

Since her days at RealLife TV, Greta has utilized a distinctly Japanese theory called Quality Management. It's meant to get everyone involved in the process of making television – from the lowliest researcher to the anchorman himself – and it's why she invites the whole staff to these meetings. Though cumbersome, Greta swears it increases the "care factor" of the employees. But as far as most of the Network staff can tell, it's backfired. There's more resentment than ever, more infighting, more back-stabbing as people try to protect their seniority. After all, trying to create a so-called "empowered team of workers" when every few weeks another job is cut is like trying to make a school of piranha jump through hoops at Marineland. Quality Management, the staff realizes, is just another of the necessary illusions that corporations in trouble sustain in order to function without revolt. So most of the staff just keep their mouths shut and hope that when the axe swings their way they'll have time to push an unsuspecting colleague forward to take the blow.

"I'll be circulating a memo later announcing the unfortunate de-jobbing of another producer from *World Report*," Greta continues, her voice settling into the comfortable euphemisms of management-speak. "I did my best to stop this bit of redundancy-making but the numbers don't lie."

Stonebane leans over and whispers something to Ludwig Zeemanvitz, who quickly scribbles a note back.

"If we want to play ball with the advertisers," Greta says robotically, "it's going to be hardball, and to come out with a win-win, we're going to have to pull together like a team and re-engineer our programming ideas. Take it day by day. Be professional about change. After all, the audience is the real boss here and we'll give them what they want."

The slurps of coffee around the room reach gruesome decibels as Greta piles on the corporate clichés. Producers exchange glances at one another, each trying to determine who will receive the dreaded pink slip later that day. Slurp.

Blow. Sip. The chorus of electric nerves plays out in the coffee cups of the Network team.

Greta looks around the room for the Indian librarian Tasso Darjun and can't find him. An unusual, but fortunate, turn of events, making her next job easier. "I must also announce that there will be some changes to the library system."

From behind the bathroom door, Tasso's head snaps up. *She never talks about the library.*

"The old library will be closed in exactly one month," she drones on unemotionally. "A centralization of the system is underway – we're linking up to a computer in the on-line department, so everyone will have to learn to use it. Digitization, bits and bytes, RAM, ROM, it's all here. Meaning, by the end of the month there will be no more Mr. Darjun around to help you out. Of course, I think everyone in this room is up to the task of a little research, it's no big deal these days. Point and click and you get what you want. I only wish Mr. Darjun were here so I could thank him personally. He's done such a heroic job over the years and we'll be sorry to see him go."

Greta's words pierce Tasso's skin like quills, deep and barbed, tearing into his body. His muscles go taut and his hand unconsciously presses the wet cloth hard on Jake's face. *Close the library?* His mind recoils at the thought. He'd been at the library for almost twenty-four years. *New computer system? Sorry to see him go? This . . . this is madness.* Panic drenches him. He grabs the handle of the washroom door as if to exit, then just as quickly lets it go. *Point and click? A little bit of research? Is that all she thinks I've been doing all these years?* He begins to hyperventilate.

"As for other changes in the schedule, those will be announced next month," Greta says, wrapping up the speech. "And that's it for this morning. Are there any questions?"

A cool feeling of relief washes over Greta, as if she's just run through a sprinkler on a hot day. She's announced the cuts and the staff are too shellshocked to begin the "dialoguing" portion of the meeting. She hasn't mentioned the shooting, opting to sort it out after she locates Jake, and it looks to have been the proper decision. Stiffening her back confidently, she looks straight ahead at Martin Gimper's slouched frame and prepares to call the meeting to an end.

But the silence is quickly spoiled.

"Well, Greta, I see you've taken your knife to the *World Report* again," Stonebane says, waving his long finger slowly back and forth in front of his face. "Cutting back on the flagship show, I don't think that's wise."

She's surprised that he still has some fight left in him after their earlier encounter and decides simply to pick up where they left off.

"Your ratings are sagging again, William. Shall we go over the book right here?"

But he backs off. "No use in arguing over a few numbers, is there? I'm sure someone as persuasive as you can find a way to keep the laxative companies from, shall we say, running away."

He smiles warmly as nervous laughter runs through the room. Greta doesn't respond.

"But I do think," Stonebane continues, feeling the crowd come on side, "I do think we all might want to get your thoughts on the, ah . . . how to put this delicately? The Jacobson affair."

"Yeah, Greta, let's skin that onion right now," yawns Ludwig Zeemanvitz as he strokes down his thin canopy of hair.

She turns to lock eyes with the corpulent figure of Zeemanvitz, the self-described "Klan-Approved, Grade-A

Kike." According to Network legend, he spent the first ten years of his life as the only Jew in a small town in Mississippi and the rest of his life consciously keeping up his beloved Southern drawl and boasting about run-ins with good ol' boys. When Greta first arrived at the Network he told her that he'd been in the news business so long that he covered the sixth and seventh day of Creation, but didn't file the story because God forgot to create a phone. It was his way of saying, "Welcome aboard, junior, don't fuck with my program." She usually enjoyed the sugary, slow pace of his speech, like watching ice cream melt on a dessert tray, but his charming words camouflaged cutting insults and hidden agendas that also made her wary of him.

"Ah did notice somethin' awful weird this mornin'," Zeemanvitz says, "what with the whole staff buzzin' round the paper like flies on a cow patty. Read that cover article by the Stanton fella, and, whew, he smoked our boy Jake like a kosher pig. I'm thinkin': There's the fan, here comes the shit, take cover. So Greta, the way ah see it is simple. We can roll up and play porcupine on this one, try ta scare off the other news media, a strategy ah personally contend is foolhardy. Or we show some *chutzpah*, grab our collective cajonees; ah'll put a few of my so-called reporters on the story and we'll lead tonight's broadcast with it. Run a special item on Jacobson, too. But it's your call, right? You're the big *macher* on this ranch, ain't ya?" He smiles at his liberal mix of Yiddish and Texan.

"As I told William this morning in my–" Greta begins, but she's cut off by Stonebane's loud voice.

"You make a good point, Ludwig. We must cover the Jacobson affair on my newscast."

"Couldn't agree more if ah said it myself – which ah just did," Zeemanvitz responds laconically, winking at Stonebane.

"After all, everything that happens in the world is news. Ah stole that little beauty from your book, Bill. Touché."

"Nicely put," replies Stonebane, always delighted to be publicly quoted. "Even if we *become* the story – or, in this case, if *one of us* becomes the story – we still must cover it. Objectivity is the very essence of the Craft. After all, we are the people to whom the whole nation turns in times of crisis."

"And sure as the Nazi's invaded Alaska, *this* is a major crisis," confirms Zeemanvitz.

"It definitely is," Stonebane intones.

"Halle-fuckin'-lujah," says Zeemanvitz, patting his bloated belly and kicking back in his chair. "So we cover Jacobson."

"We can discuss this in my office later," Greta hisses. "Are there any more questions?"

"Why not sort this Jacobson thing out while we're all here?" Stonebane asks, raising his voice a few decibels to take command of the room. "I suppose we might get an exclusive interview with Jacob. Wonderful for the ratings, if indeed he did do it. Do you happen to know where he is, Greta?" he asks innocently. "I'm surprised he's not here with us. It's such an 'interesting' news day after all."

Blood rushes into Greta's face as she scowls at Stonebane, but she says nothing and pretends to take notes. She knows there's still plenty of time to make a final decision about Jacob, and she doesn't want to have a public confrontation with both Zeemanvitz and the wily Stonebane. A silence fills the room, wrapping itself like a bandage around each person.

□ □ □

In the bathroom, Tasso is still not sure if he's heard the news correctly that his library is being closed. He shuts his eyes and senses the oppressive heat in the enclosure. No air comes through the blocked vents and his clothes cling uncomfortably to his body. The bizarre events of the morning begin to coalesce in his head into a few ugly phrases. *Suspicious-looking people . . . We'll be sorry to see him go . . . close the library.* A whirling feeling overwhelms him. He opens his eyes and shakes his head to try to alleviate the uncomfortable sensation, but it only intensifies. *What am I doing here?* he wonders, looking around him in horror. *Locked in this hot toilet with a crazy person? Have I really been fired? Fired?* The world he's built feels as if it's quickly diminishing. Suddenly it's smaller than his library, smaller than the cramped bathroom where he stands, smaller than his own body. His whole life instantly reduced to a microscopic place behind his eyes where his mother used to say God stored your dreams. This is his most secret place, his locus of identity, and he realizes that the long years at the Network have rendered it so small as to be almost non-existent. A surge of pure fear overcomes him as the last vestiges of a comfortable identity implode into a horrible realization: *My life's been stolen for the second time. Now I'll have to re-cast myself all over again.* Lost in these thoughts, Tasso isn't aware that his left hand is grinding the wet tissue into Jake's face, suffocating Jake in the process.

Jake regains consciousness when his body involuntarily kicks outwards in search of air. Lungs bursting, he inhales deeply and throws his hands desperately upwards. Unfortunately, as his left hand rockets into the air it connects firmly with the point of Tasso's chin. Stunned by the blow, Tasso falls directly on top of Jacob and lets out a wail.

The noise startles Martin Gimper, who sits hunched over in the Chair directly in front of the washroom door. For the past fifteen minutes, the Gimp has been coping with the relentless gaze of Greta Watt by practising the art of visualization. It's a trick he learned from his athlete friends, who told him that they alleviated tension by mentally replaying their favourite matches. For the Gimp that match is the unforgettable 1980 fight between Roberto Duran and the welterweight champ Sugar Ray Leonard, when, in answer to the Gimp's nightly prayers, the long-shot challenger Duran won the title on points and the Gimp pocketed a cool forty dollars from his all-too-cocky cousin Ricky. Now he sees himself sitting not in the Chair, but in Duran's corner, with only one last round of intense punishment to be endured before being crowned the champ. *The thrill of victory, the agony of defeat,* he thinks to himself as the meeting progresses, quoting the sublime voice-over to ABC's *Wide World of Sports*. It always chokes him up. So when he hears the wail from the bathroom behind him, it's the Gimp as fighter, not reporter, who leaps up and yells, "There's someone on the shitter!"

Another noise emanates from inside the little room – this time from Jake, who is trying to remove the panicking Tasso Darjun from his body.

The Gimp grabs the handle to the washroom door, but to his frustration he finds it locked. But the muffled sound of voices from the washroom sends a jolt of adrenaline through the Gimp's body and he leans back and smashes his broad shoulder into the door, breaking it open.

"A-ha!" cries the Gimp, although he's not exactly sure why. After all, he's as stunned as the rest of the staff by what he sees.

"Marty, what the hell are you doing?" gasps Janice Dawson, realizing that her on-air sports reporter has just gone berserk.

"Jesus H. Christ, look at that," mutters T-Bill, worrying that a new sex club has started without his knowledge, making his recent conquest on Stonebane's desk seem passé.

Dylan O'Sullivan catches Sudra Buchdeera's eye and winks flirtatiously as if to say, See, everyone's doing it.

What they all see is Jacob Jacobson lying beneath the recently dismissed librarian Tasso Darjun, both of them struggling to get up. Now the whole staff are on their feet, shouting and jostling, making it impossible for Greta and Stonebane to discern what the ruckus is all about.

"Please keep calm, everyone. It's just a toilet!" calls out Greta.

But it isn't just a toilet, it's Tasso and the newly conscious Jake, finally extricated from each other's tangled bodies and walking gingerly out of the bathroom and into the staff meeting.

Janice Dawson leaps forward, pulls the Gimp into the corner, and administers spin to him with such urgency it appears as if she's giving him artificial respiration. "You thought someone was hurt in there, you were just doing your job, that's all you say, got it, Marty? That's what you say when they ask."

Sudra walks over to Dylan and slaps him across the face. No one notices. All other eyes are rivetted on the dazed figures of Tasso and Jake.

"Jacob? Jacob?" Greta repeats incredulously when she finally sees him. "How did you get here? Are you all right?"

Jake stumbles forward and raises his head at the sound of Greta's voice.

"I'm sorry, Ms. President. Have I missed the meeting?" He feels drunk in a pleasant but reckless way and puts his arm around Tasso. "My man Tasso and I were doing some research on a little story and we must have dozed off. These meetings have always been so deadly, real mustard gas for the mind." He smiles at the disbelieving faces around him.

Ignoring Jake, Tasso stands perfectly still. If he tries to move he's not sure which body will perform the task: the dutiful and secure Tasso of old or this new, bastard version of himself, of which he's become aware only minutes earlier. His muscles tingle as if he's been atomized and then put delicately back together. One movement and he feels he might shatter into a million pieces, disappearing back into some form of energy. It's the closest thing to a religious feeling he's had in years.

Greta tries to think of some tactical way to save the meeting from descending into pandemonium, but this is far beyond the powers of a mere SOS. Questions about Jake swirl in her mind, all the more urgently when she notices his dishevelled appearance. Bloodstains dot his clothes and his face has a nacreous hue, the colour of drywall. But as startled as Greta is by Jake, it's Tasso who truly terrifies her. Still as a corpse, he glares at her, his two dark eyes piercing through the tumult from across the long conference table as if they'll never let her go.

"This meeting's over," Greta announces, trying to tear herself away from Tasso's gaze. "Everyone back to work."

But a hint of fear in her voice undermines her authority and no one moves.

"I want to know how many people have trouble staying awake in these things," Jake continues, his thoughts now running free and uncensored. "How about a show of hands? Oh, come on, admit it. I could sell pillows here. What was is it today? Let me guess, the same old, same old from our peppy leader Greta: someone got fired, an advertiser threatened to drop out, and we heard a few inspired comments about 'the team'? Bull's eye?"

Greta stiffens at the comments and Jake chuckles, moving slowly through the confused silence towards the boardroom table. He still can't feel his body and his legs and arms bend without regard for his mind, propelling him forward as if by a mysterious gravitational pull. Random thoughts churn in the narcotic stew of his mind, making it difficult for him to focus, but giving him a feeling of lightness, a high. It's the best he's felt in hours. He notices Stonebane purse his lips in disgust.

"Why the long face, Bill?" Jake asks, his brain alternating electrically between clarity and confusion. "Isn't the great defender of the Crap, oh, sorry, "the Craft," still keeping the little people in TV-land happy? Oh no, Bill, it's the little Pepto-Bismol people! They're coming to take you off the air." Jake's voice breaks and he cackles to himself.

Stonebane bristles. "Quite an entrance, my boy," he says as soberly as he can. "In fact, we were just talking about you. I think you have a bit of explaining to do."

"Has anyone ever told you how weird your voice is?" Jake says flippantly. He lowers his chin and imitates Stonebane's deep pitch. "Good evening, welcome to *World Report*. I'm William Stonebane and I suffer from anal retention."

"Jacob!" Greta barks sharply as laughter scatters across the room.

"You're way out of line, son!" Stonebane bellows.

"I won't have my meeting hijacked like this," Greta interjects again, trying to stop the proceedings before Jake makes it impossible for her to ever salvage his career. "Mr. Darjun, tell me exactly what's going on here," Greta demands, attempting, if nothing else, to get Tasso to take his eyes off of her.

But Tasso stays rooted to his spot. Slowly he turns his head from side to side, gazing about the room at the other staff members who stand like a crowd rubbernecking a car crash, greedy for a bloody spectacle. A rush of something pure and malevolent travels past the salt stains on his pants and up his leg, into his groin, through his waist, and then shoots through his whole body, suffusing him with cool hatred for everyone in the room. But as quickly as that feeling comes, it changes shape. From hatred to loneliness, the shortest journey. He stands as alone as he's ever been. He thinks of Goa, so long ago – and suddenly, not so long after all. He looks back down the long oak table at Greta.

"Ms. President," he says finally, his voice trembling slightly under the weight of its surprising volume. "You've made a very great error in closing the library, a very great error which you will regret."

"Excuse me?" Greta gasps, taken aback by what appears to be a threat from the usually demure librarian. "Tasso, I'm sorry, but this is purely a business decision. It's just business."

"More like going out of business," someone mumbles, too excited by the presence of real drama to remain silent.

Another burst of laughter ensues, clattering like pebbles kicked up on the road by a skidding car. Then it subsides. Finally Stonebane speaks.

"I think we're getting sidetracked here. Jacob, why don't you simply tell us all what happened last night. We're most keen to know the details. Better yet, why don't we record a statement for tonight's show? What say you to that?"

"What say me?" replies Jake, now agitated by the combination of too many people and too many pills. The reckless high he felt moments ago stiffens into hostility and his mind momentarily clears. "What say you to the idea that what happened last night is none of your goddamn business?"

"I beg your pardon?"

"You don't have to beg. What happened is between myself and Rachel and a policeman with a burnt ear." Jake flicks his left lobe with his thumb and forefinger.

"Ever the wit," Stonebane says. "But you see, young man, you've now become a major news item, a Network exclusive if you will. So a little co-operation with your colleagues would help."

"Co-operation?" Jake mutters angrily while still shaking his head. "Co-operate with who? You? What does that mean? Does that mean that I'll just plop myself down in front of a few million people and give you the hot exclusive on the gory death of my lover? That's quality thinking, Bill. Real therapeutic."

"Rachel was your lover?" Stonebane whistles. "Lucky girl. Or maybe, not so lucky after all. Take us into that office, Jacob. Tell us how you felt when you saw your lover shot to death. Tell us how you felt when Rachel's body lay in front of you. Tell us how you feel now."

The mention of Rachel's name, the way Stonebane so casually tosses it off as if it were just another headline, seems to release some powerful chemical in Jake's brain. His thoughts veer and distort until everything in the room appears hazy and unreal, covered by thick static. And then, just as quickly, they harden into new shapes, into the clarity of anger and shame. Stonebane's bald head and white face become a camera lens, the staff around him become klieg lights, shutting off and on. Their faces show no emotion, they are just acetate colour filters thrown over blank eyes, convenient moods to suit the moment. Slowly Jake detaches from his body and sees himself from above. He watches himself move forward, arms swinging crazily at his side like severed electrical cables. He climbs up onto the long boardroom table and walks slowly across the wooden surface. His head is near the ceiling and the track lights warm his brow. He thinks: *This flesh is so convenient, effective for climbing tables, for producing sensations of pleasure.*

Jake sees his mechanical body walk towards the camera that is William Stonebane.

Now he's on air. Live. This is his show. His mouth begins to move, speaking in the word patterns that have made him famous. It's doing the very thing it's paid to do – talk cleverly, ad lib, transform into an electronic signal that is everyone's favourite program. He watches his TV self like an audience member and flash cards of dialogue come into his head.

Card One: A man named Jacob Jacobson struts across a long wooden table waving his arms.

"Bill, I hate to disappoint you like this, but I can't tell you a goddamn thing about how I feel, I really can't," he hears himself say. "Maybe that means I'm not a journalist of your calibre, but I just don't believe that. I read your book, you know – more like persevered through it – but one line stood out and I often think about it. It was something like, 'The journalist must dissociate his emotions from the world, commit himself to objectively documenting the events of others.' I once believed that, really I did, but the more I work in this business the more I think it's bullshit. Who actually wrote that book for you anyway? I've always wanted to know. Was it that worm Thatchly?"

"How dare you!" Stonebane sputters.

"Will everyone please try to calm down," Greta says, this time almost to herself.

"No, really, was it?" Jake continues, watching his body stride majestically down the table. "Because I just think it's so wrong, so pitifully wrong. Surprise, Billy! TV has changed since you first went on the air. Hell, everything's changed. No one wants to watch an automaton drone on for half an hour pretending that nothing affects him. It's artificial, unreal – which is why your show's in the tank, if you want my opinion.

Your attitude, your . . . what's the phrase you use? Oh, right, your 'objective perspective.' It's a fucking pretence, Billy. No one buys that crap any more. It's over, gone with the milk man, the Berlin Wall, black-and-white TV. What people want to see is the muck on my show: the ugly, grubby reality played out by ugly, grubby people."

"Ugly is a good word for your work," Stonebane shoots back.

"Of course it's ugly, Billy. That's the point of it. Ugly is good, ugly is real. Forget the slickster packaging, forget the filters. Christ, forget the news. News is overrated, Billy boy. It's the conceit of a few rich old drips like yourself trying to impose a phony order on a world you have absolutely no clue about."

"How sweet, Jacob," Stonebane huffs. "The death of your loved ones has turned you into a squishy little liberal. What a morning you're having."

"Shut that famous trap and listen for second, Bill," Jake shouts, teetering dangerously towards hysteria. His thoughts, sharpened by the sudden rush of energy, feel crisp, organized and available. "What do people want? This is the trillion-dollar question. Do they really want to hear stories about the victims of a plane crash in India or do they just want to see a cool picture of a burning fuselage? Hell Billy, it's a no-brainer. No picture, no story. Right? It's the pornography of violence that people watch the news for, and you and I are the chief pornographers in the theatre."

"Speak for yourself," Stonebane snipes.

Around the room people exchange glances, both stimulated and alarmed by what's happening around them. Greta looks up at Jake in horror, realizing that there's nothing she can do to stop him.

"But after a while, Billy, and here's the tragedy," Jake says, moving inexorably down the table towards him. "After a while even pictures of burning fuselages don't get people off. They're too far away for the average Bubba. Bubba can't make that imaginative leap. What Bubba really wants to see is the pure chaos he knows from his everyday life. The chaos he can recognize. Indigenous terrors. Bubba wants to see the family disagreements, the lover's revenge killing, the incest and addictions. He wants the post office worker who mows down his co-workers with an Uzi because he's been laid off. Real, close-to-home chaos, Bill. The lushness of domestic violence. Mmm. Yeah. That's why Bubba likes my show. Because I'm just like him. I need what he needs. My show validates Bubba's confusion, your show condescends to it. That's the secret of my success. I'm like a fucking priest, see, I commune with the mysterious berserk inside Bubba's heart. I cross that invisible bridge you're so scared of."

"What you are is a whore," Stonebane retorts, furious at being so publicly upbraided. "Now tell us about last night before I have to call Security."

"Oh Billy, we're all whores of one sort or another," Jake says, getting closer to Stonebane. His mind races out of control and he feels a distant but insistent tug on his bladder. "You can't honestly look at me and say that you've felt something for the people you report on. I mean really *felt* something, in your bones, not just in that voice of yours you use to express some bullshit pathos. No one in this room can honestly say that."

"You arrogant little flea-sucker," Zeemanvitz blurts out, unable to tolerate the scene any more. "Ah don't have to listen to this sophomoric bullshit."

"We certainly don't," Stonebane agrees.

Picking up his cell phone, Zeemanvitz prepares to leave. "Son," he says, "ah wouldn't piss in your ear if your brain was on fire – and ah think it is."

Card 2: But the man named Jacob starts talking faster, rattling off words as if he's spraying the air with water.

"Hey, relax. I'm not condemning anyone," Jake babbles onwards. "People in glass houses, right? I'm the worst of the lot, that's the whole fucking irony here. I'm the pro, you see, the master of the electronic race. I'm Windex clean, Turtle Wax shined, burn proof, scratch proof, chip proof. I'm a one-time-offer miracle product. I'm so brand fucking new that nothing can touch me. No accident, no murder, no war. It just beads like rain on my skin and slides off."

To the horror of everyone in the room, Jake starts punching himself on the side of the head. "See," he yells. "I'm goddamn numb!"

"I asked you a simple question and I demand an answer," Stonebane growls, intent on not being thrown off by Jake's mania.

"Yes," Greta says, finally wanting an answer for herself so this madness can end. "What did happen last night?"

"You want the truth?" Jake asks, abruptly dropping his voice. His arms fall to his side, and he breathes thickly.

"The truth would be nice, I think we'd all agree on that." Stonebane's eyes dart around the room looking for allies.

Jake closes his eyes and wishes everything would slow down so he could explain how confused he actually is, how he can't find a truth simple enough to justify what he felt in that bloody hallway, how he can remember only fragments: the flashing red light, the darting shadow, the blacking out. A cloud of traumatic images descends on his mind and threatens to collapse him. He opens his eyes to steady himself.

"You have to tell us something, Jacobson," Stonebane says impatiently. "We can't just run dead air on tonight's broadcast."

Dead air. The phrase erupts in Jake's brain like a struck match and for a moment he thinks that Stonebane has hit on the perfect solution. Let the viewers make up their own version of his story; that would be truth enough for him. His mouth opens to say as much, but nothing comes out. He gazes at the faces from the Network looking up at him, all carrying identical expressions of shock, and he feels as though he's standing in a hall of mirrors, misunderstanding regressing undiminished into infinity. He keeps still, waiting for new words to spill out of his mouth, but all at once a hot sensation fills the empty space below his mind where his body used to be. The sensation runs down his legs, soothing him. He becomes lighter and lighter; if the feeling endures he imagines he'll simply float safely out the window into the cobalt sky, away from the Network and the hospital and up to the cottage where the winds of Georgian Bay howl like radio static. Warmth.

Jake closes his eyes as he relieves himself, his pants soaking dark with piss.

Later the police will discover that one of the pills in Jacob's bag was Rifampin, a diuretic drug used to cure TB. It has one noticeable side effect: it turns all fluids in the body neon orange. But even a journalist of William Stonebane's calibre could not know about Rifampin, and at the sight of the bright liquid pooling in front of him on the oak table, he flies into hysterics.

"You've gone mad, you filthy animal!" Stonebane shouts, mortified by the toxic sight. Turning to Greta, he says savagely, "This is all going on air, every last detail."

Zeemanvitz stands up and demands an immediate explanation from the medical reporter, Tamara Finley-Plaznicz. "Finley, why the hell is that boy pissin' Vitamin C?"

"It must be . . . God, I don't really know, sir," stammers Finley, realizing that now she too has been infected by the virus of scandal invading the room.

"Ya dumb-ass rookie!" Zeemanvitz hisses, shaking his head so quickly that his canopy of hair lifts off his head like a sail.

As if they were a flock of sparrows rising out of a wheat field at the approach of a thresher, the reporters flee from the room. Out flies Stonebane and Zeemanvitz, out flies Dylan O'Sullivan and T-Bill. Even Greta picks up her papers and bolts. Sudra Buchdeera claws her way through the crowd and the Gimp is practically carried out by his producer. Cell phones are left on the table as if tainted by the liquid that's now pooling around the feet of a dazed Jacob Jacobson. The doorway jams.

In the midst of the upheaval, Tasso calmly walks over to the wall and pulls the red fire alarm. Bells start to ring throughout the building, a dissonant clanging that dislodges all order from the offices and studios.

And in seconds they're all gone. Jacob and Tasso are left alone in the long boardroom abandoned coffee mugs still steaming and cell phones still beeping. The loud bell makes the room feel smaller than it is, protected in its emptiness by a massive cloak of sound. It's the moment after a child drops a vase and looks up to his mother's shocked face. It's the quiet after a family dispute, during the slow clean-up of the smashed dishes in the late-night kitchen. It's the intimacy of debris.

Tasso walks back towards Jake and mutters, "Mr. Jacobson, the meeting's over. I have to go now." His voice barely penetrates the cry of the alarm.

Jake doesn't say a word. He just stands on the desk staring straight ahead, paralysed by the miasma of images and words fogging his head. Tasso shrugs his shoulders and reaches into his pocket and pulls out a cigarette. Benson and Hedges Gold. He lights up and inhales deeply, his whole body pleasured by the delicious smoke.

He walks slowly back into the washroom, his mind emptied of thought, and gathers up the stethoscope, the bloody hospital coat, and the bag of drugs, not quite sure what to do with them. When he returns with the paraphernalia, Jake is still standing, as if transfixed by some invisible image. Tasso climbs up onto the conference table and takes him by the hand.

"Mr. Jacobson?"

Startled by the warm touch of Tasso's fingers, Jake whips his head around. "Tasso? What's happened?"

"You were right about the meeting," Tasso says carefully, as if each word were a grenade. "Someone did get fired. Twenty-four years. This is what I get after twenty-four years."

Jake nods, but says nothing. They stand in silence for a while, neither sure what to do.

"You once helped my daughter, so I'll help you now," Tasso says unexpectedly, even surprising himself. "Then I have to leave you alone."

Jake sways helplessly and then, balancing himself with great effort, he looks at Tasso closely. "You're a decent man, Mr. Darjun. Thank you."

And at that moment Tasso knows something has changed. That in the shared silence hidden within the steady noise of the fire bell, someone has looked upon him for the first time as an equal. No longer as librarian or researcher or foreigner – he's been released from those roles into another: citizen.

The fire alarm sings.

"I don't feel too well," Jake says hoarsely. "There's a cab outside waiting for me. Could you help me get to it?"

"We'll have to go out the back. Be very careful. People want to find you."

Jake lists to his left and Tasso grabs his arm to straighten him. Very slowly, Tasso leads Jake down from the table and out the boardroom door, both limping away from the reporters and the police who swarm the Network trying to get Jake's story. Down the corridors towards the side exit they move, Tasso thinking sadly of his own story, how his carefully constructed life has fallen into turmoil in a single morning, how he'll have to re-invent himself somehow, in another place. And the fire alarm keeps wailing, on and on, as if it will never stop.

REWIND

This is how Theo comes home:

"Whole world's in chaos," says the short, balding man behind the coffee shop counter when he sees Theo reading the story about Rachel Anne Poiselle in the *Gazette.* He pinches his nose to clear it and then wipes his hands on his white apron. "Every day there's someone killing someone else somewheres. You'd think there was a world war or somethin'. Cream and sugar?"

"Black's fine," Theo says without looking up. He tenses his jaw and the man notices the muscle bulge under Theo's skin.

It's early Monday morning and the frost on the restaurant window glistens as the heater inside fights uselessly to melt it. In an hour Theo will be at the small island cabin his father built, now stuck in the Georgian Bay ice like a black scab. Theo is wasted from exhaustion, his shoulders hunched as if carrying a heavy pack, his eyes rheumy and glazed. Three days ago he left Fenwick Park, stole a car and a new set of licence plates, and bolted across the country, stopping only once for a few hours in Toronto. He's wired on coffee. To keep himself from dozing off while he drives, he keeps his fingers close to the glowing end of a cigarette, the burning sensation jolting him awake before he careers off the road. Fugitive tricks. His fingers are almost completely yellow and black.

"My wife and I watch that guy on TV every night," the man continues, pointing to the article Theo's reading. "That Jacobson fella. He's real good, too. Stirs it up. You ever watch him?"

"Sometimes," Theo says, still reading the story with intensity. He'd already heard most of the details on the radio, but he wants to see how many facts the newspaper got right.

"What I want to know is, how can a guy who's got it all – the money, the fame, the whole nine yards – go and kill someone? That's the mystery to me: What's goin' on in that guy's head?"

"Give me one of those chocolate doughnuts," Theo mumbles, trying to ignore him.

"Made 'em fresh at five this mornin'," the man says, reaching down with a pair of tongs to grab one from a tray. He puts it on a napkin and slides it over to Theo. "Just last year a guy up here went zonko. Walked out to his barn and shot his horse, and then followed his wife to the school where she worked and blew her away, too. Turned the gun on himself before the cops got him. Bam! Right through the roof of his mouth. Guy used to come in here too. Corn farmer, and a good man, as far as I could tell. Took his coffee black, just like you. Up to his ass in debt, though, and I guess he couldn't handle it. Hey, we all get pushed too far, I sympathize with that. But to shoot his horse? Now what did that poor animal ever do to him? Man can kill his wife or kill another man, that's his business as far as I'm concerned, but you don't kill an innocent animal. That's just wrong. Makes me sick."

"You think he did it?" Theo asks quietly, lifting his head to finish his coffee.

"Jacobson you mean? Hell, I don't know," the man shrugs. "Probably. I watch the guy on TV is all, don't know what he's like in person. Probably nuts. You can't tell what people are really like on the inside."

"True enough."

"Take this guy up here. If I knew he was gonna lose it I would'a called the humane society and taken that horse away 'fore he got to it. Anyways, famous guy like Jacobson, he'll get off. Hire a big lawyer. Nothin' touches people like that. They're black ice, Teflon. That'll be two eighty-five for the coffee and donut."

"Jacobson won't get off easily," Theo says to the man as he flips him some change.

"How do you know?"

"I just know," Theo says and walks back out to his car.

An hour later Theo arrives at Pointe au Baril, more a collection of marinas than a town but the place where his father used to park the car and take the boat to the cottage. Instead of stopping, Theo drives past the turn-off for a few miles and then, looking over his shoulder to make sure there's no other traffic on the road, he swerves off the road and ploughs the stolen car into the bush. He jumps out and quickly covers the car with snow and branches until it blends in with the landscape. Then he grabs his bag of clothes from the back seat and heads back for town on foot. Forty-five minutes later he again sees Pointe au Baril, now just another frozen section of land where pickup trucks trail smoke like lifelines.

Everything around Theo is a swath of undifferentiated white – the sky, the trees, the ground – and in the thin border between the whitenesses small northern lives make erasable tracings. It's the perfect place to hide. In the summer Pointe au Baril dresses itself up for the wealthy city people who drive two hours from Toronto in their Range Rovers and Saabs, park at Hogan's Marina, and pick up a few groceries from the overpriced counter where Terry Hogan – pregnant again – will ask if they want to put the gas for the boat and the bags of potato chips on a summer tab. And then they jump into their bow-riders and head off towards one of the thousand scarified rocks that make up Georgian Bay's famous island retreats. In the summer the bay opens to a raw beauty, the land warm and naked, trees bent westward like suspects thrust against a wall, strip-searched by the rough hands of wind. But in the winter it reverts to more primordial rhythms. It's not a place that speaks of holidays or summer boat rides, but of endurance and the dumb intentions of survival. The land is silent, as if sound might awake the ire of the brutal wind blowing in off the frozen horizon and wreak destruction. Winter is always longest on the shores, which are protected neither by the contours of land nor the warmth of cottagers, and Terry Hogan likes to say that there's no summer season at all, just a few months of détente before winter once more attacks.

The cold doesn't bother Theo, even though he's not wearing proper clothing. He's too distracted by what the paper said about Jake to feel it. Locating a snowmobile parked in a covered shelter beside Hogan's locked-up store, Theo hotwires it and heads towards the family island. No one's used the cottage in winter since Momma started wandering, but it's always been the family refuge. Their father built it by himself when he was twenty-nine, going up every summer for three years, and it's possibly the only job he ever completed. There the boys spent their first summers, learning to sail, swim, and canoe on rough water, and Momma and Pop would enjoy a few meandering months before returning to the angular city of bad finances, alcohol, and the little erosions of daily life. But even before Pop died the place began deteriorating: the septic system blocked up and the log walls needed new insulation. The cottage went from refuge to monument, and finally, when Pop died, to talisman.

For two and a half miles the wind tears into Theo's cheeks like a scalpel as he speeds across the massive beating heart that is the bay, now packed in ice, waiting patiently to be transplanted again into the warm body of summer. The snowmobile whines loudly and as Theo guns it he thinks about the conversation he had earlier at the coffee shop. The man was upset about a dead horse. Grimacing in the wind, Theo remembers a similar conversation he once had with Jake in Algonquin Park, so long ago . . .

August again, leaves dripping with the first brushes of red and orange, air loses the weight of summer humidity and opens like a lung. It's their time to go camping in Algonquin Park, one week together unwinding into an old comfort, and they do it every summer the same way: pack the bare essentials, canoe in the nude, flash their asses to other campers if they run across them, sun themselves on hot granite rocks, swim in the cool lake water, watching turtles.

"Watch out for the snappers, Jake, they'll bite your pecker off."

"They always go for the big one first."

One summer Theo brings a shotgun. It's going to be different this year, he explains, they're going to learn to survive off of the land.

"This trip is going to be old style," Theo says as they lower the canoe into the water. "I want to experience what life's really like in the bush."

"Maybe we should try to get scurvy too," Jake laughs. "Then we can boil some bark and do shooters."

"I'm serious. There's only enough food for two days. The rest of the week we'll have to survive on what we catch."

"I can't eat fish every night, Theo. I hate fish."

"I want us to bag a bear."

Jake snorts. "Right. Well, I'm not gonna starve to death in the forest while you play Daniel fucking Boon. Now where's the rest of the food?"

Theo reaches into his bag and shows Jake his gun. "This is our food. Trust me, you won't starve."

Jake stops loading the boat and looks up at Theo. "I hope you realize that you're out of your mind. We're not allowed to kill a bear in the park. The rangers will arrest us."

Theo puts the gun back in his pack. "I'm serious about this. No one's gonna catch us. We'll skin the thing, bury the entrails, and smoke the meat, like I learned when I was up in the Arctic. Christ, we'll be miles from anyone. Come on, let's do this one right."

And because Theo is so adamant, Jake relents. He always does. They go into the bush to hunt a bear. It takes them three days of paddling to find one. Theo brings honey and peanut butter as bait and he spreads it around their campsite with some other food. Then they wait. At about two in the morning on the third night, something emerges from the bush.

"Jakey, for Christ's sake, wake up, we got one," Theo whispers excitedly from his sleeping bag. "I think it's eating the honey."

"Oh shit, Theo, don't do this," Jake pleads, groggy from sleep. "Go back to sleep."

"Get the flashlight," Theo says, unzipping the tent fly. "Quick, get up before it takes off."

"I don't want to kill a bear. For God's sake, I barely eat meat in the city."

Theo picks up the rifle and crawls out into the night. "Get up, you chickenshit, and grab the light. I think I have a shot."

Jake makes a joke about acting like cavemen, tries to cajole his brother into abandoning his plan, but Theo is already cocking the gun.

"I'm not doing this, Theo, I won't be a part of this."

"All right, screw you. I knew you'd back out anyway," Theo says, taking aim. "I'll eat it and you can starve. But at least hold the light. I don't want to miss the son of a bitch."

Reluctantly Jake gets the flashlight and shines the beam on the bear. It's a small black, with a red tag in its ear. It licks the honey greedily, making noises like the rustling of wet leaves. When the light hits its face, the bear looks up towards it and its eyes turn opaque and unfocused, like two onyx stones. Jake watches the bear bend its head to the side, curious, obviously not threatened by the appearance of two humans.

"I've got it," Theo whispers. "Hold the light, Jakey. Hold it steady."

"Theo, please don't shoot the bear, don't do it."

"Keep quiet."

"I said *don't do it.*"

Crack.

The gun goes off and the sound rolls across the glassy

surface of the lake, bouncing off the forest into the starlit night. The bear crumples, hit in the shoulder. It makes a horrible noise: a flat, painful sound that comes out like a hot flash of fire exploding and then just as quickly extinguishing. Wounded, the bear is reduced to making wheezing sounds.

Crack.

Theo shoots the bear again.

Then he's up, walking cautiously towards the animal, breathing steadily, gun still pointed at its head. Jake stays in the tent and holds the light on Theo, his hand hurting as he grips it hard. He watches his brother put down the gun, take out the hunting knife, kneel, and slit the bear's throat.

"Just to make sure," Theo calls out, turning towards the light. He breathes excitedly, gulping in chunks of air. "It's not so big. I thought it would be a helluva lot bigger."

Jake lets the light drop to the black smudge of bear, a Rorschach pattern on the white canvas of light.

Theo bends down and sits silently over the bear carcass for a minute, mumbling something to himself.

"What are you doing?" Jake calls out.

"I'm thanking the bear for giving himself to us," Theo says. "You have to apologize to everything you kill. That way the spirit of the animal knows that we respect it, that we killed it for a noble purpose."

"And what purpose is that?"

Theo looks up to the light and squints his eyes. "One thing dies so another can survive. Sacrifice, Jake, it's a beautiful thing. The law of nature."

Theo rubs the side of the knife on the side of his pants. "Now watch this, Jake. I learned this when I hunted moose with the Dene. They could gut, skin, and chop the animal up into pieces in nine minutes flat."

He takes the knife and plunges it into the bear's belly, dragging downward from crotch to neck. Like a reluctant pack mule, the windless air carries the humid scent of blood to Jake's nostrils. Jake holds the light and watches.

Thrusting the knife deep inside the bear, Theo cuts into its intestines and stomach, then reaches his arm in and yanks them out onto the ground. The bear steams.

"We'll have to bury these," Theo instructs Jake while cutting out more entrails. "You'll have to dig a hole. Make it deep so the rangers don't find it. I'm gonna take its head off."

Theo gets up quickly and walks by Jake to the tent, grabs the axe they use to cut firewood, and returns to the bear's carcass. Spreading his legs wide, Theo raises his arm up. Jake watches the axeblade catch the moon in the background and then smash down onto the bear's neck. There's a muffled sound, like that of a boot stepping into a mud puddle. It takes Theo five hits to break the spinal cord.

"A bear head!" Theo yells triumphantly. "I mean, Jesus, can you believe this? Look at those teeth, Jake." Theo holds up the head by the red tag on the ear and puts his hand inside the bear's mouth, laughing.

The black eye sockets of the bear are hollow as caves.

Twenty minutes later the bear is skinned and Theo cuts off the feet, tail, and testicles. "If you don't cut off the balls, the meat will go bad. That's what the Native guide told me."

Jake doesn't move. He stares at the hot pile of meat and bones lying in front of the decapitated head of the bear. A heaviness pulls at his eyes and he knows it isn't sleep. Theo walks towards him, his shirt off, and Jake notices the blood and hair clinging to Theo's chest. He leans into the stink of death emanating from his brother and shivers. Theo is a figure of terror, he thinks, a primitive warrior. But somehow beautiful too, as if the coruscating sweat on his body is actually cleansing him.

"What do you think, brother?" demands Theo. "Just like the pioneers. Let's go for a swim and celebrate. We'll bury this later."

"No, you go, I'm fine." Jake shines the light on Theo's chest but gazes down at the ground. He feels sick and sad.

Theo puts his hand over his eyes to block the glare and moves closer. "Come on, Jake. I'm not mad at you. It's tough to go on your first hunt. I felt the same way when the Dene took down a moose. But we're gonna eat it, not mount it. This isn't murder, it's just survival. Life has to be close to the bone, that's what the Dene used to say. You eat hamburgers at home, don't you? Have you ever been to a slaughterhouse? This is a thousand times more humane than what they do there. It's just a bit harder to watch in person. This is how life ought to be lived, Jake. No filters. No bullshit. Now come in the water. You'll feel better, trust me."

And reluctantly Jake decides to believe Theo, believe him because in some raw and difficult way Theo is always right, because his truths are always more true than the unexamined ones Jake lives by. Theo is always closer to the bone, closer to that place where Jake only feels compromise, a vagueness he's ashamed to reveal. And so he gets up and follows Theo into the lake. They swim far out into the middle of the water where the Milky Way reflects off the surface and they stay there, silently floating on their backs until they can no longer tell where the lake ends and the black sky begins . . .

The cold wind biting at his face brings Theo back from the Park. He's getting close to the cottage. The ice is covered with a thin layer of smooth snow, polished hard by the wind, and the runners of the snowmobile glide over it with ease. He needs to see Jake, needs to make Jake trust him the way he had when they were hunting in Algonquin Park. Needs to find a way to explain to Jake that what happened in Fenwick Park had a purpose, that it encompassed a more complicated truth than the one Jake showed on TV.

He pulls back on the throttle, accelerating the machine to full speed, and reflects on his work as an activist. Protesting with student groups in China, living with street kids in Calcutta, drinking with alcoholics on Native reserves, immersing himself in the lives of the people he's come to save, understanding their horror so he can help them defeat it. He learned this lesson when he was twenty-one, working at a mission in Bangkok with a priest who had spent ten years as a pimp. The pockmarked priest had faded tattoos on his arms and the other workers whispered that he had once killed a man. But the priest never apologized for his earlier life, nor did he hide it from the volunteers. "Someone asked me today if I'm ashamed of my past," he said to Theo after a long day working with the AIDS victims at the mission. They were drinking beer to cool off from the heat. "I'm not. My past made me what I am. If you don't understand sin, it follows that you can't understand redemption. All the great saints, Augustine, Jerome, they all knew this. Their lives began in darkness and emerged into light. Like us. Our job at the mission is to teach people this kind of hope: that there are wings born from sin."

These words echo through Theo's memory as he drives across the snow, because these are the words leading him towards Jake. These words will make Jake understand the terrible things he has to do. Just like he did in Bangkok. The whine of the snowmobile turns into the sound of tuk-tuks and street bikes . . .

□ □ □

"You big American, want little girl, little boy?" cries out the wiry Thai man from the bar door. Theo waves him off and keeps walking, wiping sweat from the back of his neck. He's been in Bangkok for six weeks with a missionary organization that's trying to snatch young women away from local gangs and brothels to take them back to their villages. The priest with tattoos tells Theo that pimps go out to the country and give ten American dollars to poor families in exchange for their daughters. The parents are assured that their daughters will work as maids in a hotel in the city and send money home. "Poverty makes any sale easy," the priest says, closing his eyes as if remembering it first-hand. "Within two days, the girls are sold to brothels in Bangkok or Chiang Mai. Young virgins are best. Tourists on sex trips don't want to get AIDS." Ages ten, eleven, twelve, the girls who are stupid and clean. These are the ones that Theo has come to rescue.

"You want good food, mista? I give you good food, then you take girl for night. Yes? Maybe you need two, huh, big man?" says another man in the street, grabbing Theo's arm. Theo throws him off and walks towards the mission.

But just like the priest, Theo has to know what it's like for them, has to see the girls' faces when they're in bed, has to watch how they suffer. Only then can he understand why he's here to save them, why people go to them, what this life is like. He ducks into a club and immediately sees a few girls performing on stage. One girl shoots darts out of her vagina, bursting balloons held up by another. It's less a performance and more of a game to them. They laugh gaily, ignoring the crowd. Theo tells the waiter he wants food and is quickly led into a back room and seated at a table facing a glass wall.

Behind the glass he sees two rows of girls, all wearing lime green bikinis and with numbers stuck to their chests, as if in a pageant. One to forty-five. So many girls. He notices their bodies: the hard, small breasts; the long, awkward legs of youth. They're sexy only in the sense that they're available. He looks at each of them and sees no fat of experience, none of the unique shapes of time. There's nothing voluptuous in the room; everything is similar and small, the details of desire filigreed into thin bodies and desperate eyes. The girls gaze out distractedly as if watching a film they can't understand, and Theo tries to catch an eye. He can't. For a moment he's confused by this and then realizes that the girls are sitting behind a one-way glass. He can see them, they can't see him. Looking down at the dinner menu he sees the name of the club: Aquarium.

"You ready to o'da, mista?" the waiter asks abruptly. "You o'da food first, then o'da girl you like. Pick nice girl from da tank, yes?"

Holding back his revulsion, Theo orders his food. Without warning, four young girls in lavender bikinis come to sit with him. It's a good club for customers that way, no need to ask. One of the girls, short with a blunt haircut, puts her hand on his crotch and whispers, "Take me, I fuck you good," but he pushes her away. She gets upset and runs to the corner of the club, where he spies her sniffing some glue from a plastic bag. Then she races back, shoving the other girls aside. "Buy me Coke, mista," she demands, her eyes alight.

The girls are not allowed to drink alcohol, so he buys them all Cokes, forty baht each, and little white bills pile up in a dish on the table as the waiter brings the drinks. Techno music throbs. The floorshow in the next room continues. Beside him a group of German tourists are getting drunk, lifting girls onto their laps and pinching them with fat fingers, pointing at the others behind the glass and making lewd gestures with their tongues. Theo stifles the urge to walk over and throttle every one of them.

When the food arrives, the waiter shoos away the girls and Theo eats slowly, thinking of his work with the mission and how he'll never be able to tell the others about his secret trick of honest compassion.

"41," he says to the waiter as he pays his cheque. "I'll take Girl 41." It's the same girl he saw on stage when he first walked in.

Later, in a room rented by the hour, she lies beneath him, motionless, eyes closed, her body stale like a loaf of old bread. She waits dully for Theo to fuck her. He knows she's underage and wonders if she were split in half how many rings he could count, how far her concentric circles of age would progress. Twelve, thirteen, fourteen. Underneath his sweating body, she has less life than a tree.

"How old are you?"

"Yes, you like?" she says, forcing a smile and stroking her tiny breasts quickly. Her eyes do not open.

"How old are you?" he repeats more forcefully.

He takes her hand and squeezes it, but her body turns to ashes, sending out no signals of possibility. She is suddenly ageless.

The room is small, with an adjoining bathroom and decorated neatly with classic Thai designs of gold dragons and monkeys. Girl 41 doesn't have a name. He tries to kiss her and she bends her head to the side to avoid his mouth. Her lips are chapped and dry, pressed shut like the rest of her body. He suspects that she has AIDS. Seventy per cent of the prostitutes do; that's what the mission tells him. Underneath her flaked lips and hardened skin Theo imagines the virus flourishing in her blood. Nothing about her body suggests that she might resist it, or resist anything. Her heart, her veins, her capillaries – barely expanding and contracting under his body as her breath comes slow and laboured – are all just lock systems for the rising river of disease. There's no intention in her body at all, only the expectation of discomfort. She's young, beautiful, and corrupted. He throws away his condom and opens her legs. Tonight he'll face the anonymous threat of death as she does every night. Tonight he'll understand.

"Do you have AIDS?" he asks.

"No AIDS, no have AIDS." Her eyes never open.

"How do you know?" he persists. "Have you been tested?"

"No AIDS, no have AIDS."

He enters her without a sound.

Moving slowly inside her, he watches her face, waits for it to open, as if in time he may overhear at least part of the secret it must be telling. He tries to be gentle, hoping that her body will offer some code into which he can read her pain. Even agony would be welcome. But she offers nothing. Underneath him she simply endures, almost bored. She's used to being part of someone else's story. And this is the only secret he will hear: that there's nothing in this act, just a horrible lack of meaning. A vacancy.

He doesn't come.

"Get dressed," he says, getting off her. "I'm going to help you. I'm going to take you home."

"You like it, mista? More?" Her eyes open apprehensively, as if in some way she's failed him.

"Put on your clothes. I'm going to help you."

He doesn't know any Thai and they stare at each other for a moment, not sure what to do. Theo bends down and puts on his pants, hoping that she'll understand. When he stands up, he sees her holding out her hand, waiting to be paid.

"Five thousand baht," she says.

"Listen to me," he says urgently. "I'm sorry about what happened in there. I really am. But you don't need money now. I'm taking you away from here, I'm taking you back home."

He tries to gently lower her hand, but it stays out, steady as a temple pillar.

"You pay me!" she commands, her voice as high-pitched and as sharp as the darts she used on stage. "Five thousand baht, pay me, five thousand baht!"

He gives her the money before she gets hysterical, and watches her dress. Then he grabs her arm and leaves the room. Outside the brothel owner takes the money from the girl and approaches Theo with a toothless smile.

"You like her? You want more girl?"

"I want her all night," Theo hisses. "At my own hotel. Here's twenty thousand baht. Now fuck off."

The girl bows her head to the owner. Somehow she's done her job well and he pats her ass and says, "Yes, she best girl in house. You come back tomorrow again, mista, even betta girl. Maybe two?"

Theo takes Girl 41 by the arm, hails a tuk-tuk, and speeds over to his hotel. He doesn't speak to her. When they arrive, he takes her up to his room and puts her to bed.

"You want again, mista?" She passes her hand over her crotch, but her expression is the same: dull, empty.

Again he tries to unlock her code. Gets in bed. Enters her. But she seals her body like an envelope and makes no sound. Ten minutes later, he rolls off.

"Go to sleep," he tells her, but she already is.

In the morning he delivers her to the mission where they prepare to take her home. She curses him, scratches his face and cries at his betrayal. But Theo understands now. These girls must be saved from their life. Even if they don't know it.

Four months later he's brought out forty-six girls and the priest desperately wants him to stay. But his Thai friends tell him that the gangs are following him and want to slit his throat. He's ruining business.

The day he moves home from Bangkok he goes to a pet store and buys an aquarium with one large colourful fish. He doesn't want the shop owner to tell him what kind it is. Better if he never knows. And every morning afterwards he wakes up and feeds his mysterious fish, watching it head dumbly towards the flakes of food, it's whole life dependent on a source it will never understand. Then he apologizes to Girl 41, wherever she is; apologizes out loud for using her vacant body as the opening through which he slipped and found a larger pain. Because the priest was right. This is what happens to people; they become the violent messengers of a truth they don't know they contain. And Theo hopes Jake will understand this, understand that what he has to do is not crazy, it comes from a faraway place, connected to the present through the deep memories encoded within every action.

Theo jolts back to Georgian Bay as the cottage looms ahead of him. As he turns off the snowmobile, he realizes that he doesn't have a house key. Walking around the back, he breaks a window with his elbow and climbs inside. Fatigue threatens to collapse him. He needs some rest, time to plan, time to figure out a way to contact Jake without the police finding them. Within ten minutes, he's built a fire and stripped off his coat. Then he lights a cigarette, settles into the couch, and waits for night to break open.

POSTMORTEM

"You should have been there!" Stonebane shouts into the phone while he paces furiously around his office. He's on the line with Thatchly, and his voice blasts into the mouthpiece like a jet engine. "Utterly repulsive. He actually relieved himself. He almost relieved himself on me for that matter! He's finished. Done. I'm going to bury him on tonight's broadcast."

"I think I've got something even more delicious than that," replies Thatchly giddily. Unlike Stonebane's voice, Thatchly's is unusually high and shrill, resembling that of a little boy being choked in the school yard by a bully and begging for mercy. But now he's so excited by his news that his voice peaks to the breaking point, as if the bully is about to cut off his oxygen supply. "Remember the surprise I told you about earlier?"

"What surprise?"

"I told you, didn't I?" Thatchly squeaks in bursts. "I went into Rachel Poiselle's office the night she was shot."

"Yes, yes, I already know that."

"Let me finish. While I was in there I was looking around, sort of spooked by the place really, and then I saw something shiny on the floor. Just lying there, in the far corner of the room, half covered by some papers. It hadn't even been tagged as evidence yet. I went over for peek and, William, do you know what it was?"

"Thatchly, please." Stonebane pinches his lips shut in exasperation.

"It was a gun. That's right. The murder weapon, right there! I got such a shiver, because, to be honest, I've never really seen a gun from so close. Anyway, there was so much confusion in the room, the police photographer was moving all over the place, and no one was really paying much attention to me. So I did something quite rash. I really don't know what came over me."

"And?" Stonebane grunts.

"And . . . I bent down and tossed the gun behind one of those old heating rads. Just like that. Very quickly, mind you. I don't know why, but I did. I thought the police would find it – you know how carefully they go over a crime scene – but I went back this morning, flipped the police officer my press badge, and looked for the gun again. And you know what? It was still there! Lodged against the wall."

Stonebane remains silent, shocked by Thatchly's tale.

"William? Hello?"

"Go on," he says warily.

"What I'm saying is," Thatchly's voice drops to a squeaky whisper, "I have the gun. I was half out of my mind when I saw it again and then, well, then I took it. Put in my briefcase and walked right out of there. Don't worry, I used a cloth. Jacobson's fingerprints must be on it. Can you believe it? I've got it right now."

There's a pause as Thatchly catches his breath.

"Thatchly," Stonebane says, his voice swirling with venom. "You ignorant little termite. You've tampered with police evidence! That's a federal offence, do you realize that? You're going to go to prison for this." He pauses for a moment, and then, as an afterthought, he adds, "I'm not part of this, do you understand? You did this alone. I did not tamper with police evidence or instruct you to do that either. Is everyone in this place insane?"

"But William, don't you see?" Thatchly says unflappably, having foreseen Stonebane's reaction. "No one knows about the gun but us. There's no evidence tag. So what I'm thinking is, let's turn this into a Network exclusive. We'll plant it in, let's say, Jacobson's make-up room, later today. Then we'll 'discover' it ourselves while we're 'investigating the story.' Imagine: William Stonebane scoops the police and finds the key evidence in the case. We'll hold a massive press conference. Are you with me? Jacobson will not only be caught red-handed, but we'll be the only reporters on the scene. The ratings, William, think about it. Oh, I'm dying. We have the smoking gun. This could be the biggest special since O.J."

William stands quietly, his voice circling in his diaphragm like a shark deciding whether to attack or swim away. Thatchly has the gun, he mentally repeats to himself. This is definitely out of order, he thinks, against every ethical rule of the Craft. But then again, times have changed, haven't they? Standards are falling and he needs to compete with the newer, racier shows on air. That's exactly what Jacobson was bragging about this morning, wasn't it? And if the boy-man wants to live by the sword, well, why then shouldn't he die by it? Stonebane remembers what Greta said earlier about his sponsor cancelling their contract, and he realizes how desperately he needs a spectacular story to win back viewers. Planting a gun, though? Was this going too far? His mind races through his options. If he turns Thatchly in, he will be doing the right thing, but then where would he be? Back to square one, back to low ratings, back to more cuts from Greta. A sticky situation, he ponders, but he can handle sticky situations, that's what he's trained to do. If he manages this delicately, it might turn out to be the story of a career. A journalistic coup of the first order. A burst of adrenaline rushes through his old veins like it used to when he was a younger reporter in postwar Vietnam, and the predator in his diaphragm swims off, as if distracted by more promising movements elsewhere.

For the first time since the dreadful morning meeting, Stonebane feels better, back in control. Thatchly's a bit zealous, he concludes, but then, who can blame him? He's trying to impress me, Stonebane reflects, and doing a very good job too. And really, it's not as if they're "setting up" Jacobson per se; after all, it was quite clear to him after the morning meeting that Jacobson *did* do it. Putting the gun in the desk is merely – well, merely insurance.

"You've got to be very fastidious, Thatchly," Stonebane whispers. "Get in here as quickly as you can. We'll discuss it all in detail. The police will want to search Jacobson's things, so we have to move quickly. I don't think they have a warrant yet."

"I'll be there within the hour," Thatchly squeals.

A knock on Stonebane's door startles him and he quickly hangs up the phone, sits down at his desk, and pretends to be engrossed in some computer work.

"Come in," he calls out, tapping nonsensically at his keyboard.

Greta opens the door and takes a few cautious steps inside and stops. She's clearly uncomfortable after the disastrous meeting and shifts back and forth on her feet, clearing her throat to announce herself.

"Greta," Stonebane erupts, genuinely surprised to see her. He wonders feverishly how long she's been standing at his door and if she heard anything of his conversation with Thatchly. He buries his head behind his screen to hide his anxiety. "Just trying to learn that new library research system."

"Already at it?"

"Change is good, right?" His fingers dance randomly over the plastic keys, making a flutter of noise.

Greta shakes her head incomprehensibly and coughs again. She decides to forego any preamble and get right to her purpose. "William, have you seen Jacob?"

Stonebane lifts his massive head from behind his monitor, taken off guard by the question.

"He disappeared right after the meeting," she says carefully. "No one can find him."

"Disappeared?" Stonebane leans back in his chair, relieved that she didn't say anything about the . . . he can scarcely even bring himself to think about what Thatchly has in his possession.

"I went back to the boardroom after the fire alarm was turned off and he was gone," Greta continues. "I thought maybe you might know where he . . ."

"Absolutely not. Of course, after what he did this morning I assumed you would have Security take care of him."

"Obviously I didn't. That's why I'm here."

"That's going to be a problem, then, isn't it?" he says coldly. His confidence surges back as he notes the defeated slump in Greta's shoulders. "I was fully expecting to interview him on tonight's broadcast."

"No can do," she says firmly, the defeat in her shoulders

not evident in her voice. "Nothing that happened in that meeting goes on air, is that clear? At least not until the police formally name him as a suspect."

With the news of Thatchly's acquisition still fresh in his mind, Stonebane allows himself to concede the point to her. No use in fighting over tidbits when he has the motherlode.

"Whatever you say, Greta, that's fine by me."

She tilts her head, wary of his diplomatic gesture.

"Not a word about the meeting," she repeats more forcefully, just to make sure he understands her. "I've talked to the lawyers and this is what they want. We just run with the basic facts about the shooting."

"Excellent idea. The hospital is calling a press conference in half an hour. I'll lead off the broadcast with what they have to say about the body. Is that all right by you?"

"Fine."

"Just out of interest," Stonebane ventures with mock sincerity, "have you chosen a substitute host for Jacobson on his program tonight, or will you run a repeat?"

"Interested?"

"Me? God no! I was simply wondering if you might just cancel the program altogether, what with the distressing news of the shooting."

Greta pauses, taking measure of the insidious motives she suspects are imbedded within Stonebane's question, and she decides to deflate any of his hopes. "The show stays on air no matter what happens to Jacob. I'm firmly behind the format."

"Well, then," he says tartly. "That's very good news indeed."

"I'm actually going to try out your arts producer as host."

"O'Sullivan?" Stonebane spits instinctively. "He's got the intellectual range of a dead carrier pigeon."

"Actually, Dylan's done some good on-camera work before," Greta says. "Let's give him a shot at prime time, show the audience a new face for a change."

Stonebane imagines the ratings on Jake's show plummeting after a few O'Sullivan bungles, and he quickly switches tactics. "Then again, maybe Dylan would work," he oozes. "Yes, bold thinking there, Greta. I say give the boy the show."

With one last look at him, Greta turns to leave his office, but stops before she gets out. "And William, if you find out anything about Jacob . . ."

"You'll be the first to know." He bends his head as if to get back to his work, but as soon as Greta shuts his door he springs up and walks excitedly over to his window. Down on the wintery street he can still see the Channel 7 van parked out front, waiting to get some information on Jacobson.

"Wait all you want, amateurs," he says into the window, his deep voice fogging the glass and erasing the view below. "This story belongs to me."

LEAK

"I bet they know where he is," insists Gerald Dennis-Stanton, sipping coffee in the back of the Channel 7 news van. "Someone in that place must have talked to Jacobson today."

He's been sitting with Charlene Rosemount and her cameraman Herb since they interrogated Tasso earlier that morning, waiting for the unlikely event that Jacob Jacobson will appear at work, or, less acceptable but more probable, word that the Network is sending out a spokesperson to hold a press conference. The blasting heater causes Stanton to sweat under his thick camel-hair coat, but he refuses to take it off. He adores the coat because it's new and expensive – $660 to be exact, on sale. And even though it got soaked when the policeman threw him into the snowbank, he still wants to show it off to the spectacular-looking Charlene.

Stanton's hobby – and he proudly calls it that – is being handsome. He shops for clothes with the same obsession an adopted child might search for a birth parent, doggedly scouring out-of-the-way stores for obscure fabrics and styles that match his exacting tastes. As he waits for Charlene to acknowledge him, he puts down his coffee to let it cool and takes out a portable water-resistant nourishing cream he keeps in his Sak's briefcase. Bending down with a grunt, he gives his Italian lambskin shoes a quick buff and polish to get the salt stains out. When he finishes that task, he removes his carved ivory comb from its case and pulls it through his flaxen hair, making sure the part in the side is so straight along his scalp that it looks as if it's been made by a table saw. Even his skin shimmers with care. His cheeks are hand-shaven with a triple-blade Gillette Mach 3 and shined by Armani cologne until they glisten like mirrors. ("Avoid lift-and-cut electric razors," he's always telling fellow reporters in the washroom as he examines his face for incipient signs of stubble. "The rotating blade theory is one of the great scams of our time.")

Brushing his hand over his azure eyes to wipe away the sweat he worked up after his personal grooming routine, Stanton picks up his coffee, drains it, and gives Charlene what he likes to call The Big Gaze From the Big Blues.

"Are you with me on this one, Charlene?" Stanton asks, focusing his eyes intensely on her. "They've got to know where he is."

"How the fuck should I know?" Charlene replies, sipping her coffee and glaring at her cameraman in the front seat. "Herb, do you have any sugar? This coffee tastes like B.O."

"It's my special brew, Charlene," Herb calls back. "I thought you'd like it."

"Where do you roast the beans, under your armpits?"

"Listen to me, Charlene," Stanton says, trying to grab her attention away from the coffee. "I think we should try to get inside. Shake down a few people."

"Are you on crack, Stanton?" she says. "No one in there's going to talk to us. We're the enemy, in case that hasn't penetrated your polyester brain."

"But if Jacobson whacked her, they'll have to talk." *Shake down. Whacked her. That's good print-speak*, Stanton thinks, studiously ignoring Charlene's rudeness. *Let her know he's been on the street.* Beneath his pressed shirt he flexes his abdominals, as if to confirm that he's tough enough to survive in a world where people whack other people. Silently he praises the magic of his ab-roller – although he'd never tell Charlene he actually uses one. As far as he's concerned, showing people how hard you have to work at staying slim is as embarrassing as being fat.

His portable digital phone rings, interrupting his thoughts, and he reaches into his camel-hair jacket to grab it. "Stanton . . . Yeah, what? I know there's a press conference at the hospital, I'm on my way . . . What? She's not dead! Not dead!" he yells into the phone. "Well, shit, how was I supposed to know? I wrote the damn article at three o'clock in the morning. She was *supposed* to be dead. They said she was *as good as* dead . . . Fine, I'll go right down."

He folds his tiny phone and puts it back in his coat pocket. Now his eyes are blinking furiously.

"Just my luck," Stanton whimpers. "The prof didn't die. The doctors at the hospital are about to announce that Poiselle is alive, making my article in last night's paper a major screw-up. Christ! They told me last night she was *fatally* shot in the head. I'm up *shiesen straussa* with my editor."

But Charlene isn't listening to him. As soon as she hears Stanton say that Rachel isn't dead, she dials the Channel 7 newsroom on her own cell phone and speaks to her news editor. He tells her exactly what Stanton has just heard. The doctor who operated on Rachel is calling a press conference to correct false reports in the media. Rachel Anne Poiselle is not dead. She's out of her so-called coma and worse, she's stable. It's all over the radio. Charlene slams down her phone.

"Fuck her fucking coma for fucking up my report."

"She does spoken-word poetry at night, you know," Herb comments from the front of the van, grinning in the rear-view mirror.

"And fuck you too," Charlene says, opening up the window and throwing her coffee onto the icy street. "A perfectly good celebrity murder downgraded to a celebrity shooting. I don't deserve this punishment." She reaches into her bag to grab a brush, snaps open her compact, and starts violently teasing her famous red hair.

"Don't pull out your gorgeous locks over one lousy shooting," Herb says as he watches her attack her head with the brush.

"I'm meditating. Back off."

"Just be thankful that you're not still doing the weather," Herb says helpfully, pointing out the window. "You could be standing out there."

She reluctantly acknowledges his comment with a snigger and thinks back to her first TV job, a mere two years ago, when she replaced the local weatherman, Chuck, after his car spun out in a freak snowstorm and turned him into a quadriplegic. She'd gone through so many transformations since then that it seemed like a lifetime ago when she was positioned outside the station in snowstorms and spring showers, regaling viewers with jocular tales of low-pressure systems and changing barometric pressure while she nearly froze her nipples off. Six hellish months of that and she was promoted to a full-fledged reporter, morphing effortlessly into a news junkie. She pulls a clump of red hair from her brush and reflects how her fearless style, her probing, often indelicate questions – the kind other reporters were too timid to ask – escalated her to the station's top-rated reporter. *In under a year and a half*, she thinks to herself proudly, feeling a sting in her scalp. Just three months ago she spent a fun-filled Saturday driving around the city with Herb, counting the number of billboards featuring her beautiful face and bountiful red hair: twelve of them, not including the one with a spray-painted graffiti moustache above her lip.

"If you don't stop that, you'll look like Kojak on tonight's newscast," says Herb, growing anxious as he watches Charlene's assault on her hair continue unabated. "You know how the boys back at the station love your do."

"Cretins," she snaps, calling to mind how frequently "the boys" back at the station comment on her hair. Once she made the mistake of telling another reporter that her hair was the exact colour of a summer cherry, and soon the chauvinist pigs in the newsroom were whispering that it was the same colour as the *other* type of cherry. She realizes that they're simply threatened by her untouchable looks, by her tall, slim body, by the way her clothes fit tightly. She knows they resent her evenly set black eyes, her elegantly plucked eyebrows, the tiny upturned nose – perfected by an excellent plastic surgeon who'd thickened her lips for an extra grand.

But mostly they hate her because they know she's the most dedicated reporter at the station. She covers every possible kind of story, knows how to edit on the fly, can do live hits without fumbling a word, and never comes in behind deadline. All she needs is one big national story, one that will break her out of "local 'snooze'," as she calls her genre, and put her in her rightful place as a reporter on one of the national networks.

The Poiselle shooting, she thinks bitterly, had all the elements: a famous suspect, a beautiful woman, a brutal killing. The fact that the victim clings to life is a major setback to her rising career.

Unable to hold back her frustration, she throws her brush down at the floor. "She's alive! This is just sick. So help me, I could kill that woman myself."

"Get in line," Stanton mutters.

"Ram it, typist."

"Ooh, talk dirty to me too," Herb chuckles.

Charlene knows she has a dirty mouth – foul as a septic tank, her producer says, but he gives her the best assignments because he likes to hear beautiful women swear. Sexism, she thinks as she tosses her compact back into her bag, can be a woman's best weapon. Flicking her hair back over her ears, she punches the back of the driver's seat.

"Herb, stop picking your ass and get us over to Mount Sinai Hospital now. We'll talk to the doctors anyway."

"Mind if I catch a ride?" asks Stanton, turning up his camel-hair collar, James Dean style.

"It'll cost you a pair of cappuccinos," replies Charlene.

The Channel 7 news van screeches a U-turn on Spadina Avenue and heads uptown towards the hospital.

"There's got to be more to this story," muses Charlene, holding the door handle to steady herself in the careening car. "Somebody in the Network must know about Jacobson and they're going to have to leak it soon. They can't all be loyal campers."

"Just because you've let me stay warm in your cosy van," Stanton says, shifting his body closer to hers, "I'll break the rules and let you in on a little secret. Jacobson has a brother named Theodore. There's a rumour going around our newsroom – well, actually, it's going around between me and myself – that Theo Jacobson is involved in that killing out in B.C."

Stanton knows he's impressing Charlene, and he'd rather do that than protect his own story.

"What killing?" she asks with mock indifference, galled that someone else might know something she doesn't.

"Oh God, you TV reporters are really something," Stanton chortles. "Don't you read the *papers*? A logger was killed out in B.C. last week. His chainsaw hit a tree spike. A group of radical greens have been blamed."

"Oh, that." She dredges up a vague memory of something she saw on the wires and makes a mental note to pay more attention to news on a national level – where she'll soon be. "I know about that."

"Well, I've got a friend in the police force out there who says the cops think Jacobson's brother is the perp. And they're going to go after him very soon. Now that lead, Ms. Rosemount, could cost *you* a cappuccino. And a dinner reservation."

He sits back in his chair proudly and tries to brush a salt stain off his coat.

"What the hell has B.C. got to do with this?" Charlene asks rhetorically. "Stanton, you couldn't find a story if it crawled up your ass and bit you on the brain."

"Does your mother know how you talk? I'll tell you right now, if I get confirmation on that tip, I'm going to run it in tonight's edition."

"Do it, Stanton. But you'd be better off talking to that cop O'Malley. He'll give you even less than nothing."

"Oh, him! The police come to me when they want news, not the other way around. Please."

As the van speeds towards the hospital press conference, Charlene is still unable to shake her anger. "Oh, screw this!" she explodes, again punching the back of Herb's seat. "I'm not going to the goddamn hospital. I already know what they're going to say. Herb, stop the van. I gotta get a real coffee."

Herb hits the breaks and veers towards the curb, almost knocking over a startled pedestrian. Charlene leaps out.

"I take mine with skim milk, no sugar!" Stanton calls out after her, but Charlene merely holds up her hand with her middle finger erect and disappears down the street.

"You're in love with her, aren't you, Stanton," Herb says as he puts on the hazard lights.

"Who isn't?"

As Charlene makes her way around the corner towards the Sunbucks, she notices a man in a flowing black coat walking briskly ahead of her. Immediately she recognizes him as the librarian she questioned in the morning. *He's got to know something.* She trots to catch up with him.

"Excuse me, sir, you remember me?" Charlene says, tapping Tasso on the shoulder. "Charlene Rosemount, we met earlier today, outside the Network."

Tasso almost loses his footing when he sees her.

"No cameras here," Charlene says, sensing his anxiety and moistening her usually steely voice with sweetness. "I just want to talk to you for minute. Off the record."

"I don't think so," Tasso mumbles, holding up one hand to keep her away.

It's only been ten minutes since Tasso found the cab for Jacob and hustled him inside, and all he wants to do is take a long walk away from the Network and try to make sense of his terrible morning. In his left hand he carries the black bag Jake stole from the hospital, the bloody hospital coat now stuffed inside it. In Jacob's panic to get in the cab, Tasso didn't have a chance to give him the bag, and now he's stuck with it as if it's some accursed talisman. An oppressive lassitude overwhelms him. Only the bracing cold air keeps him from sitting down in a bus shelter and collapsing into sleep. *Thirty days and I'm out of a job.* And now to be faced with this woman, it was all too much. He simply wants to be left alone.

"I was going to call you to apologize for those rude police this morning," Charlene says. "I really am sorry about that. *Really.*"

She drops her head slightly, almost contritely, and extends her hand forward. Unable to refuse a polite gesture, Tasso reluctantly reaches out and grasps it.

"That policeman's name is Ian O'Malley," she continues, not so much shaking his hand as holding it. "You might know him from his *Crime Re-Play* spots on TV. Thinks he's the cat's ass, but you handled yourself brilliantly. I've never seen anyone cut him down like that. You're very cool under fire."

"Thank you," Tasso says, perplexed by her version of the events.

"God, it's freezing out here," Charlene says, quickly grasping him by the arm. "Let me buy you a coffee as an act of repentance. There's a Sunbucks right there on the corner. Would you mind? I'd feel so much better." She moves close to firm up her grip and smiles seductively.

"A coffee?" Tasso mutters in a fluster.

"Get out of the cold for a minute. My treat."

"Perhaps." He's too tired to resist her.

"I'll take that as a yes."

She hurries him along the street towards the Sunbucks, holding his arm ever more tightly, chatting relentlessly in his ear about the various types of winters the city has experienced in recent years and how she knows about all this because she used to be a weather reporter for Channel 7 and on and on. When they get inside, she promptly takes off her coat to reveal a tight-fitting charcoal grey outfit, the silver buttons on her jacket marking a track line directly down her chest.

"Now, Mr. . . . I'm so sorry, I seem to have forgotten. Mr. Darwhalla?"

"Darjun. Tasso Darjun." Tasso gazes around him, bewildered by the frenetic activity of customers.

"Beautiful name," she says, covering her mistake seamlessly. "My third cousin just married someone from India. It was such a lovely wedding, all the women in saris, just lovely. Would you mind if I use the little-girls' room to freshen up? This cold weather is so tough on my skin. You go ahead and order."

Before Tasso can answer, she heads off, leaving him stranded at the counter. A perky boy in a green-and-white uniform instantly approaches him.

"How can I help you, sir?"

"What? Oh, I guess I'll have a coffee, please," he fumbles.

"Will that be a latte, a cappuccino, a mochaccino, an espresso, or a regular?" recites the smiling boy expertly.

"Just a coffee," says Tasso, glancing down nervously at his watch. He ought to be getting back to the library. *Oh, the library*, he thinks dejectedly.

"Colombian, Brazilian, American, Special House Blend, or one of our nine different slow-roasted flavours?" the boy continues, rattling off the names with a clipped, but somehow emotional, tone.

"Regular, please."

"O-kay," replies the boy, confused but still enthusiastic. "I'll make it Kenyan. It's really solid. Decaf or regular?"

"I said regular."

"Cream, milk, one per cent or skim?"

Tasso gazes at the boy with a baffled expression. "Nothing."

"We have lactose-free milk as well," the boy offers helpfully.

"No, no thank you."

"Well, you'd be surprised how many of our customers can't digest milk products. Sugar or sweetener?"

"Black. I want a cup of black coffee," Tasso says, trying to cut off the conversation.

"No problemo, I can do that one too," the boy says, laughing at his own little joke. "Black it is. Now, is that Petito, demi-Grandé, or El-Grandé?"

"What?"

"Oh, that's just what we call our small, medium, or large selections."

"For heaven's sake, I just want a cup of coffee," Tasso explodes in annoyance.

"Okey-dokey. Right. So will that be a Petito, demi-Grandé, or El-Grandé?" The boy smiles at Tasso again, as if it's the first time he's ever asked the question in his life.

"Petito, then, whatever. Make it a small." Tasso sighs and looks over his shoulder to see if Charlene Rosemount has returned. She hasn't.

"Do you have a Sunbuck's club card, sir?" The perky boy behind the counter is unmerciful.

Tasso grinds his teeth in agony. He's not able to understand why getting a cup of coffee is so difficult in a shop specifically designed to serve cups of coffee.

"I don't want a card."

"Well, you ought to. It can *really* save you money. We can set you up in a flash. I'll need your full name and address, your phone number –"

"I just want to *pay*."

The boy pauses and regards Tasso patiently, as if to show that he sincerely understands how a foreign gentleman might not be well versed in the nuances of the First World's booming service industry. He passes Tasso the cup of coffee, leans over the counter, raises his voice, and enunciates slowly, miming in time with his hands.

"No problemo, sir. The CASH, the place you can PAY, is at the end of the COUNTER. That way." He points, with a swing of both hands. "Just over there, sir. Near the CASH BOX. You PAY. Enjoy, enjoy, enjoy!" The boy practically throws his smile at Tasso.

At the cash register, an older man wearing a black leather jacket and Ray-Ban sunglasses complains loudly to the cashier. Tasso waits behind him, his body slumped over his beverage as if he wants to hide it.

"Do you have anything besides these flip-top lids?" the man in the sunglasses asks, his tone loud enough to suggest that he's speaking on behalf of the rest of the café customers. He's a lawyer, Tasso thinks, instantly classifying him. Or a broker. Makes over a hundred thousand dollars a year, is recently divorced, sees his children every other weekend, plays mediocre golf but cheats on a few strokes, resents the fact that he's turned forty and has started to lose his hair.

"I want one of those raised tops that you can sip from immediately."

"You mean the lids with the pre-punctured little hole, sir?"

asks the cashier. She's a young woman with a ponytail and, of course, a winning smile.

"Yes, the pop-on lids."

"Like these?" She pulls a lid out from behind the cash register.

"Not the *pull tabs*, the other ones."

"The flip tops?" the girl probes earnestly.

"No, flip tops are the same as pull tabs," the man says, growing exasperated by her incompetence.

"I'm so sorry, sir, I want to help you but–?"

"The pop-ons!" He makes a cup shape with his hand and pretends to put it on his coffee. "I want the pop-ons."

"Oh, you mean the kind that hold the cappuccino foam. Pop-ons, I see." Her broad smile broadens.

The man smiles back at her, relieved.

"The flip tops smudge my cinnamon."

"True," she nods. "So true."

Communion.

Bursting with anxiety, Tasso cuts in, throws five dollars on the counter, and flees to a seat in the back of the café. He puts the black bag on the floor beside him and unbuttons his coat. Pop-ons, pull tabs, flip tops. Everything is too specialized, too complicated, he thinks. Nothing is too insignificant for the ultimate concern of the customer these days. He regrets getting bullied into coming here by Charlene Rosemount. Why didn't he just say no, why didn't he just turn away from her and go back to the Network, wait out the day and go safely home to bed? But even going to the Network seemed unappealing, he ponders, visualizing himself slogging through his last month at work, going to staff meetings and filing stories, trying to keep up a dignified public face during the excruciatingly pitiful denouement of his career. He shakes his head and takes a small sip of coffee, but it's too hot and burns his lips. Enervated to the point of collapse, he pulls out his package of cigarettes to have a smoke, but before he manages to light up, a man at another table leans over and interrupts his thoughts.

"Read the sign, bud!" the man says nastily. "No smoking. I don't want to die from your stupid addictions."

Tasso looks over to the wall and sees a picture of a cigarette within a red circle with a thick line through it.

"Sorry," he mumbles, and quickly puts his pack back in his pocket.

He breathes in deeply to calm himself. *What is that woman doing in there?* Tasso wonders, staring helplessly in the direction of the washrooms. A nicotine craving seizes him and he thinks how therapeutic a lungful of smoke would be to offset the clean, almost boring air in the café. Tasso warily examines the other patrons, cataloguing them as he did the man at the cash. Smoke-free cafés attract a certain kind of customer, he theorizes – the kind who enjoy paying four dollars for a non-alcoholic drink and constantly gaze around the café to see who else is there, as if every other customer is a potential friend, a similar type. They all sit alertly poised, he notes, not quite relaxed but trying to appear that way, looking like extras in a living movie full of Range Rovers and BMWs, where all the main characters talk on cellular phones and rush to meetings. In this movie, most of the locations are bookstores, health clubs, and expensive non-smoking coffee shops like this one, where people wear sunglasses indoors and complain loudly about their coffee lids. As far as Tasso is concerned, it's a genre of film that plays perpetually in the psychic theatre of upwardly mobile white people. He's never chosen to be an extra in this movie: he's the wrong *mis* for this *scène*. In fact, at this moment Tasso feels very *Indian* and yearns to stand up and leave, but just then Charlene Rosemount dashes back from the washroom looking newly made-up and slips into a chair at his table.

"Sorry for taking so long," she says almost breathlessly. "Huge line. I'll never understand why they don't build more cubicles for women. Our bladders have rights too!"

Tasso nods uncertainly and again attempts to drink some coffee.

"Oh good, you got something." She turns her head and catches the attention of the perky coffee boy at the counter. "Hey! I need a double cappuccino, El-Grandé, Brazilian, two Sweet'n Lows, one per cent milk, no lid, and stamp my card later."

"Okey-dokey!" calls back the boy, delighted to serve someone so fluent in café Esperanto.

Her attention swerves back to Tasso. "Usually I have the espresso because I love the way the pressurized steam forces the flavour from those stubborn little brown beans, but I've already had two today. Feel my hand, it's still buzzing from my last hit."

She reaches out impulsively and takes his hand and lays it in hers.

"Do you feel it vibrate?" she laughs.

"Perhaps." He withdraws his hand politely and drops it to his side for protection.

"I'm sure you've had a hell of a morning, Mr. Darjun. What with the news of Jacob Jacobson being involved in the shooting." He doesn't say anything, so she continues. "You know she's not dead. The hospital is going to announce that any minute now."

"Really?" Tasso says. "I thought–"

"Some jerk reporter from the *Gazette* got it wrong," she says, thinking of Stanton sitting in her van on the street. She knows she has to move quickly. "Thank God she's still alive. I was horrified by the news, weren't you?"

"It was quite awful."

"People were shocked at the Network, I imagine."

"Very much so."

"Of course, he didn't do it, did he? I mean, he must have told your whole staff the story, right?"

"No. He didn't say much about it, really," Tasso says, remembering how Jacob walked down the long table, screaming nonsensically at William Stonebane.

"Meaning he was in this morning?" Charlene asks, floating her questions at Tasso ever so gently. "You saw him, then?"

Tasso can barely focus on what the woman is saying. He's been fired, doesn't anyone care about that? What will he tell his daughter? He thinks about the bills he has to pay for her college tuition, the mortgage on his home, how much he'll miss his beloved walk to work.

"Yes, I just saw him," Tasso says absently. "He wasn't feeling well, needed to get a taxi. I assisted him. That's all."

"No kidding?" Charlene says, holding back her desire to dive down Tasso's throat and pull out the words. The young boy comes over and delivers her cappuccino, winks, and flitters back to the counter. "And you don't happen to know where he went in this cab, do you?" she continues.

Tasso shrugs, not wanting to be so rude that he says nothing, but also wanting to expedite this impromptu meeting so he can go back to . . . to what? He takes a large swig of coffee, hoping an empty cup will politely signal an end. "He said something about Georgian Bay. Told the driver to take him to some place, I didn't really hear it, Point something or other. I can't say. They started to argue about it and so I left. I felt bad for him, you know. He was so devastated about the death of his woman. I once lost someone close to me, I know how it is. But now you say she isn't dead. He'll be pleased to hear that."

"Sorry, Mr. Darjun," Charlene interrupts. "Are you saying that Rachel Poiselle and Jacob Jacobson were together? I mean, they were an item?"

"Oh, most definitely," Tasso says, nodding his head, surprised at the naïveté of the woman. "He said as much at the staff meeting." As the words "staff meeting" pass his lips, Tasso recalls the moment when he was fired. How casually Greta had included it in her speech, how indifferently she'd summed up his life's work. He quickly drinks up the last drops of his coffee. "I'm afraid I must be going now. It's been a pleasure talking to you again."

"Just one more thing, Mr. Darjun. Please." She opens her eyes pleadingly. "Did Jacob tell you anything, anything at all?"

"As I said, he wasn't well. There was a great commotion at the meeting."

"I thought I heard the fire alarm go off. People came streaming out of the building. What happened?"

Tasso stiffens at the mention of it. "How should I know? It was a false alarm, I think," he says quickly.

"And that's it?"

"Please, I do have to get back."

"Was there anything else he said? Just think."

"I wish I could tell you more. He mumbled someone's name a few times, maybe Theo or something. But he was not right in the head."

He gets up to leave but Charlene leans over the table and, for the second time, grabs his hand. "Mr. Darjun, listen to me.

I'll pay you good money for any more information. Serious cash. How much do you need? You can remain anonymous, don't worry about that. Just tell me what you know and we can work out a deal. You win, I win, okay?"

Tasso rips back his hand and stands up, completely thunderstruck by what he's just heard. "I'm afraid I don't quite follow," he says. "I thought you wanted to have a coffee, I thought–"

"Let's not waste each other's time here," Charlene snaps, the tone of her voice switching back to its metallic edge. "You tip me off about Jacobson, I pay. No bullshit, a straight cash deal. But let's get this straight. No green for the stuff about the cab ride and the staff meeting. You gave me that for free. Now what else do you have?"

Tasso shakes his head in disbelief, not sure what has just transpired. He fiddles uncomfortably with the lid of his coffee cup and suddenly he remembers what Charlene said about the espresso – the way a certain kind of pressure extracts all the flavour from the little brown bean. He looks at his own skin. The little brown bean . . . "This isn't right," he chokes, turning to run out of the café. "No. This isn't right at all."

"Wait a second!" Charlene yells, but he's already knocking his way through the line-up of well-dressed customers, and a moment later he bursts through the glass doors and scurries up the street towards the Network.

Without pausing, Charlene whips out her pen and furiously scribbles down notes on a napkin, elated to have gleaned so much prized information from such an unlikely source. *So the prof was his lover!* she thinks. *Story's getting better. And Theo? Who was that? Maybe Stanton was right about that shit out in B.C. after all.* She decides to put it in her next report too. *And what was in Georgian Bay? Cottage country? Place to hide out?* She'll have a researcher find out if he owns something up north. "I've got the hunting instincts of a fucking leopard," she says to herself as she folds the napkin and stuffs it in her pocket. Leaving a ten-dollar bill on the table, she begins to head for the exit but stops when she notices a black bag sitting under the table, near Tasso's chair. *Did he leave that for me*, she wonders, *or did he just forget it?* She pauses for a moment to consider what conventional ethics dictates one ought to do when one finds someone else's personal property. Within seconds she's rifling through the bag.

"Holy shit!" she mutters as she pulls out the hospital coat. Her fingers touch the dried blood and she takes three slow breaths through her nose to try to calm her heart. "The librarian just handed me the motherlode," she whispers giddily to herself. "I've got a Deep Throat, my own goddamn Deep Throat!" She quickly stuffs the coat back in the bag and snaps it closed, looking around the café to see if anyone noticed what she took out. The man sipping from the pop-on lid glances up from his table and grins invitingly at her, but she ignores him. Grabbing the bag in her arms, she races back to the Channel 7 news van.

"What the hell took you so long?" Stanton asks impatiently when she jumps into the front seat. "We've almost missed the whole press conference."

"Give it a rest, Stanton. We don't work together, remember?" she replies, tucking the black bag safely at her feet, out of his sight. She mentally debates whether to reveal her prize piece of evidence in her next report, but decides to hold it back instead. Such a development in the story, she reasons, needs to be revealed at the proper time, when she can milk it for every kilowatt of attention she can get. *Let the story build,* she tells herself. *Let the fugitive chase go on, then, when the whole nation is watching, spring it on them and scoop the case.*

"You could apologize for keeping us waiting," Stanton says. "We've been sitting here for almost twenty minutes."

"Then why are you still wearing that ridiculous fur coat?" she says. "The heat's probably lowering your sperm count."

"This coat? It's camel hair, not fur!" Stanton stutters and blinks his Big Blues in embarrassment. The woman may be beautiful, he thinks, but she clearly has pedestrian taste. "Did you at least remember my coffee?"

Charlene reaches back, slides the door to the van open, and yanks Stanton by the lapel. "That's it. Out! Did you hear me? Get out! We've got work to do here."

"Wait a second," Stanton says indignantly. "You said you'd drive me to the hospital scrum. What the hell is this? Herb, come on! Tell her to chill out."

"She's the boss," Herb replies, not looking back at him.

"Get the hell out of my van!" Charlene seethes. "Or I'll call your editor and tell him that you're harassing me."

Stanton unwillingly steps out onto the cold sidewalk, the wind whipping his long camel-hair coat. "Aw, this is bullshit," he says despondently. "Don't do this. This is real rookie stuff, you know."

But Charlene slams the door and squeezes into the front seat beside Herb.

"Let's go, Herb. You're not a parking attendant. I know where Jacobson is. Jesus Christ, I've got everything. You won't believe this. We need to get a map of the Georgian Bay area and look for places beginning with the word Point. And we've got to go fast, so put the pedal to the metal and get this tub of tin in gear."

"What happened to you?" Herb asks. "I thought you were just getting some coffee."

"Well, I got a helluva lot more than that," she says, reaching down to reopen the black bag. "I'll tell you on the way. Now get on the highway and start heading north."

The van peels out into traffic, leaving Gerald Dennis-Stanton cursing them from the sidewalk, covering his perfect blond hair to protect it from the gusts of freezing wind.

THE BAY

Leon Pastiche glances back in the rear-view mirror frequently and wonders what he's doing ferrying a TV personality like Jacob Jacobson two hundred kilometres up to Georgian Bay. He thought he was through with this passenger after he waited for over two hours in front of the Network, but then the Indian man knocked on his window and begged him to go to the back of the building. Jacobson was waiting for him and seemed desperate when Leon pulled up. He offered five hundred dollars for a drive up north. Leon couldn't refuse a fare like that, no matter how crazy it seemed.

Now the sharp smell of piss from Jacob's pants fills the car and Leon opens his window a crack, the cold air snapping at his ear like a dog. Turning up the heat, he drives for two hours in silence, deciding not to ask too many questions. Five hundred dollars is a very good day. At Pointe au Baril, Leon turns off the road and puts the car in park.

"Yo, mon, wake up. Where we goin' now?"

Jacob opens his eyes and tries to sit up, but he can barely move. He's been sleeping for most of the ride and his body feels like a bag of coal: hot, dirty, heavy. Looking out the frosted window he sees the old chip wagon where in the summer his mother would stop and buy the family fresh-cut french fries with vinegar.

"Just a bit farther," Jake mutters. "Follow the sign to Hogan's Marina."

The parking lot at Hogan's boarded-up store is plowed, but not recently, and snow kicks up in the wind as Leon pulls in. The place reminds him of one of those souvenir snow globes – white flakes swirling around in an enclosed city of plastic.

"This is fine," says Jake, closing his eyes for a moment, the residual effects of the pills still making him dizzy. "Just follow the road and it will take you back to the highway."

"Mon, where you gonna go from here?" Leon asks impatiently, staring out at the emptiness. "It fuckin' cold out. You sure dis is da place?"

"I've been coming here for years," Jake replies absently.

"You da boss," Leon replies warily as snow whips round in the barren lot. "But I'm tellin' you, mon, dis don' look like a place to leave no one. You one crazy motha fucka, you know dat?"

"Thank you."

With that, Jake lifts his body up and gets out of the taxi, forgetting to shut the door as he heads directly towards the frozen water. He's intent on walking to his cottage, and his body can't feel the cold. In his mind he's already sitting by a fire with a drink in his hand thinking about Rachel, before she was smashed, before she saw him delay. The snow is deep, crawling inside his shoes, and he heads out into the screen of white making the sound of crunching bones.

From the car, Leon Pastiche watches him stumble forward. A gust of cold wind blows on the nape of his neck and he reaches back and pulls on the handle, shutting the door Jake left open. The windows start to frost over as they catch Leon's heat, and he puts the car in drive. He starts to roll away, but glances back in the rear-view mirror to see Jake out on the frozen bay. "Sheeit," he says out loud, drawing the word out in exasperation and slamming on the brakes. Leon knows he has no real obligation to try to help his passenger, he's already done his job, but he can't just abandon someone in the middle of the bitter cold. At this temperature the man could die. "Sheeit," Leon says again as his conscience stops his foot from hitting the accelerator. For over a minute he debates what he should do, the whole time watching Jake get farther and farther away, until finally his conscience wins him over, and with a burst of curses he puts the car back in park, grabs his hat, and starts running gingerly through the snow after Jake.

"Yo, Mista Jacobson, hold on!"

The wind blows hard and Jake keeps moving as if he can't hear anything. Leon catches up to him and jogs alongside.

"Listen to me, mon. Hey! Is damn cold out here, maybe you should phone someone."

"I'm going home," Jake says blithely. "I'll be safe there, don't worry."

"Sheeit," yells Leon, grabbing Jake by the shoulder. "Stop for a second. Take dis hat, okay? Put it on before you freeze your white balls off."

Leon pulls the toque over Jacob's head past his ears and stares directly into Jake's eyes.

"You sure you okay, cuz I'm leavin' now. You hear? I'm leavin'."

"Don't be a stranger," Jake responds as he strides away.

"Crazy motha."

Leon bolts back to the cab and slams his door. Willing himself not to look back, he pulls out of Hogan's Marina, and heads back to Toronto.

Alone out on the white ice. Alone inside a furious wind. Jake walks steadily as his mind concentrates on memories of Rachel, memories of her before he saw her bleeding on the floor, when they were together and true, when her hands were on his skin and for the first time he felt he could truly be known . . .

She lies beside him naked on the bed, waiting for them to make love. She likes the lights off. Likes it to be pitch black so she can look at his body with her hands. He's thin, long, a tiller she steers. Her fingers map out his topography, over his hips, down his legs. The smoothest skin she's ever touched. That's what she says. Even smells like a baby. He's innocent in the dark, she says that too, the most innocent man she's known, and he almost disappears in his innocence so she holds him tightly. Keep the lights off, she says. Her head is back, her black hair splayed on the pillow like a textile exhibit. In the bedroom it's a different kind of black than the night – cleaner, more firm – and Jake's eyes adjust to its contours. He watches Rachel move beneath him, warming the sheets. The more he watches her settle, the more he slips away, farther and farther, out her open window, into the maple tree. He becomes the anonymous rush of wind in the leaves, present only by motion. His body moves without him. Back arches up and down, slick with thin sweat. He can slip out of his skin as if it's a costume. He's perfectly frictionless, a surface that can't be invented. It has no gravity, no physics. He's surprised she can even hold it. Deep into his body, he feels his nerves recede until they might no longer exist.

"Open your eyes, look at me, look at me, please" he pleads, frightened by his vanishing, wishing he wasn't so remote.

Her eyes open wide, but then he covers her face with his hands. Now she talks softly. Urgently. Knows he's troubled.

"You have scratches on your chest again, Jake. What happened?"

"Nothing."

She knows about these markings. Knows that the only blemishes on his alabaster skin are the thin red lines across his chest, across the back of his hands. These ones are new. The scabs thread like paint splashes thrown on white canvas, like eyelashes too close to see. With her fingers she reads them as if they're Braille.

"Why do you cut yourself, Jake?"

"I don't. I told you, I fell down. Shh."

"I want to know why you do it."

He moves harder inside her to distract her, making love rhythms that are the propaganda of the body. But Rachel can't be distracted. She asks again about his scars, her questions containing no hint of condemnation. She asks only from care.

This is what Jake fears: that she'll understand something about him that he doesn't know himself. Fears she'll figure out why he takes a knife from the kitchen drawer and runs it across his chest. Why he takes the skin off of his wrist with a bottle opener under the table when they're lazily discussing a movie over dinner. Puts his hand in his pocket to hide the blood. Is he ashamed of himself? she asks him. Is he afraid of something? He doesn't answer. These minor wounds are not important. He doesn't even feel them. They don't stop him from going to work, from becoming a TV host, from rising to meet her desires like water in a rain-swollen well. He's engineered very simply this way. Things work for him. He's productive. He doesn't require deep investigation. Only this little crack, this strange rupture in his surface, signifies something else, but he doesn't want to know what that is; why he feels no pain, why the scars calm him under the hot lights of the Network studio. But Rachel sees them with her hands, Rachel is unafraid to know them, to know something about him that he might not. She moves his fingers from her face and her green eyes shine against the dark, two bruises on water.

"Can you feel us, Jacob, can you really feel us?"

"Of course." He tries to sound surprised by her question.

"Tell me why you do it then, please. I worry."

"It just happens. I don't know."

She knows not to ask more. They make love quietly and soon he feels that she's about to climax. Her body closes inward, tightening against him in full embrace. She grips his hair and whispers fiercely in his ear: "Stay right there, my love, right with me."

After she comes he pulls out of her quickly, holds his penis and remains silent. Her black-and-white cat crawls up on the bed and nuzzles him for warmth. With the back of his arm, Jake brushes the cat away.

"You didn't come, sweetheart." Rachel talks with her eyes closed.

"I'm sorry."

She rolls over and flicks on the light. "I want to videotape us. I want to record us making love so you can see."

"Okay."

"Bring your camera tomorrow," she instructs him. "It's important."

His thoughts jumble as he slips on the ice, extending his hand out to balance himself. Jake's feet are numb from the snow and he walks clumsily. He follows the route he would take if he were driving the boat to the cottage, a route he's taken a thousand times as a boy with Theo, back and forth to Hogan's Marina, off to parties and dances that occurred too long ago to trigger memory. The wind cuts through his shirt and hits his chest, freezing the sweat under his arms. He has to concentrate on Rachel as she used to be, when they were together and everything was whole . . .

Now they have a camera and the lights have to stay on. She holds it to his face as they make love. It's an odd sensation. He looks into the camera as if he's hosting his show. She explains that this will locate him. She wants him to see how his body moves. Wants him to connect his face to his limbs. The window is closed and she flicks the camera on to record.

"Don't look at the lens, sweet," she says. "Let it record what it wants. We'll watch it later. You're not on television, Jake, you're alone with me. Here, you take the camera. Record us making love. Show our legs, our feet. Show our arms locked together. Close-up on our fingers, Jake. I want to see your hand in mine."

She tells him what to do and he does it perfectly. It's like TV. He trusts her voice; it slides into the vacancies of his head, a tea bag dropped into clear hot water, blending. It reminds Jake of his producer coaching him during an interview through his earpiece. He feels his body move, making love to her. Closing his eyes, he begins to sense something pleasurable move up through his chest, into his head. It startles, like a first taste of sugar, like a cool hand touching the cheek of someone sleeping. In his mind he sees himself on the TV screen, but he's never felt this close to it. The lens is a friend, a lover. His lover. It's not glass but water, and he puts his head through the liquid screen and feels clean. He can breathe here, can breathe underwater, behind the lens where he's never been. He grabs her hair and makes heaving noises from his mouth, as if chasing something. Now he wants to come.

Stumbling in the snow, Jake's memory jars, a videotape being chewed by the recorder. The picture blurs, jumps off screen, and then clears into something different. He starts walking again, but now he can't focus on what it used to be like with Rachel. Time rushes forward and now he sees a different Rachel beneath him. Something's wrong with her. Her face is bleeding, bleeding the way it did when he saw her in the hall. She's still naked beneath him, but now she's wild eyed and screaming for help. But his body won't roll off. He lets go of her hair and stares down at her, horrified.

"Dial the police, Jake," she pleads. "Do something. Tell them I'm shot. Hurry."

She's bleeding to death on the sheets, but his body moves helplessly on top of her. He watches in shock as the picture of her face rapidly smudges and disappears, her hair sinking into the pillow, tendrils of a plant receding into the earth. Now there's just a red stain on the pillow, spreading outwards, towards their locked hands. He wants to help her, put his hands on her broken surface the way she would his, but somehow the thick glass wall of his displacement stops him. His body thrusts automatically, still wants to come, but he also wants to help her, to save her from her pain. The conflict paralyses him, and he watches Rachel's headless torso rise frenetically up and down beneath him, faster and faster, as if it's being electrocuted. Petrified now, Jake wants to stop this nightmare. He wants to stop making love to Rachel, but the window in the room is locked shut and he can't slip away. He feels every nerve in his body rise to the surface like an anemone swirling blindly in invisible tides, burning. She's floating lifeless in his arms and he watches her from far away, knowing he'll never come, knowing he'll never stop. Then something flashes across his peripheral vision, the same disembodied shape he saw in the hall near Rachel's office. A shadow that disappears too quickly for him to recognize. He sees a red dot from far away and then, between breaths, he hears the steady hum of the video camera. It's mounted on Rachel's night table next to the digital clock, pointed to the back of his head like a gun . . .

He falls in the snow and lets out a hoarse scream. *Rachel is dead, Rachel is dead.* The phrase pulses through his mind with an acute ache. He struggles to his feet to keep walking. Now his face is grey from the cold, his hands blue. He's slowly freezing into the painless uniformity, a scar of himself. He recognizes an island to his left: the Keivers'. His cottage is farther ahead, but his feet can no longer perform their fundamental task and he collapses again. He starts to crawl, almost swimming through the snow, his limbs so exhausted he feels as if he's drowning. There's a light on in his cottage, but in the snow-darkened expanse it barely registers to Jake.

Finally he reaches the island, clawing his way to the front

door. His numb hands can't grasp his keys from his pocket and after a few frustrating minutes, he stands up shakily and starts to bang on a window. He's too weak to break the glass.

□ □ □

The rattling sound wakes Theo from a restless sleep. Leaping up from the couch, he instinctively grabs his handgun from his bag and heads for the door. He's not expecting anyone out here and he fears it might be the police. He knows they will be looking for him, but he can't imagine that the B.C. force would have the wherewithal to find him all the way across the country. He sees a shape leaning against the window, but he can't make out any details.

"Who's there?" he calls out suspiciously, holding his gun to his side.

Outside the wind buzzes and spits snow, but there's no answer.

"I said, who's out there?" He shuffles closer, keeping his back against the wall.

In the next moment, the shape pressed against the cabin window lists to the left and collapses. Theo jumps forward and without hesitation throws open the front door. The cold air hits him like a fist. He points his gun down at the body lying crumpled in the snow.

"Jake? Is that you?" He can barely distinguish the features of his brother's face. "What the hell are you doing here?" Kneeling down, he pulls the toque off of his brother's head. Jake rolls his eyes upwards, barely conscious from the cold.

"What happened to you, Jake? Hey! Wake up! Are you all right?"

He tries to get Jake to his feet, but Jake's body pitches forward as if he's drunk. Theo sees that his brother is only wearing shoes, his socks covered with balls of snow like burrs in summer.

"You walked here?" Theo is incredulous. "You actually walked from Hogan's? Are you out of your . . . Get inside. You'll freeze to death."

Jake doesn't respond and Theo picks him up with ease, carrying him quickly to the fire.

"Stay awake now, Jake. You're gonna be all right. Jesus. How did you get here?"

Jake closes his eyes, his thoughts pushing on the bruise of his mind as he fixates on Rachel's damaged face. Then he falls into an icy blackness.

Theo knows what to do. Runs and gets blankets from the beds, strips off Jake's clothes, then his own, and lies with his brother next to the fire, passing his body heat to Jake's cold skin.

"For Christ's sake, Jake, stay awake."

He slaps Jake's face until Jake moans and his eyes open to slits. His speech is thick, words sunk in freezing water.

"Rachel's gone, she's gone."

Theo doesn't listen. He rubs Jake's arms, his chest, toes, fingers. He rubs them with his big dry hands, pressing his body close to his brother and whispering.

"Come on, get your heart pumping. Your blood has to circulate. Stay awake, Jake, keep talking."

Theo works efficiently. He keeps his hands on Jake's body, gets hot water bottles and packs them beside Jake's chest, retrieves the heavy wool Hudson's Bay blanket their mother used to lay over them when she would read them Hans Christian Andersen tales at night. When Jake's extremities begin to thaw, he starts screaming. He thinks his fingers are being burnt off, his toes chewed by an animal.

"Stop crying, it's your own fault," Theo says, so relieved that Jake isn't unconscious that he allows himself the luxury of anger. "You're an idiot to try to make that walk at this time of year. You could have died out there."

Jake gazes up at his brother. "Theo."

They lie in front of the fire for two hours, body to body, holding each other as scaffolding does an unfinished building, wondering how the other got there, wondering how they might protect each other from unimagined dangers. And soon they drift off to sleep.

Hours later, when the fire starts to die, Jake wakes with a start, shivering. His brain is more clear, washed by sleep. He opens his eyes and sees Rachel's face embossed on the darkness. "Rachel's dead, Theo. I saw her," he says to his brother.

Theo pulls Jake's body close, packing it hard into his own. His hands grip Jacob's hair softly.

"Listen to me, Jake," Theo says. "Stop shaking. Rachel's not dead. Don't you listen to the radio? She was touch and go, but she's going to pull through."

"What?"

"The first news reports were wrong. Typical, right? Doctors say she's going to make it. Bullet grazed her. She's going to live, did you hear that? Now get some sleep. You look like shit, and we can't stay here very long."

He let's go of Jake's head.

"She's alive?" Jake mutters, trying to comprehend what Theo tells him. "Are you sure?"

"I heard it on the radio. I told you." Theo pauses. "I'm glad you're here. I didn't know how to contact you without the cops getting on my ass. We have a lot to tell each other."

Jake lies dumbly beside him, too shocked by the news of Rachel to speak. Relaxing his grip, Theo puts a little space between them.

"Now listen to me, Jake. Does anyone know you're up here? The police? Anyone from the Network?"

Jake shakes his head.

"Because I don't want anyone to find us. I have to be alone with you for a while, Jake. Travel a bit, like we used to do. I want to talk to you about some things while we still have time."

Jake's body vibrates with a deep cold, a tuning fork that makes no sound. He looks closely at his brother, bewildered by the sight of him.

"Where have you been, Theo? God, I . . . I haven't heard from you in weeks."

"You seem to know all about me," Theo retorts, flushing again with anger. "I watched your fucking show."

"That logger," Jake rasps, his mind retrieving a memory of the news. "He got killed. I wanted to write to you about that but I was so busy with the show. Then Rachel got shot. And I thought she was . . . God, are you sure she's alive?"

"News said she is."

"I was worried about you too, Theo, really worried."

"Hard to tell from what you said on TV." Theo takes his arms off Jake. "You're a mouthy son of a bitch on air, aren't you."

"It's just my job," Jake replies quietly. "It's not personal."

"Everything's personal."

"I'm sorry, okay? I get carried away. You don't know what it's like under those lights. You start performing. You sense a million eyes watching you at once and it takes over your body. You lose yourself in order to please the audience. You do. It's instinct, that's all." He rubs his bloodshot eyes. "But that logger, Theo, the one who died. Were you–"

"Involved? No more than anyone else," Theo lies. He knows his brother won't accept what he had to do in Fenwick – not yet, anyway – and he doesn't want to scare him. "It was an accident, Jake, a casualty of war. We were trying to save a forest, as you may recall."

"Your name hasn't been in the news," Jake says slowly. "I would have seen it if you were involved. I looked. I looked every day."

"It will be. There's a guy I worked with up there named Nigel Fornhaven, he wants to bust me, which is why I had to take off. He'll probably cut a deal with the police. Give them my name as a scapegoat. That's what people do, Jake. They get scared, want to save their own skin, so they turn on people they once trusted."

"What happened out there?" Jake's feet start to sweat under the hot blanket.

"Now you ask me?" Theo shakes his head in disgust. "Too fucking late, brother. Why didn't you ask me weeks ago, when you were on air making me look like an asshole."

"You were in the bush, for Christ's sake, I couldn't even contact you."

"You never tried," Theo snarls. "Those loggers were breaking every law in the book, clear-cutting illegally, putting in roads near salmon streams. But you never put that on screen, did you? Why not, Jake? I'd like to know. Bad for the ratings?"

"A logger got killed. What the hell was I supposed to do?"

"You were supposed to support me. That's what. It's called fucking loyalty."

Jake closes his eyes, feels his body go lax with exhaustion. "I said I'm sorry," he mutters.

But Theo presses onwards. "Do you have any clue what I've been trying to do out there?" he asks. "Did you ever bother to ask me why I'm putting my whole fucking life on the line for a forest?"

And that's when Theo tells Jake everything. Holding his brother in his arms, Theo tells Jake about the old priest in Bangkok, about his long night with Girl 41, tells him what he's done during his years wandering from crisis to crisis, trying to change things. Jake listens intently to his brother's words and is soon transfixed, just like he used to be as a child, full of awe and fear and shame. Theo's terrible beauty, his brutal honesty, his righteousness lashing and tearing at Jake's flimsy life, peeling away Jake's gossamer coating of well-meaning intentions the way the hot fire devours the skin of bark on the birch logs. Jake leans into Theo's arms and tears come down his cheeks. He wants to apologize to Theo, to everyone, for being so remote, so callous, for letting everything in his life get so out of control.

"I heard about Rachel when I was driving," Theo says when he sees Jake break down. "What did the cops say? Have they talked to you yet?"

"Some detective questioned me at the hospital," Jake answers, wanting his words to be the exact ones Theo needs to hear. "I can't remember what he said. I just wanted to get the hell away from everyone. But I should really get back to see Rachel now. I should call."

"You were there, right? You saw her get shot?" Theo asks, pressing for details.

"I didn't see much. Just her face, you know, she was in the hall all bloody. I think I blacked out." Jake's voice trembles and Theo pulls him close.

"It's good," Theo whispers, almost to himself. "It's good that you saw that. Does anyone know you're up here?"

"I don't know. Maybe. I had a cab drive me. He must know where I am. And the librarian helped me out at the Network. I went there from the hospital. So he must know too."

Theo glances out the window at the blowing snow, as if expecting someone else to arrive.

"We've got to get out of here," he says firmly. "The police might come looking for you and find me, too. I'm in serious shit. How are you feeling?"

Jake glances down at his naked body and attempts a feeble joke. "A bit underdressed for a reunion like this."

Theo gets up and pulls on his shirt. "What I'm asking, Jake, is for you to stay with me for a while. Don't go back yet. Please. Rachel will be fine, right? I need you. I need you to be with me right now until I can figure out what to do."

"I'm really sorry about the coverage, Theo, I am," Jake says, reaching up to touch Theo's arm. "It's television, you know? It's just television."

"I know exactly what it is. Will you stay with me or not?"

Jake nods his head slowly, wanting to help Theo in the way Theo has helped him so many times before. "Whatever you want, Theo. I'm here."

"Good. I don't have much time left and there's still some things I need to show you."

Theo bends down and kisses his brother on the forehead, as if administering a blessing. The hot lips sear on Jake's shivering skin and he wonders what Theo means about running out of time.

CAB FARE

"Get me some mustard, would you, Rog? Not that French shit. Regular-like."

Ian O'Malley is sitting in his office eating a Polish sausage he bought from a street vendor outside Police Headquarters, and he chews the meat with considerable aggression, as if it were still alive.

"Search warrant come through yet?" Roger asks as he gets up to leave.

"Still waiting, of course. I mean, good Lord, I gave it high priority – it's an attempted murder! – and here we are sittin' on our cake holes while the bureaucrats shuffle paper. You call Jacobson's apartment again?"

"All morning. No answer. None at his office either."

"He'll turn up. And some of that sauerkraut, too – and call the lab while you're at it," he says as Roger shuts his door, cutting out the busy noise from the precinct.

The press are howling about the shooting and O'Malley

feels the pressure. Jacobson is still his only real suspect, all he has to go on until the fingerprints come back from the Identification lab – which could take days. He picks up his phone and dials Forensics to see if they have any more details on the .38 calibre bullet they pulled out of the wall of Poiselle's office, but the line's busy and O'Malley slams the down phone. "Goddamn backlog," he mutters. "Can never get through." He thinks about the bullet – could have come from anything: a Glock, a Saturday night special, even a revolver, but no one found the gun at the scene so it's a guessing game. He examines the thin file he's begun amassing on Jacobson, and even if preliminary searches have turned up empty, he feels convinced that Jacobson is his man. He doesn't like the way Jacobson pulled that phony "shock" routine at the hospital and he likes even less the way Jacobson disappeared some time after questioning. Come to think of it, O'Malley reflects, taking another bite of his sausage, he doesn't really like Jacobson's pompous show on television either – the way he sits there all smart-assed and knowing in front of his guests, as if he's somehow got all the answers.

As he waits for Roger to return with some condiments, O'Malley reconstructs the crime in his mind, weaving together the probable events as if he were writing a detective novel – no, the *series* of detective novels – based on his career in the force he promises himself to type out one day.

It's late on a cold Sunday night. (*Clancy*, O'Malley fantasizes, *I'll write like Tom Clancy – maybe Grisham. How hard can that be?*) It's 9:30 p.m. Jacob Jacobson bursts into Rachel Anne Poiselle's office. She's all curves and lips. Smart but sensual. They're lovers. He's angry. He wants to have a fight. She's been sleeping with someone else. One of her students, no doubt. His ego can't take it. (*Keep the sentences short*, he reminds himself, recalling a few of the Elmore Leonard books he's read. *Make it easy for the TV producers to turn it into a drama. God, I'm thinking of everything!*) Jacobson's a TV star, needs to be adored. They exchange words, violent words. Jacobson gets hot. Temper out of control. Takes out a gun and threatens to shoot. She laughs. She's a tough woman. She's been threatened before. Where did you get that gun, she says, the Props department? (*Dialogue, I have to remember to have a lot of good dialogue.*) Jacobson red with rage. Sweaty. Waves the gun. She taunts him. Thinks he looks stupid carrying a gun. She calls his bluff. Shoot, she says, I'd like to see that. Then, suddenly, he pulls the trigger. She goes down. Hit in the head. Now he's shit-scared. He's never seen a body. He's just a blow-dried TV dick-wad. But she's not dead. She crawls down the hall calling for help. He panics. Should he kill her? No, he doesn't have the guts to do that. Concocts a flimsy plan, like he's seen on some TV drama. Phones 911 as if he's a hero. Pretends to be in shock. Then he plays possum, lies "unconscious" beside her, as if he's injured, too. As if some imagined killer popped them both. Bullshit. Remember those Menendez boys? The case is solved within days. (*That should do it for the build-up*, O'Malley decides, taking another bite from his hot dog. *Time to move to the finale. This writing gig is too easy. I've just got to start typing it all out.*) It's your basic crime of passion. Spousal abuse. Whatever. Let the lawyers sort it out. Jacobson did it. Simple. The hero cop takes him down. Goodbye boy wonder, no more TV for you. Another case solved. *Roll the goddamn credits or whatever they do at the end of a book*, O'Malley thinks, satisfied with his work.

"Here's the mustard," says Roger, opening the door and interrupting O'Malley's literary endeavour. "Couldn't get any sauerkraut."

Oh, well, back to real life. Same shit, different stable.

"Thanks, Rog." O'Malley grabs the plastic condiment pouch of mustard. "Any news?"

"Still no word on a fingerprint match. Say they need more time, the usual cluster fuck. But the chief stopped me and he wants that report on the Hudson case finished ASAP."

"Yeah, and the Chin case and the Fabrizzi case and screw him. This is the big one, he said so himself on the news, so let's try to focus here for a second and not worry about every goddamn shoot-up in the city."

"I'm just telling you–"

"Whatever. Did you call the hospital again?"

"How many times you gonna ask me? Doc says when the woman wakes up we can talk to her."

"So she's out of the departure lounge?"

"Oh yeah, moved out of intensive into critical this morning. Apparently she'll be fine. Just a graze, but still pretty bad."

"When can we question her?"

"Not sure. Doc says head wounds are hard to predict."

"Keep checking with him. Meantime, let's play the 911 call again. I want to hear Jacobson's voice."

Roger walks over to the filing cabinet, picks up a cassette player, and lays it down in front of O'Malley's sausage wrapper.

"Easy!" O'Malley says, moving his food closer to him. "Don't get any crap on my machine, it's expensive."

Roger shrugs and presses play. They hear the nasal voice of the operator.

"911."

"Yes, there's been an accident. Someone's hurt."

"Turn it up, Rog, I can't hear the damn thing."

O'Malley bends his good ear to the machine and Roger pulls up a chair to the desk.

"You're calling from 944-4478?"

"I need an ambulance," Jacobson's voice says. He doesn't sound panicked, more distracted and annoyed than anything.

"Are you hurt?"

"No, not me, someone else. We need help."

"How many people are hurt, sir?"

"One, just one. She's bleeding. I think she's been shot."

"Is she in danger now?"

"No. Please, you've got to send someone quickly."

"Is anyone else with you?"

"For fuck's sake, are you listening to me? Someone's been shot. I think there's a gun, I don't know. Jesus Christ, why are you asking me questions? Send a fucking ambulance. I'm at the University of–"

"Stop it right there, Rog," O'Malley commands, biting his sausage and wiping his chin with the back of his hand. "Rewind a little. I want to hear that part about the gun again."

Roger presses rewind and the tape screeches, then plays.

". . . are you listening to me? Someone's been shot. I think there's a gun, I don't know."

"Stop it."

Click.

"Did you hear that, Rog? How does he know there's a gun? We didn't find any gun. Why the hell would this son of a bitch say there's a gun if there was no gun at the scene? You get someone to go back to that university and go over every inch of it, just to make sure we didn't miss something." O'Malley slams down his sausage, sending mustard spraying onto his fingers. "But I'm telling you, Rog, this is the guy. Listen to his voice. So calm and cool. Shouldn't he sound hysterical? His lover's bleeding to death. Wouldn't that freak a guy out?"

"You ever read that book by Camus called *The Stranger*?" Roger ventures.

"What the hell are you talking about?"

"It's an existentialist thing, right, where this guy is involved in a murder but he shows no emotion. Everyone thinks he did it because that's not normal behaviour. You know, he's really calm, detached-like. It's a French book."

"Are you high on something, Rog?"

"I'm just saying, it could be like that."

"And I'm saying shut the fuck up. When I find this guy, so help me, I'm gonna flick his antennas so hard he'll never get good reception again."

"Well, he didn't actually say he saw a gun," Roger says quietly. "He said he *thought* there was a gun."

"Listen to the tape, chump," O'Malley cuts in. "He basically said there was a gun. Why would a guy say that if he didn't see a gun?"

"All right. Let's say he did see one," Roger says, not wanting to argue further with his superior. "Where do you think he went after you talked to him?"

"How should I know? I talked to the staff and no one saw him leave the room. Doctors! Can't even keep track of who's in their own bloody ward. Too busy golfing. But I'll tell you something right now. Jacobson took off after I told him to get a lawyer. He knew that I was onto him. You should have seen him, Rog. Very evasive, detached-like. Typical of a psycho. Thinks he's above the law because he's on TV. So who isn't on TV these days?"

"Yeah, my wife and I, you know, we watch his show all the time," Roger admits. "He's pretty good."

"Zip it, Roger, and call the hospital again." Some juice from the Polish sausage drips down O'Malley's chin. "And while you're at it, call the Network, too, and let's find out who Jacobson hangs out with. We got to move on this before the press eats us up."

Another police officer pokes his head into O'Malley's office.

"O'Malley. Got someone here I think you should see."

"I'm busy. Send him over to Keller."

"It's about the Poiselle shooting. I think you should see him."

Leon Pastiche walks tentatively into Ian O'Malley's office, his eyes gazing down at the floor. The door shuts loudly behind him and sends a jolt of discomfort through his body. He thinks of all the unnecessary hassles he's endured by police while driving his cab, how people in his neighbourhood avoid cops the way insurance companies avoid skydivers. Contact inevitably leads to accidents. But on his way home from Georgian Bay he listened to the radio and heard that Jacob Jacobson was a suspect in the terrible shooting at the University of Toronto, and he knew he'd have to go to the police, no matter how much he dreaded it. After all, the man was in *his* cab for two hours and acting very weird.

"And you are . . .?" O'Malley says, not getting up.

"Leon Pastiche. Cab driva'."

"Congratulations, Mr. Whatever, but I didn't order a cab," O'Malley replies, rolling his eyes upwards to signal to the unwelcome guest that he has interrupted important business.

"Sir, 'ting is, I jes' drove dat guy Jacobson," Leon says nervously. "Drove him all da way up north, see."

"You drove Jacob Jacobson up north? Really?" O'Malley winks at Roger, as if to say, We get these cranks all the time on a big case.

"Dat's right."

"So, Mr. . . . Plastique, is it?"

"Pastiche. Leon Pastiche."

"That's a French name. You a Haitian?"

"Canadian cee-tizen," Leon says forcefully, throwing back his shoulders to straighten his posture.

"Hey, aren't we all?" O'Malley raises his hands in mock surrender. "So, where exactly did you drive Mr. Jacobson?"

"Georgian Bay. Place call Pointe au Baril."

"He took your cab to Georgian Bay? Interesting. I guess you get a lot of fares going that far north."

Leon doesn't answer him.

"Mr. Pastiche," O'Malley says, settling back in his chair. "Tell me the truth. Have you had anything to drink today?"

Leon sees O'Malley wink at the other officer and he shudders. The policeman's big head reminds him of the grille of an old cab, dented on one side as if it's been side-swiped and now cruising dangerously for more action. Leon realizes that he shouldn't have come. *Dis pig ain't gonna listen to no black mon*, he thinks to himself bitterly. The air from the heating unit opposite blows an unnatural machine breeze and Leon feels his throat go dry. He remembers the tumour that had been attached to his brain and wonders what unknown part of him was cut out when the doctors removed it. Perhaps some psychological reasoning device that would explain why on earth he would be insane enough to willingly walk into a police station and offer to lend them his help in apprehending a criminal. As if they would take it, stick a badge on his black ass and call him a deputy.

"Sorry for wastin' your time, mon," he mumbles, and turns to leave the office.

"Just a minute there," says O'Malley. "We're not done yet. How do you know it was really Jacob Jacobson in your car?"

"Seen him on da TV. Plus he tol' me, didn't he? I'll be goin' now."

"He just up and told you who he was?"

"You 'tink I'm lyin'?" Leon swings his head around, tired of being patronized. "Sheeit. I pick da guy up at da damn hospital, mon. Den I wait two hours for him at da Network. Right on Spadina. Den I drive him all da way up north. Said he got some home out dere, or somet'in'. Now what da hell you wan' from me? Dat's all I can say."

"Well, that's better," O'Malley says, altering his tone to something friendlier. "You might have told me that earlier. Maybe you did have him in your cab after all. What was he wearing?"

"Why da fuck am I gonna lie to you?" yells out Leon, not caring if his attitude provokes the police. All his papers are in order, all his tickets paid up. "You wanna find dis guy, go to a place call Pointe au Baril. Dat's all I know."

"Roger, take Mr. Pastiche to your office and get some more information on his trip. I've got to make a call."

Roger escorts Leon out while Ian O'Malley stuffs the rest of his sausage into his mouth. He waits for a few seconds after the door closes, then quickly dials the number for the police station in Parry Sound, the nearest unit to Pointe au Baril. He sets his face in a grin, his lips hanging like a red hammock from his pinned-up cheeks.

"Got you, Mr. TV," he whispers into the receiver as the line rings urgently in his good ear.

April 19, 1998

Went to the murder scene at the Gabinson house last night as soon as I heard about it on my bedside police scanner. It was buzzing with dispatches like an infection so I couldn't ignore it.

By the time I arrive the media's swarming the place, shoplifting bits and pieces of the house with their cameras. But there's a press ban on the details of the murders, so whatever they see will have to stay unknown to everyone but those of us right on the scene. As if the press tell people anything even when they don't have a muzzle on. Feeling cynical and distressed and don't really know why I've come, except I love to see the slutty nakedness of a crime scene before it gets dressed-up by tailored news reports. And since this might be a serial killing – at least that's what the police are saying – there's a weird dramatic patina on everything, as if every detail is drenched in significance, part of a pattern. It's cinema verité and everyone feels edgy and uninvited.

I'm wearing a Walkman so people think I'm listening to music, but I'm not. I just don't want anyone to talk to me, so the dead headphones are a trick I use to eavesdrop. It's like being invisible.

Flash my I.D. to some cop and slip under the yellow police tape to go inside and look around the house, at the diorama of the Gabinsons' life. Dirty dishes in the sink. Old kitchen table still not fully cleared, chips of wood taken out of the edges by children gouging with cutlery. They ate spaghetti tonight, from a can. Chef Boyardee. Why bother with a can, when it's so easy to make from scratch? I look in the cupboards and inspect their groceries to find out about their life. Ice cream and corn chips, Pop-Tarts and ground beef. Not a lot of fresh fruit. The Gabinsons are shopping plaza and mall people. Lots of bagged milk and a stick of garlic butter in the fridge. I go upstairs to see how they keep themselves in their private spaces. Blue throw rug in the bathroom, not bad, but doesn't match the green towels. In the medicine cabinet there are no vitamins, just Q-Tips and tweezers, a bottle of Aspirin, and prescription drugs I don't recognize. Someone in the family wears contact lenses. Disposable. I bet it's the daughter. Then again, everything looks disposable after a murder.

A cop catches me in the bathroom, but before he can throw me out I slip away and sneak down to the living room. Two cheap white leather couches make an L-shape, good for lounging, but you tend to slip on leather and that's bad for your posture. Big-screen TV in the centre – the most expensive item in the room – and a cheap Manet reproduction on one of the walls, the usual bounty of suburban shopping campaigns on full display.

In the basement people crowd around a body. The thirteen-year-old daughter. Chopped up with an axe. Electrical cord around her neck, the killer's signature. The medical examiner tries to determine the time of death by looking at her skin coloration, but there's so much trauma that he says he'll have to go back to the lab with the body parts. I walk around slowly and notice the basement walls have posters of rock bands like No Doubt and the Backstreet Boys. Teen design, ugly as always. Lots of blood.

I wander back upstairs and loiter invisibly inside the Gabinsons' house, looking at pictures of their daughter. Her face is prominent among the gallery of photos that sits above the TV. Family viewing. It's such a common exhibit, the awkwardly posed portraits curated less by aesthetic taste than by middle-class love. And I've judged their groceries, opened their fridge, seen their bent toothbrushes and their pink toilet-seat cover, their kitsch art and their beautiful daughter. Electrical cord around her neck. I've entered the story and stolen it as my own. Made this broken family part of my virtual world.

I start to feel sick by my own cruel assessment and am almost glad when a police officer ignores my press badge and throws me out. On the street I wait with the neighbours and reporters. Wait for what, I wonder? We all stare at the house, expecting something to happen, but nothing does. With my headphone disguise, I move around and watch the whispered birth of rumours. A Black and Decker drill was used to drive holes into her head, says a woman wearing a checkered kitchen apron. Bottles were shoved up her anus and broken, says her husband more authoritatively. Arm in arm they move around repeating their information. The crowd mills aimlessly, happily overwhelmed. I hear snippets of other whispers, details of imagined rape scenes, and the ever-popular, thrilling assertion that the killer is a friend, had dinner at the victim's house while the body lay hacked up in the basement freezer. Homage to the great Hitchcock, I'm sure.

Wish I didn't hate the crowd so much, but I guess they're no different from me. Reckless and dirty, that's how I feel. I start a rumour about a secret videotape of the killing and it spreads like spilled milk.

Ironically, I spent last night at home looking at newspaper clippings of the other murders ostensibly caused by the same killer. It's all stuck in my journal. Pictures of the victims. Pictures of them in high school when they were young and sweet and smiling for the high school photographer – shutter open, snap, closed, the sound of something being stolen. And the footage. I watched my video collection and relived the first hysterical moments of the serial killings. Endless footage of the grieving families and the time they spent suffering during the manhunt, how they become more frustrated with the bungled police investigations than with the random deaths of their daughters. Months have gone by with no leads – there's nothing as pathetic as bovine cops chewing the cud of excuses in front of edgy reporters. The whole story really just an elaborate apology to the public because there simply is no killer, no story. And then there's another press conference and the case expands with lawyers to protect the families' rights and the police rights and the media rights, and some even come to protect the unknown killer's rights. All this even though there's still no news of the missing bodies and no pictures of the killer and no leads. And then, of course, another girl goes missing. Tonight, it's the Gabinsons' girl.

Media marinates in the juice of protracted murder cases and I put everything in my journal, let the information sit there like food going bad in an unplugged fridge. What am I going to do with it? I realize that I hardly ever ask myself that question. Somehow it all seems important, but important to what I still don't know.

Hours later I'm still here among the neighbours, rumours rustling across the fields of our collective imagination, binding us together with intimate suspicions and fears. We huddle close under the streetlights like farm cattle, the dumb and unnecessary instinct to herd. But I also get the feeling that at any moment something might give way. A bottom drops out, a barrier collapses. The crowd becomes a mob, suddenly seething and violent. Rush the house, tear it apart, find someone to take the blame for the confusion and fear and offence. A dangerous, bubbling anger barely contained underneath the veil of guarded expressions. I've sensed this so many times before, that at the borders of crime there's always this chaos waiting to implode.

I glance sideways at the faces around me, try to determine who is a charitable person and who is a killer, who a loving husband and who a wife beater. Everyone unknowable. A woman turns away from my gaze and sips from a mug of tea. A man in slippers gives me a sympathetic nod. I think of those grim news statistics: Most emergency-ward visits are caused by domestic violence; women who are pregnant are more likely to suffer abuse than those who aren't. Who would beat a pregnant woman? What would a man like that look like? Why don't his defects show on the surface, like boils or scabs? Some mark of Cain. The fellow in slippers smiles at me, holds out his hand and offers me a candy. I take it, thank him, and soon feel a sharp, minty freshness in my mouth. What if he's the killer, I think. It's possible. I read that serial killers will mill around and watch the police go through the crime scene. Part of the thrill, I guess. I take a closer look at the man and imagine some dark, impenetrable tunnel that leads down into his heart.

Of course, I'm feeling so morbid and depressed now that I'm probably missing the point entirely. Maybe it's simpler than I think. Maybe he's just a concerned citizen, here like everyone else – the cops, the media, the neighbours – to sustain the illusion that what is lost can be regained through acts of recognition and order. Gather. Talk. The security of community and law. That's what the police tell us. That's what the press tells us. That's what we believe. But listening to the quiet neighbourhood whispers, smelling someone's barbecue, watching the traffic slow down to rubberneck the murder scene, I think this illusion is weakening. The pull of chaos is too strong. There's no order, no justice; there's just these few quiet moments in between the violence, and we broadcast them again and again until we believe that they're true. And then everything falls apart all over again.

When I go home I flick on the local news. They're live at the Gabinson house covering the murder, and a good-looking reporter is standing five feet from where I was not fifteen minutes earlier, interviewing the woman in the checkered apron. She sounds better on TV.

FAST FORWARD

The car speeds along the highway amidst the swirling snowflakes, which collide and explode on the windshield like swarming insects. Theo smokes silently, opening his window just a crack so the cold wind buzzes. Jake watches the dark colours of the pine scenery smudge in his peripheral vision. They're heading into North Bay, a town almost four hundred kilometres north of the city, because Theo wants to visit an old girlfriend. He tells Jake he needs to tie up a loose end and Jake doesn't ask for details or explanation. He wants to be near Theo and feel their old trust, the stern security of his brother's eyes, and he has too many questions of his own to start asking any of his brother. After three hours, they pull into a stubborn-looking, flat-roofed bungalow called the HorseTrail Motel. Its pink neon sign flashes vacancy against the thick canvas of sky.

"Are we stopping?" asks Jake.

"Just for the night," Theo says, backing the car into a parking spot.

"I thought we were, you know, laying low. Hiding out, whatever."

"It won't matter here," Theo replies, shaking his head as if Jake has said something stupid. "Come on, let's check in."

"I don't mean to sound vain," Jake continues, "but people tend to recognize me. Maybe I should stay in the car."

"You're a nobody up here, Mr. Letterman. Relax. You're just like me."

Jake nods his head and they walk into the lobby. The motel owner is playing solitaire and checks them in without even lifting his head from his cards. Theo gives Jake a meaningful stare and lays fifty dollars cash in front of the man, and then they go to room seven. Jake feels embarrassed about his celebrity anxiety and follows Theo silently.

"Unpack my bag, will you? I've got to make a call," says Theo, going over to the side of the bed and picking up the phone.

The room is the basic motel double: two single beds, one bathroom, an old colour TV with a broken remote, and a simple brown dresser with one drawer nailed shut. The only decoration is a dingy poster of a lake scene taken somewhere in the north, with the words "Keep it Beautiful" printed on the bottom. It appears as if the room were specifically designed to communicate transience rather than comfort.

Jake puts Theo's bag on the rust-coloured bedspread and opens it to see what his brother packed. He takes Theo's clothes and throws them on the bed: rain gear, wool socks, underwear, T-shirts, heavy sweaters, several books about social action and alternative economies. He wonders if this is everything Theo owns and concludes it probably is. Theo lives on the bare essentials. At the bottom of the bag he feels something hard and is surprised to see a video camera, complete with charged battery and fresh tape.

"Where did you get this?" Jake asks, as Theo talks on the phone to the operator.

"Yes, I'm looking for the number of a Theckla Garrow," says Theo. "G-A-R-R-O-W. No, I don't know the street."

"Is this camera yours?" Jake waves it in front of Theo's face.

"Just a minute, operator," says Theo, covering the receiver with his hand. "Yeah, it's mine."

"When did you get it?"

"I'm on the phone. Sorry, operator. Yes, I'll try that one. 553-2342. Thanks."

"I didn't know you were into taking videos Theo. I thought you hated cameras."

"I got it to record the loggers' reactions during the protest. I barely know how to use the damn thing. But you're gonna teach me. I want to make a documentary of this trip, a home movie of us. For posterity."

Jake takes off the lens cap and flicks the switch to ON. When he looks through the viewfinder he sees his brother in the centre of the digital square, bending over to dial the phone. Autofocus. Theo's body straightens as he waits for the sound of the ring. Jake zooms in on Theo's face so only the thin lips and the stubble on his chin are in the picture. He presses the red button with his finger. Record. A light on top of the camera starts to flash.

"Hey, Theo, now *you're* on TV."

Theo moves his head out of the shot, and Jake zooms out and watches Theo adjust back into the picture.

"We're live, Theo. You're on."

"Hello, is Theckla Garrow there? . . . Hey, it's Theo. Theo Jacobson . . . Yeah, it has been a long time, but I was in the area and I thought I'd give old Theckla a buzz and see if she's still alive . . . I'm fine, same old, same old . . . That's right, my brother's on TV. In fact, he's with me right now . . . Listen, why don't you meet us for a drink? . . . Tonight . . . O'Donnell's Grill . . . Sure, I can find it. Say in a half an hour? . . . See ya there."

Theo hangs up and looks over at Jake.

"Was that *the* Theckla Garrow?" Jake asks from behind the camera's eyepiece.

"Yeah, we're gonna meet her in half an hour. You remember her?"

"Theo, you dog. How did you know she was here? I mean, didn't she move to San Francisco with her father or something?"

"L.A. actually, with her husband. But we kind of get in touch every few years. Postcards, the odd call. She's been up north for a while."

"Say something for the camera, Theo. Tell me how you feel right now."

Theo gets up, pushes his hand through his long brown hair and straightens his shoulders. He stares directly into the camera and speaks very slowly, the words spaced so far apart that they seem to be strangers queuing in a line.

"It's good to be with you, Jake. I want to get to know you again. Get away from everyone. I don't want you to be afraid any more."

Then Theo puts his hand over his face and Jake abruptly turns off the camera and closes his eyes.

"You know I can't stay here much longer, Theo," Jake says quietly, almost to himself. "I've got to get back to Rachel. I don't know what's happening with her, how she's doing. Shit. I haven't even called the Network. I just can't run away Theo, I'm sorry. I can't."

Theo speaks quickly, as if he's just said the wrong thing and wants to apologize for his mistake. "I know you can't, but just wait. Please. I'll come with you and we'll see her. Just stay with me for a few days."

"I want to, but–"

"I'm asking this one favour. Don't call anyone. The police want to find me, and if they trace your call they will. I've never asked you for much, Jake. Do this one thing for me."

Jake pauses, knowing he can't refuse. "A few days," he whispers. "Of course."

Theo claps his hands loudly. "All right. We've got to go meet Theckla now. Bring the camera, I want you to record this. I want you to record everything." He puts his arm around Jake and leads him out to the car, holding him tightly to his side.

□ □ □

Theckla waits for them inside O'Donnell's Grill, sitting in one of the wooden booths that has a miniature jukebox bolted to the wall. A country and western song plays almost inaudibly next to her ear. Four shot glasses sit empty in front of her. When she sees Theo she jumps up out of her seat and throws her arms around him, hugging him with her eyes closed for a full minute. Jake lags behind, shooting it all as Theo instructed him to do. And then Theckla starts talking, her speech as fast as amphetamines.

"Theo Jacobson! Oh, hi! How are you? It's been so long, I . . . God, you look great. I missed you, I mean, Jesus, here you are in North Bay, why the hell would you come here? I mean, this is butt-fuck no-wheres-ville and I'm dying for some real company. I mean, look at these people, they don't have enough brains in this whole town to get on the road and leave, you know? Theo, you look great, where have you been? What? I haven't seen you in four years. God, do we have to catch up. Is that your brother with the camera? Oh it is, the famous Jacob, now, he's done well. Man, I remember when he wasn't even old enough to sneak out with us, you remember that? Jeez, he's a bit taller now, duh! Of course he is, twenty years later, what am I, losing my mind? I am, I actually think I am losing my mind. Who wouldn't in the middle of a town like this? But not really, maybe. I don't know. God, sit down, let's have some drinks. Hey Jake, put down that camera. What is he, like a TV junkie now? Let's celebrate, Christ, I haven't had company in ages . . ."

Theckla is vibrating with excitement and speaks as if she's chasing after her own words. Her voice rattles throughout the bar for everyone to hear and she smokes with equal intensity, inhaling deeply, then exhaling as she talks, the words coming out camouflaged by smoke. Her hair is no longer auburn, but peroxide white, clipped short and blunt over her ears, which themselves are decorated with six earrings each. A red tattoo of a flower on her left lobe resembles a burn mark, and she notices Jake staring at it.

"You like that?" she says, grabbing her ear. "I just got it. It's a flower – not a real one, but a copy of the first flower my kid drew when she was two. That's right, I've got my own fucking kid, can you believe it? Theckla Garrow is a mother, and a damn fine mother, too. That's why the tattoo's in red, 'cause my kid used a red crayon to make the flower, then she ate it, which is another story, but I thought I should make it into a tattoo and put it right there 'cause, you know, it means that I'll always remember to listen to her with a sweet ear. It's a symbol, which is important to have. In fact, my whole body should be a testament to my beliefs since no one else seems to care what I say. So I'm starting to get into tattoos, not the lousy flash art they have on the walls of a parlour, but my own stuff, see." She rolls up the sleeve of her shirt. "I designed this circle here on my arm. Take a look, it's a green circle – which is planet Earth – and in the centre is the sign for infinity, only I drew it crooked, because we're moving towards the infinite future but no one is sure what way we're going. Right? My body is a canvas for my beliefs, I think everyone's body should be, so we can be beautiful and important at the same time." She unrolls her sleeve and lights up another cigarette. "But everyone in this town thinks I'm a dyke 'cause I have tattoos and ROSCOE-WA-FUCKING-SHINSKI-LEFT-ME-FOR-A-SLUT-WAITRESS, who, by the way, used to work right here. And then I cut my hair and dyed it and started wearing big boots and now I'm known as the town dyke, even though I have a kid. Check this one out, I just got another tattoo on my belly button."

Jake and Theo watch Theckla display her body art. Then the waitress comes and Theckla doesn't bother to ask them what they want, just orders them beer and a few shots of tequila each. She keeps talking and talking until they forget that the music on the jukebox has run out, and finally she has to pause for a minute to rummage through her bag for a new pack of cigarettes.

"Do you mind if Jake shoots some video, Theckla?" Theo asks in the respite of silence. "We're kind of making a home movie."

"No, no, go ahead, hell, make me famous," she says, digging into her purse. "I always thought I'd be famous, and then I went off and married that asshole Bryant, what a mistake that was. Hey, where's the music?" She looks up suddenly, lighting up a smoke from a fresh pack. "We need some music. Do you have a quarter for the machine? I think I left my wallet in the car."

"Start shooting, Jake," says Theo, handing some change to Theckla.

Jake lifts the camera and focuses on Theckla and Theo sitting beside each other across the table. Then he decides he needs a better establishing shot and pans the bar where a group of men in snowmobile boots and plaid flannel shirts quietly drink beer.

O'Donnell's is decorated in a style Jake imagines might one day be called Art New-Road, which is to say that highway signs from all over North America are nailed to the wooden walls beside licence plates for cars and trucks, some dating back to the "classical period" of the forties. The bar is a homage to highway towns and is predictably filled with silent, thick-limbed men whose deep-lined faces look like white dinner plates recently wiped clean with a thick piece of bread. Jake turns the camera back to Theo and Theckla and sees that they are holding hands. He points the camera down and lets the tape record their fingers twining.

Theckla continues to tell her story in a circuitous, episodic way, running over years and events as if Theo knows them all already, although he doesn't, and they keep drinking and toasting each other with tequila while Jake films and films. Theckla describes how her first marriage to the actor Bryant Hillman was a fiasco, especially after they moved to L.A. where both of them tried to get into films, each doing a few B-thrillers and mostly just hanging out and living off the money Theckla's father left her after he died of AIDS in San

Francisco, which she thinks is just such an unoriginal way for him to die, but at least it's trendy, and she mentions how her father was always very much concerned about keeping up with trends, and then she describes how Bryant somehow landed a TV soap opera job playing a doctor and how that split them up because he couldn't handle being in a relationship with a junkie, which she was then, by the way, but only because she was so stressed out because she'd decided to keep the baby. And when Bryant didn't want it or her, she went and hung out with Tim Leary's crowd and a few up-and-coming stars from England, mostly Euro-trash and sons of former rock stars like Donovan Jr., and she partied pretty heavily with them, she could tell Theo stories, but not right now, and then she regaled them with how she'd been there the year before Leary died, and he told her – because she was his favourite and he loved her daughter, who's brilliant, they'll meet her later – he told her to find out about life outside of dirty Hollywood, which she did, going on the road and ending up in Kansas with a letter of introduction to William Burroughs of all people, and talking about junk with him was very interesting, but then the all-time downer – meeting some ex-Deadheads in her motel who beat her up, robbed her, and stole her car, leaving her alone and broke and stranded with the baby. Which is when she met a Polish truck driver from North Bay, of all places, named ROSCOE-WA-FUCKING-SHINSKI-WHO-LEFT-ME-FOR-A-SLUT-WAITRESS. And he fell in love with her when they met at a truck stop where she was hooking to make a few dollars, just so you know, and he'd cleaned her up and taken her and the baby back up to Canada, and now, here she is telling her crazy story in O'Donnell's bar to the famous Jacobson brothers, a long way from L.A., and an even longer way from the Rosedale golf course where she used to go with Theo to figure out how things worked in the world.

By the time she finishes, they're all pretty drunk. Theckla moves closer to Theo and feeds him tequila from a shot glass, the booze running down his chin, catching in his stubble and flashing in the hazy light. They laugh, touch, exchange sloppy kisses. Jake records it all but soon he begins to feel uncomfortable, unwanted by Theckla and Theo. It's a feeling he's used to from many years ago.

"Keep shooting, Jake," Theo orders when he sees Jake put the camera on the table. "I want all of this on tape. Theckla's story should be told for posterity."

"Yeah, make me famous, little Jake. Don't hog the limelight."

"We're running out of tape," says Jake, searching for an excuse to stop.

"I've got more in the car. Keep shooting."

"I should go back to the motel."

"What's the matter with you, Jake?" slurs Theckla. "You're not having fun? Come on, loosen up, you're very uptight for a TV guy. I thought you'd be all loose and funny."

"I guess I left my loose and funny script at the studio."

"You know what? You need to get fucked, my friend," Theckla says, leaning in close to Jake's face. "That's what you need. I have a little list in my head of people who I think need to be tied up and fucked. I think you just made it on that list."

"I'm honoured, Theckla, really, I am."

"He doesn't like me, Theo," Theckla says, pulling away. "Your snotty little brother doesn't like me. You think I'm a fuck-up, don't you, a real fuck-up. You're embarrassed to be with me, like I might rub off on you, taint your pretty TV skin with a little northern poverty. But remember, chump, we grew up together, so fuck you. I'm going to dance."

Theckla gets up and walks into the middle of the bar and starts to dance to the music on the P.A. system.

"Shoot this, Jake, stay here and shoot this." Theo gets up, walks over to the table beside them, and starts talking to two other women. The bar begins to fill with people and a few cheers go up as Theckla moves to the beat. She dances fluidly, aquatically. Shutting her eyes, she puts her hands over her head, and grinds her hips. Jake points the camera at her and presses PLAY. Someone at the bar turns up the volume and several more people stand up to dance. The men drinking beer at the counter turn to watch. One of the women Theo was talking to walks cautiously over to dance with Theckla. More cheering starts. Theo comes back and slides into the booth.

"Watch this, Jake. I just paid that woman fifty bucks to dance two songs with Theckla. This'll be great. Theckla's wild, she'll do anything. She lives without fear; that's why I love her. She's totally unconcerned with anything but pure experience. I love her for that."

The woman moves uncertainly beside Theckla, who opens her eyes and lets out a whoop. She grabs the other woman's shoulder and pulls her close, moving her hip into the woman's thigh. Then she bends her knees and dances low to the ground, rubbing her face against the woman's leg and licking the denim of the woman's jeans. The men at the bar stand up from their stools and gather closer.

The woman with Theckla glances over at Theo, confused, as if the game being played is lost on her, but he winks at her and makes a rolling motion with his hand to signal that she should continue. Jake turns the camera away from the floor and focuses it on Theo, who stares intently at Theckla and rubs his jaw with his hand. Then he looks at Jake and says to the camera, "No fear, right now there's no fear. Watch this Jake. You could learn something from Theckla."

Theckla holds the woman's head close to her own and shimmies her hips back and forth. The music plays louder and the crowd calls out "Yeah!" and "All right!" Theckla pulls the woman even closer so that their faces are nearly touching.

"You all think I'm the town dyke? Well check this out," she yells, and abruptly kisses her startled partner. It's a hard, open-mouthed kiss, and though the woman struggles, Theckla holds her firmly. After a few seconds Theckla lets go, the woman's lipstick smudged as if someone's just slapped her on her mouth.

"Oh, shit, you bitch, you bitch!" the woman screams.

She runs over to Theo, cursing loudly, calling him a pervert, a bastard, hitting him with her fists. But Theo blocks her blows with his massive forearms and signals to Jake to keep the camera rolling.

Jake does. The woman throws a beer at Theo but misses, and then she bolts to the bathroom, sobbing. Theckla lets out a shout – "Right on!" – and begins to strip. As she unbuttons her top she moves towards Jake, until she's facing him. Lifting one foot up on the edge of the table, she pushes her crotch in Jake's face.

"You need this, little Jake, just like my old hubby Bryant, the famous prude. Can't you celebrity types get it up? I think you need some tit tonight."

Jake puts down the camera and says soberly, "I don't think I do, Theckla. Thank you."

"You don't like tits, little boy, you afraid of booty?" She leans back and removes her shirt.

Theo snatches the camera and turns it on Jake.

Theckla's arms are covered in tattoos. On the right one she has a rendition of Casper the Friendly Ghost hanging from a crucifix. On the left there is a crescent-shaped moon and a star with a line through it.

"What are you looking at, Jake, my tits or my tattoos?" she asks. "You like it, huh? The moon? You know what that means, Jake? It means that when you look up in the sky and make a wish, you're bound to get screwed instead. It's an anti-wish tattoo. Wish upon a star and you don't get far. I know, I married a star."

"Very clever," Jake comments, retreating deeper into the booth away from her body and watching Casper wriggle on the cross as Theckla's skin stretches back and forth to the rhythm of her dance. It's an absurd image, Jake thinks: crucifying a ghost, mixing religion and television cartoons for no apparent purpose. Is it for the delicious emptiness of the irony? Is that enough? None of it makes sense to him. Not the series of tattoo messages, not the vibration of the camera, not the hot skin closing in on him like epiphytic vines. It all seems randomly cut into his life: interesting film footage ruined by a bad edit. He remembers what Walter Cronkite used to say at the end of his nightly newscast: *And that's the way it is.* Everything had resolution for Walter. All news items were constructed like stories. Crimes had solutions. Crises had conclusions. That's what Jake loves about his job. He can ask a question in every show and find the answer within an hour. That's why the audience watches him: he brings them resolution. But now he's incapable of summing anything up. All the conflicting strands of the last twenty-four hours conspire to overwhelm him. They stubbornly refuse to make sense. He thinks of Rachel, of watching her in the hallway. He recalls the sensation of taking a picture of her bloody head.

The alcohol in his system sends him spinning into thought, and now he doesn't care if Theckla strips or if she walks away. The end doesn't matter. It just happens. He notices that her shirt is off and that her tattoos shine with sweat. Theo zooms in on Jake's face, finds no discernible expression and records it.

A muscular bouncer in a black shirt appears at their booth and yanks Theckla by the arm.

"Put your goddamn shirt on, lady," he says. "This ain't no strip joint."

"Get your hands off me," she screams, taking a swing at him with her free arm.

Catching her fist before it can hit him, the bouncer bends her arm behind her back. Theckla lets out a short wail and kicks upward with her left leg. Dropping the camera to the table, Theo leaps on the bouncer, knocking him away from Theckla and onto the ground. They fall into a heap, but in a few seconds Theo, who is an experienced fighter, has the bouncer in a fierce headlock. Everyone in the bar presses in closer. Someone yells, "Fight, fight!"

Jake gets up, but does nothing. He continues to watch the scene around him.

"Put your shirt on, Theckla, and walk out the door," says Theo calmly, while he holds the bouncer's head tightly. Jake notices the veins in Theo's hands fill under his skin.

Taking her time buttoning up her shirt, Theckla walks over to the table and finishes her beer in one long drink. Then she puts on her coat, and before she leaves, leans down and says to the wheezing bouncer, "I have a kid, buddy. You just tried to beat up a mother."

She struts out of the bar, swinging her arms proudly beside her. Theo lets go of the bouncer, who slumps winded on the floor, then grabs the camera from the table and follows Theckla out. Just before he gets to the door, he turns back and shouts, "Jake, come on. Get the hell out of there."

Jake doesn't move. He stands still, mesmerized by the body of the bouncer, until Theo runs back in, jerks his shoulder, and pulls him outside and into the car. Skidding on the ice in the parking lot, they speed away into the night.

The windows inside the car frost up from their breath. Theckla lights up a smoke and starts talking again. She's badly drunk now, and her adrenaline is pumping.

"Did you see that? I'm just having a little fun and they go bananas. Those hicks." She rolls down the window and puts her head into the wind and screams, "WEEEHAAA, YOU HICK-TOWN MORONS!" The cold air blasts in on Jake's face in the back seat

"You're so goddamn good, Theo, you just took him out," Theckla raves. "Did you see the faces on those guys? Woohaa, I can't believe you taped that. That's fucking priceless. The expression on their faces when I kissed that girl, total confusion. Terror – big men terrified of us little girlies having a kissy-poo. Nothing is as dangerous as a kiss, that's as true today as it ever was. They were hot, don't deny it, weren't you a bit hot, Jake? Man, Theo, I miss you. Let's go back to my house and have a drink. I want you to see my kid, she's so beautiful. She's so smart. My brains, not her dipstick father's, but she got his looks, I'll admit that. Thick lips, big green eyes. But my brains. Three years old and she's drawing, she's talking, she's reading. And I'm teaching her every day so she has a better shot at this world than I did. See this tattoo of a flower below my ear? Know what that is? Oh, shit, I told you already, didn't I? Duh. Well, it's all about her now. I'm never letting Bryant fuck-face see her again, not that he'd want to. You know, he actually got married again. You believe that? To another actress, of course. Oh, you're gonna love my baby. Jade. That's her name. Jade, like the colour of my eyes and my tattoos. Take a right up ahead, I'm just at the end of that road."

Theo pulls into the driveway of a small white bungalow that has long icicles hanging from the porch. A plant holder covered in snow hangs from the eavestrough and resembles a white church bell. There are no lights on inside and the front windows look like black holes even against the sooty night. They get out of the car.

"It's not much, but Roscoe let me keep it when he left, so I call it my home," says Theckla, searching through her pockets. "Is it cold or is it just me? Where the hell is my key? Oh, here. Hey, wait, aren't you gonna put this in your movie? You gotta put my baby in your movie. Start that camera."

Jake dutifully gets the camera out and they head to the door. This is what Jake records:

Exterior shot of the house. Theo and Theckla walk towards the white door. Theckla fumbles with the keys. The picture is dark and it's hard to see the expression on anyone's face. Their bodies move in and out of shadows like fugitives. Theo helps Theckla with the lock, and she leans over and gives him a long kiss on the mouth. Finally she puts the key in and opens the door. Inside there's not enough light and the picture is dim and grainy, like images from a bad surveillance camera. Sounds of crying, a rising and falling of a small voice seems to pulse under the screen.

Theckla calls out, "Jade? Jade, honey, what's the matter? Oh, hell, where's that light switch?"

The lights go on and the picture flashes hot white, then quickly adjusts to reveal a large living room designed around one brown wooden table, a La-Z-Boy chair, and an old television set in the far left corner beside a sad-looking plastic Christmas tree. Remnants of tinsel dangle helplessly from its branches. The walls are painted off-white, only they appear more like white that has gone off with time. The carpeted floor (also off-white, in the same way as the walls, but dirtier) is strewn with crumpled clothes and toys, the kind of disarray that marks the absence of habits. In the far corner of the room a child in polka-dotted flannel pyjamas lies shivering and crying, a wet stain pooling underneath her. It's Theckla's daughter, Jade. Jake swings the camera towards her and notices something covering Jade's hands. He zooms in on the little fingers, first the soft squares that are her fingernails and then a dark substance in her palms. A moment later he recognizes it as shit. It's smeared across the pink dots on her pyjama top.

"Mommy! Mommy!" Jade cries out when she sees Theckla.

Jake's body stiffens at the room's rancid odour, but he steadies himself and continues to focus the camera on Jade. Theckla bursts into the picture.

"What happened to you, Jade?" Theckla demands, her voice pinched with edginess. "You got out of bed, you bad girl! You made caca in your pants. Is that what you did? What have I told you about that! Bad, bad girl. All over the carpet. I have guests and you've been bad. I'm too tired for this right now, Jade, too tired."

Theckla kneels down and picks up her child, stiffening her muscles so she holds Jade at arm's length. Jake moves in closer to shoot, and Theckla turns to him with the crying baby in her outstretched arms.

"He took all the furniture," she says directly into the camera lens, her eyes bloodshot and watery. "When Roger left me he took everything except his goddamn La-Z-Boy. That bastard. I'm sorry about Jade. She doesn't usually do this. I'm really sorry."

Then she puts the child on the floor and gives it a nasty cuff on the head. "Go to bed, Jade. Now! You've been a very bad girl and Mommy is angry. Go to the washroom and clean yourself up."

But Jade doesn't move. Like a stuffed doll, she falls down and starts crying again, louder and more hysterically, the keening rhythm of fear scraping and ripping at the back of her throat. Her whole face seems to leak tears onto her stained clothes and soon it glazes over with wetness, glistening as if wrapped in plastic.

Jake zooms in on Jade's wailing face and Theckla's voice careens into the picture from out of frame.

"Look what you've made Mommy do in front of her friends. Now I have to clean up your mess. You know what I'm going to do to you in the morning? Yes you do. Now stand up and go to bed! Momma's not going to help you."

Jake pulls back to get a wide shot of the whole room. He sees Theckla sitting cross-legged beside the shit stain, lighting a cigarette and throwing the match in front of her. No one says a word and soon Jade's crying is no more noticeable than the toys on the floor – part of the general disarray of the house. The ashes from Theckla's cigarette fall to the carpet and Jake notices that little black burns mark the entire room. Dull sequins on an old costume. Several empty bottles of wine and gin are knocked over under the table. *Gin, just like Momma*, Jake thinks, getting them on tape.

It's the perfect set for Theckla, Jake ruminates coldly. All the randomness of a hopeless, but not abandoned place – which makes its tragedy less conclusive. Theckla's life, he realizes, teems with resilience and failure, the two basic ingredients of a good television story. Even the bleak lighting is right. He points the camera at Theckla and kneels down in front of her.

"I'm a good mother, I really am," Theckla whispers directly into the lens. "She's such a tough kid sometimes, but I'm a good fucking mother."

Theo moves into frame and kneels down beside Theckla. From his pocket he takes out a chequebook and fills it in.

"Take this, Theckla, I want you to have it," Theo whispers, handing her the cheque.

"What is it?"

"Just cash it tomorrow, it'll help."

Theckla looks down at the cheque and instantly starts wailing.

"Oh Christ, Theo, I can't, it's too much, it's too much."

"Take it, okay? I don't need it any more. Do me a favour."

And then Theo lifts up Jade, holds her close, and kisses her on the head. He makes soft sounds that mimic the parental language of comfort and walks to the bathroom, holding her gently. Before he leaves the room, he turns back to Jake and says, "Turn it off. That's all I want you to see."

"What did you give her?" Jake asks, still holding the camera.

"None of your business. Now shut it off."

The little red light on the camera goes out, fading the picture to the black sound of Theckla crying. Jake sits down on the floor and soon falls asleep amidst the smell of smoke and shit and cold night air, just some of the things that never show up on film.

November 14, 1998

Frogs. Frogs with no legs. Frogs with legs bent backwards. Frogs with no eyes. Frogs with one limb missing. Frogs with no feet. Frogs with webbed feet grown together. Dead frogs. Blind frogs. Hermaphrodite frogs. The glass display cases are filled with frogs pinned to white boards displaying the lexicon of deformity. The woman on the podium is from Minnesota, where the frog crisis is breaking, and her voice is pitched with urgency. I imagined earlier that it would be more croaky, and I'm a bit disappointed that it's not. Even a cheap form of consistency is helpful on occasion. She's so short that it's hard to see her face behind the bouquet of microphones, but her voice penetrates into every part of the room, like the pins holding the frogs on the white boards.

The whole place has the fleshy aura of imminent disaster, but no one here can seriously understand why frog deformities in Minnesota mean that we're on the brink of utter demise. There's something nervous and medical in everyone's face, and I get caught up in the abstracted sense of fear. I like it, forget that I haven't eaten since breakfast.

Actually, all I can think about is fishing with Pop, baiting our hooks with little frogs, which he claims are the best for catching small-mouth bass. Slip the hook right under the mouth in the white skin. Try not to make it come out the eye. These are Pop's instructions, and he only gives them once. Then we cast the frogs out on the end of a three-pound test line and watch the little pebble weights drag them down to the rocky bottom where the bass feed. Mostly we don't catch anything, and after five or six casts the frogs usually die, their legs extended out in that lazy exhaustion of old bait. Every few minutes Pop tells us to get a fresh frog because fish won't bite unless they're attracted by the movement of something alive. Pop is an impatient fisherman, likes to move around trying four or five different spots every hour, changing bait, experimenting with his casting technique, reorganizing the tackle box, switching to lures, checking the anchor line. He fishes like the lake owes him something, like it's a bad debtor, and he gets frustrated when it doesn't pay up. I guess this defeats the reason for going fishing in the first place, but somehow Pop finds the ordeal relaxing. So we tear around the bay baiting frogs and casting into choppy water until the sun sets into burnt gold and the bugs come out and Pop guns the boat home with the running lights on, the wind slapping his silent face as he curses the barren lake. That's what I'm thinking about at this conference, looking at all the deformed frogs from Minnesota.

From the podium the short professor explains that frogs are a "sentinel" species, meaning that what happens inside their bodies indicates what can happen inside ours. Somehow we're closely linked to frogs on the evolutionary chain. We share the same renal systems or something. This rather complicated piece of logic doesn't go over well with the nervous crowd – they're not very keen to be so closely linked to slimy amphibians, which is why the professor is having such a hard time convincing people that if frogs are dying now, it won't be long before we start dropping off as well. Desperate for support, the professor mentions the polluted Love Canal in New York, and how residents there eventually developed abnormal chromosomes and low sperm counts five years after she noted the same problems in the local frog population. Silence. Then she reels off some frightening stats about the toxins in our ecosystem, how pesticides and acid rain have poisoned our water supply, how our biosphere is failing and blah blah blah. For all her bluster, it's hardly as dramatic as a car accident or a murder scene, and I wonder why I've dragged myself all this way to look at frogs. It's not helping me and I start to lose focus.

Then again, maybe she's right. Maybe the disaster that's going to get us all begins with frogs. Maybe it's not something dramatic like a nuclear bomb or a serial killer or a random act of violence, maybe it's just some colourless corruption that wipes out frogs, tadpoles, and all the other slimy creatures, until one day it gets all the little children, too.

I imagine whole neighbourhoods in Minnesota where kids are born with one leg, with webbed feet, half male, half female, playing on the swings with blind kids, retarded kids, and kids with crooked limbs, while the short professor runs around the parents yelling, "I told you to watch the frogs, didn't I?"

Frogs are the plague species, I remember that from childhood. At the Passover seder Pop used to sing the song about the ten plagues of Egypt and we'd join him, dipping our baby fingers in the cup of red wine and dabbing it onto our plate: one for every plague. Blood, Locusts, Darkness, Frogs . . . all the way to the death of the first-born son. Old Testament signs. Frogs. The fourth plague. Good for catching bass.

I leave the conference still thinking of fishing with Pop. We bait our hooks with the sentinel species, enjoying the few moments left on the bay when we were still ignorant of the signs of the future.

FAMILY VIEWING

Six in the morning in February's North Ontario cold is the other side of silence, everything laid open and amplified, when clouds scudding across the sky can sound like bedsheets ripping. If all hours were six o'clock, Theo might go deaf from the details of the world. He's always believed that the deepest secrets are revealed in the small actions and gaps to which no one pays attention: the pulling sound of his mother's mouth as she drags on another cigarette after dinner, the dead river snaking through the Rosedale golf course, the drip of intravenous sliding down the tubes into his father's veins. He listens for the little agonies buried under the silence of moving along and measures his truth from there.

Lying in bed back at the HorseTrail Motel, Theo watches his brother sleep, the blankets rising and falling to the meter of Jake's breathing. Jake betrayed him with the coverage of Fenwick, Theo knows that, but he doesn't blame him. Jake's simply listening to the wrong rhythms. He's deaf to his own violence so he doesn't know what he's doing wrong. Theo is here to help.

Quietly Theo slips out of bed and goes to the bathroom to drink some water. He has a gnawing hangover, but feels good about Theckla. She'll do better with the money, she deserves better. The floor's cold and Theo curls up his toes, balances on his heels while he examines himself in the mirror. He stares back at his face, moving his mouth into a smile, then a frown, like an actor warming up before a show. Opens his mouth wide and looks deep into his red throat, which is burnt raw by cigarettes. Exploring this simple facial vocabulary relaxes him, because he's spent years reducing his face to its most basic expressions: frowns, smiles, blankness. In Theo's mind these are the only gestures he requires because action, not expression, is the best form of communication. As far as he's concerned, faces are beside the point, vague and uncertain, masking authenticity with a runny set of signals no one can really interpret. Make-up, lipstick, eyeliner, skin cream, white teeth, photos – the whole industry is just about hiding a face within a face. If he could, he'd erase the human face altogether, destroy the option of image and give people more dexterous hands. Only hands can know certainty. Hands have no secrets. Over the black territory of unknowing, people send trembling hands. Hands are action, hands are faith.

In any case, his face is a poor indicator of his identity, so he closes his eyes to see his real self on the screen of memory. It projects into his mind and shimmers metallic and undeniable: a coin, a key, an axe. A solid tool that does the right thing, that doesn't cower away from its duty. For a second he reflects back on Ranklin Demoins, the horrible way Ranklin died, the blood spitting from his neck. *Was the forest worth this death?* It's an incalculable equation, but Theo believes, has to believe, that it was the right thing to do.

The air in the bathroom dries with electric heat against the cold and rises onto his face. He notices the scar under his chin and remembers where it came from. He's six years old, chasing the neighbour's dog beside the cut lawns. Trips on his shoelace. His chin hits the hot asphalt road, the pain reaching his brain along with the sound of the dog's nails clicking as it runs away. He doesn't tell his mother or father about the accident. He hides in the bedroom and hopes no one will notice the damage. Not their problem. Holding his hand under his chin, he waits for the blood to stop. Blood congeals under direct pressure, that's what Momma once told him. It still makes sense. Now that Pop's dead. Now that Ranklin's dead. Now that his own brother has betrayed him. Direct pressure, right now. He opens his eyes, splashes cold water on his face, and rinses his mouth. The water tastes metallic.

It's time to leave. Theo walks over to Jake's bed, puts one hand over Jake's mouth and uses the other to pinch his nose shut. It's a joke they used to play as kids, waking the other person by cutting off their air supply. Five seconds go by. Six. Seven.

Jake tries to exhale, then inhale, then exhale again, but the used air bounces back into his lungs and hits the inside of his face like a boot. His body jolts awake.

"What the . . ." Jake starts to say and twists his body away from Theo's hands. His eyes open wide, then retreat to a tight squint. "Would you grow up?"

"Time to move, brother," says Theo, giving Jake a light slap on the head. "Sleep is for the dead."

"Yes, master. Should I kiss your ass too?"

"We have to keep moving."

Jake closes his eyes again. The last thing he wants to do is move. He should be with Rachel, but he can't leave Theo. He needs time to think about what has happened in the last few days, to reflect on the chaos, to stand back for a moment and try to be alone. It's an impulse he often has in the city, and sometimes he drives out to a remote location, sometimes a farmer's field or a dirt concession road, where he knows no one expects him to be. Then he gets out of the car and stands perfectly still for an hour, closing his eyes and trying to find solitude. He always fails. Within seconds he starts imagining all the signals stitched deep into the air around him – the radio waves, the television waves, the sub-levels of voices – imagines how an antenna might pick up stories from hundreds of different places, might make the silent air talk, sing, move in pictures. Stories buzz in the air everywhere, pulling, scratching, tearing at his skin, making solitude and reflection impossible.

Jake opens his eyes, grabs the remote from the bedside table, and flips on the TV. On the screen a farmer dressed in a bloody gown says to the camera, "We're about to open a new abattoir because the emu and ostrich industry is ready to fly, even if the animals can't."

"Why do you have to turn that thing on as soon as you get up?" asks Theo, starting to pack his bag.

"I think my show's on," replies Jake vacantly. "They rerun it in the morning. I want to see how they're coping with my absence."

On Channel 3 a basketball coach says, "The real key to success is off-court cohesiveness, the way the players go to the movies together in their off time."

"That TV is gonna be the death of you," says Theo. His voice is low and hoarse from cigarette smoke.

Jake nods. "Whatever."

"I mean it. You think TV's part of your life, but actually, you're part of its life."

"Too early for a lecture, Theo, way too early."

"Just look at yourself. First thing in the morning surfing the tube for your own mug. Pathetic. I find this sad, I really do." He puts a toothbrush and one of the motel towels into the bag.

"Try not to cry."

"I think you should quit the show, Jake, let them find someone new to do your job. I really do. Get out of TV altogether and work with me for a while." He stuffs in a turtleneck and a few pairs of socks.

"Appreciate the offer," Jake says, trying unsuccessfully to recall what he said the day before at the staff meeting and if, indeed, they've already found someone new to do his job. *I should probably call in, let them know I'm okay. Call Rachel, too, maybe talk to her mother.* Thoughts of the confusion he left back in the city send a chill through his body and he pulls the blankets up closer to his face.

"You realize that you're starting to resemble everyone else on TV, don't you?" Theo asks, his hands packing down the clothes. "Seriously. The modulated voice. The make-up. We used to make fun of people like that. Even Momma used to mock those dicks on the news, remember? When I watched you cover the Fenwick crisis, I thought, Jesus, my brother's becoming a first-class phony. He really doesn't give a damn about what I'm doing out here."

"I said I was sorry about that."

"Tell me something. Are you even in control of what you say or do the sponsors feed you the script?"

"Yes, Theo, the big bad corporations control the airwaves, and when I say the wrong thing I find a horse's head in my bed. Oh, please, let it go."

"I don't think anyone's in control – if you want to know the truth – except maybe the box itself. I just read this book by a sociologist, can't remember his name, someone out in Fenwick gave it to me, and it argued that all of you – you actors, hosts, commercial pitchmen – all of you live for the TV itself. It gives you appetites and desires, it tells you what's acceptable and what's not, how to behave and all that. That's why you get addicted to it. The pictures own you, not the other way around. That's what the book said anyway. Wish I could remember the title." He flips some spare camera tapes into the bag.

"Taking correspondence courses in first-year media theory?"

Theo keeps talking, ignoring the comment. "You know that priest I told you about, the one in Bangkok? He owned absolutely nothing. Total ascetic. He used to say that to be free you had to give up your desire to own things."

"Thought he was a Catholic, not a Buddhist."

"He was, but that's what he believed. Just like that book says. You get so attached to the things you own that soon they end up owning you."

Jake laughs. "Sounds more like a Reverend Moon sermon. I hope you didn't give him all of your money?"

"Never had any to give, at the time that is. I would have, though." Theo rubs his jaw pensively. "So I'm just wondering why you can't shut off that tube and simply be with me. Is that so much to ask?"

"Just *be*?" Jake says, rolling his eyes. "As in, Zen-out, catch the vibes, swap auras?"

Theo puts a stray sock in the bag. "You can be as smart-assed as you like, but he's right. That box is your master."

On Channel 4 a man reads the news in Italian and pictures of a car accident flash across the screen.

"I wonder if they'll get a replacement for me," Jake ponders aloud, trying to change the subject. "Maybe I've been fired. Wouldn't that make you happy?" He continues to surf, the colours of the TV flickering outwards and absorbing into the blandness of the room, smudging the place into the colour of transience. He closes his eyes and bathes in the kinetic light, the need for sleep muting his thoughts of Rachel.

On Channel 5 programmed synthesizer music plays over an infomercial, but the signal is bad and the text unreadable. An elevator-music version of an old Beatles hit fills the room like fog.

Theo says, "Sometimes when I miss you, Jake, when I really just want to be close, I try to find your show on TV, and honestly, it freaks me out. The TV I mean. Every channel's in this weird state of apocalyptic panic. It's all 'last-chance offers,' 'blow-out sales,' and 'don't miss this final opportunity.' Do you ever notice that? But it doesn't matter in the least if you miss any of it. The same stuff will be on tomorrow, sure as the sunrise."

Jake opens his eyes and shakes his head with annoyance. "Spare me the 'Good Morning, fellow residents of hell' routine. I'm exhausted from last night's reunion tour."

But Theo continues to talk, throwing his personal items more deliberately into the bag. "All the clips of bombings and car accidents and dead bodies, I don't get it. Must terrify people, because they sure don't like to see it in real life, trust me on that. So when I'm looking for your show I get to thinking about people sitting on their couches, all shit-scared of the virtual corpses and fires on screen, muttering to themselves, 'There I go but for the grace of God.'"

"There but for the grace of God go I," Jake corrects him.

"Exactly! But the weirdest part, to me anyway, is watching some of that truly disgusting footage, and then the next thing you know, wham! you've got a commercial asking you to buy some tampons. And people do, don't they? They buy all that stuff. It's this frenzy to get as much stuff as possible before it's too late, before the end comes, before it's one of them on TV in an accident. People think they're consuming, but they're not. They're preparing for that final battle. They're stocking up." He packs some socks, batteries, and sweatshirts.

"That's a good theory, Theo," Jake says. "I'll have to remember that one. Stocking up."

On Channel 8 a wrestling match announcer screams, "Here comes the champ, the icon of icons, Hulk Hogan, to shred some muscle. Just look at that specimen!"

Jake watches the chemically enlarged blond wrestler burst through a curtain and rush towards the ring. He hasn't seen TV in a few days and it soothes him. Something about the consistency, the way it accepts every eye so readily, its generous colours and warm light, the way the random images play together to make new stories. Somewhere in that great electric mystery he suspects he'll find himself, located within the mob of images, contributing, working, communicating.

His legs cramp under the sheets as the wrestling match on Channel 8 progresses, the monstrous Hulk Hogan flexing his steroid-poisoned muscles and the crowd cheering madly. A marvellous spectacle of theatre. Jake's show plays on the next channel, and for a moment he fears clicking the FORWARD button on the converter. Will he still be there? Or has he been replaced, fished out of the invisible reservoir of flowing images and sent into space to float forever, unwatched? The curtains of the room flutter in the morning wind and for a brief moment he wishes he had never been on TV. He'd like to be part of the audience, like to let the TV entertain him, sweep him up in strange and wonderful stories that have nothing to do with his life. If he sees himself on screen it might break the peace, might bring on gaseous memories of taping and script reading, the sludgy faces of Stonebane, Zeemanvitz, Kelly Gordon. And then all the images will coalesce and become Rachel.

Theo zips up the bag and the heater in the corner snaps with an electrical charge. Jake flicks the button on the converter to his own show.

Channel 9, *The Jake Connections*. A black woman sits in the guest chair recounting in excruciating detail how she hid her lesbian affair from her husband and her kids. She wears a shawl pulled back over her hair, her high forehead bisected by one deep line, a crossbeam that seems to support the weight of her heavy facial features. He reads the red text at the bottom of the screen – "Today: Coming Out of the Closet to Your Family." The camera sways around the woman, but Jake can't remember the particular show. Something's missing from the set. The camera pulls out and pans over to where Jake should be sitting. He isn't there. Instead, Dylan O'Sullivan leans back happily, blond hair gleaming with light, mouth moving, teeth flashing. He looks just like Jake, fatuous and fit, the same as all young men on TV. Dylan's make-up catches and shapes the light to display his perfect features. In shock, Jake flicks the TV back to Channel 7 and puts the remote down on the orange blanket. He's been replaced.

On Channel 7 a beautiful woman with red hair is reporting from outside the Jacobsons' snow-covered cabin. Behind her four police officers stand in a circle around two black snowmobiles, the vast expanse of grey beyond them recedes deep into the back of the picture. Theo looks up, sees the place that he just left on screen, and darts over to watch.

". . . According to Detective Ian O'Malley, Jacobson was at this cottage only twenty-four hours ago, apparently leaving early yesterday morning. The cottage belongs to his family. Since the shooting of Rachel Anne Poiselle, the movements of Network TV star Jacob Jacobson can only be described as bizarre. Doctors at Mount Sinai Hospital report that he fled his room early yesterday morning posing as a doctor, and that he took with him a bag full of prescription drugs." A map of the city appears on screen and the location of the hospital is circled by a yellow electric pen. The woman's voice continues. "He then proceeded to the Network offices, where my exclusive source says he badly disrupted a staff meeting, reportedly attacking news anchor William Stonebane and setting off the fire alarm. When called to verify this, the Network president refused to comment." The yellow electronic line connects the hospital to the Network building. "Leaving the Network, Jacobson fled up here, to Georgian Bay, his family retreat."

The picture cuts to a few images of the cottage on Georgian Bay, and then the woman with the red hair comes back on screen. "In fact, in a bizarre coincidence, Jacob's brother Theodore, a well-known environmental and political activist, is the leading suspect in the recent death of a logger at the stand-off in Fenwick Park on Vancouver Island. Police in British Columbia are on the hunt for his whereabouts, but he too has gone missing. Police fear the two brothers might have gone underground together."

Theo grabs the remote from the bed and turns up the volume.

"A press conference at the Network is tentatively set for later today so President Greta Watt can give her thoughts on the Jacob Jacobson affair. Meanwhile, Rachel Anne Poiselle remains in intensive care at Mount Sinai Hospital. And Jacob Jacobson, her lover, and now the prime suspect in the shooting, is still at large. I'll have more exclusive coverage on the breaking story of the Network's fugitive star at the end of the hour. This is Charlene Rosemount, live from Georgian Bay for your number-one source of news, the Street-Beat, Channel 7."

"The prime suspect?" Jake sits up in bed, almost breathless. "What the hell is going on? They think I shot her? I just found her, for God's sake, I called the ambulance! That cop thinks I did it? I don't know who shot her."

"Doesn't feel too good to have your life fucked with, does it, Jake?" Theo says, a thin smile oozing across his lips. "Do you see what I mean now?" He walks over to the TV and kicks the screen with his steel-toed boot. The box shatters and buzzes. Broken glass rains onto the carpet. A grey white dust floats up and collects around Theo, glowing with an indistinct electric light, and then recedes into the orange-brown blankness of the roadside motel.

"I love doing that," announces Theo. "Should have done it the moment we got here."

Jake presses his hands against his eyes. "We really have to go back," he says. "No more screwing around. I have to see Rachel and straighten everything out."

"Then let's get going."

□ □ □

The early morning is grey-black in the unexposed negative of winter. Jake listens to the wipers swish back and forth on the windshield, shaping the salt debris into arcs and making a bandage of gauzy noise that dresses the growing tension between the brothers. The road before them is swallowed by the deep yawn of flat horizon, almost daring them to feel acknowledged by the leaden landscape. The only other vehicles on the highway are transport trucks carrying loads of goods from one place to another, moving with dumb purpose through another empty morning that measures the non-stop culture of freight. The trucks kick up salt mixed with dirty snow, which slashes hard against the car when Theo passes them. A thin, hard shield of ice covers the fields.

Theo doesn't speak. He smokes steadily until the inside of the car becomes hazy and thick. He decides to take a side-road because the redheaded reporter has put them on TV and he fears getting pulled over by police. Now the car moves urgently over the messy two-lane road, the headlights spraying light before them in loose columns which don't so much illuminate anything as put borders on the shadows: granite rock face blown through by highway engineers, winter fields, dead cornstalks half covered in snow, bent fence poles and broad barbed wire meant for cattle, not humans. Everything abandoned, waiting for warmth.

They drive by a lone transport truck and Jake thinks of Theckla alone in her house with Jade, wonders what unasked-for freight the morning will deliver to her. *Why did Theo give her a cheque*, he wonders, *saying he didn't need it any more*? The events from the past two days swirl through his mind: Rachel's bloody face, the orange piss, Tasso's helpful hands, the white toes he can't feel, his face fished out of the waves and waves of blue-green TV, the prime suspect, the thrush of the tires . . . everything charging forward out of control, and now in stark contrast to the still fury of Theo, who presses down on the accelerator and hurtles them home. Jake buckles his seat belt.

Soon they're the only car on the dark road, leaving the trucks on the main highway to speed towards Toronto. Jake gazes at his brother hunched over the wheel, smoking cigarettes, and he notices how Theo's face is veiled by severe concentration. Something in Jake stirs into an emotion he recognizes as sadness. His brother is too certain, he lacks the paranoias and distractions, the ambiguities and distortions that Jake believes are normal. He senses that something in Theo has changed. That he has hardened into some new intention, as if in the two silent months since he's been away in Fenwick Park there's been a little death, and then this new density of becoming. But becoming into what? Jake can't recognize the shape – it's too large, too amorphous – but he senses its bulk, the solidity that curves the air around Theo's shoulders. The car skids over black ice and then bites back into the road.

"Can I ask you something, Theo?"

Theo doesn't turn his head to Jake. He stares straight ahead through the slash of wipers. "Shoot," he says.

"That logger, the one that died . . ."

"Demoins."

"Right. Did you really watch it happen?"

"I told you already."

"It was quick, right? Real sudden."

"What?"

"The accident. He died instantly?"

"You're playing journalist with me, Jake. Don't do that."

"I'm interested. Was it instant or did he scream for help?"

"He just went down. That's it. Saws were buzzing all over the forest. Rain hitting the leaves. Everything so loud that I couldn't tell if he screamed or not. Probably did."

The wipers crash back and forth and Jake's thoughts flash to an image of himself. He's in the bloody hallway at the university and Rachel is crying out to him, begging for aid. He stands so still watching her, unable or unwilling to help. Down the hall a dark shape moves quickly, a red light wavers and disappears. He shakes his head.

"So you didn't try to help him?"

"Like I said, I ran over, but I was too late. Chain flew off the saw, hit his neck, and that's that." Theo snaps his fingers. "It wasn't personal. Knelt down and told him so."

"What do you mean?"

"Like the Natives used to do to fresh kill. Apologize to it for the pain. Thank it for sacrificing itself. Like we did to that bear in the park. Remember?"

"You talked to him?" Jake asks, incredulous.

"Not really." Theo ashes his cigarette impatiently. "He was already dead, or on his way. Told him I was sorry this had to happen. That he was dying for a purpose. You know, same as the bear. He spat on me, actually, all angry and confused, but anger makes you understand. It's good that way, forces people to face things they don't want to face. Still, it was too late to help, even if I wanted too."

"But did you *want* to?" Jake asks more urgently.

Theo drags on his smoke. "Doesn't matter what *I* wanted. He's dead all the same. That's what counts."

Jake reaches forward to turn up the fan on the heater and soon the thick pall of smoke inside the car starts to circulate. "What was it like to see someone die?" he asks.

Theo stares through the windshield as snowflakes explode and melt on the glass.

"Was it frightening? Sad?" Jake presses.

"This isn't your TV show."

"Were you uncomfortable, paralysed, stunned?"

Theo doesn't answer.

"Ecstatic? Turned on? You can tell me."

"Don't do this, Jake."

"You felt some pleasure. A high. Like you'd rather watch than help. Is that it?"

"That's not it at all," Theo says, his voice straining to hold back his rising anger.

"Then what, Theo? Let's talk about this."

Theo hits his hand on the steering wheel, as if to physically stop the conversation. "Let's talk about you instead," he yells. "How'd you feel when you saw your lover all shot up? You answer me and then I'll answer you."

Taken aback by his brother's animosity, Jake grits his teeth. Images of Rachel pulsate through his head. He falls silent.

"Not so cocky any more, are you?" Theo says, finally glancing over at Jake. "Too close to home."

"No, it's a fair question," Jake replies hoarsely. "I was confused when I saw her. She seemed so far away, like I wasn't even in the same room with her, like if I reached out my hand I wouldn't be able to touch her, not then, not ever. She wasn't real, wasn't the person I knew. She was so, so unreachable. And yes. Maybe there was this weird pleasure. But that's it. I stood there, watching and . . . I . . . I guess I just wanted to know what it was like for you."

They sit inside the sound of the car tearing along the icy highway, neither of them talking.

"This guy I once worked with in China," Theo says, abruptly changing the topic. His voice softens and he turns down the heater. "Brit. Bad teeth, I remember; you know, the whole ex-pat thing. I think he's dead now or gone back to London. Anyway, he'd been in Beijing for something like ten years working with dissident groups, setting up fax lines and distributing leaflets. Remember, this was when Deng was still on the ball and nasty. Before the reforms. The guy was part of the Tiananmen Square protest, an organizer, and he was right in there when the military stormed it. Saw the soldiers open up at the crowds, at his friends. Nowhere to go, he said. Too crowded to move, bullets pumping into the mass of bodies. Thousands of people went down, that's what he told me, not hundreds like we heard on the news. Said it took the Chinese authorities days to wash all the blood off the streets – and they were using fire hoses."

Theo pauses and reaches for another cigarette. He snaps his thumb over the lighter and an orange flame erupts and then dies. He tries it again and then a third time unsuccessfully until he realizes the lighter is not working. He tosses it into the back seat and reaches down to push in the car lighter on the dash. Jake watches him carefully.

"I asked him what it was like to see that, to see a real massacre, and you know what? He didn't say it was horrible at all. Not frightening, either. No. Said it was *beautiful*. That's right. Said it was like watching a painter create a work of art. So I'm shocked, right? Think the guy's lost it. But he told me, he said that all those students went there knowing that some of them would die. *Hoping* some of them would. Because that was part of it, see? They all knew that violence was the only way to make their protest successful. Turn it into something symbolic, powerful. So when the guns went off – pop, pop, pop

– and the tear gas descended, and the tanks came roaring in, and there was fear and terror and panic, my friend just stood there and observed. Like watching an opera. Said some of his young Chinese friends actually ran into the fray so they could martyr themselves. Others tried to kill the soldiers, charging them with their bare hands, clawing at the helmets before they would be clubbed and beaten. Bodies everywhere. Violence as an art form, that's how he described it to me, violence as a conduit to greater ideals. Now what do you make of that?" Theo hauls deeply on his cigarette, making a sucking sound.

"I think the guy sounds like a fucking loon," Jake replies, growing uncomfortable by the turn in the conversation. "What's the point?"

"Point is, he's onto something. Violence as media. I thought you'd get into that."

"Sorry, Theo, but on my list murder's not really a negotiable sin. Neither is human sacrifice."

"I'm talking about something more subtle," Theo says. "I'm talking about ideas."

"Was Ranklin Demoins an idea?"

"Absolutely. That's my point."

"Well, then, I must have missed it."

"Look, one moment Demoins is just some poor schmuck cutting down trees, probably lives in a trailer park or some dingy apartment, goes out for a few drinks with the boys, just another little citizen going about his little business, warding off the boredom. But the second that chainsaw cuts through his neck, Ranklin Demoins stops being a nobody."

"That's right. He's dead."

"No, no, he's alive! More alive than he's ever been. This is what I'm getting at. Suddenly he represents a whole set of vibrant ideas in a way he never could have when he was struggling through his poor schmucky life. When people say Ranklin Demoins's name now they're also saying something about cutting down old-growth forest, something about the nature of protest, something about a hundred other things that they would never have been able to say so neatly. Ranklin gives us that economy, that literacy, that *richness*."

"And that's worth his life?" Jake cuts in, repulsed by what he's hearing from his brother. "Tell me you don't believe that, Theo, because I feel that there's something seriously wrong with the point you're making." He opens the window a crack and the wind rushes in, pushing the stale car air into a whirling, hissing circle.

"Get over how you *feel* about everything and try to look at things from a larger perspective," Theo continues, his voice as steady as the sound of the tires on the highway.

"You mean your perspective?"

"No. This isn't personal. It has nothing to do with me or with Ranklin Demoins. We're nothing. But the words 'Ranklin Demoins,' they're powerful. More powerful than real people. More powerful than TV images and newspaper articles. This is the unique technology of violence, do you see what I'm saying? It's about text and transmission. It's media, Jake, real media. I wish you'd open your mind to something new for a change." Up ahead the road bends sharply, and Theo has to brake to make the curve.

"Sometimes you scare me, Theo."

"Don't be afraid to be afraid. Now shut your window. It's getting cold in here."

Jake keeps the window open and breathes sharply from his nose as he lets Theo's words settle into his mind.

"You wrote that to me on a postcard from Fenwick. 'Don't be afraid to be afraid.' "

Theo takes his eyes off of the road and gazes at Jake. "I guess now you know what I mean."

At that moment a brown shape darts in front of the headlights. Theo whips his head forward and hits hard on the brake peddle. Jake's body lurches towards the dash and then his seat belt locks tight. The car skids, slews to the side, but it's too late. A dull thud comes from under the right fender, and the car careens heavily into the snowbank.

"We hit something!" screams Jake, panic releasing through his body. "Back up, Theo, back up. Hurry. I think it's under the car."

Theo revs the engine and the bumper dislodges from the snow. He reverses two feet along the shoulder, puts the car in park, and hits the high beams. The light flickers through the barbed-wire fence in front of them and is almost too faint to pick up the details of the brown shape on the road. The tips of dead cornstalks whisper in the snow-covered field, moving shadows. They've hit a dog.

They sit in silence, gazing dumbly out at the animal in front of them. The car pants in neutral and smoke from the exhaust curls up the trunk and blows through the crack in the window. It stinks.

"You hit it, you hit that dog," Jake says slowly. "It's hurt. Look, it can't move its back legs."

The prowling sounds of winter drown out the dog's whimpering, but Jake can tell that it's making noise, its jaw opening and closing through a hot curtain of breath. Scratching with its front paws at the ice, the dog attempts to get up, but its hind legs are collapsed and they twist awkwardly, like pieces from a broken geometry set. The bumper has shattered the dog's hip.

Little tufts of fur blow up intermittently from the dog's back and its ears are pressed flat against its nape in fear. It's hard for Jake to discern what colour and kind of dog it is: a tawny yellow or shallow brown, part German shepherd, part Lab, some careless mixture of farm mutt. The black spot of its nose resembles the toe of a boot, the mouth line an untied lace. The only true colour visible from the car is the dog's long pink tongue, gaudy against the rest of the background and thick with a white varnish of saliva. Jaws open and close. Front paws scratch. Curtain of hot breath. It can't get up.

"Let's get going," Theo says.

"Get going? Are you crazy? That dog's hurt. It's going to die." Jake's voice is high with tension, as if air can't reach his diaphragm. He stares at his brother incredulously.

"What do you want to do, Jake? Pick it up, go knocking on doors and ask people if they own a dead mutt?"

"Maybe."

"It's just a farm dog. It probably has no owner, lives off barn scraps. Let's go."

The dog stares into the headlights and its eyes fill with glazed white, the colour of frost. The wind blows without sympathy.

"We can't leave it here, Theo, we can't," Jake pleads.

"There's nothing we can do," Theo replies matter-of-factly. "It was an accident, we're in the middle of nowhere, and we have to get going. Do you have any idea how badly the police want to get hold of us? Weren't you *watching* this morning?"

Theo starts to put the car in drive, but Jake grabs his arm.

"We have to kill it," Jake insists. "You'll have to run it over."

"You're out of your mind. We're leaving." He tries again to put the car in gear, but Jake holds onto his arm.

"We're not leaving that dog in pain. At least we can put it out of its misery, you know, run it over to stop its suffering."

Theo almost laughs at the suggestion. "I'm not running over that dog, Jake. No way."

"Then I'll do it, all right? I'll do it." Jake tries to speak firmly, but his voice is still pitched high, as if it's not speaking on behalf of the rest of his body.

Theo considers Jake's suggestion, and his blank face subtly changes into a mixture of expressions number one and two: smile and frown. He lights a cigarette and recalls their camping trip in Algonquin Park: the bear steaming in front of him, Jake holding the flashlight, hiding in his sleeping bag, watching. Then the warm lake water cleaning off the blood. The hot fire cooking the meat. The black colander of sky, leaking light through the stars. Pioneers.

"You're not getting behind this wheel, Jake," Theo says slowly. "But if you want to kill that dog, grab the tire jack out of the trunk and get out there and do it yourself. Otherwise we're out of here."

Jake tries to process Theo's words, but squints his eyes, unable to.

"You mean, beat the dog to death?" he asks raggedly. "Is that what you mean?"

"I mean what I mean," Theo says, nodding. "There's a metal handle in the trunk. Take it and put that mutt out of its misery. Or don't. What do you want, Jake? Do it, or we get on our way. Doesn't matter to me."

The density around his brother that Jake sensed earlier seems to shift. Now it's darker and moving his way. It has changed like the weather – inevitable, atmospheric. He doesn't want to notice this.

"What's the matter with you, Theo? Run over the dog, run it over so it doesn't have to suffer. Come on, stop screwing around."

"Up to you, Jake," Theo replies, butting his cigarette casually. "Let's see you do something for yourself. No cameras, no audience, no commercial breaks. Just you doing the right thing all alone. Like I do all the time. Unafraid to be afraid. Kill the dog, Jake, put it out of its misery yourself. One swift hit to the head and you'll end its pain. It's God's work, Jake, go do it."

Theo taunts Jake, wants to see his brother experience the certainty of anger, wants him to know the blood price of doing good work. He watches Jake's breathing thicken into heaving rolls. The windshield starts to fog.

"You're crazy, Theo. What the hell's happened to you? This isn't about me, or you, it's about a dog. That's it, just a goddamn dog."

"So do it. You want to stop its pain, learn to do it yourself. Stop talking for once in your life and do something."

Jake hits the dashboard with his hand in frustration.

"Do you ever listen to yourself?" he yells. "I mean, all morning you've been talking about death and violence like you're the first person who's ever seen it. What about Pop? Do you remember that? I sat with Pop all night while you went off making funeral arrangements or whatever. Where the hell did you go anyway? I sat with his body, I held his hand, so fuck you and your moral high ground. You don't have a patent on pain."

"The dog, Jake, there's a dog outside."

"And Rachel," Jake continues, the heat of anger flushing his face. "I saw her pain. Real pain. I know things that you'll never know. Everyone suffers differently. Death isn't your private club."

"Stop making clever sound-bite speeches and go help the dog, Jake." Theo shoves Jake on the shoulder. "It's in pain. Go deal with it."

"You don't think I can, do you?" Jake replies, swiping away Theo's hand. "Why? Because I'm not a self-righteous activist? Because I'm a talk-show host? Because I didn't want to hack up some park animal just to feel like a macho pioneer? You're sick, you know that? Sick. Now open the trunk, open it!"

In a fury, Jake jumps out of the car and runs to the rear, banging on the trunk with his bare hands. "Open it, open it!" he screams hysterically.

The trunk clicks and Jake pulls it up and grabs the tire jack. Then he heads for the fallen dog. Inside the car, Theo quickly reaches back into his bag and takes out the video camera. Removing the cap, he pushes the red power button to ON and lifts it to his eye. He wants a record of this, too.

Outside the car the cold presses against Jake and his fingers start to sting against the metal handle of the jack. Exhausted by its futile effort to stand, the dog falls still and emits a low whine that mingles with the wind. Jake can see its rib cage pounding and feels his own fall into sync. The headlights of the car blaze into him as if they have weight. He looks back towards Theo but is blinded by the white light. He doesn't want to do this. He doesn't want to hit the dog, doesn't even know how. Swing the metal handle of the jack down on its head, or into its chest? How many blows will it take? Maybe the dog will live, maybe he should pick it up and force Theo to find its owner. The cold air bites into his fingers and he swings the metal jack through the air to get his circulation going.

The dog looks up at him with its big, disc-shaped eyes, intelligent enough to communicate real pain. It's half dead already, Jake thinks, remembering his father's body, how it seemed to be in between states. What is that called, Jake wonders, that liminal moment between life and death, when neither side takes precedence? He stands at this gap, gazing at the dog, at the invisible border between life and death, between sleep and dream, water and steam, two bodies making love. Rachel's body, unconscious somewhere, half alive, half dead. He stares again at the dog, at Rachel in the hall, both sets of eyes blazing with intensity. That same look, in perfect facsimile, replete with the paradoxes of need. *Click.* He can take the dog's picture, lie it next to Rachel's and compare them. No blood on the dog. *Click.* The pink tongue soft with sweat. *Click.* Needing his help and beautiful for it. *Click.* Both in between, at the gaps, undefinable.

The wind and light close in on him, some natural architecture of intimacy, dragging his attention to the dog. He can hear its quick breath and he has the urge to kneel down and touch it. Something elemental in him shifts. He wants to hold its head in his lap, stroke it, whisper words it cannot understand. But there's no vocabulary in this place. It's wordless, soundless. Pure white. Now he doesn't want to take a picture of this. He wants to stop the pain. If he stays here and waits maybe a meaning will appear, a revelation about himself he can track. If he waits long enough near the hurt dog he might learn something. He puts the jack on the ground and bends down to touch the dog's head.

And just then the car horn erupts, fracturing the moment.

"Come on, Jake, let's go," Theo yells from the window. With his right hand, Theo presses on the horn again, holding it down. The discordant sound pushes the intimacy from the air and howls out flat, loud, almost shaking snow from the cornstalks.

Jake starts to scream. "Shut up, Theo, shut that fucking horn up!" Picking up the jack, he runs back to the car, raises it high over his head and brings it down viciously on the hood. The car rocks under the blow, but Theo keeps one hand on the horn and the other holding up the video camera. He records the jack handle hitting the hood again and again. He zooms in on Jake's face. Records the creases around Jake's eyes getting deeper, Jake's mouth stretching to hold the anger, the burn in his cheeks smeared like jam. The horn continues to wail.

"The dog's in pain, Jake. Kill the dog, not the car," Theo calls out from behind the windshield. "The dog, put it out of its misery. Go on, do it."

The headlights and the sound of the horn surge around Jake in waves and he turns quickly back to the dog. Now! he urges himself. Go beyond the border. Close the gap. Right now. He lifts the handle into the ashen sky and brings it swiftly down on the dog's head. He hears the bones crack like pressure ice on the lake in early spring. He starts crying and screaming, swinging the handle violently again, up and down like a sump pump.

"I'm sorry, goddamn you, I'm sorry," Jake cries as the jack hits the soft body of the quiet animal.

It goes on for seconds, but the light and the cold and the metallic noise of the horn bend the time into a smooth disc, holding Jake for what seems like hours. He's inside the Möbius strip of pain, swinging the handle down again and again and crying, a record needle skipping on one off-note.

Then the horn stops. In the echoing silence there's a new sound. Machinery. A high whine and then nothing. Two men suddenly emerge from out of the cornfield, wearing snowmobile suits and black helmets. Theo quickly gets out of the car and moves up beside Jake, putting one hand inside his coat and holding the video camera in the other, low, around his hip. He's still rolling tape. A pair of snow machines are parked just along the fence alongside the field, almost hidden in shadow. Jake doesn't notice anyone. Splattered with blood, he leans over the corpse of the dog like a canopy, spent and empty.

"What the hell are ya doin' to my dog?"

An inert, blunt voice startles Jake, and he looks up to see two men standing over him.

Silence.

"I said, what are ya doin' to my dog?" the man repeats. His words are clipped by the wind, buzz-cut short.

The men hold their helmets in their hands like granite rocks. They're farmers, or look that way from their muted features – weathered and blank, as if they've never known the pleasure of surprise. The first man's sharp nose appears to have been broken several times: it dodges left under his brow, then takes a sharp right above his thin mouth. His light blue eyes are covered in a watery film and carry no discernible wisdom, even though he looks about fifty. His hair is cut so short that Theo can see the veins in his skull. The other man – taller by a good half foot but twenty years younger – hasn't shaven in days, and his yellow facial hair bristles like hay. Father and son, Theo concludes, although it's hard to tell. They're as featureless as the land around them, geologic in their simplicity. Body heat rises from their heads as the men examine the scene methodically.

Theo says nothing, but stares evenly at the men, unafraid. The older of the two wipes his nose with the back of his glove. As if on cue, the younger man in the black snowmobile suit walks towards Jake and grabs the jack handle. Jake backs off, unsure of how to react.

"Who the hell are–" Jake starts to say.

"Shut up," the young man hisses, snapping the handle viciously into Jake's stomach. Jake collapses over the dog, his breath expelling like a solid ball of heat. Then the man lifts the metal handle over his head with one hand and brings it down brutally on Jake's back. Jake cries out and then starts to moan with pain.

The younger man looks over to his father, as if waiting for instructions, and through some invisible communication, starts to move towards Theo.

"I don't think so, bud," Theo whispers, opening his jacket to reveal the handle of a gun. The son stops, but doesn't change his expression. It's the same as Theo's: blank, deep, and durable. From his hip, Theo keeps the camera pointing at Jake. Recording. No one speaks.

The older man sniffs loudly through his twisted nose and nods again to his son, who shuffles over to Jake and kicks him off the dog with his boot. Dropping the jack handle, he bends down and picks up the dead animal, holding it gently next to his chest.

With one last, almost curious look at Theo, the two men move quietly back into the field with their dog, and then the sound of their snowmobiles rattles the air and they disappear into the cornstalks, leaving Jake and Theo alone on the side of the highway.

Some morning light starts to leak up the skyline, brightening the bottom edge of the grey horizon. Pointing the camera at Jake's prone body one last time, Theo zooms in close on Jake's closed eyes until they fill the frame. Then he flicks off the POWER button and puts the camera back in the car.

Jake coughs up blood. Theo walks over to him and helps him up slowly. Jake can hardly breathe, and buckles over in pain. He starts crying from confusion and shock. As they make their way carefully over the ice to the car, the headlights blind them and Theo pulls Jake close, holding him tightly with his hands against the big light, saying close to his ear, "You did good, Jake. I'm proud of you."

And then they pull away from the field and race towards Toronto, where morning is breaking and everything is starting to rise.

PRESS CONFERENCE

Reporters, producers, and police crowd the foyer of the Network, all preparing for Greta Watt to begin the press conference. Five camera tripods from different television stations stand near the entrance like guards, while four more people with heavy Betacams slung over their shoulders roam near the podium. Sound technicians wire microphones to the stand, twisting the little square station logos so they face forward like drink boxes on a supermarket rack. Photographers wind their film, journalists check their tapes, cell phones ring, beepers vibrate, klieg lights flash on, video-mounted sun-guns blaze, hundreds of wires hum and murmur with newly connected circuits of electricity, ready to beam everything out into frenzied radio waves and digital bits, separating into nodes and transmitters and then shrinking into one small story: the Jacob Jacobson affair.

"Don't take any shit in the scrum, Herb," Charlene Rosemount instructs her cameraman. Since her report last night from Georgian Bay, Charlene knows that she's the lead reporter on this story, and she's intent on not losing her position. "I want the best shot, front and centre. I don't care if you have to trample someone's baby to get it."

She flips open the mirror of her green compact to apply some more red lipstick when out of the corner of her eye she spots Gerald Dennis-Stanton.

"Oh, Christ, Herb, it's Stanton," she mutters. "He's going to be pissed at me for running that bit about Jacobson's brother. Do something, ask him where he bought his coat, I don't know. We don't have time for his preening."

Stanton pushes his way through the crowd towards Charlene, his Big Blues clouded by irritation. She's really going to get it, he seethes, not giving a beaver's ass what she thinks about his six-hundred-dollar coat – which, he reminds himself, is all class, at least to people in the proper circles.

"Too late, my lovely vixen master," Herb says, grinning at Charlene. "The print man cometh."

Stanton waves his hand frantically in the air to catch Charlene's attention, his notebook pages flaring out and rustling.

"Hi Stanton," she says coolly, checking her face in the mirror.

"Don't 'Hi Stanton' me," he bristles. "You stole my story! How dare you rip me off." Stanton throws back his head in what he hopes is a handsomely indignant pose.

"I have no idea what you're talking about, but I have work to do now," Charlene replies without looking up. "Why don't you give me a call and we can sort this out over a nice, long dinner?"

She tilts her head and smudges her lipstick between her lips sensuously.

Dinner? Stanton thinks, taken off guard. *Is this an opening?* He pauses while his vanity fights with his professional integrity for control of his mouth. For once, the latter wins out.

"No, thank you," he says furiously. "You took my tip about Jacobson's brother Theo and ran it yourself. You scooped me on my own story, and that, well, that's just not cricket where I come from."

"This is the news, Stanton, not one of your daddy's country clubs. Wake up, for Christ's sake. Besides, now that the story is on TV, people might actually read your article."

It's a cheap shot, but one Charlene knows will annoy Stanton. It does. He thrusts his notebook indignantly into her face, the Big Blues glowing with fury.

"I work for the number-one paper in this country!" he sputters. "And that was my source. I told you about Jacobson's brother. *I* did the work for that angle, *me*. I got to Theo through sheer, old-fashioned reporting skills."

"You're whimpering, Stanton," Charlene accuses, pointing with her finger. "That's so unattractive for such an attractive man. Isn't he attractive, Herb?"

"Gorgeous, just gorgeous," Herb says, patting Stanton on the shoulder. "That's a damn fine coat you're wearing, too."

"How would *you* know?" Stanton snaps, shooting a condescending glance at Herb and then turning back to Charlene. "I bet you didn't even verify that source. Did you even bother to phone the Vancouver police?"

"Why would I do that when the tip came from such a brilliant newspaper reporter?" she asks, oozing crocodile charm. "I knew that you must have checked it out, and that's good enough for me. I only steal from the best."

"You got that right," Stanton blurts out, his vanity making a sudden recovery and wresting control of his mouth. "Well, you owe me dinner for the tip. I know a nice little bistro on–"

Ian O'Malley's hand clutches Stanton's shoulder and interrupts him mid-invitation.

"Hey, handsome, two minutes for looking so good. Why don't you stand over there? I've got to talk to Ms. Rosemount for a minute."

Stanton examines the hand on his new coat (the second hand in less than a minute) and notices the mustard smeared on O'Malley's fingers. *Damn it.* It'll cost twenty dollars to dry-clean the coat – and that might just be the beginning of a long, sartorial nightmare. Mustard is, as Stanton has heard so many times from his dry-cleaner, one of the real enemies of quality clothing. *This is all too much*, he thinks. *I've won awards, for God's sake!*

"I don't think the police should be playing favourites with the press, detective," Stanton says, lowering his shoulder and twisting his body away from the offending hand. "Whatever you say to her, you can say to me."

Another detective moves past O'Malley, and Stanton recognizes him as the man who pushed him into the snowbank the day before.

"Call off your goon, O'Malley," Stanton cries out in an effort to be tough.

"Stanton, you should stop watching so many bad cop movies," O'Malley laughs. *Goon*, he repeats to himself. He wouldn't use that kind of crap dialogue in *his* book. "Let him be, Roger," O'Malley says. "Stanton can stay if he wants."

O'Malley turns to Charlene and rubs his jaw slowly. He needs to be delicate, charming. Turning slightly to the left, he gives her a better view of his good side. *Make sure she doesn't see the burned ear. Establish trust with smooth bedside manner, be debonair and dangerous, intimate and intimidating.* He pauses before beginning, giving himself just enough time to think, *What a fucking good cop I am!*

"Nice touch with the lipstick, Ms. Rosemount. I know how the camera loves the colour red," he says huskily, using his TV knowledge as an opening.

"Looking for a job in make-up, O'Malley?" she asks, barely acknowledging his presence with so much as a peek up from her compact mirror. "I think there's a job at the station." A little burst of powder comes off her face as she dabs her cheeks with a round make-up pad.

"Not exactly what I had in mind," he replies. *Look at me when I'm talking to you*, he thinks, offended by her arrogance.

She avoids his eyes.

"I was quite surprised to see you up north at the Jacobson cottage, Ms. Rosemount."

"I do love the lake country, detective." She quickly winks at him, baiting his temper, and then continues dabbing her face.

O'Malley breathes deeply. "What I mean is, we had just got tipped off that Jacobson was up north and less than an hour later, you're already on the scene. Now, do me a favour and tell me how you found out about that place so quickly?"

She doesn't respond, hunching over her compact mirror as if to examine a minute blemish on her perfect skin.

"I think you and I have to start sharing a bit of our information," O'Malley presses. "That might help us both out."

"Herb, is somebody talking to me?" Charlene says, still engrossed in her own reflection. She flutters one hand near her ear. "I keep hearing this voice . . ."

Herb tries to suppress a laugh and can't.

Barely able to conceal his rage, O'Malley imagines what fun it would be to lock Charlene in a room and turn a high-powered fire hose on her. He tries to hide the nasty thought with a smile, as if to show her how much he appreciates her verbal jousting.

"You're funny, Ms. Rosemount. I like funny. Funny's good. I just think you and I have some information to share about a very urgent case, and I think we should do that right now."

O'Malley clenches his jaw tightly in an effort to sustain his artificial smile, and Charlene is reminded of an amateur ventriloquist testing out his technique. She thinks of how dearly he would like to get his hands on the black bag Tasso left behind for her at the café. Lifting her head, she stares him down.

"In case it hasn't filtered up to your cholesterol-clogged brain, O'Malley, I work for Channel 7, not the police department. You don't come near my information."

O'Malley forces himself to chuckle, as if she's just let slip another witticism, and he keeps the smile cemented to his face. He thinks again of the fire hose, how quickly it would wash away her cockiness and make her respect his position. *Smile,* he tells himself. *Smile.* "Again, you amuse me. But the comedy hour is over. How did you know Jacobson went up to Georgian Bay? How did you get there so quickly? No one knew about that tip but me and the squad from Parry Sound, and yet, you were there before any other reporters. That's fine detective work, Ms. Rosemount, I admire it. But again, I want to know how you got your information."

"She stole my tip about Jacobson's brother, detective," Stanton says, cutting in. "That was my lead."

"Shut up," O'Malley hisses at Stanton, then reverts back to

his pleasant tone. "Did, by chance, a cab driver named Leon Pastiche give you a call, Ms. Rosemount?"

"What cabby?" Charlene asks, with genuine interest. "I don't know of any cabby. Do you actually know something that *I* don't?"

The cement under O'Malley's smile finally gives out and he sucks on his teeth. "Listen to me, Miss Barbara fucking Walters, this is not a game. If you're holding back information or know of a witness, I'll book you as an accessory to the crime."

Charlene bursts out laughing.

"Read the law, buster; that is, if you can read," she snorts. "You can't threaten me. For one, you haven't even made an arrest yet, and for two, I was just following a tip. You want to control the press, send your résumé to China, I'm sure they could use a guy like you. In the meantime, I'll have my people fax you some notes on how the press gets treated in this country. It's quite instructive. Herb, roll the camera on O'Malley. I might as well interview him, since he isn't doing anything important." She seamlessly switches into her TV-interview voice as Herb swings around with the camera.

"Detective O'Malley, do the police think the Jacobson brothers are now working together?"

As she asks the question, she pulls a comb from her purse and starts to tease her hair.

O'Malley instantly puts his hand in front of the lens.

"You better tell me who you're talking to, because I think you're interfering with a police investigation," he growls.

Charlene ignores him and asks another question.

"Is the Network hiding information about Jacob Jacobson in order to protect him?"

"Don't mess with me, Ms. Rosemount, I'm warning you."

"Have you found the weapon used during the shooting?"

"I want to know your source!" O'Malley yells, almost lunging at Charlene. She doesn't move.

"Okay. Cut, Herb, this is a waste," she says, shaking her head at O'Malley's unco-operative manner. "Listen, O'Malley, obviously you know nothing I don't know. So here's the deal. If the woman finally dies and we can get ourselves a bona fide murder case, and you stop picking my ass and actually make an arrest, then I'll help you out with whatever I can. As it is, all we've got is a lot of rumours and one decent suspect. Once we get a body, then we can all cosy up and make some news together. Until then, it's every woman for herself, and that means you, too, Stanton."

Out of the corner of her eye, Charlene spots Tasso Darjun standing silently near the front of the room, leaning against a wall on the fringes of the press scrum. Breaking away from O'Malley, she starts to make her way over to Tasso, wanting to thank him for his tip-offs and maybe even milk him for some more news. She waves her arm above her head. Tasso sees her coming towards him. She winks and nods her head as if to silently affirm a solidarity, but he turns away with a bewildered expression and presses his body closer against the wall.

But before she can squeeze through the people and reach him, Greta Watt walks out to the podium to begin the press conference. She's followed by Ludwig Zeemanvitz, William Stonebane, and Dylan O'Sullivan.

"Oh, shit," Charlene spits, spinning on her toe away from Tasso and heading back to Herb. "It's starting. Shit. Shit. Go Herb, get to the front, right now." She seizes Herb by the shoulder and nearly throws him forward into the best position.

□ □ □

From his spot on the podium, William Stonebane happily observes the massive crowd settle into place in front of him. A smile blossoms from his lips, not the quick smile public etiquette requires, but a smile that conveys a deeper pleasure: the pleasure of power. He feels younger because of it. *All those people waiting to hear some news from Greta Watt*, he thinks, *and here I am with the most explosive news of all.* Every part of his body is still, as if by moving he might disrupt the scene unfolding in front of him. He sees the Channel 7 cameraman poke his way to the front of the scrum, he sees the policeman with bad breath pace behind the crowd, he sees Greta Watt standing in front of the podium preparing her speech for the greedy journalists who don't have anything new to put in their stories. The pleasure he feels suffuses his entire body and he understands how the stillness of anticipation is also the foreplay of the saboteur.

Greta Watt breathes deeply to calm her nerves and puts her hands on the sides of the podium. As soon as the police announced Jacob as a suspect in the shooting, she knew that she had no choice but to call a press conference and give a statement. Full disclosure, that's what the Network lawyers advised her to do – that is, full disclosure with the exception of the fact that Jake peed on the boardroom table and disrupted the meeting. They also told her to put a gag order on the staff until Jacob showed up and they got a decent explanation from him as to what actually occurred on that fateful night at the university. *Full disclosure?* Obviously the legal subtleties of the term were lost on her, but she concurred with the lawyers' strategy anyway. Still, unsettling questions whisked through her mind: *How did that reporter from Channel 7 find out that Jacob went up north? How did she get there so fast? Was there a leak at the Network?* But she knows she's not here to answer these questions. She's here to do some damage control, and in that regard, confidence is more important than truth.

She clears her throat into the bank of microphones and high-pitched feedback pierces the air, causing a few soundmen at the front to throw their headphones off in pain. Pulling her prepared speech from her pocket, she smooths it out on the podium and sends herself an SOS.

"Ladies and gentleman," she begins. "I've decided to call this press conference to clarify some questions raised in the media regarding the status of one of our flagship programs, *The Jake Connections*. First of all, I'd like to announce that Dylan O'Sullivan is going to be the full-time stand-in host for Jacob Jacobson." From the row of people behind her, Dylan O'Sullivan steps forward and nods his blond head, pursing his lips as if he's just accepted a serious mission from his commander in chief. *Nice work, Dylan*, she thinks. *So far, so good.* "Naturally, all of us here are deeply concerned about Jacob Jacobson's absence. He has been through a traumatic experience, and until the police present us with solid evidence that might change our position, he still has our full support."

She gazes around into the glow of faces and lights. *Snap* go the cameras. *Whir* go the cassette machines. *I'm not giving up on him quite yet*, she thinks, knowing she has too much invested in Jake to let the first scandal scuttle his career. Now to the more difficult part of her "full disclosure." She sets her jaw and straightens her posture, remembering the conversation she had with Stonebane in his office. He did agree, she assures herself, not to mention anything in public about what happened with Jacob at the staff meeting. *Good. Just get on with it*, she tells herself.

"As for the recent reports on Channel 7 alleging that Jacob Jacobson disrupted a staff meeting and assaulted some of our staff, we categorically deny this." She pauses for dramatic effect. *Confidence is better than truth.* "It's this cheap and sleazy kind of reporting that gives journalists all over the world a bad name. Jacob Jacobson did appear for a brief moment yesterday morning – *before* he was named a suspect – but only to tell me that he wasn't feeling well. He needed some time off, which I granted him, given the circumstances. Subsequently he went home to rest. We don't know what happened to him since, as our job is to run a TV station, not a police investigation. You have my personal word that our policy at the Network has always been to treat everything as the news, even if something directly affects one of our own staff. But we only report real news, not cheap allegations."

At that moment William Stonebane's immense voice explodes. "In that case, I feel that I must speak up!"

Greta twists her head back to him, her knees almost giving out in surprise. "William! What are you doing?" she whispers fiercely, although it's picked up perfectly by the microphones.

"I'm doing what I've done as the Network anchorman for almost thirty years," he cries out heroically, strutting to the podium. "I'm telling the truth!"

He almost shoves her aside. "Thatchly," Stonebane says, his arm extended sideways. "Bring me the bag!" He rolls the R in *bring* like a laird.

From the side of the room the tall, beakerlike figure of Thatchly scurries past Tasso and up to Stonebane. He's holding a plastic satchel out in front of him as though it contains something poisonous. The cameras turn as one massive beast and follow him with a seething electronic gaze. A jolt of excitement stuns the room, as it dawns on everyone that something unusual is actually happening at a news conference. Real news.

"I'm sorry to intrude, Greta, but this has all happened so quickly," Stonebane continues, using his massive voice to capacity, thereby preventing anyone from interrupting. "Only moments ago I received an anonymous tip on the phone. The person told me that the weapon used to shoot poor Rachel Anne Poiselle could be found behind the set in a certain studio right here in our hallowed building." Pausing to let Thatchly climb up onto the stage, he takes the bag from his assistant. They've choreographed this performance all day. "That studio is the one used exclusively to record a show called *The Jake Connections*, a show, as most of you know, that is hosted by the prime suspect in the shooting, one Jacob Jacobson." Again he pauses as the cameramen jostle madly for better position. "Indeed, he *was* here yesterday morning, and he did attend the meeting. But he also did something else." Stonebane reaches into the bag and with a swing of his arm pulls out a gun. "He tried to hide his weapon! I am here to personally present it to the police."

Holding the gun up high above his head, he luxuriates in the wash of light from the flash bulbs. Thatchly applauds quietly.

Tasso watches Stonebane's speech intently, but something in his peripheral vision makes him turn his head back towards the crowd. He sees a woman clawing her way up to the front of the room, wielding her microphone like a police baton. *Charlene Rosemount*, he thinks in horror. He notices something else, too. In one arm she's carrying a black bag, the same one that he found with Jacob in the board room. His mind reels. *Oh my God, I left it at the coffee shop!* He puts his hand over his mouth.

Before any of the reporters can blurt out a question to Stonebane, Charlene Rosemount springs out of the crowd and bolts up to the podium. Pushing her way to Stonebane's side, she waves the black bag over her head.

"Charlene Rosemount, Channel 7 Street-Beat News. I've just been given the key piece of evidence in this case," she announces breathlessly.

Another volley of flashes.

"What is this? Who do you think you are?" Stonebane demands, still holding the gun in the air.

"I'm the one who's just broken this case wide open, that's who I am." Charlene scrutinizes the gun in Stonebane's hand, her eyes venomous. Raising her arm higher in the air, she sticks out her chest, giving the cameramen below an extra incentive to focus exclusively on her evidence.

Stonebane studies her in disgust. "You've got nothing but a bag, you silly girl. Now scat, go away." He flicks his long fingers at her.

But Charlene leans in front of the microphone bank and says loudly, "Only minutes ago I was given this bag by a secret source. In it I discovered the bloody gown that Jacob Jacobson wore the night of the shooting, when he fled from police at the hospital."

She lets the black bag down for a second and snatches out the hospital gown, waving it like a cape.

Holding their evidence up, Stonebane and Charlene stare each other down like matador and bull.

"This is way out of order," Greta shouts, trying to put herself between them. "Both of you get down right now."

But Stonebane won't be stopped. Unleashing his voice as if it alone might remove both Greta and Charlene from the podium, he bellows, "I have the *smoking* gun!"

"And I have the *bloody* gown," Charlene counters.

They begin to jostle with each other for the centre position and the crowd of reporters presses forward. Caught off guard by the sudden mêlée, Detective O'Malley tries to rush the stage to seize the new evidence. But the reporters, each desperate to get the best spot, won't let him through. Like a mad wrestler, he yanks them one by one, throwing them aside in order to clear a path to the podium. As he gets close to the front of the pack, he grabs the shirt of one cameraman so hard that the man spins around.

"What the fuck do you think you're doing?" cries out Herb as O'Malley's big hand tries to pull him out of the way. As he swerves around, Herb instinctively smashes his massive Betacam down to ward off the attack, assuming the assailant is a competitive cameraman seeking a better spot in the scrum. But he's wrong. When he takes his eye from the viewfinder, he realizes that he's just cracked his camera directly on Detective Ian O'Malley's nose.

"Holy Jesus," he breathes.

Throwing his hands up to his face, O'Malley emits a muffled scream. Blood pours over his mouth. O'Malley stares through his fingers at Herb and snarls, "You just bought yourself a jail sentence, you little tapehead." And without further pause, he leaps towards the podium. *Get your nose broken by a camera and then just move the fuck along*, O'Malley repeats silently so he won't pass out from the pain.

Herb swings his camera back up on his shoulder and resumes shooting. If he misses this scene Charlene will dismember him, and that, he decides easily, would be worse than any jail sentence. His video tape rolls and rolls.

Now the podium is in chaos. Greta Watt tries to get to the

microphones to stop the press conference, but Thatchly pushes her away in an attempt to protect his mentor. Zeemanvitz grabs Thatchly in order to find out what's actually happening but Dylan O'Sullivan, who's turned to flee the stage, is caught in his way. In the traffic jam of bodies, they all struggle uselessly. The only one not caught in the jam is Ian O'Malley. Almost blind with pain and rage, he rockets up onto the stage.

"Give me that gun!" O'Malley screams, his body now a massive projectile heading for William Stonebane.

Stonebane lurches to get out of O'Malley's way, waving the gun in the air, but he's too slow, too old, and too cornered by the other people on the stage to escape. O'Malley hits him like a jackknifing tractor-trailer, catapulting Stonebane into Charlene. She lets out a howl.

"Don't touch that coat!" she cries, as if anyone at that point is still paying attention to what she holds in the air.

But the bloody coat is no longer in the air. In the panic of the moment, Charlene lets go of her evidence and it falls from her hands. Everyone begins to collapse. High-pitched feedback again fills the air as the passel of microphones go smashing down onto the stage floor, taking with them both the podium and the disoriented crowd of people.

And then there's an odd moment of stillness as William Stonebane, Ludwig Zeemanvitz, Charlene Rosemount, Ian O'Malley, and Greta Watt intertwine in a tableau of confusion. The photographers capture an almost undifferentiated mass of human flesh tilting to the left, the long arm of William Stonebane sticking straight up out of it, still holding the gun. Flashbulbs explode. Afterwards some of them will say that the scene resembled the photograph of U.S. marines raising the flag over Iwo Jima. But a second later the inertia of the falling bodies takes over, and the next pictures portray something far less monumental than the famous image of victory. They show something more like an orgy. Stonebane's hand holding the gun disappears into the welter of bodies.

No one really knows what happens next. Days later, Stonebane will claim that he let the gun drop. O'Malley will plead that, while he indeed touched the gun – his fingerprints will be the only ones found on it – it had, by that time, already been fired. In any case, somewhere between eye level and the ground, the gun goes off with a loud, percussive explosion.

Dylan O'Sullivan reacts to the gunshot like any self-respecting journalist who cut his teeth covering cultural events like ballet openings: he throws himself to the floor. He has a horrible premonition that his embryonic on-air career is about to be cut short by some recently downsized employee on a psychotic revenge mission. The only person who beats him to the ground is Gerald Dennis-Stanton, whose primal instinct is not only to protect his perfect white skin, but also his perfect camel-hair coat. *Let the camera people be heroes*, he thinks as his chin hits the floor. *I'll write the roundup.*

Greta Watt, who has landed on her back, opens her eyes and finds herself gazing two inches from the face of Ian O'Malley. He's lying on top of her. His face gushes blood and she assumes he's been shot.

"Oh my God, you've been hit!" she yells.

"Who?" O'Malley answers, trying to extricate himself from the pile of bodies in order to pull out his own gun. "Who's been hit?"

"You, you!" Greta replies as the hideous face in front of her continues to bleed.

O'Malley manages to struggle to his feet and whips his revolver from his holster. His eyes have already swelled into purple bulbs and he can barely see.

"Nobody move!" he cries out, because there's nothing else he can think of saying.

Lying prone on the stage with his face partially covered by the hospital gown Charlene dropped, William Stonebane gazes down at his shirt. It's smeared with blood, and he can feel a slight burning sensation in his side.

"Thatchly, I think I've been hit," he moans.

Diving towards Stonebane, Thatchly drops to his knees.

"Don't move, William, stay very still," he squeaks, caressing Stonebane's head. "You might have a spinal injury. Can you feel your extremities? Talk to me. I'm doing all I can. You're a hero, William. Now stay conscious, let me hear that deep voice of yours."

"Call a goddamn ambulance, Thatchly," Stonebane rasps. "What are you waiting for? You twit!"

"Thataboy. You did wonderfully up there," Thatchly purrs, not moving from Stonebane's side. "Now stay lucid, don't fade away. Wriggle your toes if you can."

Positioned next to Stonebane and sensing a large bruise beginning to form on her hip, Charlene Rosemount manages to grin.

"That your little boy toy, Stonebane?" Charlene mutters, getting to her feet. "I've always suspected you batted for that team."

From his prone position Stonebane twists his head towards her. "How dare you say such a thing!" he gasps.

Thatchly lifts his hands from Stonebane's head in protest. "I'm his assistant! He's wounded, for God's sake. We need help."

Charlene smiles wickedly. "Look, I don't care if you're a back-door man, Stonebane. I'm open-minded – but I'll bet your viewers aren't."

"That's slander!" Stonebane barks, half sitting up.

"Maybe, but you lay off this Jacobson story or a nasty rumour about you might find its way into the tabs. Complete with pictures of this light-in-the-loafers young man stroking your head. You know how that can look."

Stonebane's mouth drops open. "You wouldn't dare stoop that low."

"Try me," she snarls, grabbing the bloody gown from the floor. "And keep this in mind next time you try to steal my story." With that, she jumps off the stage and heads towards Herb, who has the camera pointed directly at her.

Reeling from the threat, Stonebane touches his chest and instantly realizes that he's not, in fact, hurt at all. His hands fumble over his body until they locate a tiny rip under his armpit where the bullet must have passed.

"It missed me," he mutters, stretching out his arm as if to test its function. "It's just a scratch, that's all. Less than an inch and I would be dead."

"Thank God," Thatchly whispers, unsure of what to do. "Can you walk?"

"Of course I can." Stonebane pushes himself up, and they both dash quickly, and separately, through the pandemonium towards the exit.

Still on the stage, O'Malley cradles his nose in one hand, the gun in the other. "Nobody move! I said, nobody!"

But everyone in the room wants to get as far away from O'Malley as possible. Panicked by the gunfire, the savvy media types conclude that the one-eared man waving the gun on stage must be the lunatic who let off the shot. They flee for the exit.

Charlene seizes Herb by the sleeve, demanding, "Did you get everything? Did you get me going down?"

"Yeah, yeah, everything," Herb replies, still shooting.

"I want that tape on air in fifteen minutes! This is the big time." She dashes towards the door dragging him behind her, already thinking of her opening line. "I need a shot of me outside of the building," she instructs. "I'll do my introduction there as the police cars arrive. It'll rock. Let's go! I need a live link *now*."

The rest of the people in the room follow her out. Even Greta gets up and departs, fearing for her life. O'Malley chases the pack out the door, his gun aiming wildly while he howls for everyone to stop.

And then the room is empty. The only lingering sound is of someone breathing. It echoes in the room like wind in a conch shell, powerful but placeless. It's the sound of Tasso Darjun, who lies on the floor near the corner of the stage where the podium fell. The microphones that Greta Watt spoke into are splayed out towards him, amplifying his breath. A stinging sensation bites into his arm, and he notices a pool of blood collecting beneath him. He's been hit. Grazed by the bullet beneath the shoulder, in the fleshy part of the arm.

He knows he's alone, once again forgotten in the riot of activity, discarded from the main story, which has moved outside the Network building to the exact place where, for twenty-five years, he's peacefully lit his nightly cigarette. Habits are broken. A new life begins. He listens to the microphone broaden his breathing, in and out, in and out, until it fills the vast hall, holding him inside his own rhythm. He closes his eyes into blackness and wonders why his life is being so senselessly destroyed.

HOME MOVIES

Pearlescent with thin white clouds, the mid-afternoon sky brightens with diffusions of sun. The stalking cold of winter lets up, uncharacteristically shy and mute. An unseasonal rain falls on the snow-covered ground, now gleaming silver. The air smells of earth and water, pinching the horizon, as if the gap no longer exists between land and sky. It's still more than two months before the naming of spring, when the gardens and lawns of Hogg's Hollow will awaken to colour, but winter seems to have made an unexpected retreat.

Theo parks the car in front of the fence at the fifth hole of the Rosedale golf course. In the summer he and Jake used to climb over the fence and wade through the Don River to collect stray golf balls, trying to sell them to passing foursomes to make some change. In the winter, they tobogganed on the rolling hills. This is where Theo discovered love with Theckla, where Jake first saw it painfully unfold from his hiding spot on the banks. The openness of the land holds memory lines like scars snaking beside the river. Now memories of two other boys, another time. Only land changes slowly, Jake thinks. Everything else flashes with accidents and damage.

The rain taps on the roof of the car and Jake listens to its staccato beat, measuring the dull throb in his body against it. Pain everywhere. Fingers and toes stinging from old frostbite. Stomach, hips, and back aching from the jack handle. His body wants to relinquish its duty of support. Rest. He lays his seat back and Theo hands him a bottle of Johnnie Walker.

For hours they drink silently in the car beside the fence, neither of them sure if the time measures a new intimacy or a new dislocation. Theo lights cigarettes, and the smoke curls out the window and splits in the rain. He thinks of Theckla, how such a strong young woman ended up so broken by the very wildness she so loved. Hopes his money will help her to rediscover that strength he used to see so often waiting beside this fence.

The house they grew up in is a five-minute walk away – a brown, streaked, shingled box sitting in front of the forest where the spring floods come down. Momma's there, they both know that. She's always home now. Theo says he wants them to see her together, wants to remember something about how they used to be, but Jake can't imagine what memory might have foreshadowed this moment, drunk in the car, lurching from violence to violence.

"I smoked my first cigarette here with Theckla, you know," Theo says softly. "Right here. Almost choked to death. Stole a pack from Momma."

Jake nods and closes his eyes. He'd rather Theo didn't talk, but he's too tired to stop him. The scotch moves around in his stomach, hot and solid.

"Theckla never wanted you around," Theo continues. "She wanted to be alone with me, teach me about things, maybe grab a kiss or two. But I knew you were following us. I knew you were always somewhere in the bushes, tagging along, and it made me feel better to know that. Less scared of her or something. Just to have you near, that's all I wanted, to have your eyes watching me. It was about that, you know, not about Theckla, or getting kissed; it was always about us. Knowing we were in on the same secrets, the same discoveries. I never told you that, did I? I guess I just believed it was our special understanding, a silent promise to watch over each other whatever it takes. I miss that, Jake, I really do. You messed things up with that show of yours, you know that? You really did. Anyway, we're both in trouble now." He points to the golf course. "Look at this place. Momma says they've cleaned up the river now. She says they got all sorts of ducks and birds, even fish. Fish in the Don? Theckla wouldn't believe that, poor kid. I loved this place, I really did."

Jake listens to Theo talk and recalls the camping trips they used to take, talking for hours under their tent domes, rolling joints on the rocks, swimming in the cold, clean water, sending words out into the night sky like messengers, as if next year those same words might return to them with news of the future, carrying proof and wisdom. Year after year those same trips, everything tranquil and meandering, everything young and without urgency and innocent with untested plans and ideas. It was always like that: Theo talking and Jake listening to the curves and bends of conversation, letting Theo's ideas insinuate into his muscles and relax him. Jake usually in agreement because he believed Theo always did the right thing. Theo helped people – had that brute kindness, that simplicity that Jake could never articulate. The love that transcends detail, the love which is beyond category. But Jake senses how much they've both grown up. Not wiser. Just susceptible to judgement. As if every detail, every word counts for something.

The pain in Jake's body dulls as he absorbs the scotch. He thinks about getting hit by the two men, how it didn't hurt, how it felt almost owed to him, as if the men were in on the joke Jake had been playing on himself for years. But now, sitting in the car with Theo, another sensation emerges. He can hardly define it and he's not even sure he wants to recognize it. Like anxiety, only more solid. Spiky with intentions. He wishes Theo would stop talking about Theckla and their childhood. They aren't children now, and it's useless to pretend. They can't go back and steal from the past, use it to forgive the present. He watches the fence to the Rosedale golf course distort through the rain-covered windshield.

"Let's go see Momma," Jake says, sitting up. "I want to see how she's doing."

"Cops will be watching," Theo warns. "Bet on it. We'll have to go through the forest. Cut through the backyard."

Jake gets out of the car and heads towards the ridge of trees overlooking the ravine. Theo grabs his bag and follows, the ground soaking through their shoes and snow-covered trees bending under the cold rain. After picking their way through the woods, they finally arrive at the old house, hop the wood fence, and scurry across the yard to the back door. Jake stops to listen to something and Theo pulls in behind him. They can hear music playing from inside.

"What's in the bag, Theo?"

"Video camera."

"What's with that all of a sudden?"

"I want a record of us for posterity," Theo answers quietly.

"Maybe you'll turn it into a little TV movie of our trip. A documentary of who we really are. What's the matter, don't you like cameras any more?"

Jake doesn't answer. He unlocks the door and walks into the house, calling out to his mother.

"Momma? It's Jake and Theo. We've come over for a visit. You home? Momma, where are you?"

Theo hurries to the front window and peers outside for any sign of the police. The street is empty, and he breathes a sigh of relief. Lifting up the camera, Theo points it in front of him and presses PLAY. The picture jumps up and down spasmodically as he walks, following Jake into the den. A music video plays on the TV, blasting the song through the house. Theo focuses the video camera on the TV screen and records what he sees: some thrash band playing live, the performers stage-diving into the seething mosh pit of dancing fans.

"What the hell is she watching?" Jake mutters, glancing over to the white leather couch. His mother is asleep in her clothes: her left arm thrown over her forehead, right hand clutching a rock glass with a lemon jammed at the bottom. Her mouth is slightly open and her respiration is thick, like water sloshing at the bottom of a boat. An ashtray full of cigarette butts lies on the floor beneath her, and grey ash is scattered all around it.

"Just finished the twenty-minute workout, I imagine," Theo comments, reaching down and taking the glass from his mother's hand. "Does she ever stop with this exercise routine?"

"You want a drink, Theo?" Jake asks quietly, moving towards the built-in bar where their mother keeps a cache of gin.

"Yeah. And another for Momma. I think her step class starts any minute." Theo laughs sadly and points the camera at his mother, zooming in on the bright spittle at the corner of her mouth.

Jake pours two gin and tonics. The all season family drink.

"Money says the press has been phoning her every minute, asking about us," Jake says, sipping from his glass.

Theo sits down on the edge of the couch beside his mother and strokes her hair. He rests the camera on the coffee table, propping the lens up on some books so it faces Jake. The red RECORD light flashes.

"I haven't talked to her in weeks," Theo says. "Stopped calling when I left B.C."

Jake examines the framed pictures of his family resting on the shelf above the television. There's Pop, standing at the steering wheel of the motorboat, holding up an empty hook in his hand and grinning as if to say, Skunked again. The dusky sky behind him is almost purple. There's Momma and Pop at their wedding, the old photo so faded by sun that Momma's white dress is almost bleached out of the picture, Pop just a stiff shadow in his pressed tuxedo. Both drifting into background. There are the boys, posing awkwardly in the backyard with Momma and Pop, the only family portrait ever taken. Theo ten, Jake eight, kneeling on the cut green grass, hair carefully parted to the side and both of them wearing the same blue shirt and brown corduroy pants. Doing their duty as members of a happy family and, for that moment, believing it. Jake takes a long pull from his drink, remembering the boy that was himself.

Music blares from the TV. Jake finds the remote under a stack of entertainment magazines and presses MUTE. The band plays silently as the bodies throb and muscle to some primal rhythm. Leaping from the stage, the singer is caught in slow motion as he descends onto his screaming fans. The film speeds up as the crowd holds his prone body over their heads and pass him from hand to hand, sharing his weight. Jake watches the singer let his body go perfectly limp. The energy of the crowd seems to enter the performer like a spirit, his body twitching unconsciously. Jake sees that the man is drenched in sweat and almost glides frictionlessly over the thrashing frenzy with eyes closed, trusting that the anonymous bodies dancing below will keep him aloft. Jake thinks of Latisha, how she held him on her raw voice. "You never wanted to come down from her arms and see what was really happening on the dirty old ground of our house"; that's what Pop said once when they were out fishing, reminiscing. *Pop.* Jake stares at the picture of his father on the mantelpiece and misses him, misses the tired face he got to know so well during those unlucky fishing trips.

"Almost two years since Pop died," Jake says. "Two years next week."

"That long?"

"Momma still misses him, I really think she does."

"Probably."

"Me too. Two years. Christ. It's still so clear. That night I sat with him. Every detail of his body. The blue veins in his hands. The colour of his teeth. He had really white teeth, you remember that? Even with all those black cavities at the back of his mouth. Two years. Seems like two days."

"Doesn't it."

"I never got to say goodbye to him, you know. He just trickled away. Water through a sieve, that's how Momma described it. Remember?"

"Right." Theo shrugs and wipes the spittle from his mother's mouth.

"His will to live just gave out," Jake says, shaking his head. "And that was it. Even the doctors couldn't understand it."

"What do doctors know?"

"They never even found the final cause of death. He just stopped breathing. How does that happen?"

"No one ever knows what's really going on, do they? Those doctors work on a different plane, way up in the clouds, too busy to fuss with us little people on the ground."

Jake stops and stares at Theo. Theo's words hit him sharply, like a spade breaking through frozen soil, unearthing the old memory of what his father said about Latisha on that day when they were out fishing. He lets his memory churn for a moment, going deeper until he senses something solid emerge, a question buried in a memory field he's let lie fallow for too long: *What was really happening on the dirty old ground?*

"You were there," Jake probes carefully. "You saw him go."

"Momma and I. Yeah."

"Where was Dr. Packjay? I thought he was on call."

"Another emergency pulled him away, I think. And then Pop stopped breathing. We went crazy, but the nurse couldn't revive him."

Jake pauses, turning the pieces of his memory around to examine them in a new light as an archaeologist might do to the fragments of a shattered urn. "It was so strange, because you didn't even stay around to talk to me, did you? I got there so quickly after my show, but you and Momma were already gone. I never understood that. Leaving me alone with Pop all night."

Theo's eyes are fixed on his mother's splayed hair.

"Momma asked me to make funeral arrangements," Theo replies quietly.

"At three in the morning? That was so weird."

"That's what Momma wanted." Very gently, he presses his mother's hair over her ear.

The singer on TV is passed from hand to hand, the crowd underneath him like an ocean. "I still don't understand why no one called me at the studio when his vital signs dropped," Jake says, forcing the matter. "No one told me he was so close to dying."

"You were doing your TV show, Jake. It happened too fast to call."

"But the doctor said he was stable. He told me it was all right to leave. I must have asked a dozen times that day."

"Pop was in a lot of pain, Jake," Theo says, trying to placate his increasingly agitated brother. "He hated those tubes sticking out of him. The liquid food. The oxygen mask. The buzzing machines. The hospital stink. He was probably glad to die, anyway. He wanted to go."

"How do you know that?" Jake's voice is too loud. Again he glances over at the picture of his father in the boat, his father enjoying himself despite his perennial bad luck. Pop got beat by that lake every summer, but he never gave up trying. Never. Then Jake thinks about the dog, how Theo urged him to beat it to death, to put it out of its pain, how Theo held his hand on the horn and urged Jake on. Theo's too certain about everything, Jake thinks, too righteous. *What's happening on the dirty old ground?* "Pop didn't want to die," Jake blurts out. "He wasn't like that."

"You're gonna wake up Momma if you keep yelling."

"But that's a stupid, arrogant thing to say, Theo. How do you know what he wanted?"

"Just shut up," Theo snarls, his face losing its red hue and becoming milky and stern. "There are some things you don't want to see, okay?"

"Like what?"

"Like everything. Pop had debts to pay, problems you never knew about. Real problems, too big to solve."

"So tell me, Theo, tell me what those problems were. What do you know that I don't?"

Theo keeps moving his hand over his mother's hair, to the rhythm of her breath.

"You're drunk, Jake. Settle down."

Jake grabs Theo's hand and squeezes it tightly. "What don't I know? Tell me."

"Persistent little journalist, aren't you?" Theo hisses, twisting his arms and pulling his hand free. He picks up the video camera and aims it at Jake. "Give us that famous smile, Mr. Jacobson. You're on film."

"I want to know about Pop. Right now, for fuck's sake." The booze burns in his belly, heated by his growing anger.

"Don't swear, Jake!" Theo admonishes. "I'll have to edit that out for the Network." He winks, but Jake stands silent, waiting.

"All right, listen to me," Theo says, his tone quickly changing. "Pop was in a lot of financial trouble. I mean bad loans from bad people, the whole nine yards. When he got sick, he knew he'd never be able to pay his debts. So he told Momma that the only way she'd ever be able to live was on his insurance money. If he ever got to the point where he couldn't work, he wanted her to put him out of his pain and collect. You get it? Now come on, smile for the camera."

"Put that goddamn thing down, Theo."

"You don't like cameras now? Maybe you're in the wrong job after all."

"Pop never told me any of that. No one did."

"Once again, my big reporter brother has missed the real story."

The picture on TV goes out of focus, blurring the colours of the crowd into a stylish, soupy oil.

"How do you know so much?" Jake asks, trying to sort through Theo's cryptic explanations.

"Momma told me before Pop died. You want to ask her yourself?" Theo laughs bitterly and gestures to their passed-out mother.

"Put him out of pain? I don't understand. What does that mean?"

Theo zooms in on Jake's face. "Are you thick, Jake? He didn't want life support. Wake up. He wanted to make sure Momma had some money to live on. It was his way of telling her that he still loved her, I really think it was."

"Jesus," Jake whistles. "Why'd you never tell me before?"

"Can't you just smile? I'm filming. You're ruining my movie."

"You're being an asshole, Theo. Put that thing down."

"Who's the asshole, Jake? You don't want to know about Pop. You never did. You're a good-time guy, Jake. Always leave the messy stuff to me. Now shut up and mug for the camera. Be that famous, charming celeb."

"I need to know, Theo, I need to know what really happened to Pop."

Theo keeps the camera rolling, but stands up, circling Jake.

"You really wanna know?" Theo says. "Okay, big boy. Time to grow up. I'll tell you. But even Pop didn't want you to know. Said you wouldn't understand. Too cruel for a sentimental guy like you. Momma said so, too. And they're right."

"Understand what?"

"We stopped it, Jake. While you were out doing your show, we stopped everything."

"Stopped everything?" Jake repeats. "I don't get it."

"The fucking machines, the life support," Theo explains calmly. "Momma and I turned everything off. Let him go in peace. There, that's it. I promised Momma I'd never tell you, and now I've broken my promise, you asshole. Are you happy now? Is that something you really wanted to hear?"

The picture on TV clears back into focus as the crowd pushes the singer back up to the stage. He jumps to his feet, waving his arms like a windmill, whipping up the crowd into a frenzy.

"You killed Pop?" Jake asks slowly, letting the idea bleed into him. "Are you telling me that you killed Pop?"

"I'm telling you that we did what he wanted us to do. That's all. He wanted to go like that, with some dignity. Can't you understand that? He was in pain. This is what he wanted. Now wave to the camera, Jake. Wave to Momma. You're on TV."

As the tape rolls, Jake shakes his head back and forth, unable to grasp the enormity of what he's hearing. Images loom and mingle – his dead father lying in bed, Ranklin Demoins cut down in the forest, the wounded dog – and something in him gives way, as if the invisible hands whose support he's taken for granted for so long have finally parted. Everything in him starts to fall away. He sees Momma walking across the ice, sees her disappear into sky, sees Theo disappear with her, sees Rachel in the hall, sees Theo in the hall beside her, Theo everywhere, in every memory, inhabiting everything he does. And suddenly he has to see Rachel. Has to know what exactly happened to her that Sunday night.

"Fuck you, Theo, fuck you," he says, hurling his glass of gin at the shelf above the television. He runs crazily for the front door, not caring who sees him as he steps outside and takes off down the street.

This is what Theo's camera records: Jake's body bent forward, moving like a line of colour quickly out of frame. Then the automatic focus adjusts on the shelf, where Jake's gin and tonic drips down the family pictures, spilling fish-eyed drops onto the silent band playing on the TV screen below.

What the camera doesn't record is Theo standing up, kissing his mother on the forehead, and following Jake out through the back of the house, slipping into the woods so he can get back to his car and head directly for the Network.

FLOWERS FOR RACHEL

In the hospital, drunk and in search of Rachel's room.

Keep your head down. Don't look at anyone. Avoid the doctors. Find her. Find her alive. This is what Jake is thinking when the taxi drops him off and he slips through the hospital doors. Too many people know his face, have seen him on TV, seen the reports of the shooting, consider him a suspect. Jake wishes he had the hospital coat, some kind of disguise. *Hard to focus, too much booze. What's happened to Theo? Out of control.* He can't remember where the doctors took Rachel the night she was shot. *Floor seven? Right. Follow the green line, remember the stretchers along the wall, the people in faded blue gowns rolling by in wheelchairs. Everyone in slippers and soft shoes. Just like with Pop. Pop . . . Keep your head low. A nurse. Ask her.*

"I'm looking for the critical care ward," he says, coughing into his hands to cover his face. "My wife had a head injury."

He calls Rachel his wife. It feels strange to lie about this, to appropriate a promise in a place where he's broken so many.

"You're on the wrong floor," the nurse says. "Neurological intensive care is on eight."

Off the elevators on eight, he scurries past the staff at the round reception desk. *Follow the blue line. Look for names on the wall.* But there are no names on floor eight. Pop had a name on his door, Jake remembers that. His mind lurches back to Theo. *We stopped everything.* He tries to shut out the thought. He's come for Rachel. Here in intensive care, where everyone is trying to recover from some unasked-for event. Here where young bodies get old, where there are bandages and casts, machines and tubes, black screens with thin green lines and hanging bags of translucent intravenous. Indiscriminate. *Where's Rachel? Have they moved her? Ask someone, ask a nurse.*

"Ms. Poiselle? Is she–"

"New ward."

"Sorry?"

"Just this morning. Upgraded to neurological ward. Down the hall, take a left, fourth door on the right."

The nurse is too busy to notice him, moves on to other emergencies. People here give priority to the person in the most pain, sensitive to a threshold beyond Jake's reach. The whole place permeated with bland alarm and bleached danger. Take a left, fourth door on the right. Rachel's room. To his relief he sees that there's much less activity here than in critical care. Fewer nurses, no family members, no police. It's a private room, just like the one they gave him the night she was shot. *Go inside. Shut the door.*

Rachel lays upon an adjustable hospital bed, the top half slightly raised so he can see her head. She's asleep. Moving closer, the new details on her face reveal themselves to him. The plastic tube going into her nose. Her half-shaved scalp. A thicket of bandage and gauze protruding from the left side of her head. A black bruise dipping beneath her eye like the shadow of an awning. The white sheets are perfectly pressed, folded down on the green hospital gown that covers Rachel's breasts. But what he notices most is a smell, so pungent he can almost see it. Not the hospital smell of stale food and sleep, but something sharp and alive. Flowers.

There are flowers everywhere around her. Around the metal handles of the bed, on the window ledge in front of the blinds, crowded on the little table beside the food tray, the dull green Jell-O and the plastic water cup. Roses and tulips, Queen Anne's lace and carnations, chrysanthemums, baby's breath, lilies and irises – chaotic with slashes of yellows and reds and pinks. White cards sticking out of the bouquets like birds. The smell envelops Jake's liquored body. There are literally hundreds of them, stamens coursing green and wet, petals soft and bending, filling the room as if planted right in the white walls and the grey light, protesting the aura of sickness in a riot of wild odour, almost floating the bed. Jake moves close to Rachel to watch her sleep. But she's not sleeping. Her eyes open quickly, as if she's sensed a disturbance in the thick air.

"Look who's here." Rachel's voice is strong and clear, not wounded as Jake imagined it would be.

"Rachel," Jake whispers demurely. He's not sure how she'll react to his presence.

"I've been wondering when you'd come." There's no condemnation in her voice, no judgement. Like when she feels his scars. "Everyone else has been here."

"I see that." Relief washes over him as he senses her warmth, and he moves closer to her through the heavy air. Still, he can't bring himself to make eye contact, and he pretends to study the various bouquets.

"I get so many flowers, every day," she says, lying perfectly still. "I don't even know the names of them. It's embarrassing."

"No, it's not." He touches the wet petal of a white rose.

"Did you bring me something to add to the collection?"

Jake purses his lips into a painful grin, trying to summon up some of their old humour. "Do you like topiary?"

"I don't even know what that means. I'll have to start gardening when I get out."

He turns his eyes to her, reaching up tentatively to touch her cheek. But then, as if the gesture would be presumptuous, he pulls his hand away. "How are you doing?"

The IV tube drips liquid into her vein and she closes her eyes for a moment, letting some pain pass through her. "Been better, haven't I?"

"Are you going to recover?" It's a stupid question, he knows it, but it's all he can think of to say.

"I'm alive. I'm told this is lucky." She shifts her feet under the sheets, pulling them down to reveal more of her long body.

"It is."

"At least I know I can take a bullet. A major asset for a rising academic."

In a half-laugh he mumbles, "Publish or perish, right?"

They try to sidestep the awkwardness by reverting to their old habit of banter, but it comes off tired and sad. Rachel smiles as if she feels sorry for him and brushes some hair from the one side of her face where it still falls. Jake wants to apologize to her about something, but it's something too large or too vague to be held by a single word, and he sits silently on the edge of the bed, breathing her in. Wanting to be helpful, comforting.

"Where have you been, Jake?" she asks. "You should have been here days ago."

He gazes again into the chaos of flowers. "I don't know. Away. I just left."

"Bad answer."

"I'm sorry."

"You're always sorry."

"It's true."

"You break my heart, you shit. You really do."

They don't talk for some time. Jake can hear Rachel's lungs work air through her nose tube. It sounds as if she's sighing.

Her lips are chapped and bruised and she licks them gingerly. "They told me I was in and out consciousness for ten hours," Rachel says. "Don't remember much. Amnesia, I guess. When I finally woke up I asked for you and the doctor said you were gone. *Are you all right?*"

It hurts Jake to know how hard she's trying to make him feel comfortable, to set him at ease, even though he can sense her obvious disappointment. Still helping him, even now.

"I should have come earlier," he mutters lamely.

"Yes."

"I'm so sor–"

"Don't say it again."

"But I am."

"I spent two hours yesterday getting grilled by the police." She points to the bandage on her shaved head. "They still don't know who did this to me."

"I should have been here. I know."

"They asked a lot of questions about you," she continues. "Like where you went, if we'd been fighting recently, if you've ever threatened me, if I had another lover – you know the kind of crap they ask. They think you did this, you know, they think it was you." She reaches up with one of her hands to adjust her breathing tube and winces. "Detective was an asshole, badgered me till I felt nauseous. The doctor had to chase him out."

"It's all so crazy."

"Tell me about it. I'm surprised they let you in, what with the police and all," Rachel says, disguising her bitterness with a brittle laugh. "How did you get here?"

"I just snuck in. People too busy to notice." He ducks his head, embarrassed by his predicament.

She tries to sit up but after a few strenuous seconds she collapses back on her pillow, her breath rasping through the tube. "I'm so weak, it's frustrating. And my head spins with images. You at the end of the hall. Watching me as I bleed. Tell me you actually tried to help, Jake. Tell me I'm wrong to think that you just stood there like a tree, because I've spent two fucking hours with the police convincing them what a good man you are. You are a good man, aren't you? Tell me I didn't make a fool out of myself. Please."

She's too weak to muster any real anger, but Jake can sense how hard she's trying. He stalls for an answer, gazing around at the flowers which are such obvious and confident declarations of love. "I don't know what to say. I froze. I'm sorry."

She reaches out and wraps her fingers around his, trying to raise her body, but again she fails. "They've got me on a lot of codeine and they mention names like Ducolax, Lorazepam, and Elavil. I know more names of drugs than I do of flowers. Isn't that tragic?"

"No," he says.

She coughs quietly and her eyes flicker shut, then open.

"You don't realize how much of sickness has to do with loneliness until you're stuck in a hospital bed," she says.

"Gwendolyn came by yesterday with about five million flowers to tell me that 'the accident,' as she calls it, has tripled book sales. She has such good intentions, but she had this look of resentment on her face, she couldn't help it, and it was just so infuriating. As if I'd *dragged* her into a stinky hospital ward on purpose! Everyone is like that when they visit. Not just Gwen. And they make you feel worse, I'm sorry but they do, so you tell them to leave. You get rid of them and – this is the absurd part – then you lie in your bed counting the seconds until they come back. It's pitiful, really. There's no dignity to spare here, I'll tell you that."

"My father said the same thing," Jake says, remembering how belligerent Pop could get when he was bedridden, telling Jake to go home only minutes after he'd arrived for a hospital visit, throwing the *Time* magazine that Jake had brought him to the floor. *Momma and I turned everything off.* Theo's words sear into Jake's body and he starts to perspire under his jacket.

"You know what's strange, Jake?" Rachel says. "I dream all the time, even when I'm awake."

"Good dreams?"

"Nightmares. Codeine-induced, I bet. It's as if all the things I was scared of as a kid have come true. Like this rickety old swing set my parents set up in the backyard. I dreamt I was on it, swinging back and forth, making all sorts of crazy creaking sounds, as if the swing was screaming in pain, and then the chains let go sending me flying off into space, spinning away into nothingness. It's one of those falling dreams, when there's no ground below you, and it's so terrifying because you know you're about to die, but you can't tell when. It's just blackness and falling, and you think you can be rescued, but you can't. I keep having that dream."

Jake doesn't say anything, just holds her hand tightly, the heat softening their skin.

"The water?" she says. "Can you hand me–"

"Sure." He reaches over and grabs a glass of water from the stand beside her bed and brings it to her lips.

"I can do it myself." She clutches the glass in her free hand and takes a small sip, then passes it back to him. He sees the intravenous tube sticking in her arm and she notices him looking.

"Attractive, isn't it? Goes with the shaved head and black eyes."

"Don't."

"Does it repulse you?"

"No."

"This other dream, I have another dream, too," she says.

"Another nightmare?"

"It's you. You're here, you're lying beside me, not running off, abandoning me in this goddamn place." She stares at him with her hard green eyes and then, as if some lever in her body had been pulled, they instantly become two stones in pools of rising water. "I'm scared," she says, her voice turning weak and yielding. "Going out of my mind. Who would do this? Who? What do they want?"

"I don't know," Jake says, squeezing her hand, wishing he had something concrete to tell her.

She swallows, blinking the tears from her eyes, and says, "In the dream we make love, but there's no camera. You don't need it any more. We're in bed and you're making love to me and you're very present. Finally in tune, like we always wanted. But then I realize something's wrong. I can't feel anything. I'm dead, you see, in the dream I'm shot dead but we're still making love. We can't stop. It frightens me, Jake, and I don't understand it. I want it to go away, but every time I close my eyes, there it is."

"You should rest," he says, stricken by the similarity between what she's telling him and the vision he had while he was walking across the ice. "I'm going to go. You're tired."

"No. Stay. I need you, I do," she insists, grasping his arm frantically. "I want to know that you're really here. Need to feel it on my skin."

"I'm not sure I–" he starts, but she cuts him off.

"Your body. I want it beside me. I'm scared, Jake. Please. Lie here. Be close to me. Please."

He can hear the need clawing at her voice, as much out of love as out of desperation, the wild yearning for comfort of a child lost in a mall. It chills him to see her so vulnerable, so naked, and he knows he won't be able to refuse her bizarre request. Still, he tries.

"I can't," he says lamely, motioning to her tubes, trying to communicate the impossibility of climbing up onto the bed without hurting her.

"You don't want to touch me," she says, twisting her head on its side and closing her eyes. "Don't tell me that, Jake. Tell me I'm still beautiful and that you love me. Take off your shirt and lie here. Beside me. Let me feel you. This is what I need."

Jake lets go of her hand and stands beside her for a few moments, unsure of what to do. The air smells heavy and sweet, ceremonial. Rachel rolls over, the desperation in her voice hardening to impatience.

"Don't stand there deliberating," she commands. "The nurse checks on me every hour or so. I'm asking you to do this one simple thing. Take your shirt off, close the curtain, and lie with me. Can you at least do that?"

He has to obey her, has to find a way to apologize for hesitating in the hallway. He reaches over and pulls the green curtain shut, the little wheels sliding noiselessly along the aluminum track.

"Take off your pants," she instructs without moving her body. "Socks too. No socks in bed. Good. Hurry up, Jake, I don't want the nurse to come. You'll get in trouble. Now come here. Carefully. Don't yank the tube."

Now his clothes are strewn around the bed and he stands in his underwear, feeling clumsy and awkward. But he follows her directions, bumps against her as he climbs over the high metal bar into the bed. Her face twitches in pain as his weight hits her and he shifts to the side.

"Closer Jake, careful," she mouths. "Let me feel your body. Lie on top of me. Gently." She recoils for a second when his face comes near hers. "You reek of booze, Jake. I can smell it even with this tube up my nose. What time is it?"

He doesn't answer her. His eyes are shut into fragrant blackness, exploring her body with his nose, smelling the sweat of her recovery. Her hands make contact with his skin, moving over it, mapping him. She touches the bruises where the jack handle hit him. Pain throbs through his body out into his skin, and he presses close to her, blood to blood.

"What happened to you?" she whispers, passing her fingers over the swollen marks on his back. "You've cut yourself again. No, those are bruises, welts. Did you do this to yourself?"

"No," he says. The warmth from her body stirs in his groin as the urge to touch her inexorably grows more powerful. "My brother did it to me."

"Theo?" she asks.

"He's come home," Jake replies, trying to block Theo out of his mind. He feels his blood move into his penis, a hot, steady rush, hardening it against Rachel's skin, and he's ashamed by it, embarrassed that he would desire her now, in this bed, while she's so fragile. He tries to move off of her, but she holds him firmly in her hands, their bodies weighing on each other in silence. And soon the rhythm of his breath unites with hers and he starts kissing her face, tentatively at first, around her edges, her chin and her bottom lip, her earlobes and eyelashes, then the plastic tube going into her nose. He can taste the antiseptic of the bandage gauze.

"They do the strangest things to you in Emergency," she says as he prowls her surface with his mouth. "They cut my clothes off with big scissors. Like gutting a fish, right up the middle."

"I know," Jake says, wanting her to keep talking, wanting to feel her body beneath him. He knows she's slightly high on codeine, her thoughts running astray, but it doesn't matter. Her words penetrate him as if they are a blast of heat, melting Theo's revelations and beating back the cold memory of her cries for help in the long marble hall. She keeps talking, her mouth so close to his ear that he can barely understand her.

"Be careful, Jake," she says almost dreamily. "They put a finger up my bum in Emergency, rattled off all sorts of medical words. I wanted to tell them that it was my head that got shot, not my ass. I'm thinking all these crazy things, you know, babbling like an idiot, and they're just moving me from bed to bed in Emergency, ignoring me."

Her voice fills his head, humid and steady. He kisses her forehead and her neck, wanting to cover her whole body with his tongue, taste her, breathe her, bring her close so she can feel safe. He turns his hip to open her legs slightly, as he used to do when they would sleep at her house, his groin pressing against hers.

Rachel's hands move over Jake's back, down his buttocks and his legs, and she says, "I had bad vital signs when I got in. The doctor told me that today. I'm trying to pick up on all this medical speak, maybe for another book. Shot in the superior portion of the left temporal lobe. Near where they say we all store memory. The body has all these mysterious places I never knew of. Secrets from ourselves. That's where the bullet went though, near what they call the deep white matter. Deep white matter. I love that phrase. It's like the soul or something."

Jake listens to her voice in his ear, but soon he stops trying to decipher the words. He doesn't want details. The urge to be inside her grows more intense as she talks, as if her voice were turning up an electric current, and to enter her as he's done so many times before would complete the circuit. For a second he fears someone might come in the room, catch him on top of her. What would they think of that? Screwing a gunshot victim. They probably have some medical term for people with such perverse inclinations. But as quickly as this thought comes, it dissipates, dissolved by his powerful desire to touch her. He grabs the cold metal bar on the side of the bed with his left hand to support himself, and with his right he reaches down to place the tip of his cock near her vagina. He realizes that she's not wet and lifts his hand to his mouth, licking his fingers so he can moisten her.

She says, "Nothing makes sense. My mother's actually on holiday, you know that? Can't even reach her. No one's around for me. And then you disappear, Jake, and the police are asking me about you, and honestly, I don't know what to say. They told me that you took off. God, to hear that shook me up even more. What happened in there, Jake? What did you do that night when you found me?"

The words run out of her mouth over his damp skin like a cool breeze and he can barely absorb them. She talks fast, overflowing with language; it swirls in the floral air, sends him spinning back to the hallway when he saw her crying for help. In the distance he sees that little red light flashing and a dark figure dashing into her office. He can almost make it now, it's something he recognizes, but somehow, too, something he doesn't want to recognize at all. His cock is hard, the warmth of her surrounds him as he pierces her surface. He moves to penetrate more deeply but her body recoils, tries to pull away.

"Don't," she says, pressing her legs together. "Not now."

But he thrusts into her anyway, hoping she'll recall the sensation, even as he feels ashamed of himself for doing it.

"You don't deserve this," she says, but her body slackens and she exhales as if relieved. "I can barely feel you, Jake, I'm on so much codeine. We shouldn't do this."

Jake keeps moving his hips, drawing in and out of her, clenching his eyes so tightly that he sees coloured dots. White and red, wavering like the light at the end of the hall. He starts to breathe in short gulps, trying not to change his rhythm, feeling the bed shake. He wants to tell her that he loves her, that he's sorry for abandoning her, but he's not sure if the words still belong to him, if giving them to her would have any meaning now. Her body is still under him, and he senses the flowers shine and glisten around the room.

Rachel's eyes are closed, too, her breathing getting heavy as Jake moves gently inside her. She says, "The man kissed me, Jake. I just remembered right now. He kissed me on top of my head."

Jake stops his motion, his penis enclosed within her. "What are talking about?"

"The man who did this to me," she says, her voice halting,

as if repeating something that's being parsimoniously dictated into her brain. "I never saw his face, but he kissed me. Like you were just doing."

"When?"

"Right before he smashed my face on my desk," she says, eyes still closed as she immerses herself in the new memory. "That's why my mouth is so bruised. It's strange how I blocked all of this out. The doctor said things would come back. But that's it, isn't it? Put the gun to my head and then he kissed me. I was so scared, but that freaked me out."

Jake grows soft inside her, but he doesn't move for fear that he'll distract Rachel, jolt her out of her memory.

She pauses, her breathing becoming difficult through the tube. "I was in my office, marking some papers," she says. "Waiting for you, right? We were going to grab a bite. And it just happened. Like a nightmare. Someone is behind me. He clamps his hand over my mouth. I froze. Couldn't even scream. That's when he smashed my head down. And then something else. He whispered something in my ear."

Jake lifts his head and examines her closely. The tube in her nose. The eyes, wet and shimmering green. Alive. Distressed. "What did the man say?" he asks urgently.

But somehow Jake knows what she's going to tell him. It's what he's avoided all along, what he's blanked out since that very night. The vagueness that's surrounded him for the last few days suddenly, brutally coalesces. The blurred scenes in his mind focus into perfect clarity. The red light. The dark shadow. He knows who it is.

"I can't remember exactly," she continues. "He told me I was going to die for a purpose. I think he said that. That he was sorry and that I would understand if I got angry or something. It was so crazy. I flipped out. No, no. He kissed me on the head again, that's it, and then I tried to get away, kicked back to throw him off and tried to run. Then this loud explosion in the side of my head. The next thing I remember is you, standing in the hallway, and then nothing. Black." She stops, her mouth gone dry. Then she pushes him off her body.

And now Jake knows. He lets her words cling together in his head like bits of magnet, re-arranging themselves to form the same sentence he heard from his brother two days earlier, when he asked about Ranklin Demoins. *"You're dying for a purpose, but I'm sorry. Be angry, then you'll understand."* The dark shape running down the hall was Theo. The red flickering light his video camera. Seeing him, but not seeing him. Not wanting to. Blacking it out for days, but now letting it come down in full light. Theo everywhere: in the forests of Fenwick, beside Pop, at the university with Rachel, out of his mind and dangerous. Desperate and vengeful. He thanks his victims before killing them, like the black bear so long ago in Algonquin Park. Theo on the run from the police, says he's out of time. And as Jake lies among the flowers, he knows there will be something more, that his brother is not quite done with his insane mission. That before the police track him down for Ranklin Demoins's death, Theo will do what he has been alluding to Jake all along: something violent, something larger than life. Something that Jake will never forget. The hot sensation around Jake's face returns and he starts to cry, as if every second since that moment in the bloody hallway rushes out of his body, flowing through his skin out into the perfumed air. Boiling.

CHANNEL SURFING

Three minutes to broadcast. The red ON AIR light glows outside the studio and Dylan O'Sullivan prepares for his second day as the replacement host of *The Jake Connections*. His make-up gleams under the studio lights, skin perfect and smooth, his demeanour full of the controlled ardour that gives a host the manufactured image of confidence. Slouching into a Larry King-like attack position, he leans forward and pulls down the back of his blazer so that the collar flattens neatly against the nape of his neck. He thinks gleefully of his envious co-workers, how they're all sucking up to him now that he's an on-air personality, and not merely a behind-the-scenes producer. How T-Bill Cantor insisted on buying him a bran muffin and "flavoured" coffee – an extra eighty cents! – at the cafeteria this morning, how Sudra Buchdeera sent him a deliciously seductive e-mail reminding him of his sex fantasy on the anchor desk, for which she was suddenly willing to chuck aside her annoying feminist ideals. Well, no need to join *that* club now. In fact, Dylan has lately made a point of ignoring his old colleagues in the hallways, rubbing his unlikely success in their faces like hot wax. On-camera people, Dylan theorizes, ought to associate only with on-camera people, go to on-camera parties . . . sleep with on-camera women. Straightening the useless notes in front of him into a perfect pile, he practices his read from the TelePrompter. Earlier that day, Jacob's old producer, Kelly Gordon – now *his* producer – explained that viewers like to see a host hold a paper script because it lends the show the desired "reality factor." He's even supposed to glance down at it occasionally, as if he's actually reading. A few good tricks like that, he tells himself, and soon the show will be called *The Dylan Connections*.

In the next studio William Stonebane is finishing his nightly newscast. Dylan tries to remain calm as he waits for his cue. This is the nightly routine, the passing of the electronic baton from one show to another in the seamless weaving of perpetual television stories. On the little monitor built into his desk, Dylan watches Stonebane read the news. *Copy his perfect composure*, Dylan thinks. The appearance of pure objectivity, the weighed pauses, the occasional smile. *We're kin*, he concludes happily. *Fellow hosts. Real on-camera people!*

Two minutes to air.

□ □ □

"Move cam one into the wide-shot position," Greta Watt instructs the bearded man controlling the robotic cameras. "Good. I want to make sure everything goes right tonight for Dylan."

Greta sits comfortably in the director's booth above the studio and observes her latest protégé on the multiple screens in front of her. Wiping a long, mascara-coated lash from her eye, she wonders about the strange reversals of fortune in the last few days. Television loves a scandal, that's what she always believed at RealLife TV, and it was no less true here at the Network. What with the shooting of Poiselle and then the wild antics at the press conference, record numbers of viewers were tuning in to find out what's going on at the Network. Of course, she reminds herself, there was still some messy fall-out to clean up. The hemorrhoids people threatened to cancel their multi-million-dollar contract, claiming that the stress and anxiety caused by "the incident" was unhealthy to a client-base with sensitive stomachs. But once they saw the numbers, they backed off. A mass audience justifies the worst behaviour.

The police were another story. She recalls the exhausting morning she'd just spent down at the police station, Stonebane by her side, answering a barrage of questions from the police chief. A mild-mannered balding man with a reedy voice, the chief displayed grave concern about various issues of evidence tampering and how, exactly, a gun managed to go off at a press conference. Stonebane, she had to admit, was brilliant, eloquently defending his actions, noting how he had anonymously received a package containing "the evidence" only minutes before the press conference and so had used the public forum to turn it over to the authorities. Cagey veteran. "Well, I suppose the matter can be settled," the police chief had said cautiously, "that is, of course, if Mr. Stonebane doesn't move to press any charges against Detective O'Malley in the matter concerning the accidental discharge of the firearm in question. A little quid pro quo, perhaps, Ms. Watt?" She chuckles out loud as she recalls how fast Stonebane jumped at the offer, ending the interrogation minutes later.

Resting her hands on the switcher, she feels the warm plastic of the button. Her fingers tingle. Punch in camera three. Check the close-up shot. Zoom in on Dylan.

Still, in the wake of so many unsettling events she knows her job is to reassure the staff that all is well at the Network, that she's still, to use one of her favourite managerial clichés, "in the driver's seat." Directing tonight's show herself will, she knows, be a fine example of her Tony Robbins-like sense of purpose. Give young Dylan a boost, too. She'll guide him through the latest breaking story, "Upload to Heaven," the image-friendly tale of a mass suicide of some California Internet cult whose members wiped themselves out simultaneously without ever meeting in person. A scrumptious news piece, full of death and technology.

She watches the lighting engineer test the kliegs when the phone beside her rings.

"Yes?" She hears her secretary's voice on the other end.

"It's Carmella. Just checking in as per instructions."

"Any news on Jacob?" Greta holds her breath for a moment.

"Still haven't heard anything. The police are as frustrated as we are."

Greta exhales, ruminating over the situation. The evidence against Jacob is still very slim – there's no sign of his fingerprints on the weapon – but, as the lawyers pointed out, he hasn't done much to boost anyone's confidence regarding his innocence. No one has heard from him in days, and the press are getting hysterical, the *Gazette* actually calling him the most famous fugitive alive. And even if he does finally show up, she reasons, it will be next to impossible to rehabilitate his career. *You really can't rely on anyone but yourself.*

"Ms. Watt?" Carmella says. "Are you still there?"

"Yes, I'm here. What about Mr. Darjun? How is he?"

"The bullet only grazed him and he was released from the hospital within hours. He's already back at work."

"He's a resilient old bat. Good for him. You sent him his letter of dismissal, though?"

"He should have received it yesterday."

"Was he satisfied with the offer?"

"I really don't know, Ms. Watt. Again, he was at the hospital, remember? The bullet injury–"

"Right, right. Probably slipped his mind. Leave a message on his phone to remind him. Anything else?"

"Wire reports just came out saying Ms. Poiselle is recovering nicely. Nothing new."

Greta shrugs. "Still, it's an inspirational story. Upbeat. People like good news. 'Heroine Survives Maniac,' that sort of thing. Tell Zeemanvitz I want a colourful piece on her progress for tomorrow night's broadcast. And if you hear anything about Jacob, and I mean anything, call me immediately. I'll be here until the end of the show."

She bangs down the receiver and begins her final scrutiny of the studio. The phone lines are ready for callers. The guests are booked over the satellite in California. The floor director is checking the mikes. The robotic cameras roll into pre-set positions. The lighting grid blazes. Dylan is primed to go. Everything is working out, and Greta feels lucky to be in charge. The Jacobson affair is essentially over, and she's played it brilliantly in the Network's favour. She punches in a tape for a Javex bleach commercial and relaxes as the pleasant jingle plays into her headset.

Thirty seconds to air.

□ □ □

In the darkness behind the wooden facade that makes up the set for *The Jake Connections*, Tasso lights up his tenth cigarette of the day. He's been chain-smoking in his special spot for over an hour, ever since he put on his long black coat and closed the library. Now the coat seems heavy on his body, weighing down his rounded shoulders as if it's trying to smother him. He should be on his way home, he realizes that, but he can't bring himself to make his way to the exit and begin the long, cold walk along the streets. Home means phoning his daughter, telling her that he's been fired. He can't keep it from her forever. It's all so shameful, so diminishing. Better to hide away here, in his little smoking refuge, among the half-used paint cans, solvents, and varnishes the set designers leave piled in the corner – in a badly unsystematic way, he notes bitterly.

He lights up another smoke and regards the pile of cigarette butts and ashes that grows steadily beside him, listlessly arranging the mess into a perfect circle with his finger. His left arm throbs where the bullet wounded him. The doctor told him it wasn't serious, bandaged him up quickly, gave him some painkillers, and sent him back to work the next day. "Work?" he mutters sourly. "What work would that be now?" Reaching into his pocket with his good arm, he takes out a bottle of tablets the doctor prescribed, opens it, and pops two pills in his mouth. In less than a month he's supposed to pack his bags and leave the library, that's what the letter from President Greta Watt said. One year short of his full-benefits retirement package and they let him go. No farewell party, no gold watch. Slipped out as invisibly as he'd slipped in, as if he'd never been here at all.

His mind runs back over his twenty-four years at the

Network, and to his dismay, he finds there's not much to remember. Almost a quarter of a century filing stories, letting the events of the world glide past his helpful hands; here he is at the end of his career, and nothing stands out but the crushing routine of daily news: Nixon resigning, the SALT treaty, the October Crisis, AIDS facts, Three Mile Island and Chernobyl, the royal wedding and, later, the public divorce, supply-side economics and Hinckley, various fish crises off the coast, the Berlin Wall, the Gulf War, O.J., Clinton's cigar, Flight 111 . . . every event in history passing through his fingers, but he never left a mark on any of them, and, he has to admit, they never left a mark on him either. He wonders how he might measure his life-long connection to the world at large, but he realizes that no science has yet been devised to measure a connection that minute. A watcher, an indexer, a space in between the things that matter. *This is what I am*, he ponders sadly. *An expendable life.*

The pulsing sensation in his arm dulls as the painkillers begin to take effect. He throws his cigarette away in disgust at his self-pity. *Twice!* He's lost everything in his life twice, so why, he wonders, trying desperately to be optimistic, why is he so afraid to lose it all again? His daughter's almost fully grown, certainly she's independent enough. And he has a few dollars salted away in the bank. To a certain degree, he reflects, he's free. Free to do what he wants, to express himself in any way he pleases. To be born again into a new life, a new career. A new skin. Taking out a fresh pack of Benson and Hedges from his shirt pocket, he leans back against the wooden flat along which the studio cables run and lights up. The smoke is instantly sucked away by the air filter. He shuts his eyes, trying in vain to imagine a new future without the library, without the morning walk to work. Without his pension. But he can't. The distant pounding in his arm beats against the blackness of his mind, penetrating into his unsettled soul.

□ □ □

Jake remains in bed with Rachel, feeling her body soften into a codeine sleep. He's heavy with too much information, wiped out by Rachel's disclosure and what that disclosure has forced him to accept about Theo. Anger and confusion slash inside of him, fierce pains hammer in his chest like a butcher pounding into a piece of meat. He considers pressing the CALL button to summon the nurse and tell her who he is, tell her to dial the police so he can tell them what Theo has done. Have Theo arrested and bring everything to an end. But he can't do that to Theo. Despite everything, he still can't turn in his own brother.

The digital clock on the table says six thirty-five and Jake absently reaches over to the table, grabs the TV remote, and clicks on Channel 6. He presses the MUTE button so he won't wake Rachel. His show is playing, but something is going seriously wrong on the set. There's a terrible commotion, the camera jumping back and forth between Dylan, whose hands are in the air, and someone else. Jake sits up sharply, a quick intake of breath hissing from his mouth as he sees Theo's image on screen. The emotion swirling through his body coagulates into a thick gelatin that's no longer anger, but a sense of total loss, a sucking, suffocating pull on every organ, every muscle, every emotion as he finally accepts the fact that the brother he once knew is gone and has been replaced by this new, evil abstraction, this dangerous maniac who he's now watching on his own TV show. His skin starts trembling and tightens into little bumps as if he's cold. This is what he sees:

In the middle of Dylan O'Sullivan's opening monologue, Theo bursts onto the TV set, pulls out a gun, and points it at Dylan's head. The camera zooms in for a close-up, then switches to another angle in a panicky, jerky fashion. Dylan throws his hands up in surrender and freezes with a distressed expression on his face, as if someone has just sprayed him with liquid nitrogen. Quickly the camera cuts away from this most untelegenic example of cowardice, but it's too late. The image of Dylan blanching in fear is already in homes across the country. The picture cuts back to Theo, who's now tearing around the studio in a fury, waving his gun this way and that to make sure no one breaks in and tries to disarm him. The cameras keep rolling. Leaping onto Dylan's desk, Theo kicks the water jug onto the floor, droplets exploding silver and blue in the gleam of lights. Theo is yelling something, Jake can tell from the gesticulations, but he can't hear what Theo's saying. He's heard all he needs to from Theo, anyway, and can't bring himself to turn on the volume. It's enough to watch Theo in mime, pointing the gun to Dylan's head, terrifying and exhilarating the viewers.

But even without the volume, Jake is mesmerized. The remarkable footage lends a terrible order to what only minutes ago Jake suspected was a random series of events: Pop's death, Ranklin Demoins's death, Rachel's shooting. "Pattern recognition," Jake repeats to himself, just like Rachel said. Theo's famous righteousness finally turned vicious, protecting the things he loves by destroying them, and now, on TV, destroying himself, too. *But it's my turn, isn't it? Now he comes after me.* Jake knows that he has to go back to the Network, has to go after Theo and try to stop him, but he can't lift himself off the bed and leave Rachel. Abandon her again. He lies perfectly still, almost in a trance, staring at his brother as he unravels on TV in front of him.

Jake shifts his body on the bed and pulls Rachel close, the smell of unconsummated sex with her lingering faintly among the scent of flowers. On screen Theo holds up the video camera he's carried everywhere, and Jake realizes that he is going to force the Network to run the tapes of their journey. Footage of Theckla dancing and Momma passed out, footage of the man hitting him with the tire jack. Even then, Jake doesn't move. A familiar remoteness envelops his body. But now it doesn't feel foreign. More like a paralysing intimacy, as if helping Theo now would be as shameful as not helping Rachel that Sunday night. And it's at this moment, when Jake can no longer distinguish between love and betrayal, revenge and justice, that his body comes alive. Like photographic paper after it's dropped into developing solution, he feels a picture begin to emerge: borders of a body, features of a face, details of hands and feet. A picture of himself, charged with colour and smell, vibrating with intention, propelling him to go after Theo. He bends to kiss Rachel on her dry lips and then gets out of the bed and hurriedly puts on his clothes. He pulls back the green curtain and opens the door, bolting out of the room past the nurses in the hall. In ten minutes he'll be at the Network, where the viewers always expect him, where his brother now owns the airwaves.

□ □ □

"I need everyone working together now," Greta says to her frantic crew, her fingers flying from button to button to make sure she captures everything happening on the floor. "Don't panic, most hostage crises end without violence." She leans forward and speaks steadily into the mike connected to Dylan's earpiece. "It's okay, Dylan, try to relax. You're going to be fine out there, I'll steer you right through this. No one's going to get hurt if you keep your cool. Now, very slowly, lower your hands. Come on now, listen to me, Dylan, you're doing fine." Even as she reassures her new host that he won't get shot, she has to admit to herself that this is the exact kind of television she loves: live and unpredictable. Being an executive so removed from the action doesn't give her the rush of breaking news. She starts to miss it even as she makes it happen.

Dylan doesn't respond to her words, but she doesn't let that faze her. She turns to the white-faced crew in the booth. "Let's stay sharp here, people. If this guy offs O'Sullivan – God forbid, but we have to consider all options – if he does, we cut to Stonebane for commentary." The switcher nods warily. "Kelly, make sure he's standing by," Greta continues. "If Stonebane leaves his set, he's fired." *This is why I'm here*, she thinks confidently. *Everyone else is going to pieces and I'm busy releasing the giant within.* At that moment Theo's voice comes in loudly over the booth speaker.

"My name is Theo Jacobson," he says carefully, as if he were pouring hot oil into an engine. "If anyone comes onto this set, your host dies. If you try to take me off the air, he dies. I want the doors to this set shut. Is this clear? Now, I have a videotape of the Poiselle shooting that I know the Network will be interested in showing. I want it on air in five minutes. Send someone down to pick it up. Very carefully. Right now. I want it on the air. No tricks or your shithead is meat. I want to see everything on the monitor."

Greta rolls back in her chair to consider her options, but almost immediately realizes that she has none. Until the police arrive, there's nothing she can do to stop the lunatic. Nothing, that is, except keep broadcasting. *It is news, after all*, she reflects, remembering the hard decisions she had to make when she programmed *AfterLifeTV. Must stick to our mandate.* She rolls her chair back to her position and runs her fingers through her hair as if to strip out any stray thoughts. "Kelly, this is your job," she says to Jake's – now Dylan's – producer. "It's your show. Now get down there and grab that tape."

Kelly Gordon doesn't move. The request is not only absurd, but also life-threatening. She stares at Greta imploringly, trying to communicate the obvious fact that retrieving material from terrorists is not part of her job description.

"I know this is difficult," Greta says, "but we have Dylan to think about here, too."

Kelly still doesn't move, but tries to make eye contact with others in the room in order to garner some support. In true Network fashion, everyone looks away.

"Obviously Ms. Gordon is no longer interested in being the producer of this show," Greta announces to the astonishment of the crew. "Who would like her job tomorrow night?"

The room is silent. Reluctantly, Kelly makes her way out of the booth and down the stairs to the studio floor where Theo holds the Network airwaves hostage.

"I'm going to give that woman a raise," Greta announces.

□ □ □

The studio bakes under the high wattage of the lights. Theo perches himself on the end of the desk while he waits for someone to retrieve his videotape. Leaning back towards Dylan's blanched face, Theo whistles sharply. "Hey! Look at me, chump." He waves the gun in front of Dylan's face. "How do you like my brother's shitty job?"

Dylan doesn't say a word. His hands are still in the air, and he's too frightened even to hear the voice of Greta blaring instructions in his ear. He turns his head away from Theo and a whimper escapes from his throat, picked up clearly by the sensitive microphones.

"I said, look at me!" Theo hisses. Dylan's heads whips forward, but he bends his body away, as if he expects Theo to hit him at any moment.

"Good boy," Theo says, reaching into his pocket to grab a cigarette. He lights it and then tilts his head up to exhale. The TV lights burn on his face and his vision flares white with spotted brightness.

The robotic cameras whir and vibrate as they move to different positions on the floor, and Theo can vaguely hear a tinny voice buzz in Dylan's earpiece. He notices how every surface in the studio is unnaturally smooth: the hard black desk, the glass lens of the camera, the grey wooden flats of the set, the big black TV monitors sitting on top of the rolling stands flashing back pictures of himself, gleaming with light. Nothing sticks to surfaces in the studio, everything sliding glibly over everything else, like water on a waxed car.

He waits in silence for someone to take the tape from him, knowing that silence is the thing television people most fear. The mystery of dead air, which always signals a breakdown of some sort, a sense that something else is in control. He inhales on his cigarette, watching the smoke twist purple under the lights, patiently waiting for everything to unfold as he imagined it would.

□ □ □

"We've got dead air!" Greta calls out. "I want Stonebane on for commentary." She hits a button on the console in front of her, linking to Stonebane.

"William, this is Greta. Can you hear me?"

Stonebane presses his finger in his ear to hear the voice of Greta more clearly.

"We're done for the night, Greta," he says, reaching up to take off his microphone.

"Don't get out of your desk," she commands. "Do you see what's happening in the next studio?"

Stonebane looks down at the monitor built into the surface of his desk and instantly recoils. "What's going on? There's a man with a gun in there!" Images of the bullet sizzling by his chest a day earlier flash through his mind.

"Listen to me, William," says Greta deliberately, praying that Stonebane will be in a co-operative mood. "We've got a terrible situation on our hands. Jacob's brother has somehow broken into the studio and is holding Dylan hostage."

"Jacob's brother?" Even the great Voice cannot hide a tinge of fear. "Well good God, woman, call the police."

"Someone already has," Greta reassures him. "But we have to stay on air or Dylan will lose his life. That's the demand Jacob's brother is making. Now, I want you to do the live commentary, William. I *need* you to help me out here. There's no time to argue. I'll patch you through so you can hear what's going on in the next studio, but we're going to you in thirty seconds on a split screen. I'll be in your ear the whole time, so don't worry. Are you ready, William? Can you do this?"

His mind reels. After the mêlée at the press conference, Charlene Rosemount's threat, and the painful police interrogation about the gun, he's more than ready to put the whole Jacobson affair behind him and move on.

"I don't think I can help, Greta," Stonebane says, still gazing down at the monitor where Theo holds Dylan hostage. "This is your problem, not mine."

"Unacceptable, William, you're going on air!" Greta snaps, trying not to lose her temper and failing. "This is the biggest story of the year and we're goddamn well going to broadcast it. This isn't the time for pettiness, Bill, you got that?" He remains stubbornly silent so her tone changes to something more pleading. "Work with me, William, just this once. Please. This is a winner, I guarantee. International awards. If you do this I promise you, no more cuts to your show this year. Is it a deal?"

Every fibre in Stonebane's being tells him to get up and walk away, even as he realizes the monumental nature of the story. He frantically debates whether Charlene Rosemount is ambitious and unscrupulous enough to actually leak some horrible rumour to the tabloid press about his sexuality. If she sees him on air now – as she surely will – might he wake up tomorrow and find all sorts of foul gossip about his sexual peccadilloes? News anchors are not supposed to have peccadilloes of any kind, least of all sexual ones. He's lived by that rule all his life. He shifts his weight, preparing to leave, when another thought occurs to him. It's not Dylan who's being held hostage, it's actually *him*. And he's not being held by a man with a gun; more pathetically, he's being held hostage by a journalist – a *local* journalist, at that. *My God*, he thinks, planting himself back in his chair. Revulsion courses through his body, followed immediately by shame, and for a split second he has the urge to apologize to Greta for letting down the Craft, letting down the whole sacred Network. Of course he'll go to air. After all, this is breaking news, the kind of news for which he's been training himself for decades. *People's lives are on the line*, he thinks with renewed purpose. *People's careers.*

"Cut to me whenever you're ready, Greta," Stonebane says, and he notices how the floor director stares at him with new admiration. At the side of the set Thatchly gives him a thumbs up. *Troublemaker*, Stonebane mutters to himself, but he quickly flashes Thatchly the sign back. Inhaling deeply as the thundering introduction music swells, Stonebane prepares the Voice.

"Let's make some television," Greta says, the relief palpable in her voice. Her fingers fly across the dials and the monitor in front of her breaks into two halves. Dylan and Theo on one side, William Stonebane on the other. "All right, William. Ready on my count. Five to the intro. Four, three, two, one. You're on."

"This is William Stonebane back with a breaking news story," he begins majestically. "What you're seeing on the screen beside me is a live shot of a hostage crisis taking place in a studio not ten feet from where I sit. Only moments ago a man claiming to be Theo Jacobson, the brother of our own missing host, Jacob Jacobson, burst onto the set and, pistol in hand, took Network reporter Dylan O'Sullivan hostage. We still don't know what his demands are, or just what he intends to do. But I *can* tell you this. I will not be leaving this chair until the crisis has abated."

Greta listens as Stonebane expertly outlines the events of the past week, and she marvels at his professionalism. *He's really good, the old bastard. Perfect.* She watches the split screen closely and speculates on the blockbuster ratings she must be pulling in.

"Where the hell is Kelly? She should be in there already?" she shouts to the people in the booth. "I want someone to call every other station in the country and tell them what's happening. I want viewers, people, get moving." The machines around her flash with images as Greta whispers information into Stonebane's ear, which he in turn spits out in perfectly formed, well-modulated sentences.

□ □ □

From behind the set of *The Jake Connections*, Tasso tweaks his nose. He smells smoke – not his own, but the odour of a different brand of cigarettes. Someone yells from the floor of the studio, and he hears a commotion of sorts. Part of a new show format? Lines are blurring. Nothing is routine any more. His hands shake so badly from his shot nerves that he drops his lit cigarette onto the floor before he can take a drag. It rolls under the wood flat, near the electric cables. His whole body quakes as if he's running a fever, and his limbs feel clammy and cramped. Again, the thought of walking home occurs to him, but his limbs won't lift him off the floor. In a daze he grabs another cigarette, leans back against the set for support, and lights up. Images from the last few days boil and burst on his mind like water drops on a hot skillet. He clamps his hands over his face and hyperventilates, gulping back air, swallowing and then exhaling, just as he would as a child in Goa when he wanted attention from his mother. For a few desperate moments he tries to force the tears from his eyes, but nothing comes. He realizes that he can't even cry. He's forgotten how. In a state of high anxiety, Tasso doesn't notice the thin wisp of smoke that begins to emerge from the wooden set.

□ □ □

As delicately as she can, Kelly Gordon steps into the studio to retrieve the tape from the person the soundman just described as "Charles Manson with a gun." She suspects the idea of admitting to Theo that she's produced Jake's show for two years is not going to endear her to him. *Better just to get in and out of there as quickly as possible.* She absently tucks in her blouse and runs her hand nervously through her long hair, as if preparing for a job interview. *They don't teach you this shit at journalism school, do they?* Her tongue flicks out and wets her lips as Greta's words replay through her mind: "We have Dylan to think about, too." *Yeah, right,* Kelly thinks as she inches forward. *I'm risking my ass for some rookie stand-in. I've got fuckin' seniority on that guy.* She dredges up the mantra all producers learn when they first get a job: The talent is expendable.

Theo slips off the end of the desk when he sees Kelly edge across the wall of the studio and he slides the video cassette across the floor towards her. "That's on air in five minutes or monkey-boy over here dies."

Kelly picks up the tape and examines it closely. "Oh my God!" Her cheeks flush red. "We have a problem."

"What?" Theo levels the gun at her.

"I'm sorry, sir," she stammers, her eyes staring down at the hard black floor. "But I'm, uh, I'm afraid we're going to have to dub this tape before it goes to air."

"What the fuck are you talking about?"

She fidgets with the bottom of her shirt. "This is a videotape, you see," she explains slowly, her voice cracking. "And we'll need to transfer it to beta if we want it on air?" She ends her sentence as if she's asking a question.

"Your point?" Theo says, still not understanding.

"I'll have to go to another edit suite to do that," Kelly continues delicately. "That takes time. And then the machine has to dub it and code it and, well, that also takes time. Then it depends on how much footage you have and . . ."

Up in the booth, Greta almost dives through the monitor at the image of Kelly. "TAKE THE BLOODY TAPE FROM HIM, YOU FOOL!" she yells. But Kelly can't hear her.

"What I'm saying, sir, is that, well, this won't get to air in five minutes." Kelly shrugs her shoulders, aware that she may have just got herself killed.

"What the hell is she talking about?" Theo says, cuffing Dylan lightly on top of the head.

"It's, it's kind of a TV thing with tapes," Dylan says, swallowing after every few words. "We use a certain format, and your tape is not the same one and–"

"I can hook it up to this monitor here," Kelly mumbles, pointing to one of the televisions on the set floor. "That is, if we have the proper cables."

"The set guys can do that," Dylan chimes in a little too loudly, hoping to distract Theo. "I think they have some cables over there."

"In the box?" Kelly asks, pointing to the far corner of the studio.

"Yeah, the red-and-black ones," answers Dylan, finally lowering his hands. The banal talk seems to calm both of them.

"What kind of camera does he have?" asks Kelly, moving back towards the box of cables.

"Sony three chip, I think," answers Dylan, examining the technical details of Theo's camera.

"That old . . . I mean, um, that's fine, perfect."

"Would you two mechanics shut the fuck up?" Theo says, exasperated by the conversation.

"Language!" Greta mutters. She guides the robotic cameras to follow Kelly. "He's live for God's sake, we're going to get complaints from the sponsors. Let's go to Stonebane for comment." She hits the SWITCH button.

"It looks like the terrorist Theo Jacobson wants to play some sort of tape," Stonebane says, right on cue. "In order to protect the life our brave colleague, we've decided to comply with his demands. The police are on their way as I speak and no one is quite sure what we're about to see. Viewer discretion is advised, but please don't touch that dial."

Greta cuts back to the studio where Kelly fiddles with some cables.

"Did you know my brother well?" Theo asks Dylan while he butts his cigarette out on the desk.

Greta boosts all the mikes so Theo's voice will come out clearly on air. "Answer him honestly, Dylan, pretend you're at the dentist," she coaches.

"Did you two work together?" Theo asks again.

Dylan is completely thrown off by Greta's advice. *When was the last time the dentist held a fucking gun to my head. Jesus!* He tries to refocus, unsure what answer might provoke Theo's ire. "Together? Sometimes, I guess."

"So you're part of it too," Theo spits. "Part of this bullshit machine."

"No, no, I'm just the back-up . . ." Dylan stutters. *Don't shoot*, he thinks, *don't shoot*.

Sensing Dylan's panic, Greta offers more words of encouragement. "Perfect, Dylan, you're doing fine. Breathe deeply. This is the hard part. Just like a root canal. Very basic surgery." She can see his chest heave in and out under his suit.

"He's a complex guy, my brother, did you know that?" Theo says slowly, getting up and walking behind Dylan.

"Complex?" Dylan says, trying to process the notion that root canals are somehow relevant to the situation at hand.

"I'm asking you."

"What?"

"If he's complex."

"Exactly."

"Exactly what?"

"I don't know!"

"You dip-shit."

"Ok," Dylan gasps, baffled by the conversation.

"I thought you had to have brains to get a job like this." Theo rubs his chin and the robotic camera rolls to get a tighter angle on him. "Jake loved it on air," he says. "Loved it too much. You got to watch out for that, boy-o, this place can seduce you."

"Not me," Dylan squeaks, realizing how quickly the charm of being on air can wear off.

Theo expertly twirls the gun on his forefinger. "Jake always had a knack for performing. Used to entertain the family at the dinner table, imitate people, tell jokes. Make us laugh pretty hard." As he talks, Theo starts to circle Dylan with a methodical pace, his tone slowly growing more agitated. "Then he got this show and he changed. Just like that. It was all that mattered to him, nothing else. Performance, entertainment. Stopped writing me letters, didn't even have time to stay with my father when he was sick. Too busy, he said. Yeah, right. I'm his goddamn brother, I know him! I watched him change. Seduced. He was seduced by this place. Even turned on me, out there in Fenwick Park doing something good. He sat in here mocking me for other people's pleasure. I almost went nuts. Did he tell you I was out there?

Dylan tries desperately to give the right answer. "I think so. Sure. Maybe not, though. Did he?"

"He knew, he knew I was there," Theo says, ignoring Dylan. "Tried to sabotage my operation with some bullshit reporting on his show. Why didn't he just come out and see me, ask some questions? Find out the truth? It's so beautiful out there. Untouched forest, uncorrupted land. My father used to fish in places like that, never got lucky though. Wish I could have taken him out to Fenwick, guarantee him a good haul of salmon. You fish?"

"Fish?" Dylan replies, startled by the change of topic. "Well, sometimes. Small-mouth bass. Just casting, mainly."

Greta finally loses her cool and screams into the mike connected to Dylan's earpiece. "O'Sullivan, the red light is on, and you're talking about *fishing*? Millions of people are watching! You're live, damn you. Live!"

Instinctively, Dylan repeats what he hears in his ear. "But why am I talking about fishing? The red light is on. Millions of people are watching. This is live TV."

Greta presses her fingers tightly against her temples. *Rookie host. Rookie host.*

"I bet you read Jake's girlfriend's book," Theo says, switching topics again. "What was it, *Pattern Recognition* or something?"

"It's live TV," Dylan repeats pointlessly. He's barely staying alive just trying to cope.

"High-class crap, that's what it was," Theo continues, getting more worked up. Beads of sweat glimmer on his face under the lights. "She mesmerized Jake with her so-called theory about 'meaning' being found in chaos. What does that bitch know about chaos, sitting behind her mahogany desk? She ever get out into the real world? Another phony, like all of you. But I guess she knows something about chaos now, doesn't she?" He thrusts the gun closer to Dylan's head and drops his voice to a whisper. "Boom! That's chaos for you, boy-o, and it ain't some fucking video game."

Dylan's mouth opens and shuts with no sound, panting for air.

"You done yet?" Theo says, turning his attention back to Kelly, who's still trying to hook the camera to the monitor in the corner.

"A few more minutes," she calls back, resting Theo's camera on top of the big TV set and frantically searching for the right cables.

"Dylan!" Greta howls. "Get back in the game. Ask him what he knows about the Poiselle shooting."

Dylan's head snaps up. "Your brother met Rachel at one of my parties," he blurts out. "Women love him, you know."

Up in the booth Greta lets out a moan and slouches back in her chair.

"Thanks for the info, shit-for-brains," Theo says. "But when I need your opinion I'll shoot you." Theo points to a row of red buttons in front of Dylan. "Those. What are those for?"

"Callers," Dylan mumbles. "This is a phone-in show and, uh, people can call and . . . talk show. Right?"

"I've seen Jake do that," Theo says. His tone changes to curiosity. "Well, we seem to have some time on our hands. Let's bring someone on."

"Now? I don't know if–" Dylan sputters.

"Do it."

Dylan instantly punches a button.

"Hello, you're on the air . . . with Dylan O'Sullivan." He steals a glance at Theo, not sure if using his name as host is the correct etiquette under the circumstances. An exasperated caller comes in over the speaker.

"Can you tell me what the hell's going on in there?" asks the caller impatiently. "I had a question about the California death cult."

"Did you know anyone in that cult?" Theo answers for Dylan.

"Who are you? You're not the regular host."

"I asked you a question. Did you know anyone in that cult?"

"No, but I want–"

Theo cuts him off. "Then why the fuck do you want to talk about it? Don't you have anything else to do?"

"What! Screw you," the caller shouts and hangs up.

"Take another call," Theo orders, waving the gun towards the panel of red buttons on the desk.

Dylan quickly presses one. "Hello, you're on the air." He closes his eyes and waits for the bullet.

"Hi. First-time caller but long-time viewer, and I have a question for the man with the gun."

"Go ahead," says Theo.

"I never miss this show. It's always so exciting."

"Your question?" Theo replies. He moves around Dylan.

"I just can't believe I finally got through. You know, I've tried for weeks –"

"Do you have a question or not?" Dylan snaps, feeling Theo's presence lurk ominously behind him.

"I was calling about that cult situation because I once had a friend in a cult, but since you have Mr. Jacobson's brother on the show, can he tell me anything about Jake's involvement in that shooting?"

"I can tell you everything," Theo answers, raising his face up to the heat of the lights. "But you'll have to wait for the tape to play. Everything is on the tape."

Greta's voice blasts into Dylan's ear. "Ask him about the tape!" she says. "Ask him for details."

"Can you tell us about this video?" Dylan repeats softly.

"You just keep pushing the buttons, boy, and clam up. Take another call."

Dylan nods vigorously and shoots out his hand to bring another guest. A man's excited voice comes in over the speaker.

"Yeah, I wanna know if this is for real or just one of those dramatization things. My buddy here says that gun is fake and that you're not gonna shoot anyone."

Theo bounces the gun in his hand, as if measuring its weight. "Do you think I ought to shoot him?" he asks, a slight grin curling up the sides of his thin lips.

The caller contemplates the question. "Well, it *would* be kind of cool if you did," he says finally. "I mean, no offence to the new guy behind the desk, but I've never seen a live shooting on TV. They always cut it out or sell it on video. I'm not saying I want you to *kill* him, I just mean, if you're gonna do it . . . well, show me the money, right?"

"Thanks for calling," Dylan gasps, and disconnects the line. Sweat pours down his brow in long rivulets, cutting through his thick mask of make-up until his face resembles an aerial shot of a flood zone. Beneath the desk his legs twitch frantically, sending tremors up his body.

With reptilian deliberation, Theo moves closer to examine Dylan's pallid face. He says, "Apparently some of your viewers would like me to shoot you. An interesting proposition. Should we take a poll?"

"A poll?" Dylan rasps. *I'm going to die at the hands of a psycho*, he thinks. *I'm not supposed to die like that. I'm a middle-class Catholic, for God's sake. We die of heart attacks and cancer, not bullets to the head on TV. This is not happening, someone please tell me this is not happening . . .*

"A poll's a very democratic idea," Theo explains, walking across the studio floor. "We'll ask callers to vote on your life. Why not? That's what they really want. Something dramatic and entertaining. I think even Jake would approve. What does his girlfriend like to call it? Interactive viewing. So how about it, partner? Up for a little death poll?"

In the booth Greta puts her hand over her mouth and for the first time the gravitas of the situation hits her. *Someone might actually be executed on air.* She's broadcast thousands of funerals, hundreds of acts of euthanasia, but a death poll! She marvels at the ghoulishness of the idea. It's almost Romanesque in its grandeur. Before she gets carried away, she checks herself. *Is it wrong?* she wonders, her mouth poised over her microphone, *is it crossing the line?* As if looking for an answer, she glances over at the switchboard and notices that it's lit up with callers.

"What are we going to do, Greta?" the nervous switcher asks, picking up on her train of thought. "We can unhook the callers, you know that? Don't let anyone through until the police get here."

"No," she says with forced solemnity, knowing she's at the helm of a historic moment in television and giddy at the prospect. "No. Let's do it. Follow his demands. We're going to take some callers. It's the best thing we can do, *for Dylan.*"

The switcher rolls his eyes. "Yeah, right. For Dylan."

"Zip it," Greta says between pressed lips and leans forward to talk to her new host. "Dylan, listen to me. We're going to go along with this poll thing of his. The police are on their way, so just do your best. I've been in many, many similar situations," she lies perfectly, ignoring the glares from the rest of the crew. "Viewers always side with the host, so there's nothing to fear."

Dylan, ashen-faced, nods his head. "Okay."

"Then let's take another call," Theo says, buoyantly. Under the heat of the lights he senses his world blend into Jake's. The studio feels like the forest where Ranklin Demoins died, a locus of pure action, beyond ambiguity. Every watt of studio light burns on his skin, every smooth surface reflects his face, every detail courses through him as if he's an antenna, sending his signals beyond the studio, out on the dazzling airwaves. In this moment he understands what Jake might love about TV, how live performance mimics the more intense reality he craves on the front lines of the world. The little enclosed space under hot lights, staring into the black round lens of the camera where every error counts. There's something fantastic about it. But even as he revels in the moment, he knows it's not enough. In the end, there's nothing genuine at stake. He trains his mind back on pictures of Ranklin Demoins and Nigel Fornhaven, of Bangkok and China, of every other moment when he's plucked people out of their oblivion and made them matter to the world. *The little deaths, the great becomings.* The wonderful technology of violence that Jake's world will now have to see. One last time, for Jake. *Our state of grace*, he thinks, *televised.*

Now everything around Theo seems alive. The gun feels soft in his hand and he grips it tightly, letting the sweat of his hand moisten the handle. The smooth surfaces of the studio bend towards him like leaves in the forest. He leaps up on the desk, startling Dylan, and steps on one of the buttons with the toe of his boot.

"Caller, you're on the air," he calls out into the rack of blazing lights. "Do you think I should kill this man?"

"I think you need help, buddy," yells back the voice of a caller. "You're crazy."

"I'll take that as a no," Theo says, disconnecting the line and gazing down at Dylan. "One for you, mister beautiful, and one for me. All tied up. Let's take another call." He presses another button with his foot. "Hi, you're on my brother's show, and our question of the day is this: Should I shoot this blow-dried piece of crap in the head?"

The caller hesitates, unsure of how to answer the question.

"Hello?" Theo repeats.

"Yes, hello, my name is Fran Gerny. I'm from Niagara Falls, and I think you people are going too far this time. I'm complaining to the Network president."

"About what?" asks Theo cheerfully.

"About your foul language," she says sternly. "I've got children watching."

Theo steps on the button and the line goes dead.

"I'll give that one to you, Dylan. Let's try again. You're on the air."

"Hi. I'm calling from a bar, and we've got a bet going here that you won't do it," the caller says excitedly. "Two hundred bills says you're bluffing. Come on, cock the gun if you're really such a hot shot–"

Theo hangs up the phone again, cutting the man off.

"That's definitely one for me. What a loyal audience you're building. Two all." He calls over to Kelly. "I want that tape on air! How long?"

She jumps back from the monitor, clutching a tangle of wires and connectors. "I'm going as fast as I can."

"Don't fuck with me. Hurry up." His attention veers back to Dylan. "Okay, pretty boy. Time's running out. Let's make this one the deciding call." He steps on a button to open a line. "You're on the air with our death poll. Go ahead."

The line goes dead. Deftly Theo kicks another button with his boot. "You're on the air. What's you're decision? Does this man die or not?"

"Hello, Theo." The voice on the line is so authoritative,

so powerful and rich, that it almost fills the room. "I've heard so much about you from your brother, Jake. We're very close, you know."

The voice belongs to William Stonebane, specially patched through by Greta in the booth. It's an inspired bit of television producing, Greta knows this, more of an epiphany than just a mere idea – having her star anchor on a split screen with a terrorist, negotiating for a man's life via the phone-in. Live. Her fingers whirl across the control panel, moving the robotic cameras into a new position, all the while feeding questions into Stonebane's earpiece.

"Keep him on air as long as possible, William," she instructs. "Talk to him, distract him from Dylan. We'll run your sponsor's name as a banner on the bottom of the screen."

Theo listens to the deep voice on the speaker and vaguely recognizes it. "How do you know my brother?" he asks suspiciously.

"Old friends," replies Stonebane, coolly. "In fact, he told me all about your little adventure in British Columbia. I'll bet neither the loggers nor the police are very happy to see you on TV."

Theo smiles, relishing the idea of a little resistance. He remembers similar moments: the crimson spit of Ranklin Demoins running down his face, the scratching fingernails of the rescued Thai girls. Normal manifestations of ignorance and fear. "Are you a cop?" he asks.

"No, heavens no," Stonebane chuckles. "My name is William Stonebane. I'm the anchor here at the Network. I'm sure you've watched me many times."

"Can't say that I have," Theo lies. He's seen Stonebane before, but refuses to give any television personality the charity of recognition.

"Oh, come now," Stonebane insists, incapable of believing that the Voice – never mind his face – is not instantly recognizable. "You must have watched the nightly news with me. I'm the number-one show in the country."

"Don't watch the news."

"I just can't believe that," Stonebane says dismissively. "I covered the story at Fenwick, too."

"So you're a fuck-up like my brother. Congratulations."

"Hardly," Stonebane huffs, rattled by the comment.

"Move on, Stonebane, move on," Greta commands. In the background of the set, Greta notices a haze of some sort, slowly moving through the glow of lights, but she ignores it.

"You should know that the police are on their way," Stonebane says, getting back on track. "So I suggest you put down the gun, tell us where your brother is, and turn yourself in. End this silliness."

"Fuck you," Theo answers. "I'm making the rules here, and you're interrupting my death poll. You tell *me* something, whoever you are: Ever see someone get shot on live TV?"

Stonebane pauses as he considers what answer would make for the best television. He pretends to write something down on a piece of paper, making sure he appears calm and professional for the audience, knowledgeable though not arrogant, firm yet friendly – much like his well-groomed colleague Ted Koppel. Let them know how seriously he's taking the situation, but, of course, drag it out as long as possible to give himself maximum exposure. "Over the years I've seen a fair bit of televised death," he replies studiously. "We don't show it to the public, of course, because it can be so disturbing. In the edit suite, however, it's quite common. Does death disturb *you*?" He takes a gamble and throws the question back at

Theo, an old interviewing trick that allows him to seize control of the conversation.

"Are you looking to find out?" replies Theo as he paces back and forth on top of Dylan's desk.

"Well, in my extensive experience, I've always found death to be profoundly disturbing to most people. Why do you think that's the case?"

"I'm not on *Jeopardy* here, bud," says Theo. "All I know is that the people calling in want me to off this guy and I'm inclined to agree."

"Yes, some would, I suppose," Stonebane replies, unruffled. "When Ronald Reagan was shot we did big numbers. Would have done better if he'd actually died. Still, it was compelling. Death is a popular item for us, but it can also be a dud. When it has no meaning, for example, people turn away, they don't care. Death must be handled delicately on TV – but I'm sure you know that by now."

"I know what I know," Theo says guardedly.

"But you agree that death must have context. Yes? Without context it's nothing more than another commercial. Bubble gum, dish soap, bullet to the head – it's all the same without order, without a story. This is the value of Network news. We don't just *report* on events, we create stories."

"Stories is right," Theo spits, thinking about Jake's coverage of the Fenwick situation and growing more angry at the Stonebane's intrusion. "Bullshit, lies."

Greta's voice crackles in Stonebane's earpiece. "Don't get into a philosophical debate with this guy, William. For Christ's sake, I hope you know what you're doing."

Stonebane nods to let her know that, indeed, he does know what he's doing, and continues speaking to Theo. "There are many hacks in our business, I'll admit it. But real journalists – people who love the Craft, people like me – are different. We take random events and shape them, create narratives that resonate with people's inner emotions. This is our task, our holy mission. To make people *care*." He rubs his thumb and his forefinger together, as if trying to capture something elusive in the air around him. "Isn't that what you're trying to do, too?"

"Don't patronize me," Theo says, stamping his foot on the desk. "I don't call getting off on people's pain caring. You're a fucking voyeur, just like Jake. You fake sympathy for a second and then move on to the next story. None of you people deserve to be on air. You really want to make people care, put yourself on the line, newsman." His face flushes red, and in a sudden fury he bends down and yanks Dylan viciously by the hair. Dylan yelps, his neck muscles popping, and Theo shoves the gun barrel into Dylan's mouth. "So let's play by my rules for a change. Make people care about this piece of shit right here. How you gonna do that?"

"Don't push him too hard, William," Greta gasps into the mike. "Back off a little."

Stonebane gazes at the monitor steadily and clears his throat. "No need to hurt the young man," he says soothingly, taking Greta's advice. "We're just talking here."

"Talk, talk, natter, natter," Theo answers, growing more impatient. "Just like my brother does. You said you make people care, so let's hear it." He shoves the gun deeper into Dylan's mouth. "Tell me a story!"

"Be careful, William," Greta urges, her voice dropping to a whisper. She licks her lips. "Every channel is picking up our signal now. Make this last. You're doing beautifully."

Stonebane leans back in his chair and considers his double position as anchor and hostage negotiator. If he actually talks the nutter into dropping the gun, he'll be the hero, won't he? And even if he doesn't, even if Dylan gets . . . well then, this will still be the most famous broadcast in history. Win-win, the perfect odds. Straightening the Windsor knot on his tie, Stonebane pitches the Voice higher than usual, shaving off some of its authoritative edge to make room for a more conciliatory tone. "Well, the story would have to begin long before your so-called death poll, wouldn't it?"

"You tell me," Theo says, his grip on Dylan's hair tightening. Dylan's Adam's apple bobs up and down as if he's gagging, but Theo doesn't remove the gun from his mouth.

Stonebane says, "Yes, it would. It would have to start with some background on Mr. O'Sullivan. Tell the viewers that Dylan's been the star arts producer for seven years here at the Network. A handsome, clean-cut man, dedicated to his work. Show attractive photos of him – this sounds trivial, but the truth is, good-looking people make for better TV stories. Evoke more sympathy. That's tragic, but true. Then I would find out a particularly telling anecdote about how Dylan yearned to become an on-air personality, how he studied your brother's on-camera manner in the studio late at night, long after the other staffers had departed."

"Is that true?" Theo asks, examining Dylan's wide, frightened eyes.

"It doesn't really matter if it's true," Stonebane replies quickly. "We're just telling stories here, right? It's hypothetical. Where was I? Oh, yes, then I would speak about his big break, sketch out how your brother suddenly left his job. Outline the shooting of Ms. Poiselle – stop me if you want to fill in the details."

Theo shakes his head, but he takes the gun from Dylan's mouth. Dylan pants for air and then he freezes. Very slowly,

Theo strokes the barrel of the weapon along Dylan's left cheek, making a thin line of spittle and smudged make-up which glistens in the light.

Stonebane's voice floods unstoppably into the studio. "But I'd always tie it back to poor Dylan," he says. "That's very important. Link the story back to the main subject. Don't lose focus, Dylan is our main character. Then I would introduce you into the story. I'd talk about all the trouble with the dead logger in Fenwick Park. Yes, I imagine you have your reasons for that, too. I'd have to find out why you came here, why you sabotaged your own brother's show. I'd propose a theory, suggesting that you wanted to reap some kind of revenge on the 'evil media,' part of this backlash phenomenon we've been hearing so much about lately. How betrayed or angry you feel, or whatever the most suitable word is. You can correct me if I'm wrong."

"Keep talking," Theo says. As Stonebane's voice pours into the studio through the speaker, Theo pushes Dylan's head down onto the desk. He presses the gun behind Dylan's ear.

"But it's crucial," Stonebane says, "it's crucial that, through it all, Dylan comes off as the innocent bystander in a conflict he doesn't understand. His role is that of the young, handsome professional whose dreams are fulfilled and then, just as quickly, shattered by this tragic turn of events. Perhaps I'd call the story "Shattered Dreams" . . . or "Talk TV Tragedy," something like that. We have very good people who do that sort of thing – not to worry – and, given some time, we'd build all sorts of lovely graphics, too. Make it human, all too human."

Theo leans down and puts his mouth next to Dylan's ear, hot-breathed and intimate. He whispers, "You're dying for a purpose, Dylan, but I'm sorry. Be angry, then you'll understand."

It's loud enough to be picked up by the microphones.

"He's going to do it!" Greta ejaculates. She presses a button, then the robo-cam zooms in and five screens on the monitor wall above Greta instantly cut to a close-up of Theo's finger pressing on the trigger. Everyone in the booth stops moving, standing perfectly still inside the ambient din of the working machines.

Stonebane watches the monitor with mounting tension, but he keeps talking, keeps describing how a TV show might better produce this death. Whatever happens, he knows he's about to be catapulted into history.

Suddenly there's a noise from the corner of the studio floor. "The tape is ready to roll!" shouts Kelly Gordon, who has finally managed to hook Theo's video camera up to the monitor on the floor. She starts running for the exit.

But at that moment the sound of the gun explodes through the microphones and everything stops.

This is what the viewers see: On the wide shot of camera two, Kelly bolts into the picture, out of focus, her right hand stretched forward in a gesture that appears to be a wave, as if she's trying to catch Theo's attention. A split second later the gun goes off and Kelly's blurred body hits the polished studio floor in the classic motion of self-protection. What's in focus is a picture of Theo holding the gun, legs akimbo over Dylan's slumped body, a grey cloud of smoke and dust holding the light around him in the shape of a ball, twisting and contorting with the vibration of sound. And then Theo looks straight into the lens of the camera and says simply, "Play my tape."

They do.

□ □ □

The concussive sound of the gun rips through the studio and Tasso is jolted out of his daze and leaps to his feet. Instantly he notices something new: fire. The wooden set beside him is blanketed by smoke, small flames climbing quickly upwards over the paint and the dried glue. A spark jumps off the wall and lands on his coat, burning a small hole into the black wool, and then another and another, and the next thing he realizes is that he's on fire. He rips his coat from his body and presses it against the set flats, frantically trying to smother the flames, but it's already burning too heavily. He throws the coat to the floor, where it smolders. *I dropped my cigarette*, he realizes frantically. *My God, the whole place is alight.* The powerful air vent sucks the smoke away from the main studio, but Tasso inhales a lungful and starts to choke. Behind him there's a loud bursting sound and then a feverish hiss and sputter, like the sound of a hot grill. He swivels on his heel to see the electrical box connecting the studio cables explode, sending a shower of sparks and embers onto his body and the set walls. He jumps back, almost into another part of the growing fire. Two wires short-circuit and snap, dancing crazily in the air, lashing at the back of the wood flats before hitting the ground like wild snakes. Instantly more flames spit up, the air filter sucking in most of the smoke, preventing the fire alarm from going off. Tasso panics and scurries backwards, but his foot inadvertently knocks against a huge can of paint remover stored by the set builders. It spills to the ground. As the liquid seeps out it immediately springs into red and blue flame, spreading the fire throughout the whole area Tasso once used as his private refuge. Paralysed with fear, he stands perfectly still, feeling the heat beat back the chills racking through his body.

All other sounds from the studio are absorbed into the discord of crackling flames. Inexplicably a strange serenity overcomes him. He gazes into the fire, watching the chemical of colours melt into each other: orange into red, blue into green. All at once he has a vision, as if he's no longer looking into the fire, but peering down a long, bright tunnel, his beloved mother standing at its end. He hasn't seen her for years, all the family pictures long destroyed or left behind, but now she's perfectly vivid, her diminutive frame wrapped delicately in a light green sari. The silver bangles on her wrists glimmering in a phosphorescent light. Then his father appears, wearing a cream-coloured jacket. His hair is jet black, perfectly combed to the side as always, the lenses on his round glasses enlarging his milky brown eyes. They both look young, younger than Tasso is now, and they take each other by the hand and smile peacefully, as if the horrible death they met with during the Goan war never happened at all. His father nods his head solemnly, not so much a greeting as a sign, and Tasso realizes that his father is blessing his life; that somehow in the simple gesture he's telling Tasso how proud he is that his son did his duty, took such good care of their grandchild during the difficult years. Tasso stares at them in awe. His mother reaches up with a bejewelled hand and delicately touches the spot between her eyes, the dream spot she showed him so long ago. And then she takes her hand from her forehead and throws it open into the sky as if releasing a bird, her bracelets jingling sweetly. And Tasso knows that his dreams have been mysteriously shared by those he loves most and found to be more than just sufficient, but abundant. The fire crackles and a spark flies out and hits him in the forehead. He smells his skin burning and shakes his head at the piercing sensation. Instantly the vision disappears.

Beside him a bottle of solvent explodes and the fire sprays up the wall. Tasso watches it eat into the wood, rolling in tiny orange waves up towards the ceiling. Another feeling courses through him, a lightness, as though layer after layer of his skin is dissolving, leaving him with nothing to distinguish himself with but his bare white bones. Bones of a life. A real life. An adequate life. Very slowly, he lowers himself into the middle of the circle of cigarette butts he made earlier. He crosses his legs, tucking his feet in neatly under his salt-stained pants. The colours dance around him and he gazes hypnotically at them, eyes wide and watery, unblinking. Thick smoke starts to envelop him. The ends of his hair singe, giving off an acrid smell. Then he feels the heat touch his skin. First a prickly impression on his back, then on his legs, his arms, and soon hundreds of stabbing pains all over his body. Lifting his head to the grid of lights above, he puts his hands over his lips so he won't scream. Now he's aglow, a penumbra of fire outlining his rigid form, tearing into him, dissolving him, but he keeps all his muscles taut, his back straight, until the poisonous black smoke smothers him and he disappears into it without a sound.

August 1, 1999

I'm sitting beside the front window of the cabin resting my leg and watching the heavy chop on Georgian Bay. The water rips upwards in waves, shredding its blue skin into frothing white crests that roll towards the shoals and collapse, breaking back into a momentary wash of tranquillity. Theo and I spent our summers riding these waves, navigating our way over half-submerged rocks and paddling wildly to stay upright in the swell. Pop hated to see us out there, warned us that the bay was too cold and too rough, that we would surely drown if we ever capsized. But Theo always ignored him, took us out so far that our cabin would disappear into the horizon and we'd be all alone, adrift in the heaving, thrashing water. Which is exactly how it felt that day, months ago, when I left Rachel's bed and fled from the hospital towards Theo.

I arrived at the Network and the first thing I noticed was panic. Sirens and horns enveloped the place like a wet tarp. A mash of police cars, fire trucks, and the special terrorist unit cluttered up the front entrance, lights flashing crazily. A large policeman holding a bullhorn stood on a podium barking out instructions, his voice echoing as he commanded the crowd of people to stay back. Swirling columns of smoke were visible through the windows on the fourth and fifth floors and most of the building had already been evacuated. I caught a glimpse of William Stonebane standing near a Network satellite truck with a camera crew, continuing his live broadcast. Media people from all over the city were pouring in, swarming the place like pollen-drunk worker bees around a dying queen, setting up a scaffolding of wires and mikes that would support the story of my brother's undoing. A half-dozen helicopters from stations around the country were swooping dangerously back and forth against the sky taking aerial footage.

Even as I picked my way around the pandemonium I realized how foreign this was. This wasn't like the Gabinson murder or the wet night with the three dead prostitutes. I couldn't be an invisible spectator any more. Lowering my head, I quickly slipped into the side entrance of the building with my pass key and made my way towards the studio where Theo was holding the Network airwaves hostage. What I didn't know was that the persistent Charlene Rosemount and her cameraman Herb had caught a glimpse of me, and they dashed through the doors in pursuit.

I took the elevators up, realizing that the fire alarm would keep people on the stairs, and by the time I got to the studio floor, the whole place was deserted. I was surprised the firemen and the police weren't there, but as I learned later, they were outside debating how to untie the Gordian knot posed by a major fire complicated by a hostage crisis. According to Charlene's sources, as revealed in her subsequent one-hour TV special, *Burn, Baby, Burn!: The Rise and Fall of Network Star Jake Jacobson*, the police wanted to break into the building to go after Theo, but Captain Cormac Holiday of the terrorist unit vigorously objected, apparently wanting to save his team from the potential public relations disaster that might ensue from an all-out gun assault on a major television station. "I wasn't about to direct some half-baked sequel to the Waco disaster," he told Charlene solemnly. Holiday believed, falsely, as it turned out, that the fire would force Theo to surrender of his own volition.

This is all I remember:

I'm running, running as fast as I can towards my brother. Down corridors roiling with black smoke, I move past the abandoned newsroom and its empty terminals and computers, lost in its own purpose. Across from the make-up room, I see the red ON AIR light of the studio and I swipe my pass card and push open the door. Fire everywhere, that's what I recall, heat leaping onto my face. I ignore the instant shock of it and move inside. Above me a light in the grid explodes and hot glass falls like hail, the shattering sound buffeted by the mounting roar of fire. A voice screams for help and I head for it, dodging the flames and gagging on smoke. I see someone crawling on the floor, desperately trying to get out. It's Kelly, my old producer, her face black with soot except for two blurred white streaks where tears pour down her cheeks. When she sees me she wails, cowering as if she's afraid I'm going to hurt her. Despite her protestations, I heave her up in my arms and carry her through the fire out into the hall. When we're out of imminent danger, I try to set her down on her feet, but she collapses instantly into a protective ball.

"He shot Dylan," she sobs. "Right in front of me. His brains, I saw his brains everywhere!"

Before my mind can even process that information, I hear another voice from down the hall. "Mr. Jacobson! Mr. Jacobson!"

It's Charlene, rushing towards me with her cameraman close behind. "Channel 7 News," she says frantically. "Did you shoot Rachel Poiselle? Does your brother know you're here? Do you know he just killed your replacement?" She lunges forward, shoving her microphone under my nose. "Give us a statement!" she demands.

Her cameraman swings around to get a closer shot of my reaction, the light on his camera shooting out through the smoke like a fist and blasting into my eyes. For a second I think it might actually knock me down, but the sight of these two local apple-polishers barrelling down on me in search of a sound bite brushing past Kelly's quivering frame without so much as a glance sends me into a frenzy. I charge Herb and grab the camera from his shoulder, smashing it onto the floor. "Out! Out!" I scream like a madman, whipping my arms around my body in hopes of inflicting some type of pain on them. "Get out of here!"

"You son of a bitch," Herb mutters, gaping at the sixty-thousand-dollar debris that was once his camera. But I'm wild, out of control, kicking the walls, screaming murderous threats, flailing away, and he keeps me at arm's length. The noxious cloud in the hall grows more intense and it becomes hard to breathe.

Charlene holds her microphone out like a weapon, guarding herself in the event that I turn her way. "Retrieve that tape, Herb," she snarls to her cameraman, though her eyes never leave mine. "Retrieve it right now before I stick this mike up your arse and interview your colon." The heat causes her heavy make-up to run down her face, black eyeliner melting into her skin-toned cosmetics making a sickly, almost voodoo mask. "Oh, and the woman too," she snaps, pointing at Kelly. "For Christ's sake, get her out too."

Herb ducks his head and carefully lifts his broken camera from the floor. He backs away towards the exit, but then, like someone checking out of a hotel room and at the last minute spotting a lone sock lying in the corner, he flicks out his arm and yanks the nearly hysterical Kelly from the ground. Together all three of them lurch down the hall and vanish into the poisonous haze.

I bolt back into the studio, calling out Theo's name. The fire grows steadily along the walls, moving towards the centre of the room where I used to host my show. I stumble in the blackness, unhinged, groping my way through the flames. Something soft catches my foot and sends me sprawling to the floor. A hideous pain sears into my leg, but the adrenaline coursing through my body keeps me conscious. I look down and see that a large piece of glass from one of the shattered light bulbs has lodged below my kneecap. Groaning in agony, I clamber to my feet and look back to see what I've tripped over. It's the charred remains of what seems to be a heavy overcoat. Just then a gunshot explodes to my left and my head snaps around. Another shot, this time right overhead. I squint my eyes and peer through the warping smoke. And finally I see him. Theo. He's standing on my desk in the middle of the massive studio, firing his gun into the lights, knocking them out. Behind him the flames consume the set flats. He looks half-crazed, his hair dishevelled, his face grimy with ash. Blood spots, still wet, glisten all over his body. But more then anything I notice his eyes. They're not focused on anything in particular, just staring into the rack of lights, watching the smoke thicken, as if he's in some kind of trance.

My leg almost collapses from pain, but I push on towards him.

"Hello, Jake," he says calmly, gazing down at me as I emerge from the gloom. His eyes are wide and unblinking, as if unaffected by the smoke, and there's no sense in his voice that he's surprised to see me. Just that same eerie certainty he exuded in the car trip home from North Bay. "I figured you would show up," he says, pointing the gun at the monitor in the corner. On screen I see the footage he took of me standing mute in the university corridor while Rachel calls desperately for help. "There you are, brother. The real you. What a proud moment. I brought it for your whole audience to see."

My heart is pounding wildly with rage, slamming itself against my rib cage. I get closer to Theo and see Dylan's dead body slumped over in my chair at Theo's feet. Blood is trickling from a gaping hole in his head, spilling off the surface of my desk and onto the studio floor.

"You crazy bastard!" I scream to Theo. I make a move to go after him, to launch myself at his thick legs and wrestle him to the ground, but as soon as he senses my aggression he levels the gun at me, pointing the barrel directly into my face. I stop, my eyes locking onto his, just as they did so long ago in the Rosedale golf course when he found me clinging in the reeds, spying on his private date with Theckla. But this time I don't think he's going to let me go as easily. This time there's none of that childhood compassion and understanding, no inclination to allow the moment to become part of our ancient cache of memory. His face is cold and unforgiving, a winter sky of endless blackness and pale, receding light.

"You're gonna shoot me too, Theo?" I yell, letting the emotion inside me detonate. "You're an animal, that's what you are. What happened to you? Tell me what happened to you!"

"What happened to *me*?" Theo says as if the question offends him. His face grows even darker and I can almost see the light behind his eyes withdraw further away. "I think it's high time you did a little self-examination." With a jerk of his arm he lifts the gun a few inches and fires a shot over my head into the fire, disorientating me. "This place messed you up," he says, still unruffled, as if there's no fire at all, as if he's just paddling in a canoe and not holding a gun to my head. "Look at yourself on that tape and think about it. It even turned you against me. What was I going to do? Leave you here? Come on, Jake. I'm your brother. I came back to help."

"Help?" I ask, the words tearing out of my throat. "How did you do that? By shooting Rachel? By setting me up?"

"I *woke* you up." He laughs hoarsely at my rage, but once again aims the gun at me. "Made you care again. A lesson, a simple lesson. That's all Rachel was. Don't play dumb with me." He kicks Dylan's body with his shoe, knocking it from the desk to the floor in front of me. "Poor, stupid, handsome boy," he says, shaking his head. "You knew him, right? Imagine your audience wanting to see him dead. You call me an animal? These are the people you represent."

Theo's placid voice and twisted logic terrify me and the fire begins to close in, the heat rippling the air.

"But Rachel was innocent," I say desperately, backing away from Dylan's twisted corpse. "You stood there after shooting her and videotaped me. It's sick."

He surveys me with a look of pity on his face, as if he's incapable of understanding why I'm being so difficult. "Had to get you off the air, didn't I? See things from the other side of the camera. You're angry, that's good, it'll help you understand . . ."

"Don't give me that bullshit!" I smack my hand on the desk, my palm imprinting with Dylan's blood, but Theo just nods his head up and down in some mysterious gesture of approval.

Everything around us moves with heat, a shadow play of monstrous and unrecognizable shapes. A set flat collapses, sending up a mist of orange sparks. We stare silently at each other, it can't be for more than a few seconds, but time is so poorly measured in these moments and the seconds seem to contain multitudes of memory, lifetimes of things said and terrain crossed, letters sent and secrets revealed, all transmitting from his eyes to mine and back again. But then, as if the distance between us is too vast, the signal weakens and goes dead. He lowers the gun to his side and his eyes become opaque. The flames burst and slash around us. There's a creaking sound from above and suddenly a heavy light from the grid comes crashing down. Theo raises his arms up to protect himself, but he's too late. The light strikes his head, tossing him to the floor. A bloody gash opens across his forehead.

I kneel beside him on my good leg, staring at the red frame of blood that catches in the corner of his eyes and runs down his cheeks. It makes him look sad, and for the first time I can remember, vulnerable. My first instinct is to help him, alleviate his pain, because he's my brother, the person I've revered my whole life, but I can't bring myself to touch him. My hands reach out and then stop, as if hitting a transparent screen of glass. He gazes up at me and his mouth splits into a smile, a triumphant smile I remember from so long ago when he convinced me to swim with him under the stars in the dark water of the lake, right after he gutted the bear.

"You understand now, don't you?" he mutters, still holding the same expression. He tries to get up, but he's unable to, and his head falls back on the hot floor. Some smoke catches his lungs and he coughs. "I'm trying to help you, Jake. Trying to help everyone."

I sit in the blackness of liquefied heat, my leg aching, and watch him bleed. The horror I felt before doesn't abate, but seems to turn over on itself. I'm not scared of him any more, but scared for him, wondering how he must feel to realize that after so much effort he's now lying here amidst this carnage, utterly helpless and failed and lost. And that's when I know about betrayal. Right there. It's not something you choose, like I said at the beginning, it's something that chooses you. It lifts you up and carries you away from the people you once loved, but can no longer believe.

His face coils in pain and he stares up at me, pleadingly. "Get us out of here, Jake."

I rise to my feet slowly, not uttering a word. Again he attempts to stand, but his body won't respond.

"For Christ's sake, give me your hand." He tries to grab at me with one arm, but I back away.

"You're my brother," he says, his eyes now glassy, fading. "Don't walk away from me. You can't do that."

But I do. I turn away from him and limp towards the exit. The flames burn at my skin and behind me I hear him calling out my name like a letter he's starting but will never finish. When I get out into the hallway I stop. Then I reach back into the ferocious heat and pull the heavy studio door shut.

I don't remember much about what happened next. Emerging from the Network building I entered another kind of chaos. A fireman rushed forward and threw a coat over my shoulders, just like you see in the movies. Reporters recognized me and swarmed like attack ants, their microphones mandibles jutting into my face. Cutting through the crowd, Detective Ian O'Malley viciously cuffed my hands behind my back and lead me to his police car. I recall feeling very still in the midst of the tumult, listening to the heavy rap of the helicopters overhead, watching the faces of all the pedestrians who'd taken time out of their lives to watch a fire and catch a glimpse of someone else's misfortune. I know the feeling well.

As O'Malley pushed me towards the car, I distinctly remember seeing a young family of three standing behind the yellow police tape. They'd pulled their Land Rover over to the curb to watch the disaster, all three of them gazing up at the circling helicopters. The father wore oval glasses and an expensive purple Fila ski jacket. In one hand he clutched his five-year-old daughter and the other his beautiful young wife.

"Look, Daddy," called out the blond daughter excitedly, pointing to the decal on the side of one of the choppers with one of her little fingers. "That's Channel 5."

"No, honey," the father replied sweetly. "That's a four. Channel 5 is over there. And see that one? That's a six. That's Channel 6 in the blue. Now, show me where Channel 7 is. What does a seven look like?"

Her finger shot up over the mess of sirens into the blue sky. "Over there."

"That's right, honey. Seven is sort of like an upside-down L."

"Again, again!" the child sang.

I watched the little girl learn her counting lessons from the textbook of a media disaster as the *thwack, thwack* of rotating helicopter blades severed the air into strips, and suddenly I felt sadder than I'd ever felt in my life, just so heavy and disappointed and wasted. And then O'Malley pushed my head down into his car and minutes later we were on the wet streets, making our way away from the Network.

After several hours of interrogation, O'Malley was forced to release me after seeing the tapes from the Network's robotic cameras. Greta had astutely left them running when she abandoned her post and they recorded the whole scene in the studio, clearly revealing Theo's admission that he shot Rachel. Charlene Rosemount's footage of me dragging Kelly from the blazing studio turned her into a media sensation too. It's all very well shot, edited heroically with dramatic music, and it received extensive national play. I've since heard that Charlene won an award for best local news reporting. I was urged by my lawyer to hold a big press conference to declare my innocence, and I even received a call from Greta telling me that I could easily rehabilitate my career back at the Network. "Your brother was crazy," she said again and again, as if to convince me that I really had nothing to do with what happened. But I didn't hold a press conference and I turned down Greta's job offer. As soon as I could, I headed back to the bay.

I talked to Rachel yesterday, only the third time in the six months I've been up in Pop's cabin trying to finish this story. She's still away on a long sabbatical, trying to recover. She won't tell me when she's coming home and I don't ask. Momma calls me frequently, tells me she's attending AA meetings, but I can't bring myself to see her right now. Maybe when a little more time passes I'll let her read what I've written and she'll understand what happened, at least the way I saw it all unfold. But it's not like this is going to bring me some sort of redemption, the kind of neat little ending you see on TV. I wish it was like that, though, I still do, but I guess these are the things you can't escape: people lost, identity unbecome, love shared briefly before it slips away into the fictions of your own heart, and that's only for the lucky ones. For the rest of us, everything's just a moving picture, grey and static with hope and confusion, shot through with the discomforts of our own dead air.

I take off my shirt and prepare to go swimming, running my fingers over my chest. The skin is soft, all the scabs finally healing. And outside my father's cabin, the water is blue and warm, for the first time in days threatening to remain calm.

ACKNOWLEDGEMENTS

I am forever grateful to my editor, Ellen Seligman, who has always believed in this book. Also to my staunch friend Jennifer Baichwal, for her tremendous help on the early draft. Any many thanks to those people who have always given me their invaluable support: Nadine Kriston Csathy, Andrew Heintzman, my agent Bruce Westwood, Sally Catto, Michael Levine, Malcolm Brown and all the wonderful people at *Shift* magazine, Craig Offman, Kate Fenner, Barry and Wendy Gordon, Michael McGowan, Stephen Smith, Andrew Johnson, Alison Gzowski, Michael Downie, Alice Hopton, Maria Mironowicz, CBC Newsworld, Alison Brown, Roy Graham, Geoff Roberts, Nick de Pencier, Melanie Barter, Doug Bell, the Quinn clan, Charles Stuart, Anita Chong, Sheila Heti, and Chris Blair. And finally, for my grandmother Rhoda, and my grandfather Mort, who was the first writer in our family.